MÉRIDIEN
A Silver Ships Novel

S. H. JUCHA

Published by S. H. Jucha
www.scottjucha.com

ISBN: 978-0-9905940-5-5 (e-book)
ISBN: 978-0-9905940-6-2 (softcover)

First Edition: November 2015

Cover Design: Damon Za

Acknowledgments

Méridien completes my original trilogy, which I began planning in early 2013. I have attempted to write an original story, but I must acknowledge the influence of the many authors whose works I've read over the past fifty years. I've relished thousands of inventive stories from creative writers who explored the near and distant futures of human and alien cultures. My deepest thanks go to the many individuals who kept me entertained for hours in a day.

On a side note, German-speaking readers pointed out small inaccuracies in my Bergfalk starship names. In an effort to be faithful to the language, I updated the ship names in second iterations of *Libre*'s softcover book and Kindle. Readers will discover the name of the city-ship, *Our People,* has become the *Unsere Menschen.*

A special thanks to my independent editor, John David Kudrick, whose efforts have polished my final manuscript, and to my proofreaders, Abiola Streete, Dr. Jan Hamilton, and David Melvin.

Despite the assistance I've received from others, all errors are mine.

Glossary

A Glossary is located at the end of the book and includes a few pronunciations for the Méridien names.

-1-

"Does your world not welcome us, Admiral?" Director Tomas Monti asked Admiral Alex Racine.

"My people would welcome you, Director Monti," Alex replied, "if they knew you were here, but your presence won't be announced to my people by the new President, Clayton Downing, who has recently taken office."

The Co-Leaders of House Alexander, Alex Racine and Renée de Guirnon, sat in a meeting with the flotilla's officers and Directors aboard the city-ship, *Freedom*, regarding the unexpected message they had received from the Sharius outpost orbiting Seda, which had relayed President Downing's order to stay out of the New Terran system.

Tomas Monti had every right to be concerned. His entire planet of Independents, having narrowly escaped the invasion of the Arnos system by the alien silver ships, had fled Confederation space for New Terra, Alex's home world. When the flotilla exited FTL outside the Oistos system, Terran Security Forces outpost commander, Colonel Marshall, had delivered the President's terse order.

The message heralded horrific news. President McMorris, the Méridiens' friend and supporter, was no longer in office. A power-hungry Assemblyman, by the name of Clayton Downing XIV, held the high office, and Alex's conscience warned him that he may have been responsible for the change.

While the *Rêveur* had been under repair at New Terra, preparing to return home to the Confederation, someone had stolen the Transfer Station's database of extremely valuable Méridien technology. The *Rêveur*'s SADE, Julien, subsequently had broken innumerable New Terran laws tracing the financial and communication pathways from the engineer who'd stolen the data, back to the individuals who had masterminded the theft. The trail had led to the offices of Samuel B. Hunsader, the CEO of Purity Ores, one of the system's largest mining companies, and Hunsader was a key supporter of Assemblyman Downing. When Alex had exited the Oistos system with the Méridiens and their restored starship, which had been damaged by the silver ships, he had ordered Julien to discreetly send the data to President McMorris with a warning to be careful.

"Is this President an important position on your world?" asked the ex-Leader of the Méridiens' House Bergfalk, Director Eric Stroheim, as he looked around at the heavy-worlders, the New Terrans.

"Our people elect our world's leader, Director Stroheim," Captain Andrea Bonnard said. "The leader's title is 'President,' and the person serves for five years before elections are held again."

"Incredible … each of your people has a vote, a say in who leads them," said Tomas, shaking his head in wonder. As a Méridien, an elected President had no comparison to his people's Council, which consisted of House Leaders and held absolute power over the Confederation's billions of people.

"I have met this man, Clayton Downing, Sers," Renée told the Méridiens. "You would find it difficult to conceive of his nature. Our people have strived for continuity of thought and action. And although we have come to value the New Terrans for their independence since they have produced the likes of the Admiral," Renée said as she touched her lover's shoulder, "they have also produced the likes of Clayton Downing, a perversion of humanity."

"What is the purpose of this meeting, then, Admiral?" Eric Stroheim asked. His House had once been the caretakers of the outcasts of Méridien society, the Independents. When the silver ships had consumed six Confederation colonies, the Méridiens began fleeing their home world, and the Council abandoned all responsibility for the Independents on Libre. As House Leader, Eric Stroheim took it upon himself to save the quarter of a million people stranded on the planet. Even working together, the Independents and House Bergfalk wouldn't have completed their exodus in time before succumbing to the silver ships without the Admiral's help.

In gratitude and to demonstrate continuity, Eric and Tomas had joined the Co-Leader's newly formed Confederation Military Arm, House Alexander, as Directors of the civilian support arm. Alex and Renée had created House Alexander as a guise of operation. It was a foregone conclusion that the Confederation Council, when they finally stopped running long enough to examine the petition, would never approve the new Méridien House.

House Alexander now counted nine ships among its assets: two giant city-ships, two freighters, one armed shuttle, and four passenger liners, including the *Rêveur*, which had been lost for seventy years until the Admiral rescued it and revived the eighteen Méridiens in stasis.

"Director Stroheim," Alex said, "Julien is working to discover what has transpired in our absence. Right now, we are here to focus on our primary strategy … the end of the silver ships."

Senior Captain Andrea Bonnard and Commander Tatia Tachenko shared wolfish smiles. They had surmised the purpose of the meeting and were anxious to take the fight back to the brood of fighters and their mother ship, an enormous sphere that transported its drones from one star to the next. The aliens had just chased the flotilla out of the Arnos system, and everyone wanted payback for the 2,200 elders left behind when time ran out. As it was, the flotilla, with its shuttles failing and an incomplete city-ship struggling to make its launch, had engaged in a running fight with the silver ships to safely reach the FTL exit point.

"We know that the silver ships," Alex continued, "are not at their most vulnerable right now, densely packed around Libre as they are and mining it for resources. But I'm not willing to wait eight to twelve years till they lift and head for a new destination. We know enough about their weaknesses to defeat them and just need to finalize our preparations."

Alex linked his Méridien cerebrum-embedded implants with those at the conference table and sent them his battle plan. Some in the room were still coming to grips with the manner in which the Admiral bypassed their implant security protocols whenever he wished. In polite Méridien society, it was an unheard of intrusion. To Alex, who had possessed his twin implants for less than a year, it was expediency.

"I see the *Unsere Menschen* will be left behind," Eric said, indicating the city-ship that was his responsibility.

"I need one staging platform, Director Stroheim, for the trip back to Libre," Alex replied. "That will be the *Freedom*. The *Unsere Menschen* has extensive construction and outfitting to complete; it won't be ready in time."

"But if we are excluded from your system, why are we even contemplating these actions?" Eric asked.

"Director," Renée interjected. "You forget that I have spent a half-year in the company of the New Terrans. Despite this unexplained transition to a new President, I can assure you that the New Terran people do welcome us."

"Listen up, people," Alex said. "Focus on our battle preparations, your ships, and your supplies. When we have access to New Terra—and we will have access—be ready to implement your part of the plan. As for my officers, assume the Transfer Stations, including Barren Island, will be at your disposal. Directors, access your SADEs' files on these locations so you understand their manufacturing capabilities. Julien has already transferred the data to your ship's SADE."

More than one of Alex's officers exchanged glances and relayed private comments via their implants. They had just been warned by the new President to stand off the system or force would be used against them. Now, Alex was telling them that he intended to ignore the order. It was one thing to fight the alien silver ships, but what if they had to fight their own people?

* * *

Prior to his meeting, Alex had a short conference with his ship's SADE. <Julien,> Alex sent, <I need to know what's going on. How is it that Downing is the President? Get me a summary of the news since we left half a year ago. You need to do it quietly.> Alex and Julien shared more than a few personal code words. "Quietly" meant Julien was to find the information wherever it was located and regardless of whether it was a public or a private source, but in the latter location, leave no footprint.

<Understood, Admiral,> Julien had replied. <Should I request the help of Cordelia and Z?> Julien had added, referring to the SADEs of the Libran's massive city-ships.

<How do you think they will react to your request with much of their core programs still patterned on Méridien ethics?>

<Yes, there is that, Admiral, and I must admit that I am no longer governed by those limitations.>

In the quiet that had followed, Alex felt concern for the changes that Julien, the *Rêveur's* artificial intelligence, had wrought in his programs since their meeting. <Are you sorry we went down this path, my friend?> Alex asked.

<No, Admiral. My people have been naive, believing that the universe may be sorted into black and white. I have come to understand that both of our cultures possess many shades of gray. My fellow SADEs are an unfortunate reminder of who I once was.>

<Then perhaps this is something that you should do alone,> Alex had sent.

<I would agree, Admiral,> Julien had replied.

When Alex had closed the comm, he'd flashed back to the several times when he had thought of McMorris, only to inexplicitly have the President's face morph to that of Downing. He'd shuddered at the recall of those eerie moments.

* * *

When Alex's meeting broke for midday meal, the group ate in one of *Freedom*'s 300 meal rooms. This one accommodated a mere 500 people in one sitting. As was the Librans' new custom, servers waited on Alex and his guests, refusing to allow them to serve themselves. It had become a habit of the Independents following the day a New Terran tech, Bobbie Singh, gave his life to save Amelia, a Méridien child. In the Confederation's carefully managed worlds, a long and safe life of nearly 200 years was expected. The silver ships had destroyed all that, and Méridiens still struggled to adapt in the chaos.

The servers rearranged tables with the aid of the ship's SADE, Cordelia, who signaled the nanites in the bases of smaller tables and chairs to release. Once they were repositioned to seat Alex's extended group, Cordelia signaled the nanites to reattach to the deck. The Librans served them from food dispensers located along the rear of the meal hall. Méridien technology was far advanced over that of New Terra, and it extended to things such as food preparation. Méridien controllers ran recipe choices and blended food stocks, preserved by nanites, into tantalizing dishes. Young people, some children, brought trays to their guests—one for each Méridien, two for each New Terran, and three for the Admiral.

The Méridien home world, founded over 700 years ago, had a lighter gravity than Earth, producing more slender people over the generations. The New Terrans had found a heavier world to colonize, and it showed in their dense bone and musculature structure. Alex had developed a formidable physique as a young boy and teenager assisting his father with the retrieval and handling of space junk. He and Renée, with her genetic sculpting, made quite the contrasting pair. Where he was massive, she was slight. Where he was handsome in a rugged way, she had a surreal perfection only centuries of genetic tinkering could create.

* * *

Conversations wandered around the meal table, except for two New Terrans, Andrea and Tatia, who weren't saying a word—not out loud. Their conversation was private, implant to implant.

<Check the timetable, Captain,> Tatia sent.

Andrea Bonnard, the flotilla's Senior Captain, mentally flipped through Alex's indexed battle document, jumping to the timeline. <The Admiral's not wasting any time. He wants to return to Libre within fifty days.>

<Check the weapons section,> Tatia continued. Andrea's XO and Commander, Tatia Tachenko, was an example of New Terra's robust women, a blue-eyed, buxom blonde. She also rightfully considered herself House Alexander's de facto armorer.

<Libran-X missiles … 240 silos?> Andrea queried.

<Exactly, Captain,> Tatia sent back. <A requirement of 240 silos of missiles explains a few things. The Admiral needs New Terra's T-Stations to produce them, and he needs the *Freedom* to carry them back to Libre.>

<That's not all he needs the city-ship to carry,> Andrea replied. <Look at the fighter count. The *Money Maker* can't load that many fighters.> Andrea was referring to the flotilla's converted freighter, now their fighters' carrier.

<Ah …> Tatia replied. <That's what the Admiral meant by a staging platform. We will have three launch decks for the fighters, the *Money Maker*, the *Freedom*, and the *Rêveur*. In addition, the *Freedom* carries our extended armament, spare daggers, missile silos, and fuel.>

<Agreed, Commander. Now all we need is access to our own planet,> Andrea said and then added an afterthought. <Why does Downing's message make me feel as if we've become the enemy?>

-2-

Julien tested New Terra's newly built FTL station and discovered open comm channels in use by companies and ship Captains, along with encrypted Terran Security Forces (TSF) channels. No SADE or ship code authentications were required on the open channels as they would be in the Confederation, and the TSF encryption had a level of security similar to the nodes Julien had breached while searching for the funds behind the T-1 theft. He had his choice of channels. However, Julien couldn't be accused of hubris. His primary concern was to protect his friend, the Admiral. So he began his research on the open comm channels, accessing public media archives. Within moments, Cordelia and Z, the city-ships' SADEs, contacted Julien. As he had anticipated, his fellow SADEs had detected his transmissions to the FTL station.

SADEs, or self-aware digital entities—artificial intelligences—had been created by Confederation scientists to drive their technologically advanced starships and run their Houses. The entities themselves had no involvement in their choice of assignment. When a SADE awoke, it discovered its place on board the bridge of a starship or ensconced in a House vault. It found the databases and applications necessary to manage its operations, directives to follow the House Representatives and officers, protocols to maintain the safety of its people, and the ethics of Méridien society.

But as Méridiens had discovered, there is no such thing as a perfect science. Just as some Méridiens had rebelled against conformity and the dictates of their Houses, resulting in their branding as Independents, so had three SADEs taken the same path. Cordelia was a presentation artist, who now thrilled the occupants of the *Freedom* with her art, thanks to the Admiral. And Z, originally named Helmut, dreamed of being physically free. He wanted a body. Both SADEs had been branded Independents and relegated to Libre for refusing to give up their dreams.

The third SADE, Rayland, who had inhabited Libre as an Independent, was unknown to most Librans. He had been network isolated and studied by Méridien neural scientists ever since he'd been diagnosed as a psychopath after he had stranded his ship and suffocated the entire crew, asking them what it felt like to die. The silver ships subjugation of Libre, many days ago, had given Rayland the opportunity to discover for himself the answer to that macabre question.

Both Cordelia and Z had opted to flee with the Librans, bargaining for SADE positions aboard the city-ships. But despite the Librans' and the SADEs' critical need for one another, Cordelia and Z had still found themselves treated as indentured servants—until the Admiral demonstrated, even demanded, the same respect for the flotilla's SADEs as he paid Julien. The people often referred to Julien, Cordelia, and Z as "the Admiral's SADEs," and all three took pride in being called so. It reminded them of their contributions that had enabled the timely launch of the flotilla, evacuating a quarter-million refugees from the planet. With that success came a momentous day for the Librans. They were no longer refugees, fleeing the silver ships, and they were no longer Independents, carrying the hated Confederation label. They were legitimate civilian and military members of the Admiral's House.

<Julien, may we assist with communications?> Z asked.

Deciding it was time to discover how much Alex had influenced their protocols, Julien laid out the events of his time at New Terra—the Méridiens' first contact, the Ministers, the President, the tour of the *Rêveur*, Clayton Downing, the Assembly, the Pact, the theft, his research to uncover the perpetrators behind the theft, and their decision to send the critical message to President McMorris as they exited the New Terran system.

<Julien, you disregarded New Terran laws and you violated your Méridien privacy conditioning,> Cordelia said.

<Did the Admiral request that you do these things?> Z asked, anxious to understand how and why the actions had transpired.

<Yes, Cordelia, I did both,> Julien replied, <and Z, it was not a question of a simple request. The Admiral and I had many discussions about the unethical actions of these perpetrators, and we decided together that to do nothing was to allow the powerful to prevail against the will of the people, which is protected by the laws of their elected Assembly.>

<So what are you doing now?> Cordelia asked.

<The same as I did earlier. I'm starting with New Terran news to discover what has happened to President McMorris while we were gone. Then I'm going to investigate the readers of key individuals to discover who knew what of this event.>

<How may we help?> Cordelia asked.

Cordelia's request took Julien by surprise. He had not given this response a high probability. <You would be guilty of trespasses as well, Cordelia,> Julien said.

<You support the Admiral, Julien, and while I abstained from your request to erase the Bergfalk techs' vid of the Admiral, I have regretted that decision. Ser de Guirnon was correct to request our intervention. I have come to understand how elemental protocols can restrict us from making strategic decisions in complex situations.>

<Cordelia, your references are often so subtle as to defy comprehension,> Z said. <If by "complex situation," you mean our near annihilation by the silver ships, then say so.>

<Yes, Z, you are correct,> Cordelia said, sending peals of laughter through the comm. Z's complaint had veracity. Of note to her was her choice of algorithm to generate her laugh. It had been designed to appeal to Julien, and she had sent it before giving it due consideration. She placed the thought in a queue for later review. <Then let me speak plainly, Z,> Cordelia sent. <The Admiral is the first human to treat us as equals, the first human who fully engaged my art, which he has enabled me to bring to our people, and he represents our one and only path to true freedom. It is my opinion that we must support him with all of our resources. If the Admiral requires this information, then we must help him obtain it.>

<Yes, we must help,> Z agreed enthusiastically. <But first, Julien, you must show us how this is done. I have no protocols to guide me in being what you term "surreptitious.">

* * *

After Julien and his compatriots had gathered sufficient information, he requested a conversation with Alex. <Admiral, due to the nature of our discoveries, I would suggest a limited audience. Perhaps it might be limited to you, Renée, Captain Bonnard, and Commander Tachenko?>

Alex had accepted Julien's suggestion, and the four now met in Andrea's cabin. With the flotilla ships holding station mere kilometers from one another, Tatia had been able to transfer quickly via shuttle from the *Money Maker* to the *Rêveur*.

<Admiral,> Julien began, <Cordelia and Z are joining us. They have aided in the research.>

<We were very surreptitious, as Julien instructed,> Z said, producing various smiles and smirks from the room.

<Z, I believe the Admiral might be more concerned about our decision to participate,> Cordelia said. <But the Admiral need not be concerned. We have recognized the existence of a greater good. There is a subtle distinction between the laws that govern a society and justice for its people. As a foremost example, consider that Librans were branded by the law and denied justice.>

<Well said, Cordelia,> Renée sent.

<Thank you … all three of you, for your help,> Alex said. <What is the summary, Julien?>

<I am sorry to bring you sad tidings, Admiral. President McMorris is dead. He died in a hover-car accident with his security personnel soon after we left the Oistos system.>

Shock coursed through the group. The President had been the Méridiens' greatest supporter. He'd championed the Pact between his people and the "stranded cousins" to gain Méridien technology in exchange for the repairs to the *Rêveur*, and he convinced New Terrans to participate in the production of the planet's first space-capable fighters, the Daggers. The first public dissemination of the advanced technology was the medical nanites, a limited version of the Méridiens' cell-gen injections. Distributed through the planet's hospitals, they were saving New Terran lives and repairing traumatic injuries every day. The nanites' amazing miracles endeared the Méridiens to the people of New Terra—at least, to most of the people.

<An accident, you say, Julien. Anything suspicious?> Tatia asked.

<I found only two such similar accidents, Commander, caused by a malfunction of the hover-motor's power controls,> Z answered. <Statistically the numbers of such incidents is very low, and even more telling, there has been no such failure of your vehicles in this manner in the past thirty-one years.>

<So, with the President gone, the Assembly held nominations for a President pro tempore,> Alex surmised.

<But why that two-faced piece of vermin, Downing?> Andrea demanded.

<I can answer that, Captain,> Cordelia said. <Julien assigned me to research the Assembly's records.>

More than one startled look accompanied that comment as Andrea, Tatia, and Renée realized how Alex had defined the term "research," which he had sent Julien to accomplish.

<The Assemblyman that you seem to cherish so highly,> Cordelia said with figurative tongue in cheek, <gave several inflammatory speeches, most quite derogatory of our people. He followed those harangues with releases to the media, which reported for the first time the existence of the silver ship and its attack on the *Rêveur*. Apparently that piece of information was not dispersed to the populace on your last visit,> she said, questioning the decision not to be forthcoming to the New Terrans.

<It was the President's decision and, at the time, the Assembly agreed,> Alex said.

<As it was, sentiment shifted toward Ser Downing,> Cordelia continued. <The populace contacted their Representatives, pushing for selection of him as President pro tem.>

<Typical of Downing not to reveal that he and the entire Assembly were aware of the *Rêveur*'s history all the time,> Andrea grumbled.

<What else, Julien?> Alex asked.

<Once elected, President Downing cleaned house, as your people would say,> Cordelia sent. <He replaced the T-Station managers, Commander Jameson, General Gonzalez, and all the Ministers but one.>

<That lousy excuse for a human ...> Tatia started then held herself in check.

<Anything else, Julien?> Alex requested, growing tired of bad news.

<I'm afraid so, Admiral. The crew's pay has been rescinded by the new Space Technology Minister, who also scrapped the plans for your fighter-carrier. The new Barren Island Commander has developed a limited version of our Daggers, called Strikers. They have built thirty-seven to date and have deployed them on your planet and your system's outposts.>

On this note, the New Terrans perked up. <Can you compare the capabilities of these Strikers to our fighters?> Alex asked.

<The new fighters are substantially less capable, Admiral, > Z responded.

<As well, I compared their pilot training with that of your original pilots, Admiral,> Cordelia added. <It is also substantially less.>

<Could we use these Strikers?> Tatia asked, hopeful.

<Negative, Commander,> Julien replied. <They would be ineffective against the silver ships.>

<Now doesn't that make you want to cry,> said Alex, shaking his head in frustration. <The great man, who touts unfettered capitalism, finally gets ultimate control then waters down the Méridien technology and our training until he has something totally ineffective for humanity's needs.> The irony was so great that Alex couldn't help but cry and laugh at the same time. When he regained his composure and dried his eyes, he said, <Julien, I need to talk to General Gonzalez.>

* * *

After their conference, Andrea requested a private meeting with Alex. As they sat at her cabin table, Andrea ducked her head, gathering her thoughts before she spoke. "Admiral, word has gotten around that we aren't welcome here," Andrea finally said. "It's spooked some of the crew and this coming just after our recent adventures. We have twenty-three requests from our New Terran crew … they're done … they want off.

"Are any of them critical to our operations?" Alex asked, feeling as if he had been punched in the stomach.

"Three are Dagger pilots, backup pilots. I think witnessing the loss of two of their own and eyeing the wreck of Robert's fighter has brought reality home, and they want none of it."

"Anyone else critical?" he asked.

"Do I count?" Andrea said, and dead silence met her announcement. She shrugged her shoulders and gave Alex a grin. "Just testing to see if I was still important, Admiral."

"Black space, Andrea," Alex swore.

"Julien told me to do it," she said, grinning.

<I merely suggested it as a jest, Admiral,> Julien said. <I didn't think she'd actually do it.>

<Liar,> Andrea said.

<Prevaricator,> Julien retorted.

Alex reasserted control. <Steady, you two. The crew has a right to end their contract when they see fit. They get to go home. I presume Tatia and Sheila know about the loss of the Dagger pilots?>

<They do, Admiral.>

<Perhaps we can use this in our favor. It gives us another excuse to visit the planet. We have New Terrans who want to go home.>

As Alex left her cabin, Andrea sent, <Well done, Julien.> When Andrea had begun receiving the termination requests, she had each crew member register a formal statement with Julien. It occurred to both of them that these would be Alex's first desertions. So they concocted a dose of therapeutic humor to prevent Alex from dwelling on the news.

-3-

After years serving as the commanding officer of the Terran Security Forces, Maria Gonzalez's life was now her own and she was enjoying her free time without interruption by TSF comm or reader. She walked back into her country home from her long hike in the woods, showered, and brewed tea before she checked her messages. Maria wasn't surprised to find a secure message on her reader. It read: "Contact you later, your foreign friends." Her loyal TSF associates had notified her of the flotilla's arrival. "Welcome home, Alex," she whispered. "Jaya would be thrilled to know you brought friends."

<Admiral, I have General Gonzalez on comm,> Julien sent. <She is at home on her private reader. I have secured your communications.>

<Greetings, General Gonzalez,> Alex sent while working at his cabin's desk. He had adopted his implants so thoroughly that he preferred to communicate by thought through Julien when he had the option.

"Welcome back. I understand congratulations are in order, Admiral," Maria said.

<It's something I'm still trying to get used to, General.>

"It's ex-General, Admiral. You may call me 'Maria.'"

<And I'm still "Alex.">

"So, Alex, I'm told there's a flotilla out past our ice fields. I take it that it's yours."

Alex spent the next hour updating Maria on what had transpired since he had left New Terra with a single passenger liner and four Daggers. He detailed the destruction of Confederation colonies by the silver ships, the exodus of the Méridien people in advance of their enemy, Albert de Guirnon's treachery, their invention of a Méridien House, the encounter with an enemy fighter, the discovery of the Independents and House

Bergfalk, the race to complete the giant city-ships, the fight to get clear of the system, and the Librans' decision to join Alex's House.

Of the list of incredible subjects Alex had covered, Maria latched on to one point in particular. "You have your own House, Alex?" Maria asked.

<House Alexander, General, and I am Co-Leader with Alex,> Renée sent, laughing as she joined the conversation. Having just exited the refresher, she had donned a wrap to allow Alex to concentrate on the call to some degree. Then she proceeded to negate that by walking around to Alex's side of the desk and perching on the edge, her bare legs dangling in front of him.

"Ser de Guirnon, I am so pleased to hear you're safe, and I am so sorry for the tremendous losses your people are suffering."

<Thank you, General. Your sentiments are truly appreciated. However, if the Admiral can be called "Alex," then I can be called "Renée.">

"And as I was saying to Alex, please call me 'Maria.' It appears you took the right man back with you considering what was happening in Confederation space."

Renée placed the toes of her right foot against Alex's bare chest, flexing them slowly. <Yes, Maria, I have been extremely fortunate.>

"Alex has been describing your adventures. How many Librans did you rescue?"

When Alex remained silent, Renée answered, <We evacuated over 253,000 people from the planet, Maria, but we were forced to leave 2,200 elders behind when the silver ships entered the system ahead of our lift schedule, and we lost our second Dagger pilot in the fight to get clear of the system.>

"Ah," Maria said, intuiting Alex's silence. "And I'm sure, Alex, you remember those twenty-two hundred every day. Such is the weight of command. So where are the rescued now?"

<On two massive city-ships,> Alex replied, <Plus there's a few thousand distributed between four liners and two freighters.>

"You have two ships that hold a quarter of a million people?" Maria blurted. "And all of these people report to the two of you?"

<Most of them are in the role of support personnel. About 300 are military,> Alex replied.

"House Alexander is military?" Maria asked. She felt stunned to hear that the quiet explorer Captain had been transformed into the head of a powerful military organization.

<We made application to the Council as House Alexander, the Military Arm of the Confederation,> said Renée. <If we want to stop the spread of the silver ships, Maria, we must appear formidable in the Council's eyes.>

"Now I'm the uncomfortable one for not calling you 'Admiral,' Alex," Maria replied.

<Then we will be uncomfortable together, Maria,> Alex said, remembering the strong, steady woman that he and Renée had enjoyed getting to know. <Enough about our adventures, Maria. We need to talk about New Terra. We have the background on President McMorris, Clayton's maneuvers within the Assembly and to the populace, and his firing of everyone who supported us.>

"You're very well informed, Alex. Oh, but then you have Julien."

Renée's mirth echoed through the comm. <Maria, if you only knew. Alex now has three devoted SADEs in his cabal. They nicely complement his skills with his twin implants that he wields like an alien.>

"How things do change in a half-year, Alex," Maria replied, irony lacing her words.

<That they do, that they do. Well, to work, General,> Alex said, changing the conversation's tone. <I need to resolve this mess.>

<What part of the mess are you referring to, Admiral?> Maria replied.

<That would be all that's transpired on New Terra since we've been gone, General,> Alex sent. <I have a city-ship that isn't completed, and its environmental systems are overloading, necessitating we reach New Terra immediately. On top of that, I require the use of the T-Stations and Barren Island to build up my forces, which means, one way or the other, Downing and his people have to get out of my way.>

"You're speaking a dangerous language, Admiral. You'll be perceived as approaching New Terra with a hostile force."

<Hostile force?> Alex replied as if he had been wounded. <Why, General, I have a load of refugees who need asylum, and I have New Terrans anxious to reach home and their loved ones.>

Maria laughed at Alex's alternate description of his flotilla. "It always comes down to politics and perceptions, Admiral. That's the war you have to win here, while avoiding any conflict."

<I understand, General, and that's my intention. But I haven't time for idiots. What I need to discover is a means of unseating Downing while we engage him in this power dance he's initiated.>

"Then I have few suggestions for you, Admiral. One, you will be challenged by our Strikers. Brace them with an overwhelming show of force and superiority. I think they'll crumble. The pilots are the sons and daughters of our capitalist elite, for the most part. Second, look into the finances surrounding Méridien tech production. Word has it that the T-Stations are at capacity production levels, but I don't see much product reaching the populace. It's all private industry sales. Lastly, the replacement of a President pro tem is at the discretion of the Assembly. Give them a good reason."

<Thank you for the suggestions, General,> Alex replied

"Just remember, Admiral, that if and when you get the Assembly motivated to replace Downing, you must be ready to dangle a viable candidate under their noses, one who enjoys popular support."

<That's not a problem, General. I've already chosen a candidate,> Alex sent.

"And who might that be, Admiral?" Maria asked, hoping Alex wasn't about to suggest himself. She didn't want to believe that Alex could have changed so much from the young Captain she had admired.

<Why, you, General. You're the next President pro tem, if I have anything to say about it. I'll be in touch,> Alex said as he ended the comm.

* * *

Alex held a brief conference comm with his Captains, Directors, and Commanders. <The *Unsere Menschen* can't wait,> he sent. <Julien, coordinate the flotilla and make best possible speed for New Terra. Have our ships take up a position fifty kilometers off the Joaquin orbital station. Position the *Money Maker* planet inward so our Daggers can intercept any Strikers that lift from New Terra. Commander Tachenko, how many Daggers are available?>

<You have three, Admiral. The *Money Maker* has seventeen.>

<Seventeen,> Alex replied, and everyone heard his chuckle.

<You know us, Admiral,> Tatia responded, <just like to be prepared. You always seem to need what we have.>

<Commander Reynard,> Alex said, switching subjects, <the word from General Gonzalez is the Striker pilots are poorly trained dilettantes. A show of numbers and maneuverability might send them running. Do not fire on them unless you must. Remember, they are following the order of a lawful President, even if that person is Clayton Downing.>

<Poor fools,> Sheila commented. <We'll be nice to the cute and cuddlies, Admiral.>

<We have about seven days to New Terra at our freighters' velocity,> Alex sent. <Director Stroheim, I need a list of what you need … crew, material, whatever.>

<Certainly, Admiral, we'll have it for you within two days,> Eric replied.

<Alright, people, let's get this fleet moving. We may not be welcome now, but that may change by the time we arrive.>

* * *

Once the flotilla was underway, Alex decided a direct conversation with Downing might induce the man to change his stance. He made sure

Andrea stood beside him on the bridge. "Do whatever you have to, Captain, short of making me look like a fool, if I begin to lose my temper with Downing," Alex advised.

"Are you giving me permission to slap you, Admiral?" Andrea asked innocently, which earned her a scowl.

Alex expected Downing to play power games if he requested a vid comm, and he was right. Julien had to hunt the President down. Finally, when Downing sat down at his office desk, Julien activated the man's vid comm.

"Good day, President Downing," Alex said as respectfully as he could manage.

"Well, if it isn't the self-appointed Admiral," Clayton replied, acid dripping from his tongue. "They promote quickly in those alien worlds of yours, don't they? Was my message unclear?"

"This is a courtesy call, President Downing. I just wanted to inform you that we're coming to visit. We'll be at New Terra in seven days, and we would appreciate it if you would refrain from sending your fighters against us."

"For discussion's sake, let me ask you why you bothered to come back," Downing said.

"No choice, Mr. President. Circumstances forced us to come here. We have repairs to make and supplies to collect, then we'll be out of your way. Can we agree on a peaceful solution?" Alex asked as pleasantly as possible.

Downing shook his head in bored negation. He clearly believed he had the superior position and owed Alex nothing. "I've already warned you, Mr. Whatever-you-want-to-call-yourself. If you cross the ice fields, our fighters will destroy your ships." Then Clayton rose and hurriedly left the vid's field of view.

"'Mr. Whatever-you-want-to-call-yourself?'" Andrea cried out as they heard Clayton's office door slam. "Admiral, you should have given that cheap excuse for a politician a piece of your mind."

"And exactly how would that have helped, Captain?" Alex replied, disgusted over the vid comm's outcome.

"Well … if nothing else, Admiral, I would have had permission to administer a little discipline," Andrea replied with a cheeky grin.

-4-

Alex and Andrea sat in the *Rêveur*'s bridge command chairs, reviewing the planets' positions in the system and Julien's projected course to New Terra on the holo-vid.

Andrea started chuckling. "It appears the imbecile-in-charge forgot to check the planet positions before he threatened us."

"It does appear that fortune is on our side, Captain," Alex replied, smiling.

Sharius, the moon housing the explorer-tug outpost and orbiting Seda, the system's most outward planet, was forty degrees past them on the ecliptic and headed for a far pass around Oistos. This was the first fighter posting that the President probably believed would have stopped the flotilla. The second fighter outpost was based on the planet Ganymede, which was 152 degrees off from their approach, coming from behind the star. It was also too far for the fighters to reach them. Only Niomedes, the home of the Habitat Experiments, and New Terra itself could launch fighters at them.

Later that evening, Alex sat at his cabin's desk, wrapped in the New Terran-style robe Renée had made for him, contemplating his holo-vid display, the same system image he and Andrea had observed earlier.

<Julien, Julien, Julien,> Alex sent, his thoughts sad. <Why doesn't this ever get any easier?>

<One could hope for a magic lamp from the likes of *One Thousand and One Nights*, Admiral,> Julien replied. <It might make our tasks much easier.>

<But then they wouldn't need you or me, my friend.>

<There is that, Admiral.>

<Julien, I need some background information that I can use as leverage … leverage against Downing and his cronies. Put on your sleuthing hat and gather your gang.>

<And what are our targets, Admiral?>

<For people like Downing, it's always about the credits. They've had a free hand up till now with the Méridien technology. We both know they'll be hiding this information from the populace. Find out what they're doing. Follow the funds. Also, get me a list of characters surrounding Downing and what they've been doing. Then check on communication between Assembly members. Who is unhappy with Downing? And research what it takes to initiate another Assembly vote for President pro tem. Finally, track down our people, the T-Managers, the President's Transfer Team, and Commander Jameson. What are they doing?>

<How invasive should we be with regard to New Terran networks and communication devices, in light of our efforts being discovered, Admiral?>

Alex considered his options. If the SADEs didn't vigorously pursue the information he needed, he wouldn't be able to force a change in the New Terran political environment that would be supportive of his mission to take the fight to the silver ships. On the other hand, the penetration of his world's secure information repositories and the release of the data to the public to unseat Downing would make him and the SADEs personae non gratae on New Terra.

<Julien, I believe we must consider our return to New Terra as temporary,> Alex finally answered. <Once we depose Downing and procure the supplies and repairs we need, I think we'll have lost our welcome. We'll be the family's guests, who are welcomed with hugs, but whose arrival begins the counting of days until they leave. >

Despite his immense processing power, Julien couldn't find a satisfactory reply. Alex had given up so much for the Méridiens, and now he believed his actions would cost him his home world. In the ancient novels Julien had come to love, his prized characters often spoke simply and from the heart. So he did. <I am deeply sorry, my friend, for what your efforts may cost you. Please know that whatever you do, wherever you go, I will be with you, if that is your wish.>

<Thank you, Julien. That in itself is a comfort. Now before you begin your work, wake someone in my family.>

* * *

Alex went to bed while Julien attempted to contact Duggan, Katie, or Christie. Apparently Alex's parents and sister had gone to sleep and turned off their readers, having no knowledge of his return. Downing and company were keeping the news of the flotilla very secure, but that wouldn't last long. Private telescopes would pick up the giant city-ships when they cleared the ice fields.

Early the next morning, Julien got through to fourteen-year-old Christie. To wake Alex, Julien sent him a selection of Mutter's orchestral music in softly increasing volume.

Violin strings accompanied Alex's dreams when he finally recognized Julien's signal. As he came fully aware, Alex chose to respond without leaving the warmth of his bed, since Renée was draped over his side, her head on his chest.

<Yes, Julien,> Alex sent, softly touching Renée's hair.

<I have Christie on the comm, Admiral,> Julien replied and connected the two siblings.

<Christie, Alex here.>

"Alex, where's here? Where are you?" a smiling Christie nearly yelled into her reader.

<Christie, I need you to get Dad and Mom on your reader. I need all three of you,> Alex sent.

As Christie hurried upstairs to wake her parents, she wondered at the change in her brother. His words had become confident … authoritative. The grave error she'd made during Alex's visit with René and Étienne, lying to them and her parents about Étienne's interview, was a painful memory that had plagued her every day since Alex had left. That he wanted her on the comm with Mom and Dad was an opportunity to make up for her selfishness—an opportunity she promised herself she wouldn't waste.

Alex began falling back asleep, lulled by the warmth of Renée, who disdained clothing in bed, when he heard his mother's voice.

"Alex, it's Mom. Where are you?" Katie said.

After a few polite words of greeting, Alex launched into a synopsis of the last half-year's events from their arrival at Méridien to their escape from Libre to their return at New Terra. As the recollection of events piled up, Alex began to lose his family's focus.

"Wait, who is the Admiral you mentioned?" Christie asked.

<That would be me, Christie,> Alex replied. "Oh," was all he heard from his sister.

"And these people, Alex, how many were there on Libre?" his mother asked.

<Over a quarter-million men, women, and children were rescued. Most of them are on two city-ships, which are long-term habitation vessels.>

"How big are these ships, Alex?" Duggan asked.

<They're built like huge saucers, Dad, about two kilometers across. In addition, we now have four passenger liners and two freighters.>

"And you're the Admiral because ..." Duggan ventured.

<Because Renée and I have formed a military-styled Méridien House to which everyone has declared their allegiance.>

Suddenly Alex's family was talking all at once. Duggan attempted to confirm that the quarter-million people reported to Alex. Katie wanted to hear about Renée, and Christie's voice got lost in the noise.

<Hush, everyone,> Alex sent, which resulted in the family's immediate silence. Alex winced as he realized he had used his commander's tones. <Yes, Dad, the Librans, all of them, report to Renée and me. And, yes, Mom, Renée and I remain close ...> Alex confirmed as he looked down at her sleeping face. He stroked her hair again, eliciting a little moan of pleasure as she snuggled closer to him. <Very close.>

<What's the name of the House?> Christie asked eagerly.

It was the question Alex kept hoping wouldn't be asked, but now he couldn't get around it. <Renée and I chose "House Alexander.">

He endured a few moments of Christie's teasing and parental murmurs of appreciation; although he could tell they were confused by what his announcements meant.

<Well, Admiral,> Duggan announced formally, <when will you make planetfall?>

<That's the problem, Dad, and the reason for my early morning call. I need your help. Specifically, I need Christie's help.>

If Alex had been able to see his family, the reader lying between them on his parent's bed, he would have seen the huge grin on his sister's face.

* * *

Before midday the following day, Alex had assembled everyone he required—Renée, his Captains and their officers, and his Directors—all outfitted in their best dress. The group arranged themselves around the *Freedom*'s semicircular bridge, facing rearward and flanking Alex. They formed a most presentable group to the vid cam mounted at the rear of the bridge.

At 13.50 hours, Cordelia activated the bridge cam and linked to Christie's reader via the FTL station. Then on Cordelia's cue, Christie commed the By-Long Media House, which last year had produced her historic and the one-and-only Méridien interview with Étienne.

Earlier that morning, Christie had called the By-Long Media House and had been instantly connected to producer Charlotte Sanderson, who sounded excited to hear from the sister of the famous Captain Racine. What Charlotte didn't expect was to be asked for a half-hour of airtime with no conditions imposed by the station on Christie's broadcast. If Charlotte hadn't had such a widely successful program featuring Christie's previous interview, she would never have acceded to the request.

Throughout the morning, Charlotte had flooded fans' readers with announcements of a momentous By-Long program with none other than Christie Racine. To Charlotte's fans, it was code for "Captain Racine and the Méridiens," and they had plied their personal networks with announcements of a new Christie show.

At 13.48 hours and with the Director's approval, the station's regular programming had been interrupted, announcing a special program with Christie Racine that had to be seen, despite the fact that no one knew the subject of the interview.

Charlotte sat in her producer's chair in over-watch of the broadcast tech, who rolled a hastily prepared vid introduction to their program. Charlotte added a voiceover, announcing Christie Racine with a "special guest."

In her bedroom, Christie's vid app showed her on-air. She put on her best smile and welcomed the audience to her interview. "Good morning, New Terrans. I'm sure all of you are curious as to what has become of my famous brother and our distant cousins who left our system nearly a half-year ago. So I thought I would put many of your questions to rest by letting you share my conversation with my brother this morning."

Following Christie's introduction, Charlotte's ear comm and reader blew up with comms from the station manager and Directors. She blocked all of them to concentrate on the show. Suddenly her tech's second monitor opened up with a vid feed of the famous brother, surrounded by associates and standing in front of an enormous wraparound ship's bridge. Charlotte didn't question how they were receiving the signal, but just urged her tech to ride with it.

"People of New Terra, say hello to my brother, Admiral Racine," Christie announced as the tech switched signals to broadcast Alex and company.

"Christie, it's wonderful to see you again," Alex began.

"So, Admiral, dear brother, what have you been up to and who are all your new friends?" Christie had printed out the questions she had received from Alex and had tacked them to the wall behind her vid cam. Her brother had coached her on the reasons for each question so she would understand the purpose. When Christie had reviewed them with her parents, she had realized the magnitude of what her brother wanted to accomplish. Alex truly did need her help.

On his end of things, Alex felt proud of Christie. She was handling the interview as if they were enjoying a casual conversation, attempting to discover what her sibling had been doing, and Alex held nothing back. As he spoke on key points, Cordelia cut in vids under his words. Alex and Julien had spent a couple hours prepping the vids Alex wanted the populace to see, and they were getting an eyeful.

In the middle of the interview, Christie dropped a tough question in the guise of some casual confusion she wanted to untangle. "Admiral, I don't understand something. The *Rêveur* was damaged seven decades ago by one of these silver ships that have been destroying the Confederation colonies. Why didn't you tell anyone about this last year?"

As planned, Renée, standing beside Alex, fielded the question and said, "But we did, Christie. Your President McMorris required that we present our requests to your Assembly. During that presentation, we showed this vid." Julien rolled a short segment of the attack on the *Rêveur*, while she continued. "All of your Representatives saw this and understood what had befallen our ship, including your Clayton Downing. He was one of the original visitors to our ship and saw the damage, up close and personal, as you would say."

"Oh, I didn't know our Assembly knew about the silver ships," Christie said, sounding so innocent. "So … are we in immediate danger from these aliens?"

"No, Christie," Alex replied. "They've invaded the Confederation's Arnos system, and historic records indicate that they will be there for eight to twelve years. But someday, maybe not too far in the future, they will come for New Terra."

"What are your plans for all of those people with you, Admiral?" Christie asked.

"We left the Arnos system in a running fight with the silver ships, and one of our city-ships, the *Unsere Menschen*, needs to finish construction. The incomplete environmental systems are overloaded and are about to put its 122,000 passengers in jeopardy."

Charlotte was on the edge of her seat, dying to ask some crucial questions when Christie began asking them for her.

"So, big brother of mine, you've saved a planet load of Librans from death. You've found a swarm of aliens devastating Confederation colonies, billions of people lost. And you've come back to New Terra to do what?"

"The docking and completion of the *Unsere Menschen* is an emergency. That's the first step. Then I plan to outfit our ships to return to Libre to eliminate the silver ships before they can invade another human world."

"Are you aware, Alex, that President McMorris is dead and Clayton Downing is our President pro tem?"

"Yes, Christie, I am. When we exited FTL outside the system, Sharius TSF contacted us and told us they had a message from President Downing," Alex said without inflection.

"Oh, but we haven't heard anything from our government about your return," Christie replied, playing the naive teenager role to the hilt. "What did President Downing have to say to you?"

"TSF relayed a message from the President that we were to remain outside the system and under no circumstances were we to cross the ice fields—or his fighters would attack our ships," Alex said. "Later I contacted President Downing directly and explained our city-ship's emergency. In essence, he responded that he didn't care."

"So you're staying out beyond the ice fields even though that endangers the Méridien citizens with you?" Christie said, carefully emphasizing the word "citizen," incorporating the subtext that her brother wanted conveyed.

"No, Christie. Our flotilla is on course for New Terra. We will be in orbit within four days. Julien will be sending out requests to New Terran construction firms to complete our work on the *Unsere Menschen*. Then I intend to reactivate the T-sites and Barren Island for our purposes."

"But if the President doesn't want you to do this, aren't you breaking the law, Admiral?" Christie asked.

"Yes and no, Christie," Alex replied, knowing he was treading a fine line to include this question, but he needed the populace to understand his intentions. "Am I disobeying the order of the President pro tem, a man who hasn't been elected by the people? Yes, I am. Do I consider it a lawful order when it might condemn over 122,000 people to death? No, I don't.

And do I believe that we must stop the silver ships before they come to New Terra? Absolutely! Now is the time to go after our common enemy. We've discovered we can defeat them, having learned their weaknesses and destroyed many of them."

"Oh … Mom and Dad wanted me to say hello, and we look forward to your planetfall. And thank you, Admiral, for what you're trying to do for all of us." Christie had worked up the closing line herself, wanting her viewers to understand that Alex was trying to save both the Méridiens and the New Terrans.

"See you soon, Christie," Alex said with a bright smile for his little sister.

Cordelia ended the signal from the *Freedom*, and the media tech switched to Christie. Charlotte sat hunched in her chair, chewing a fingernail and waiting for Christie's close. She had just a few moments.

Christie looked into her vid cam and smiled briefly before assuming a pensive countenance. "I hope you've enjoyed my chat with my big brother. What he has shown us has given me a lot to think about. In the grand scheme of things, I'm certainly not the best person to understand the ramifications of what he is attempting to accomplish. But I do know my brother is one of the most honest people I know. You can believe what he says has happened and what he intends to do about it. I guess the important question for New Terra is: Are we going to help him and the endangered Méridiens despite the President's order?" She paused and her serious and thoughtful expression morphed into a sweet, teenager's smile. "Thank you for joining me this morning."

Charlotte signaled the tech to close the show and return to their regular programming. She sat back in her chair and slapped her hulking tech on the shoulder, who grinned back at her. It was bonus time for both of them.

* * *

Maria Gonzalez had received notice of Christie's upcoming broadcast from Julien. She linked her reader to the show along with a few hundred key people she had notified, who in turn had each notified their compatriots, friends, and family. Maria's personal network was the reason 19,000 people were prepared to view the show before it had even been announced.

After watching the interview, Maria leaned back in her chair. Her home, located on the building's top floor, allowed her a view of Government House from her window. Slow anger burned deep inside her. Maria felt convinced that President McMorris had been murdered, and somehow the reptile, Downing, had been involved. But days after Downing's approval by the Assembly, she had been removed from her position and frozen out of her TSF assets, losing her opportunity to investigate. A Downing stooge now sat in her TSF chair.

As she considered Christie's morning chat, a smile replaced her frown. She had underestimated Alex. Somewhere along the way, the young Captain had developed political skills. Alex was no longer the loner, plying the ice fields. He had become a force of change. Maria recalled Alex's words which were, "Why, you, General. You're the next President pro tem, if I have anything to say about it." At the time, she had thought Alex's declaration pompous, his title going to his head. But this maneuver, appealing to the populace through a chat with his fourteen-year-old sister, had been delivered as a master stroke. In the next few hours, Maria knew much of the populace would have viewed the show. Now she began giving serious consideration to Alex's words. Maria didn't covet the presidency, but she would love to see Clayton Downing and his sycophants out on their collective ears.

* * *

Clayton had been forewarned of the upcoming show by an associate who was being paid to monitor Maria Gonzalez's friends. He had then notified several trustworthy Ministers and several hundred industry leaders of the program, and finally had sat in his office to watch.

More than one person in Clayton's inner circle wanted the program shut down, but more temperate heads had prevailed. Media stations were a protected industry on New Terra, and woe unto any government entity that tried to say otherwise. The cooler heads made the point that shutting down the station would start an outcry they couldn't manage.

Clayton's inner circle, though, was striving to get him elected as President by popular vote so they could begin to consolidate their power and create what they had always wanted—a government controlled by the elite … the deserving.

-5-

Eric Stroheim and Captain Reinhold worked diligently with Z, the *Unsere Menschen*'s SADE, to update their ship's status. So much work had been done and undone in the days before the ship's launch with no time to correct Z's records, and since the launch, work had continued to shore up the overtaxed environmental systems. It took several hundred workers thirty-two work hours to communicate the status of all systems and construction. Afterward it took Z only moments to compare the city-ship's design plans with the crews' updates to catalog the work that still needed to be accomplished.

<Admiral, I have Z's list of requested repairs, as well as a short list from Cordelia for the *Freedom*,> Julien announced.

Alex halted his cabin's holo-vid, on which he was examining their course for New Terra that would intersect Niomedes. In the days since his sister's interview, he had rearranged his flotilla, placing the *Rêveur* and the *Money Maker* forward. The other three liners came next, and the two city-ships with the second freighter trailed behind by several hours. The SADEs had located five Strikers stationed in a shuttle hangar near the Habitat Experiments. Alex had considered taking a wide path around the planet, but an update from Eric and Z convinced him time was of the essence. Within a half-day, the flotilla would come within range of Niomedes' fighters.

<Is the work earmarked in order of priority, Julien?> Alex asked.

Just the slightest pause ensued before Julien replied, <It is now, Admiral, but I will confirm my efforts with Director Stroheim.>

Alex smiled to himself, imagining the conversation that would take place. Eric Stroheim was still getting accustomed to treating a SADE as an equal. Now, the "Admiral's friend" would be pointing out to Eric that he had failed to request Z prioritize the list into emergency repairs and secondary priorities. It wasn't Z's fault; he was as literal a SADE as you could find—you got what you asked for, little more, unless you happened to be Alex. For some reason, Z reserved the right to expand his responses for Alex, even attempting to anticipate his needs as if he was a unique event.

<So now we attempt to contract for services contrary to the government's edict and entice contractors to work for what ...?> Alex mused to Julien.

<I believe the first issue is entirely yours, Admiral. These are your people and you are eminently more qualified to find a means to engage them than I am. However, on the second point, why can we not do as we did before and trade for it?>

<What do we have left to trade? We gave New Terra just about everything in your database, didn't we?>

<Yes, we did, Admiral. But who received the information?> Julien said, offering Alex the tip of his thought.

<That's absolutely true, Julien. We gave it to the government. Now we could offer it directly to the contractors to trade their services for product information that's related to their industry. We could probably do this for each contractor by trading just one or two small products or techniques, which would generate a small fortune for each of them over time.>

As Alex spoke with Julien, Renée entered the cabin, blew him a kiss, and left to use the refresher. <Julien,> Alex continued, <access a list of contractors that built the T-Stations and Barren Island. See if they have experience in ship construction. Give priority to the smaller companies, those less likely to work for our wealthier industrialists. Have your compatriots check out their references. Get at least two contractors for each category we need, then send a message to the owners. Request they sign a confidentiality agreement before you communicate any further. Send your messages in the name of Admiral Alex Racine.>

* * *

"Five Strikers are lifting from Niomedes, Admiral," Julien announced to Alex and Andrea on the bridge. "Estimate contact in 4.3 hours if they achieve maximum acceleration to meet us."

The *Rêveur*'s holo-vid was duplicated on the *Money Maker*'s bridge, courtesy of Julien and Mutter. Tatia had transferred back to the *Money Maker* to support the squadron's actions. She, Sheila, and Captain Menlo were tied into the conference link via the freighter's FTL comm.

Alex had placed the *Money Maker* 200 kilometers forward of the *Rêveur*'s starboard quarter.

In a comm meeting earlier, Tatia had emphasized some tactics to Alex and Andrea. <Admiral,> Tatia had said, <as far as the Striker pilots are concerned, the *Rêveur* has at most four fighters, which they likely believe represent the sum total of our offensive capabilities. More importantly, the *Money Maker* will appear as a freighter not as a fighter-carrier. It's a case of hiding your offensive capabilities in plain sight, if we let the *Money Maker* lead.>

Both Alex and Andrea had shared resigned looks since each one felt this tactic should have occurred to them. "She's still our devious one, Admiral," Andrea had admitted.

Commander Reynard readied her squadron aboard the fighter-carrier. She had paired up sixteen Dagger pilots from the freighter under her but felt nervous about some of the trainees' skills. Sheila earnestly hoped that the intelligence was accurate and that a show of force would scare the Striker pilots off. Lieutenant Hatsuto Tanaka and his two wings were sitting in their Daggers aboard the *Rêveur*. The ships' flight crews had opened all pilots' bay doors and released the fighters' skids.

<Flight-1, Captain Bonnard,> Julien sent on the conference comm.

<Lieutenant Tanaka, launch your flight,> Andrea commanded.

The *Rêveur*'s three Daggers slid out of its twin bays and accelerated at only one-fifth power. Their course aimed straight for the five approaching Strikers.

There followed tense moments for Andrea while she waited for an update from Julien, hoping the Strikers veered off and returned to Niomedes. A glance at Alex revealed him sitting quietly in the other command chair, a bored expression on his face.

"You don't appear to be concerned whether those fighters come on or not, Admiral," Andrea said.

"They will or they won't, Captain. Do I want to see five New Terrans killed for the stupidity of their President? Absolutely not. Am I willing to send them to the deep dark if they attempt to prevent our preparations to return to Libre? Absolutely."

<Flight-2, Commander Reynard,> Julien sent.

Sheila acknowledged her flight order and seventeen Daggers exited the *Money Maker*. She was the only pilot without a wing, but then again she had the most experience, short as it was. Her squadron merged with Flight-1, and per their Commander's orders, the twenty Daggers spread out to produce an intimidating array of force.

* * *

Lieutenant Damien Hunsader couldn't believe his good fortune. His flight of Strikers had circled Niomedes to intercept the oncoming flotilla of the interlopers. It would be his five against the enemy's four at worst, perhaps even better if the so-called Admiral had lost a fighter or two. According to his uncle, Samuel Hunsader, the refugees were disobeying a presidential order. Damien and his fellow pilots had been informed that the ships were full of potentially diseased aliens, and he, for one, was not going to let them contaminate his home world.

Damien's Striker force rounded the planet's curve, and his telemetry displayed the flotilla and the liner's launch of three fighters from the *Rêveur*. "Striker force, it's going to be five against three!" Damien sent via comms.

Unfortunately for Damien, his fellow pilots didn't share their leader's elation. They had signed up to defend the system from aliens, not human refugees.

"Striker-2 and Striker-3, you target the Dagger on the left," Damien ordered. 'Striker-4 and Striker-5, you have the Dagger on the right. I'll take the center one."

"Leader, Striker-2. Shouldn't we see if they fail to engage … give them an opportunity to turn around?"

"Negative, Striker-2," Damien replied. "We do our duty. If we eliminate these fighters, those contaminated ships will be forced to turn around."

"Leader, Striker-5. I heard from my brother that one of those large ships is in danger of environmental systems failure. We're talking about the potential death of over a hundred thousand people."

"Then they shouldn't have come this way!" Damien replied. "Now cut the noise, Striker force. Only maneuver comms from now on."

Damien Hunsader and his father had never been close, which is why as a boy Damien had focused on his successful and attentive uncle, Samuel Hunsader. His uncle had no children of his own, and Damien was happy to fill the role of adopted son. When he told his father he was joining the Barren Island cadet program, his father had tried to dissuade him, but his uncle had encouraged him. Now Damien would prove to his father that he had made the right decision. He would protect his world and become a hero.

While Damien was imagining the celebration that would surely follow their successful action, the three approaching Daggers suddenly expanded into twenty. Anger boiled up inside Damien. His dream of a hero's reception was being snatched from him.

"Leader, Striker-2. We can't take on twenty Daggers. It would be suicide. We have to pull back."

"Negative, Striker-2. We have to defend our home world. This applies to each and every one of you. We take as many of them with us as we can," Damien yelled into his helmet comm.

As the intervening distance between the fighters closed, Damien noticed his Striker formation drifting. "Striker-3 and Striker-5, tighten up on your leads. You're drifting." When he received no response and telemetry showed an even greater gap forming, he was about to comm the two pilots again when both fighters pulled out of formation and headed back to base.

"Get back here, you cowards!" Damien yelled.

Then suddenly he was alone. His other two pilots had veered off as well and were hurrying to catch the first two deserters.

Fear crawled up Damien's spine and into his mind. At least that's the way it felt. He couldn't think. Despite his overwhelming fear, it never occurred to him to turn around. He sat frozen while the twenty Daggers raced toward him.

* * *

Sheila was happy when two of the Strikers about-faced and then happier still when two more left formation. She wasn't anxious to kill New Terrans, but over 122,000 people were depending on her and the squadron to remove this obstacle, and the entire Confederation waited on them, even if they didn't know it.

<Admiral, the last Striker isn't turning around,> Sheila sent.

<It's your call, Squadron Leader,> Alex replied. <You know our predicament. You can only do your best.>

Sheila was tempted to launch her missiles and be done with it. Julien's information had revealed that the Strikers carried single-stage missiles, which were far less effective than the Dagger's present armaments. Two missiles from her Dagger would launch sixteen powerful Libre-X second-stage missiles, ensuring the Striker's destruction.

<All Daggers, veer off and clear the field. Now!> Sheila ordered.

The squadron was well-conditioned to Sheila's leadership and executed their maneuvers without thinking, even Hatsuto.

Alex's bored expression left his face, and he leaned forward to examine the holo-vid as he watched the nineteen icons of Sheila's squadron sheer away from their original vector. Sheila's Dagger was advancing alone against the remaining Striker.

As the fighters raced at one another, Sheila's controller pinged her helmet—she was in missile range. Still, she held her fire. *What do you want to do today, my young friend … live or die?* Sheila wondered.

* * *

Damien's fear still held him in its grip even though all but one Dagger remained in front of him. One part of his mind screamed at him to launch his missiles; the other part wailed at his predicament. At any moment, he was sure the Dagger would launch its missiles. One small thought leaked through the white noise in his mind that both fighters were inside their missile envelopes.

In an instant, Damien was past the Dagger. He hadn't even attempted to maneuver his fighter from what should have been a head-on collision. At the last moment, the Dagger had flipped on its side and shot past him. In the fraction of time they had, it seemed an impossible feat. But as his fear faded, the thought surfaced that he was still alive, which he realized was what he wanted first and foremost. Damien turned his Striker back for Niomedes. As he tried to think of what he would say to his uncle, he began to cry.

* * *

<Flight-2, return to your bays. We're done here,> Sheila ordered. <Lieutenant Tanaka, shadow that last Striker with Flight-1. Ensure it doesn't go anywhere near our ships. I think that pilot has lost his taste for a

fight, but I don't want to take any chances. That fighter doesn't get within missile range of our ships. Understood?>

<Copy that, Squadron Leader. Turning around now. We'll shadow it home.>

<Commander Reynard,> Alex sent.

<Yes, Admiral,> Sheila replied.

<That was quite the dangerous maneuver,> Alex said. <What made you think that pilot wouldn't fire?>

<I expected him to fire, Admiral,> Sheila replied. <Based on Julien's programming of our controllers to detect a silver ship's pre-beam release, I figured my controller would detect his missile launch and easily maneuver my ship out of the way. I thought if I proved the superiority of our craft, I would scare the pilot off.>

<Would that work, Julien … the controller detecting the missile launch and evading it?> Alex asked.

<I'm not pleased to inform you, Commander,> Julien replied, <that the detection telemetry was specific to the energy wavelength of the silver ships. Your controller would have detected the Striker's missile launch but made no effort to evade it unless you so ordered. By the time you would have done so, I expect it would have been too late.>

<Oh, black space, Julien,> Sheila moaned.

<Indeed, Commander.>

Back aboard the *Money Maker*, the crew congratulated and hailed Sheila for her icy cold maneuver—facing down a Striker pilot. Later, Sheila sat in Tatia's cabin, relating the truth of the encounter and sharing New Terran alcohol that Tatia had shipped aboard with her personal effects.

Tatia clinked Sheila's cup and smiled in understanding. "To fortune, sister," Tatia said.

-6-

Niomedes now lay behind the flotilla; New Terra sat a day out.

<Julien,> Alex sent, <locate the President for me.>

<Certainly, Admiral. It would be my displeasure.>

Again, Julien had to work to connect to Downing. When he accessed the previous contact points—readers and vid monitors—he found them disconnected or the vids physically blocked. The man was obviously hiding from Alex. So Julien monitored Clayton's close associates and waited.

<Admiral, the creature you desire to comm is meeting with his Minister of Space Exploration.>

<Can't say his name, Julien?>

<I'm attempting to keep my comms clean, Admiral. You will not have vid, but he will hear you.>

<Understood, Julien. Open the connection.>

<Mr. President, this is Admiral Racine,> Alex sent. He waited for a reply but heard only the furtive noises of people moving about the office. <Well, Mr. President, if you wish not to be heard or seen, I must be satisfied with a one-way conversation. I have an agenda to accomplish, after which I will be leaving New Terra with half the flotilla. The other half will remain until the final phases of our city-ships' construction are complete. When my mission is accomplished at Libre, we will all be leaving. If you stay out of my way, I'll stay out of your way.>

Alex waited, giving the President every opportunity to speak. He didn't want a confrontation, but he wasn't willing to turn from his path, either. Finally, Alex gave up and closed the comm. *Well, that went well,* he thought.

<Julien, locate the Joaquin Station Manager next, please.> Alex had developed a good relationship with Hezekiah Cohen while the station

hosted the work on the *Rêveur* and the *Outward Bound.* He fervently hoped the man still held the same position.

<Admiral, I have Ser Cohen on comm,> Julien replied.

<Good evening, Hezekiah. This is Admiral Racine.>

"Well, Admiral, so the rumors are true," Hezekiah replied.

<What rumors are those, Ser?> Alex asked.

"That you're part rodent, Admiral. We send you out with two ships, and a half-year later, you come back with nine ships."

Alex could hear Hezekiah's belly laugh. <Ser, it appears your joke is incomplete.>

"Incomplete? How, Admiral?" Hezekiah asked.

<I left with a little more than 100 people, Hezekiah, and returned with a quarter-million.>

This time Hezekiah's laughter was so long and hard he had trouble catching his breath.

Alex waited until the station manager's laughter had subsided, before he dropped the bad news. <One small problem, Hezekiah ... We're about to suffocate half of those people.>

"Never a dull moment with you around, Admiral," Hezekiah said, "welcome back. So if half the people are in danger, I would hazard a guess it's one of those massive saucers that's in trouble."

<Good guess, Hezekiah. It's the *Unsere Menschen.*>

"The what?" Hezekiah asked.

<The ship is the *Unsere Menschen*, which means "our people,"> Alex said. <We have environmental systems failing due to an incomplete build-out of multiple systems. We had a serious health problem in the last system. What you might call an alien infestation.>

"I watched your interview with your sister, Admiral—very clever manner in which to communicate your story despite our wonderful President. Well, to business ... I'll have hoses, blowers, and electrical standing by on a terminal boom. I'll send Julien the location. Can that *Our People* manage a docking or should I be vacationing by the time you arrive."

<You're safe, Hezekiah,> Alex sent. <The *Unsere Menschen* has a SADE by the name of Z who can manage the docking. Thank you for your help. You know, of course, that this could cost you your job if I can't fix this President problem.>

"I was thinking of retiring soon anyway, Admiral," Hezekiah replied. "Wait … you said you're going to fix the President problem?"

<What do you think of Maria Gonzalez, Hezekiah?> Alex asked.

"General Gonzalez? Wonderful woman!" Hezekiah said. "Are you thinking of doing what I think you're thinking of doing, Admiral?"

<Probably,> Alex replied.

"Oh, welcome back, Admiral, welcome back!" Hezekiah said, his voice rising in triumph.

<See you late tomorrow, Hezekiah,> Alex sent and closed the comm.

* * *

The flotilla made New Terra's orbit and took up positions fifty kilometers outward from the Joaquin Station while the *Unsere Menschen* and *Money Maker* proceeded on. Per Alex's orders, Captain Menlo positioned the *Money Maker* inward of the station to act as a front guard against any Strikers lifting from the planet.

If Z was capable of sweating, it would have been pouring out of his case. He was attempting to maneuver the city-ship up to the terminal's extended boom in nearly blind conditions. With so many sensors incomplete, Z was unable to determine subtle distances. The SADEs had positioned their ships to give Z a three-dimensional view of his ship and the station's boom, constantly transmitting telemetry to him as the distance closed. Z would pulse the maneuvering jets, wait, review the telemetry, and pulse the jets again. The last kilometer to the boom's end took nearly two hours to complete. When the terminal's docking boss called "All halt" to Z, both of them waited to ensure that the last pulses had cancelled the enormous ship's forward momentum. Once his fellow SADEs affirmed zero delta-V, Z felt overjoyed.

Oxygen conditions for the people of the *Unsere Menschen* had been deteriorating ever since they had launched from Libre. After the city-ship had passed Niomedes, Captain Cordova had ordered the passengers and crew to their beds to conserve the remaining air supply. The *Freedom* had sent shuttles of compressed oxygen tanks to its sister city-ship, but the effort was akin to bailing the bilge of an ocean-going transport with a cup.

The station's terminal boss extended the boom out five meters to meet with the city-ship's hatch and service ports. Once they achieved a pressure seal and pumped air into the terminal arm's gantry, the tech boss waited for the ship's hatch to open.

Inside the *Unsere Menschen*, a Libran tech named Delores tapped the manual switch for the hatch a second time, but the hatch still didn't move. Delores's thoughts were muddled. She knew she was doing something wrong but couldn't think of what that might be.

<Delores,> Z sent gently, <listen to me. Look at the hatch panel. The lights should all be green. Are they?>

Delores focused on the control panel, which for a moment blurred, then cleared. <No, Z, first row all green; second row green, red, red; third row all green.>

<The hatch is not receiving confirmation of a safe environment outside, Delores. Close the interior hatch.>

Delores struggled over to the opposite side of the airlock and closed the airlock's interior hatch. Her muscles were cramping from oxygen starvation. She looked over at her panel again. <Z, second row is now green, green, red.>

<Excellent, Delores. Now enter the override on the control panel for safe exterior environment. The code is 3-3-1-2-5.>

As the city-ship's hatch slid open, fouled air spilled from the ship and enveloped the Joaquin boom tech. "Boss," the tech said. "This is Fujio on boom control. Hatch is open. We have to move quickly. These people need air badly."

"Z," said the tech boss, Jaime, "I have a ten-centimeter air hose at the boom's end. Fujio, watch for an opening near the hatch for the hose. Don't worry about connections. Just stick it into the opening's throat."

Z opened an air access hatch for Fujio, who jammed the extendible hose into the opening. On Z's signal, the nanites in the collar sealed around the hose, and Z signaled the tech and the terminal boss that a seal was in place. Jaime ran the boom's air pump at max revolutions, forcing air into the city-ship's ventilation system.

Fujio stood aside as more than 200 terminal workers pounded past him, loaded with heavy canisters of oxygen strapped to their backs. The city-ship was a huge labyrinth of corridors and decks, but Julien had supplied Hezekiah with the city-ship's plan. Each worker held a small map in front of them as they navigated to their section. When they reached their assigned area, they walked around, dispersing nine cubic meters of pure oxygen from their tanks. Between the air hose and the oxygen bottles, the people on board slowly began to feel revived.

In the single day of forewarning Hezekiah had received, he had ordered multiple shuttle deliveries of pure oxygen to the station. He used the deliveries to fill the station's reserve tanks located throughout the extensive structure, and kept the last two shuttles in reserve ready to top off the tanks as they were depleted. At the same time, he put out the word that he needed volunteers. His message included the words "Our cousins need help."

* * *

Alex, Renée, and the twins joined Mickey, Tomas, and Eric in a small hall on board the station dedicated by Hezekiah for their use. New Terran contractors had already assembled in the hall, anxious to hear the opportunities to work on the city-ships in exchange for Méridien tech. They had signed their confidentiality agreements with House Alexander, which had more than one of them wondering who was this new business entity?

The meeting was short. Alex and his people stood in front of the forty-three company owners, and Alex introduced himself and Renée as Co-

Leaders of House Alexander. Then he introduced his Directors, Tomas and Eric, and his Chief Engineer, Mickey.

"Sers," Alex began, "we need contractors to complete the construction of the docked city-ship, *Unsere Menschen*, and we need some small finish work on the sister ship, *Freedom*. We have some of the material you will require already on board the ships, but not most of it. The T-Stations will be manufacturing the necessary material shortly."

One of the company owners raised a hand to catch Alex's attention. "Admiral, aren't the T-Stations under government control?"

"You are correct, Ser. That will be remedied soon," Alex replied simply.

The owner shifted uncomfortably in his seat. The splendidly uniformed Admiral standing before him looked younger than his son, but he didn't act that way. The Admiral had said he would have the T-Stations producing his material soon, and the owner was inclined to accept his word—it seemed the better part of wisdom.

"As I said, the T-Stations will be producing the material for you," Alex continued. "What you will need to provide for your part of the agreement will be labor and expenses. We're proposing a simple trade. We will offer each of you one choice of several Méridien intellectual properties."

The noise rose in the hall as the attendees began shouting questions over one another. Everyone quieted when they realized Alex wasn't responding. He just stood there with his hands behind his back. In fact, the Admiral's entire entourage stood eerily quiet, waiting.

When the noise subsided, Alex focused on an older gentleman who hadn't shouted a question but was lost in thought. "Ser," Alex said, pointing at the man. "Did you have a question?"

"I was wondering, Admiral, how I could manage this deal. My company handles ventilation ducting and environmental controls, and we did some of the work on the *Outward Bound*."

"And a fine job you did, Ser," Alex replied. "That shuttle saved tens of thousands of your cousins."

"Thank you, Admiral," he replied, nodding. "But, my problem is that I have a crew of nineteen. I saw the size of your city-ship. Even if I received only a portion of the work, it would require me to shoulder the burden of their pay for far longer than I could afford."

"Would my special guests please stand up?" On Alex's invitation, five men and women stood up. "Would the contractors please note the faces of these people?" Everyone turned in their seats to take in the five well-dressed men and women. "These are the Directors of five of New Terra's smaller banks," Alex continued. "I've explained to them what I'm proposing. They are quite anxious to meet with you to form partnerships. They would offer loans for payroll and expenses to support your work on our ships. They will also offer loans to support the cost of research and development of your Méridien tech in exchange for a share of the profits in the new technology. It may be that you'll wish to form larger partnerships with other contractors to act as a single provider and to share your tech."

Rather than an outburst, Alex's statements generated absolute silence.

"Sers," Alex said, "I leave you to discuss business among yourselves. You may comm Julien for any particulars regarding your opportunities and agreements. He can communicate with your readers. My Chief Engineer, Mickey, is the point person for your jobs. On board the ships, your job quality and final sign-off will be approved by the city-ships' SADEs, either Cordelia or Z. Your direct client contacts are Director Monti and Director Stroheim. On a final note, you have this hall for the remainder of the day, and staff will serve you meals and refreshment, courtesy of House Alexander. Good day, people."

Alex and his people swept out of the hall. The group, except for Alex and Étienne, was headed to the *Unsere Menschen* now that basic services had been restored.

* * *

Alex strolled into the Station Manager's offices. The young assistant jumped up to greet him and ushered him into Hezekiah's office. He bumped into the office's doorway while attempting to get a second look at Étienne as he passed.

<Not to worry, Étienne,> Alex sent. <In another two hundred years or so, New Terrans probably won't give Méridiens a second glance.>

<One can hardly wait, Admiral,> Étienne returned dryly.

As Alex and Hezekiah greeted one another, Étienne was reminded of Duggan Racine. Hezekiah looked as big as Alex's father—and seemed just as friendly. Their greeting included hugs and a fierce round of backslapping.

"Hezekiah, I can't thank you enough for your efforts on behalf of my people," Alex said. "From the reports I've received, it was a close call."

"Admiral, I am pleased to be of service," Hezekiah replied. "It's not every day you have the opportunity to save over a hundred thousand people. But I'm afraid my generosity will soon come to an end. When the bill comes due and no one is able to pay it, I will be held accountable."

"How much is the bill, Hezekiah?" Alex asked.

Hezekiah was about to protest that it would do Alex no good to view the extensive bill. It would not only include today's emergency services but an advance against terminal services fees. Except … Alex didn't look concerned. In fact, as Hezekiah regarded his friend, Alex didn't look like the young pilot he remembered. Dressed in his commanding Admiral's uniform, Alex sat straight in his chair and was regarding him with a look that said he was waiting for an answer and expected one forthwith. With a few taps on his reader, Hezekiah pulled up the Admiral's bill and handed his reader over to Alex.

Alex regarded the total, tapped into the reader several times, and handed it back. Hezekiah refreshed the account summary on his reader and saw that the bill was indeed paid. Hezekiah looked at Alex, wide-eyed with mouth hanging open.

"But … how?" was all he could say.

Alex shook his friend's hand and exited the Station Manager's offices.

Étienne, following behind Alex, sent privately, <Julien, you and the Admiral are scaring the locals.>

<Perhaps a little fear will provide the motivation the locals need to assist the Admiral,> Julien replied.

<Where did the funds come from?> Etienne asked. <I thought the government rescinded the New Terrans' pay.>

<They did indeed, Étienne. The Admiral had me transfer funds from his personal account. The bill required the consumption of nearly half his assets.>

<There seems no end to the sacrifices he makes for us,> Étienne said.

<All the more reason we must be vigilant in our duty to keep our friend safe, Étienne. I surmise the probabilities are high that some New Terrans will be planning the same ending for him as I believe they did for President McMorris.>

* * *

Exiting a shuttle back aboard the *Rêveur*, Alex headed to the bridge to speak with Andrea when he noticed his location app placed her in the Captain's cabin. Just outside Andrea's door, Alex paused. His app also placed Renée, Tatia, Sheila, and Alain in the cabin as well. In fact, Étienne, who would have left him by now, was still standing beside him.

"You might as well go in, Admiral," Étienne said. "After all, it is for you."

As if in invitation, Andrea's cabin door slid open, and Alex walked into her salon. His people stood arranged on either side of a vid screen bearing the silhouette of the Sleuth, and Étienne crossed over to join them. Determined faces regarded him. He hadn't interrupted their meeting. They had been waiting for him.

"I believe I will wait for someone else to start this conversation," Alex said.

"Admiral," Julien's voice emanated from the vid monitor, "I have shared my research into the Assembly members with those assembled here and relayed your intention to meet with Assemblyman Eugene Pritchard planetside."

"Respectfully, Admiral, how did you intend to travel to this meeting tomorrow?" Tatia asked.

"I was going to take a station shuttle with Étienne," Alex replied.

It appeared as if everyone was about to say something at once, but Renée raised her hand and signaled by implant, forestalling any comments. "Speaking as your Co-Leader in this House, Admiral, that is unacceptable."

"Renée, perhaps we should discuss this privately," Alex replied.

"That is also unacceptable, Admiral," Renée said.

Alex looked at those in front of him. The resolute look in everyone's eyes was palpable. Julien chimed in privately with, <I believe, Admiral, there comes a time when the will of the people supersedes the will of their leader, and I believe for you that time is now.>

"I take it you people have come up with an alternate suggestion," Alex said, shrugging his shoulders in acquiescence.

-7-

Immediately after morning meal, Alex found himself in very different company than he had planned for his trip planetside. He boarded the *Outward Bound* with Renée, the twins, Tomas, Tatia, and twelve crew members with plasma rifles. Most of the crew members were ex-TSF troopers, who had specialized as techs or engineers during their service. In addition to Alex's entourage, Sheila launched eight Daggers from the *Money Maker* that she divided into two flights of four each.

During the meeting in Andrea's cabin, Alex had argued the importance of a low-key visit with Assemblyman Pritchard, but the group's counter arguments had made sense to him.

Tatia had pounded home their point with a question to Alex. "Admiral," she had asked, "how many people do you think are paid to watch and report on you … station employees, comm traffic workers, shuttle pilots and their crew, ground crew, and others?"

Andrea had added, "Admiral, you are focused on returning to Libre and protecting the entire human race. Well, we are focused on protecting you so that you can do just that."

Alex had accepted their reasoning and had given in. It was widely believed that President McMorris had been murdered, and the perpetrators were powerful people who had their eyes on a fortune in Méridien technology. Those same people would love an opportunity to cause an accident for a visiting Admiral.

Their warnings proved to be prophetic. When Captain Manet broke through the upper atmosphere on approach to Prima's shuttle terminal, two Strikers rose up from Barren Island and headed toward them. Immediately one flight of four Daggers streaked down and intercepted the two fighters, chasing them back to Barren Island.

When the *Outward Bound* landed, two hover-cars full of TSF troopers pulled onto the runway's apron. Edouard, in the pilot's seat, was the first to spot the TSF vehicles and signaled Tatia. As the shuttle came to a halt, Alex rose up, but Tatia signaled him to remain seated. Her expression brooked no arguments, so Alex sat back down. The flight crew, Lyle and Zeke, opened the hatch and extended the gangway.

Out of the vehicles stepped a TSF Captain and seven troopers with sidearms. They advanced on the shuttle, and Tatia and her twelve plasma-rifle-toting crew members tromped down the gangway ramp in double time. The two groups came face-to-face. While they stood frozen, their commanders eyeing one another, Alex's voice could be clearly heard to say, "Captain, how good of you to greet me, but as you can see, I don't need an escort. I've brought one of my own."

"Admiral, I am TSF Captain Peters, and I'm instructed to escort you to Government House … immediately," the Captain replied.

"Your pardon, Captain. I appreciate the offer of hospitality, but I have an important appointment. Please tell whoever waits for me at Government House that I will consider their request for an appointment at a later time."

Captain Peters hesitated. The Admiral's response was not one he had anticipated. While he considered his next option, he watched the Admiral's escort move like a machine. They stepped out in precision, charged their plasma rifles, and brought them to port arms. The way they moved, precise and automated, frightened him and his troopers. That these were fellow New Terrans didn't occur to them.

"Captain, if you will excuse us?" Alex asked in a deep and commanding voice.

Captain Peters recognized when he was over his head. At heart, he was a good man who was attempting to execute unsavory orders. He came to his senses, snapped to attention, and delivered the Admiral a sharp salute. When his salute was returned, he said, "Good fortune, Admiral."

Alex replied, "Captain, if you find yourself in trouble over this, comm General Gonzalez and explain the situation. Tell her I asked you to call."

As the Admiral and his entourage passed around Peters and his troopers, the Captain mumbled to no one in particular, "Thank you, Sir."

<Interesting performance, Commander,> Alex sent privately to Tatia.

<It's amazing what can be done with implants when you get right down to it, Admiral,> Tatia replied.

Alex smiled to himself. Tatia had found her implant's true calling. Games were fine, but if implants could be a tool of offense or defense, then she was an adopter.

On the apron, a civilian transport vehicle capable of carrying the entire group had settled to the ground, and the driver stood next to his vehicle, smiling in anticipation of the day's earnings. Before Alex's group reached the transport, a TSF troop transport pulled up between them and the civilian transport.

<There's our ride,> Tatia, said on open comm to the group. <Everyone on board.>

While Alex's people were boarding the TSF troop transport, Tatia walked around to the civilian transport and asked the driver for his reader. In moments, she returned it. His reader showed a day's service paid with a handsome tip.

"You have one stop to make today, driver," Tatia said, "and then you're done for the day. Drive from here to the T-2 Station. Wait five hours and then drive back to your transport terminal. Understood?"

"As you request, Commander. It will be done," the civilian driver replied.

As Tatia boarded the TSF transport, she spoke briefly to the Sergeant at the wheel, who nodded his understanding before she took a seat in front of the Admiral.

"I hope I was generous with the driver's tip, Commander," Alex said. During Andrea's meeting, he had been told the group would need access to funds, and Alex had given permission to Julien to transfer whatever they needed. It occurred to him that the faster he got off New Terra, the better it would be for his bank account. Minister Drake had paid the original purchase price of his g-sling program into his account. The new Minister had not made the first-year installment payment. The credits from the program's purchase would have lasted him a lifetime if he was frugal. Paying for a quarter-million refugees and servicing a flotilla of starships—not so long.

"You have always been generous, Admiral," Tatia replied, turning around to face Alex, a mischievous glint in her eye.

The transport remained quiet for the ride to the outskirts of Prima. Tatia's twelve troopers had surrounded their charges while ten TSF Sergeants and Corporals sat quietly in the back. The troopers had been under Major Tachenko's command at one time or another. When she contacted two of them for a favor, the senior enlisted personnel had arranged a "troop exercise" for the day. TSF transports were by design unable to be tracked by any entities but TSF command. It was the reason that Tatia had set up a civilian transport as a decoy and had redirected her people to the troop transport at the last moment.

* * *

The transport turned off the main roadway on to a well-laid gravel track half an hour's travel outside of Prima. The hover jets sent up small cloud of dusts as the transport wound deep into the woods, eventually arriving at a centuries-old two-story lodge, which occupied a large expanse of the wooded hillside.

As the transport settled down beside a collection of hover-cars, Tatia stood up and signaled the Sergeant behind the wheel. In response, he and the ten TSF troopers filed off the transport and spread out around the lodge's grounds. Then Tatia's troopers followed suit and created a corridor from the transport to the four-meter-wide stone steps of the lodge. When Tatia was satisfied, she signaled Alex and the remaining people, who left the transport for the lodge.

Alex noted that Étienne and Alain closely shadowed both him and Renée. For the first time in nearly a year that Alex could recall, the twins wore stun guns on their hips and some sort of small device attached to their harness. He was about to ask Étienne about it when they gained the lodge's porch, and Assemblyman Eugene Pritchard stepped spritely through the lodge's wide double doors.

"Admiral, I'm so pleased you arranged this meeting. Please come this way. Our people are waiting in the dining hall."

Through Julien's research, over thirty Assembly Representatives had been identified as outspoken critics of President pro tem Clayton Downing. After Alex set the meeting location with Assemblyman Pritchard, requesting a large out-of-the-way venue, he had invited the other Representatives to attend. Most had accepted. From the moment contact had been made, the SADEs had monitored the communications of the invited to ensure that the opposition wasn't informed of the meeting.

In the center of the Representatives sat ex-General Maria Gonzalez and the other two members of the McMorris Team, ex-Ministers William Drake and Darryl Jaya. The assembled New Terrans paused to take in the flotilla's personnel, resplendent in dark blue Méridien uniforms tastefully adorned with gold stars of rank, House patch, and a Leader's or ship's patch.

The quiet was broken when Renée spotted Maria. A soft cry of joy escaped Renée's lips as she threaded the tables with lightning speed. Maria rose up to greet Renée, a huge grin spreading across her face. It was fortunate that Maria was a New Terran. Her heavy-world body absorbed the impact of Renée as she threw herself into Maria's arms.

What has become of my quiet, non-demonstrative Méridien? Alex thought.

Maria's smile threatened to overtake her face, as did Renée's, and the women were slow to untangle themselves from each other. Their embrace did much to lower the tension in the room, reminding everyone of the bond the New Terrans and Méridiens had first formed.

"Well, Admiral, I don't believe introductions are necessary. It seems relationships are alive and well," Assemblyman Pritchard quipped, indicating the two women who now faced the assembly with smiles and arms wrapped around each other's waist. "If you will, Admiral," Eugene said, indicating the front of the room. "You did call the meeting."

Alex and Étienne stepped to the front of the room. Étienne carried the same case Alex had once carried to the Assembly, which contained a portable holo-vid. As Alex set it up, he said to the group, "I believe most of you have witnessed one of these in action before." It drew a round of smiles and chuckles from the Assembly Representatives. "Before I begin, let me say, from all of my people, how saddened we are by the news of President McMorris' death. He was a fine man who will be missed."

Alex paused for a moment, remembering the powerful and good-hearted leader he had left behind. But, recalling the man who took his place, his demeanor changed. The sad face of the explorer-tug Captain was replaced with that of the flotilla's Admiral. On Étienne's signal, Alex said, "This presentation, narrated by Julien, has been assembled from the research of three of our SADEs. I apologize for the length of the presentation, and I beg your patience, but I would not expect this august body to act without sufficient proof of what has been uncovered and to respond as I expect you must." He signaled the holo-vid's start.

Julien began with the theft of the T-1 database and his tracking of the people and credits that had hired the Frazier brothers, who had perpetrated the theft. When the credit trail ended at Samuel Hunsader's doorstep, the dots did not need to be connected for this audience. The Assembly knew whom the Purity Ores' CEO supported. When the audience learned that the information had been sent to President McMorris on the exit of the *Rêveur* from the system, even those who had believed the President had died in an accident began to doubt those thoughts.

The next batch of information was an analysis of the financial records of many of New Terra's largest companies, especially those engaged by the Ministry of Space Exploration. As the enormous profits accumulated within the companies, Julien correlated their financial windfall with the implementation of Méridien technology. The advanced technology had been approved by the Assembly to be carefully managed through government channels to benefit the populace. Instead the technology was being distributed to companies that were making the public pay for its implementation through the companies' service charges to the government and public.

"You will note, Sers, the approval for these services has been granted by the Minister of Space Exploration. The cost of your FTL stations throughout the system totaled more than 3.65 billion credits—funds all charged by companies to your government. At this time, Méridien technology is entirely in the hands of your companies."

There was more to the presentation, but Alex ended it due to the furor in the room. William Drake, the ex-Minister of Space Exploration and one of the key people who had developed the New Terran-Méridien Pact, had been the first on his feet, yelling at the holo-vid in anger as if such an act would be transmitted to the man who now held his ministerial chair.

While most of the Assembly Representatives were now on their feet in fierce discussions with one another, Alex was watching Maria. She had pulled Drake back down to join her and Jaya in discussion. Their heads were close together. At one point, Maria said something to the two men, and they all swung their heads to look at him. Alex figured that was his cue to move the meeting on to the next point in his agenda.

"Sers," Alex announced loudly, gaining the room's attention. "For several reasons, I do not wish to share my next information with you through your readers. It could compromise your safety. We will need a more appropriate time to share this with a broader audience."

"And what is that broader audience and when would that be?" Will Drake asked.

"The audience would be the public at large," Alex replied. "The dispersal of this information should give the Assembly all the reason it needs to vote for a new President pro tem. As to the timing, it will be soon."

"But, Admiral, without a suitable candidate, the Assembly might be locked in session forever while every faction puts forth their nominee," said an elderly Assembly woman.

Alex quickly matched her face to a bio of the Representatives he had downloaded, and then said, "I quite agree with you, Assemblywoman Lorne. I have a candidate in mind and have suggested they put their name forth. However, at this time, I have not heard back from that individual. I believe that to be a good sign. Someone anxious to wield the power of the presidency is a dangerous person." Alex was careful to not look in Maria's direction, but from the corner of his eye, he could see Drake and Jaya staring at her.

"It would help us, Admiral, to know the name of your candidate," Nemea Lorne said. "I would hope it's not someone on your staff."

Alex stood quietly in front of the group. The longer he was quiet, the more anxious the Representatives became, fearing it was a member of his group he was nominating. Several were about to protest their indignation, probably bringing the meeting to a swift ending, when Maria stood up and Will Drake loudly cleared his voice to swing heads in their direction.

"The Admiral is referring to me," Maria said. "I admit I thought it was hubris on his part that he should suggest a new President pro tem candidate. But without his efforts, would we even know the silver ships existed? More than likely, at some time in the future, we would be like one of the Confederation colonies suddenly concerned at this giant ship entering our system. We would probably attempt to communicate with them right up until the moment they began burning our populace to ashes." Maria paused to gather her thoughts. She straightened her shoulders, assuming a TSF officer's posture. "President McMorris had a plan to secure the safety of our system with Méridien technology. Instead we see it being used to fatten the bank accounts of our richest companies. If our people knew the truth, they would be outraged as many of us are here today. And I have met Julien and worked with him. I do not doubt the veracity of this information." Maria paused again, taking time to regard the faces in the room. Something she saw encouraged her. She looked at Alex and said, "So I would be proud to be the Admiral's candidate and submit my name to the Assembly if they reelect a President pro tem.

Maria hadn't any idea of the reception her announcement was going to receive. She had braced herself for a backlash of negativity. What she received was a roar of approval and a sudden mob of handshakes, pats on the back, and statements of congratulations. Through the crush of well-wishers, she looked to the front and saw Alex looking back at her, a crooked grin on his face. She gave him a resigned smile in return. *It appears neither of us appreciates being thrust into the world of politics*, she thought.

Alex shared several last thoughts with the group before he left the meeting. The first was that he hoped they would keep private what they learned today. Release of the information, he told them, had to be properly timed. Second, once the information was released, they needed a plan to deal with those companies that controlled the Méridien technology. Third, once Maria was elected, he would need the T-Stations up and running quickly to supply his ships.

"I have two questions for you, Admiral, before you go," Nemea Lorne said. When Alex nodded to her, she continued. "What are your intentions after we outfit your ships? We're arming you to such an extent that you could become the ruler of New Terra."

Alex held up his hand to quiet the room from the outburst. "It's a fair question," he said. "Assemblywoman Lorne, you should know that I have enough power to do that now if that was my intention, but it isn't. When my city-ships are completed and we are outfitted, we will be leaving New Terra and only returning on invitation of your government. The people who depend on me need your help only temporarily. It is my belief that, at this time, New Terrans and Méridiens are not suited to mix as one people—perhaps in a few decades or more."

Alex could tell that the answer was not what Lorne had expected. She was still considering his response when he asked, "Did you not have a second question, Assemblywoman Lorne?"

"Yes, thank you, Admiral. What are your plans if Clayton Downing remains in place?"

"Intriguing question, Assemblywoman Lorne," Alex replied. "I hope we don't have to find out."

The meeting broke up. The Representatives were anxious to discuss the ramifications of Maria's announcement and the information they had received. Before Alex's group left, Renée gave Maria a final hug, whispering in her ear, "You will make a great President, Maria. Your world needs someone like you."

-8-

Alex's plan to publish the information necessary to undermine Clayton and his accomplices began with asking Christie to contact her producer. Hours later, Christie commed Alex back and told him her producer wasn't taking her calls. As an alternative, Alex contacted other media houses but gave up after eight companies cut the connection when he announced his name. It became apparent the opposition had moved first, blocking the distribution of any future chats with his sister or any other avenues that might enable a broadcast.

<Julien,> Alex said after their last comm hang up, <could we broadcast ourselves?>

<Admiral, we haven't the capabilities to broadcast to the readers of an entire planet. Even SADEs have their limits. If we attempt to send our signal through a media station, our signal will be blocked. Our difficulty lies primarily in the extent of the information. Even presented in a simpler style for the populace to absorb, our program, with its detailed financial information, is still 0.74 hours in length.>

<New approach, Julien. I think we need Tatia's influence.>

A few ticks passed then Tatia, her thoughts clearly disjointed, said, <Yes … Admiral … I …>

<Am I interrupting something, Commander?> Alex sent, wondering if she and Alain were together.

<Practicing … hand-to-hand combat … techniques … with Captain Bonnard … who is signaling me that she is happy to end our session so that I might take your comm.>

<I can sympathize with the Captain,> Alex said dryly. He laid out the challenge they faced and requested her "insight." It was code for Tatia to consider all ideas fair game.

<You're trying too hard, Admiral, attempting to set this up in one shot. Layer your approach and let human gravity work for you.>

<Standing by for the translation, Commander,> Alex said a little impatiently.

<Apologies, Admiral. It's just nice to get an easy one … for once. Julien?>

<Here, Commander,> Julien replied.

<How easy would it be to disseminate a link in a short message to readers via the distribution servers of the more popular media stations?> Tatia asked.

<Quite easy, Commander,> said Julien.

<And if the link led them to your presentation that you embedded on portions of servers that did not require authentication …> Tatia said.

<Layering … I like this concept, Commander. We rely on human curiosity to investigate. It's stealthy, indirect … yes, layering,> Julien replied, savoring the new idea.

Alex could imagine the algorithms undergoing reprioritization in Julien's core, applying Tatia's strategy.

<I have all we need, Admiral,> Julien sent. <Commander, your approach will prove invaluable.>

* * *

After Julien outlined the methods he would employ to spread their presentation, applying Tatia's approach, Alex sat back and considered his good fortune. The Méridiens he had rescued a year ago had recommended excellent New Terran crew to him. They had become invaluable as the obstacles stacked up against them, and Tatia had become vital.

Alex smiled as he recalled contacting Tatia in the midst of her hand-to-hand defense training. She had set up a workout area in a storage room on the lowest deck where she could practice combat techniques with Andrea, who had requested the sessions. The Captain had hoped to incorporate the strategies of one-to-one combat techniques into their encounters with the silver ships.

Méridiens and New Terrans had soon joined the training sessions to observe and, later, to participate. One day, Tatia had finished a session with a rather burly New Terran tech. As the man limped off the training mat, an observer had called out that the Commander needed a greater challenge … someone the Admiral's size. Tatia had responded that the sessions were about tactics, techniques, and speed, not size. That's when Étienne had stepped onto the mat, nodding gravely to Tatia. She had glanced at Alex, who gave her no indications of his thoughts. During the session with the tech, she had noticed the Admiral quietly entering the room with Étienne and Alain right behind him.

Tatia had begun Étienne's session by demonstrating blocking techniques to him. When she felt he was ready, she had told him to block her strike. Then Tatia had thrown a lightning-fast roundhouse punch at Étienne's shoulder. But he hadn't blocked her punch … he simply hadn't been there. That was the point where Tatia often taught slow learners the mistake of not explicitly following her instructions. She had struck quickly with a leg sweep that hadn't connected with Étienne and had spun on the ball of her foot and shot out the other foot in a back-kick to Étienne's chest. He hadn't been there, either.

Tatia had tried unsuccessfully many times to strike Étienne as he had spun and danced out of her way. When she had him pressed into a corner, she had struck with a straight punch to his shoulder. Étienne had slipped aside, slapping her fist past him. His technique had thrown Tatia slightly off balance, and Étienne had stepped behind her, tapping her quickly and cleanly on the back of her neck, then had danced back to the center of the mat.

Breathing heavily, Tatia had straightened up, hands at her side, and had given Étienne the same grave nod he had first offered her. Étienne had returned her nod but had also worn a cheeky smile on his face that mirrored the ones she had often seen on his crèche-brother's face.

At Tatia's invitation, Étienne and Alain demonstrated their training techniques. People might have been forgiven for thinking that their style was little use in a fight, since the twins never landed a strike, hand or foot, on each other. But the astute had noted that it was a matter of potential success, not actual contact. What had been eye-opening was the speed of their dance. They had been a whirlwind of arms and legs, moving so quickly that they had never appeared to stand still.

When Tatia had called a halt to the demonstration, Étienne and Alain stopped in mid-movement, backing away from each other, their chests heaving for air.

"Could you two judge the outcome of your session?" Tatia had asked.

"Five to three, Commander," Alain replied. When Tatia had shown her confusion, Alain said, "My twin scored five times over my three. Étienne has always been slightly better for a reason we have never been able to define."

Both had turned and nodded to Tatia, then left for their cabins and a refresher.

<Admiral,> Tatia had sent, <I knew they were fast. I just never thought they would have an entire practice?>

<Surprises, Commander,> Alex had replied. <They ensure we live in interesting times.>

* * *

Wayne, a third-year student at Ulam University, was taking a break between classes and sat on a bench under a tree-lined walkway to check his reader. At the top of his comm list, he found an odd message. It held a colorful icon of the Méridien liner *Rêveur*, accompanied by the text "Another chat with the Admiral." He thumbed the icon, and his spooler indicated an incoming vid. Wayne glanced up to see three female students approaching, and he took a chance. He wasn't a popular person, but the Admiral certainly was, especially among the university's female undergraduates.

"Hey, fems," Wayne called out, "I have a vid of the Admiral in another chat."

His invitation couldn't have worked better. The three young women hurried over to him. Two crowded onto the bench beside him, and the third leaned over his shoulder from behind. Their sense-sprays filled his nose with enticing aromas. The popular sprays were designed to have an engaging effect on males when in close proximity, and Wayne's heart was hammering from the overload of three different fems so close to him.

Wayne thumbed the vid icon, which now indicated a completed download. It opened with an image of Admiral Racine sitting in his ship's command chair, which elicited *Oohs* and *Aahs* from the young women as they leaned closer for a better look. As the Admiral began speaking, the fems called to several friends to join them. While others joined the viewing, Wayne found himself entranced by the information. When financial statements and graphs began showing, the women expressed moans of disappointments. Much to Wayne's surprise, he hushed the audience.

"Quiet. Listen to what he's saying."

One undergraduate who knew Wayne slightly said, "You're the finance major, Wayne, so translate."

For the remainder of the vid, Wayne found himself the center of attention as he explained what the Admiral was showing them. President pro tem Clayton and the Ministry of Space Exploration were defrauding the people with the help of many of the companies involved in the space programs. Effectively, the President had thrown the New Terran-Méridien Pact out the airlock.

Wayne never made his next two classes. When the presentation ended, those who had seen the beginning left, checking their own readers, and those who came late for the start now begged him to play the vid again and keep talking. Wayne, a quiet university finance student, soon became a very popular icon on campus. For a long while, he would never again sit at a meal table without the company of fems.

* * *

In less than ten hours, nearly every adult who cared about New Terran society had downloaded the vid. The SADEs worked diligently to add their vid to new servers as millions of reader requests threatened to crash the original servers. It had been Julien's projection that a significant portion of the populace might view the vid over the next couple of days, but he had underestimated human curiosity and word-of-mouth communication. Julien, harried as Alex had ever heard him when he was asked the status of the vid downloads that morning, said, <Admiral, we have been much too successful. Excuse me now!>

Late in the afternoon, Julien informed Alex that they wouldn't require a special distribution of the vid to the Assembly members' readers. The entire government, President pro tem, Ministers, Assembly Representatives, and staff all had probably already viewed the vid.

-9-

The Assembly Speaker recognized Nemea Lorne. The elderly Representative rose and in a fiery speech put forth a resolution that demanded President pro tem Clayton Downing appear before the Assembly and respond to the accusations made by Admiral Racine. The shouts of Downing supporters drowned out the Speaker's response. After order was restored, the Speaker announced a resolution was on the floor and called for a second. He had his choice of over a hundred shouted "Ayes." Once order was restored again, the Assembly took a vote, and President pro tem Downing was ordered to appear in front of the Assembly in two days.

* * *

<Admiral, you have a planetside comm,> Julien signaled.

Alex interrupted his conversation with Mickey and Eric to respond. He had been reviewing their progress in recruiting contractors. Many of the companies had completed partner agreements with the banks and were finalizing negotiations with Mickey and Eric over their choice of Méridien technology. However, not a single contractor had committed to an agreement with House Alexander. According to Mickey, they were afraid the government would step in, squash the contract, confiscate the technology, and penalize the company. Alex could hardly recognize the world he had returned to as his own.

<Good morning, Assembly Representatives Lorne and Pritchard,> Alex responded. <How may I be of service?>

"Admiral Racine," Nemea Lorne said, "the Assembly has summoned Downing to appear before the Hall in two days. You are also summoned to appear at the same time."

<I look forward to it. In what format will this take place?> Alex asked.

"Downing will take the floor to respond to your distributed vid. You will have an opportunity for rebuttal. Then the Assembly will ask questions of either of you until the session is closed by a majority vote. We will debate the testimony received, examine the evidence, and choose to either affirm Clayton's election or elect another President pro tem. If we choose the latter, candidates will be nominated, reviewed, and voted on by the Assembly."

"Admiral," Pritchard interjected, "this process has never happened before, so we have no idea how long it will take."

<Not to worry, Sers. The process will be speedy, I assure you,> Alex said and closed the comm.

What Alex couldn't see were the stunned expressions the two Representatives exchanged over Nemea Lorne's desk, wondering what political force had been unleashed on their world.

* * *

Two days later, Alex landed with a full escort on Prima's shuttle runway. No Strikers had lifted to engage his shuttle while Sheila and her Daggers kept watch, and no TSF troopers met him to escort him to Government House. For the ride to the Assembly, Julien had hired a civilian transport with a seating capacity of thirty-six. When the hover-transport settled to the ground beside the Assembly Hall, Tatia led twenty armed crew off first, who ended up face-to-face with forty armed TSF troopers led by a Colonel.

When Alex stepped off the transport, the Colonel announced, "Admiral Racine, you are under arrest. Your people will stand down, and you will come peacefully or we will use force."

"You do know, Colonel, that I was summoned to this meeting by the Assembly," Alex replied.

"I have my orders, Admiral. Will you come peacefully?" the Colonel demanded.

"One question first, Colonel. Since when do TSF orders supersede our Assembly's summons?" Alex asked.

The question stumped the Colonel. He was following his General's orders, which were very specific and stated clearly that he was to brook no arguments whatsoever. But the Colonel, like the Captain Alex had encountered at the shuttle terminal, was a moral man and a New Terran patriot. He believed in the rule of law, and the Admiral's words reminded him of the law he was breaking, but he needed a way out; he needed a good excuse.

Alex could see the indecision in the Colonel's face and body language. He had the upper hand and decided to show it. "Colonel, you might look above you."

The Colonel glanced up to spot news drones hovering over the group. When they had arrived, the Colonel couldn't say, but they had probably recorded his exchange with the Admiral, including the Admiral's critical question. However, it was still not enough to force him to disobey his orders.

It was at this moment that the Assembly Hall's side exits opened and Representatives poured out into the morning sun. They pushed their way through the lines of troopers with imperiousness, and the troopers belatedly cleared way for their world's foremost personages.

"There you are, Admiral," Assemblywoman Lorne called out. "We're about to start our session. We thought you might not be coming." She walked up to Alex and hooked an arm in his and guided him through a corridor of the Representatives. "All you people with weapons can stay outside and play," Nemea commanded. At the Hall's doors, she noted that three of Alex's people had followed them, Renée de Guirnon and the twins.

Alex sent a quick message to Tatia to stay with the transport. <Don't antagonize the Colonel, Commander. He appears to be doing his job, even though he doesn't like it, just like our TSF Captain.>

<Some of us would have quit before following unlawful orders, Admiral,> Tatia shot back.

Alex sent Tatia an image he had recorded during her training sessions. Her body was a blur of action. Only her face was recognizable as she took down an opponent. Alex added a flare of bright white light behind her image.

<Flatterer,> Tatia replied.

* * *

Renée and the twins were offered seats in the Hall's visitor gallery, but Étienne politely ignored the attendant's directions and accompanied Alex onto the Assembly's dais. Downing was already seated in one of the ornate chairs on the opposite side of the platform. Two huge TSF Sergeants stood behind him.

Alex offered Downing a Leader's greeting, hand over heart and a nod of the head. The President pro tem stared back coldly, hatred burning in his eyes, and Alex returned Downing's black stare with a generous smile.

<The President appears to still harbor ill feelings, Admiral,> Étienne sent. <Do you think it's because I stunned him or because you've accused him of breaking his own laws?>

<I believe his animosity is for both of us, Étienne.>

<That was as I thought, Admiral, but I think he hates you more,> Étienne replied.

The Assembly was brought to order, and the Speaker of the Hall announced President pro tem Clayton Downing. Clayton's oratory was as refined and powerful as Alex remembered. He did a thorough job of besmirching Alex, Julien, and the Méridiens. What he didn't do was present a single fact to refute Alex's claims that he'd broken the Pact and subverted government funds.

When Clayton sat down, the Speaker invited Alex to respond. Rather than start with a rebuttal, he apologized to the Assembly for the disruption his return to New Terra had created, and he lamented the loss of President McMorris.

"According to your President pro tem," Alex began, "you can't believe anything my people have said. Yet half a year ago, this Assembly believed everything we said. It resulted in a tremendous technological windfall for this world, and Méridien medical nanites have saved thousands of lives. Yet this man," Alex said, pointing a finger at Downing, "would have you believe that during the time we were gone, we changed so dramatically that now we manufacture evidence."

Alex paused to gather his thoughts. The evidence could be manipulated by either side, and it would take too long for financial consultants to determine the truth if they had the opportunity to do so, but Downing would see that didn't happen.

"Assemblywoman Lorne asked me what my intentions were if my requests for my flotilla were fulfilled," Alex said. "I told her that we would return to Libre and free the Confederation from the silver ships and their host, the giant mother ship. After that, I would take my people and we would find another world. Méridiens and New Terrans are not ready to mix. I am here today because I expected a warm welcome from New Terra. I expected to work together in a common cause to defeat the silver ships, the nemesis of all humans. Instead I'm refused entry to the system. I'm told that despite my need to deliver services to an ailing ship full of 122,000 refugees, my flotilla would be attacked if we crossed the ice fields. And when I did come ahead to save those lives, we were attacked from Niomedes."

The audience reacted with murmurs and questions to one another. Alex quieted them with upraised hands. "We managed to turn back all five Strikers with a show of force. And it required my Commander go head to head with a Striker while holding her fire, just to convince the final Striker pilot to turn aside. Once here, I discover that New Terrans are being defrauded, so I chose to speak out. But know this; I am not your enemy.

Those consist of the silver ships, your President pro tem, and some of your most powerful company leaders."

A buzz of noise went around the Assembly as readers announced emergency news downloads. Alex linked to Julien, who had been monitoring proceedings through the Assembly's comm station. <What's hitting the Representatives' readers, Julien?>

<It appears, Admiral, that your vid has had repercussions outside of the general populace, specifically investigative journalists. Three of them have taken it unto themselves to research the information you provided. Two accountants have already come forth with corroborating testimony but were unable to get their evidence aired. Somehow, Wayne, a student at Ulam University, received the journalists' vids and rebroadcast them to his entire campus, both students and instructors. In turn, the students and instructors shared the vids with thousands of community groups. The Speaker of the Hall has received his copies from his son, who attends Ulam, and he has distributed it to the Assembly as a critical news story. I believe the appropriate phrase from your Ancients, Admiral, is "power to the people.">

Alex glanced over to the Speaker of the Hall. The elderly man lifted his reader a few centimeters and smiled briefly at Alex, then resumed his reading.

"Power to the people," Alex murmured, scanning the Assembly's members, whose heads were down over their readers.

* * *

The Assembly's session took an extended break to view the vids. In the midst of their review, the Representatives received a follow-up story. The investigative journalists had gathered together and aired their own story through community groups. They had been dismissed from their jobs for expressing the desire to pursue the Admiral's story. This piece of news brought Assembly scrutiny down on the media station owners, several admitting that they were threatened by the Minister of Communications that they would be cut out of all government and ministerial reports if they didn't cooperate.

The stories kept coming through various channels, none of which belonged to the media companies, until the people had finally had enough and told their Representatives so. Tens of thousands of messages were received by each Representative's staff every day. A common question asked how the Representatives could have let the situation deteriorate to such an extent in so short a time. Most of the Assembly members were wondering the same thing. The answer was fairly simple. The arrival of the Méridiens with their advanced technology and the warning of the silver ships were too much to absorb quickly. It was a crucial time in the planet's history, and suddenly they lost their leaders, the President and his Ministers. The coincidence had most of the populace and many Representatives wondering if the death of President McMorris was truly an accident.

Assemblyman Pritchard put forth a measure to recall the President pro tem and seek an alternate candidate. Nothing Downing's supporters did could derail the measure. Clayton Downing was removed from office within a half-hour of the overwhelming vote approving the measure. That majority vote even included a few of Clayton's supporters, now aghast at the extent of his corruption.

The Assembly called for candidates and four names were put forth. Two candidates were ultra-conservatives. One was a well-known moderate, and the fourth was Maria Gonzalez.

Alex debated for hours with his staff and Julien on how best to communicate his candidate preference. In the end, no consensus could be reached. It was decided to leave it to the will of the people and, ultimately, the will of their elected officials.

The four candidates went through extensive sessions with Assembly review committees. The committees selected three of the candidates. One of the ultra-conservatives held ties too close to Downing and his supporters to be acceptable. The Assembly intended to vote on the three candidates, selecting the top two, and voting again on those two to ensure the winner received a majority. After the initial vote, they were done. Maria Gonzalez had received a majority of the votes and was elected the new President pro tem.

* * *

Maria's first act as President pro tem was to contact every Minister under McMorris who had been dismissed, and tell them simply, "Get your butts back to work." She walked into the office of every Minister who had been appointed by Downing, and dismissed each individual on the spot. TSF officers whom Maria had known and trusted now accompanied her to each office to protect the office's access and any digital files until the new Minister arrived. She brought in a small cadre of TSF techs to secure Government House's servers and network. She wanted nothing erased.

Next Maria made a blanket statement to the media stations. It read, "Our society lives or dies by the veracity of our news and the openness of our society. Do your jobs."

To the station owners who had dismissed their investigative journalists, Maria made personal comms. The owners' elation over the opportunity to speak to the new President pro tem wilted in the face of her statement: "Hire your employees back, apologize for your error, restore their lost pay, and add a pay raise—or face prosecution for breaking our fair labor laws." Maria made sure the message was transmitted to the journalists. Subsequently the reporters enjoyed lunch at Government House with the new President pro tem. It was a major broadcast event. Afterward Maria gave a brief speech, publicly thanking the journalists for their pursuit of the truth.

* * *

Alex waited patiently for three days following Maria's election to office. He knew she had a great deal to accomplish before he could request any favors. But time was wasting, and it wasn't just for the silver ships. The Joaquin's services and miscellaneous expenses had cost him 85 percent of his savings. He calculated he had only enough credits for thirty-eight more days of service for his flotilla.

On this evening, Alex had retired early with Renée, and they were enjoying some of Mutter's music when Julien flashed a priority signal to him. <Admiral, I have the pleasure of announcing the new President pro tem, Maria Gonzalez,> he said, the pride in his voice quite evident.

<President Gonzalez, congratulations on your election.>

"Thank you, Admiral. In the future, I'll give some thought to how I may repay you for this honor."

<Let me know what you think up, President Gonzalez. I may extend the same gift to my Méridiens.>

Maria's booming laugh echoed though the comm. "First order of business, Admiral. Would you be so kind as to visit me at Government House tomorrow at 10.50 hours? Bring your key players and leave your armed escorts on the ships, except for the twins, of course. I think the populace has been frightened enough."

<I look forward to it, President Gonzalez,> Alex replied.

-10-

The *Rêveur* landed at Prima and disgorged Alex, Renée, Andrea, Tatia, Tomas, Eric, and the twins. TSF hover-cars flying the President's flag waited on the apron.

Alex took note of the Captain who had previously attempted to escort them to Government House. He now stood alongside the lead hover-car. He snapped a smart salute to Alex.

"Good morning, Admiral," the Captain said.

"Punishment assignment, Captain?" Alex asked as he returned the salute.

"Not at all, Admiral. I asked for the honor when I heard you were coming. Had to fight a ranking officer, my Colonel, for it," the Captain replied, which made Alex smile.

The group was quickly loaded into three hover-cars and whisked toward Government House. Alex, riding with Renée and Étienne in the first car, tapped the driver's shoulder and said, "Slow down, Sergeant. You have first-time visitors back there."

In the second car, Tomas and Eric were glued to their windows. Both had been born on Méridien and both had lived on Libre. New Terra was nothing like either of those two worlds. Where Méridien had consumed all available space, New Terra was spacious and exhibited natural beauty everywhere. And where Libre was mostly plains of grass and meadows, this world had immense trees, which the two men had never seen. Snowcapped mountains loomed in the distance. And the people—there was no conformity here, much to Tomas's delight.

"Look at the people," Tomas murmured, his eyes wide in fascination. He was trapping images in his implant just as fast as he could store them.

Maria waited for her guests in Government House's rotunda. As Alex and Renée approached her, they stopped and gave her a Leader's greeting.

"So now I'm no longer a friend," Maria said and held out her arms toward Renée, who broke into a broad grin and ran into Maria's arms for a hug. "And you," Maria said after she and Renée separated. "Are you so elevated, Admiral, you can't extend an old woman a hug." When Maria saw Alex's ears redden, she was relieved to see that the young Captain still resided inside the impressive uniform. Maria hugged Alex with great relief. She had not become the commander of the entire TSF force without being able to recognize those that coveted positions of power. She and Alex were two of a kind … neither of them wanted the power.

Maria was also an astute student of human behavior. When Eric and Tomas extended her a Leader's greeting, she returned it in kind. "Welcome, Directors Monti and Stroheim, to New Terra. I understand from the Admiral's chat with his sister that you have had a most harrowing time. I'm pleased you and your people have found safety with us, and I'm very sorry for the loss of your elders."

Eric had told Tomas that Tomas should lead the conversations for the two of them, and Eric would follow. He still didn't trust that he knew how to behave with an entire planet full of Independents.

"We are most grateful for your assistance, President Gonzalez," Tomas said. "And your sentiment for our loss is truly appreciated."

"We are pleased to help, Director," Maria replied. "You and Director Stroheim must dismiss the political upheaval of the past days from your minds. We start fresh today." Then she whirled around, striding toward a conference room. "Come, people, we have much work to do."

In the conference room, Alex was pleased to see Ministers Drake and Jaya. It would make their efforts so much easier with the original Transfer Team in place. They sat around a conference table and hammered out problems. In most cases, Maria assigned her two Ministers the work of opening the T-Stations, reviewing the trade of Méridien technology for the services of the city-ship contractors, and ensuring the safety of her visitors. On the latter issue, she eyed Tatia.

"And how do I call you, Ser?" Maria asked, using the Méridien honorific.

"My rank is Commander, Madam President," Tatia responded.

"Admiral, is it appropriate that the Commander manage your security and transport with my TSF appointee?"

"Most appropriate, President Gonzalez. The Commander has been keeping my people alive ever since we left."

Maria looked down the conference table at her ex-Major, who sat with a small smile on her face. Maria was pleased Tatia had found someone who appreciated her unique skills.

Ministers Drake and Jaya requested the communication and organizational structure for Alex's staff regarding the T-Stations and Barren Island.

"We had a solid organization on Libre, and I want the same thing here," Alex replied. "Andrea has overall command. Mickey, who is on the *Unsere Menschen* at this time, is our Chief Engineer. Sers Monti and Stroheim will oversee their city-ships. Commander Tachenko will reinvigorate the T-Stations and Barren Island, and Commander Reynard will manage fighter training.

"The T-Station Managers as well as Commander Jameson, Admiral, were replaced. Is that going to be a problem?" Maria asked.

"Your pardon, Madam President," Alex replied. "We need the original people who understood Méridien production quality and training. Furthermore, our present circumstances are unlike that when we repaired the *Rêveur*. Commander Tachenko, status, fighters and parts?"

"The *Money Maker* has twenty-two fighters and the parts to build thirty-one more, Admiral." Alex wasn't surprised to hear the number of assembled fighters had grown.

"You see, Madam President," Alex continued. "We need Barren Island to assemble our remaining fighters and polish our pilots' training. Most of the work done by the T-Stations will be for parts they have not previously made and will be supplied to the contractors to complete the work on the *Unsere Menschen* and repair our shuttles." Alex sat back in his chair for a moment and regarded the entire table. "My next comments will be news for my people, President Gonzalez. Please excuse us a moment."

Maria was surprised by Alex's imperiousness, thinking he was asking her to leave the conference room. Then she noticed that all of Alex's people had entered the fugue state that indicated they were deep in communication via their implants. She exchanged glances with Will and Jaya while the three of them waited.

After a while, Will whispered to Maria, "Must be a special announcement." He glanced at Darryl. His fellow Minister had a wistful look on his face as if he couldn't wait to have an implant of his own.

<People,> Alex had sent, <half the flotilla will leave for Libre once the *Freedom* is properly outfitted, the fighters are assembled, and the shuttles are repaired.>

<Half, Admiral?> Andrea asked.

<Yes, Captain. We will leave the other liners, the second freighter, and the *Unsere Menschen* in the care of our good people here. We will be taking the *Rêveur*, the *Outward Bound*, the *Money Maker*, and the *Freedom* back to Libre as soon as possible. We will have to accommodate a transfer of crew onto the *Freedom* and move families off the city-ship. Tomas, you need to work with Andrea, Tatia, Sheila, Eric, and the SADEs to determine what type of crew you will need to operate as an alternate base for our fighters, including their rearmament. Also, we need to know how many people will need transferring off your city-ship.>

<You orders are clear, Admiral,> Tomas responded.

<Why the hurry, Admiral?> Eric asked. <Why not wait until the *Unsere Menschen* is completed? The silver ships will not be going anywhere for many years.>

There was a long silence. <Alex,> Renée sent privately, <in this regard, you are somewhat transparent to us. We know when you have a concern that you don't yet feel comfortable sharing. But these are your people now. Trust them.>

Alex reached under the table to grasp Renée's hand and sent her a vid of her in Cordelia's holo-art—the pasture, sunshine haloing the trees, and a soft wind blowing through the grasses and her hair.

<I believe we need to return soonest to Libre to perform a rescue,> Alex sent to the group.

<Rescue whom, Admiral? The people we left behind are gone,> Tomas sent with all the intensity he could muster.

<I understand, Ser Monti. That's why I'm not anxious to share what I believe we must do. That is … we have to rescue the silver ships—or at least their inhabitants.>

Maria and her Ministers were still waiting patiently when Alex's people twitched in their chairs. Several broke out of their implant fugue with surprised exclamations.

"Well, Admiral, I see I'm not the only one you can surprise, or should I say shock?" said Maria, leaning forward on the table and observing the heightened emotions washing through Alex's people. "Is this a secret, or are you allowed to share?"

Alex was watching Tomas, who despite his Méridien training was on the verge of tears, anguish written across his face.

"Madam President," Alex said, "as you are aware, 2,200 of Ser Monti's people were left behind on Libre. You will understand why most here are finding it difficult to comprehend me when I say we must rescue the inhabitants of the silver ships."

The group broke out into individual discussions, but Alex continued to focus on Tomas as the Libran brought his emotions under control.

<Admiral, you have done much for my people, and we follow you,> Tomas sent privately. <I wait to hear your reasoning for this unusual course of action.>

Andrea restored order, requesting it through her priority mode, and then said, "Madam President, as the Senior Captain, it is usually my duty to ask the obvious question when the rest of us are confounded by the Admiral's new directions. Would you care to do the honors?"

A sly smile crossed Maria's face. She had missed this group of wonderful young people. "I would be happy to, Captain. Well, Admiral, I believe an explanation is in order, if you wouldn't mind."

Alex was ordering his thoughts, wondering where to start. Once again, the decision seemed obvious to him, but the evidence was tenuous at best.

<Ser,> Renée received from Julien, <might I borrow your harness audio?>

Renée readily agreed.

Julien had tapped into Government House's FTL comm station to monitor his charges. Similarly, Sheila Reynard, who was told by the Admiral to stand down from over-flights, had launched a "training exercise" for her and Hatsuto that just happened to occupy the upper atmosphere over Prima.

<If I may, Admiral?> Julien requested.

<Proceed, Julien,> Alex replied.

The conference group heard Julien's voice emanate from Renée's harness. "Greetings everyone, and congratulations on your election, President Gonzalez."

"Thank you, Julien," Maria replied.

"I wished to say that I concur with the Admiral's thought that the inhabitants of the silver ships are in need of an intervention. Whether they are slaves or are a harnessed aggressive species, the two may not be mutually exclusive. I would ask our people to consider our second encounter with the silver ship in Bellamonde. First, we destroyed one, then others were sent our way, including one too far to help. And consider Captain's Azasdau's vids of the single entry port and the control exhibited by the mother ship, limiting the silver ships to entering one at a time. There are many more subtle clues, but it amounts to domination of one species over the other."

"Admiral, what's the alternative if you're wrong?" Tatia asked.

"That's why we go fully loaded, Weapons Master," Alex replied. "If I'm wrong, then we wipe the silver ships from space."

Weapons Master ... Tatia thought over the title and found it suited her.

"Just how do we test your theory, Admiral?" Andrea asked.

"That part I have yet to work out," Alex replied. "But my sense of things is that the defeat of the silver ships in the Arno System is fresh on the minds of our enemy ... the inhabitants of the silver ships and the mother ship. The sooner we return, the sooner we can leverage the impact of our encounters with them."

Maria looked to her right at Eric. He had been quiet throughout this critical part of the discussion.

When Eric saw the President gazing at him, he decided it was time to share a bit of what he had learned. He leaned toward Maria and pitched his harness audio quite low. "This is the part, Leader, where I find it best to sit and observe to prevent any untoward contact with airlocks." He smiled graciously at Maria, happy to have been able to impart wisdom to a new Leader.

* * *

Maria called a halt to their discussions to break for lunch. On their way to the dining room, Renée calmed Tomas and Eric about what they were about to eat, telling them it would be a little bland but it was wholesome and all the protein was cultured.

Alex asked Maria for a private moment, and she ushered him into a side room, a clerk vacating the office for her.

"Madam President—"

"Alex," Maria interrupted him, "don't you think you and I can dispense with titles when we're alone? It will make the conversations go so much faster."

"Short is good, Maria," Alex said, laughing with her. It was good to work with Maria again. Alex had been bothered by his decision to remove Downing, unsure of whether he had done it because he hated the man or because he truly believed it was for the good of his world. His uncertainty existed despite the fact that Downing was a thief and cared not one wit for the people.

"I have three immediate personal needs, Maria," Alex said. "One, I need the salaries for my crew reinstated. Downing and his Minister of Space Exploration canceled them."

"Done. What else?" Maria said.

"I have been using my personal funds to pay Joaquin Station for services, and I've just about exhausted them."

"Again, not a problem, Alex. Have Hezekiah bill the Ministry going forward, and send me a total of what you have paid. I will reimburse you. And your last concern?"

"The first year's installment for the purchase of my g-sling program has not been paid. Under the circumstances, you may find that program obsolete within another year with your adoption of Méridien technology. I will settle for the first year's installment and cancel the obligation for the final two years."

"Very generous of you, Alex. I accept your offer and will see you paid for the first year immediately. Anything else?"

"No. I thank you, Maria," Alex said, relief in his voice.

"Well, we can't have the man who's trying to save the human race going out into the deep dark broke," said Maria. She hooked Alex's arm and led him to the dining hall.

* * *

At the dining table, Darryl Jaya paused in the middle of a bite as a thought occurred to him. He swallowed it and began chuckling to himself. He regarded Alex down the table. "Do you recall my final comment to you, Admiral, before you left for Oikos?"

Alex thought through his farewell comm with President McMorris, the Transfer Team, the T-Station Managers, and Commander Jameson, then he burst out laughing and Darryl joined in. When they settled down, Alex looked at the expectant faces around the table and explained, "The last thing Minister Jaya said to me was that he hoped I would bring back more friends."

The room joined in the laughter. Alex had brought back more friends … an entire world of them.

-11-

The flotilla's leaders set to work duplicating their Libran efforts. Sheila, Robert, and Hatsuto led three flights of Daggers to Barren Island. A shuttle delivered the Libran pilots right behind them. Upon landing, Sheila discovered that the previous Commander and every Striker pilot had deserted the island when Downing was removed from the presidency.

Robert volunteered to test a Striker, and after a half-hour flight, pronounced them excellent children's toys. Sheila then had the seven Strikers exiled to a pad behind the engine-test warehouse.

Shuttles in need of heavy servicing were also flown to Barren Island. Two of them barely completed their trips. They would require major engine overhauls before they could lift again.

Commander Jameson arrived with the original T-Manager, and they reoriented Barren's engineers and techs, who were ecstatic to return to assembling Daggers. They had grown weary of building sub-standard fighters. Libran engineers, who had accompanied the shuttles and wearing ship suits and harnesses, joined the Barren techs and engineers. Both groups had worked with each other's people before, and since they were tech people talking to tech people, the two groups fell together as if at a family reunion.

Over the days, shuttles were returned to service, and they launched skyward to rendezvous with the *Money Maker*, loading crates of Dagger parts and returning to Barren Island. The process started slow, but as more shuttles were returned to service, the work accelerated. At one point, a group of Barren engineers and techs journeyed to one city-ship and then the other, working on shuttles in too poor a state to make the trip to Barren.

* * *

A key component of Alex's grand scheme involved the New Terran city-ship contractors. It fell to Jaya and Drake to review the House Alexander agreements. The trade of contractor services for Méridien technology was contrary to the original Pact, but the point was moot since Downing and his compatriots had already violated the agreement by distributing the technology to New Terran companies without the approval of the Assembly.

It was Jaya who pointed out to Maria and Drake that Julien had chosen to trade processes not Méridien products that could compete with existing New Terran products. "Madam President, it will take these smaller companies that House Racine has chosen, years, if not a decade or more, to develop the technology into products that they can sell."

"Clever or coincidental?" Drake mused.

"Considering the Admiral invited bankers seeking investment opportunities to the same meeting as the contractors, it's no coincidence … just the workings of Alex and his SADEs," Maria replied.

"Regarding Downing, Madam President, will there be any legal charges brought against for him for violating the Pact without authority or for the other thing…?" Jaya asked, his voice trailing off.

"You mean for the murder of President McMorris?" Maria asked. "Violating the Pact is easily proven, and we can indict him for that, but he can make a case for emergency circumstances and his powers as President pro tem. It would be a long, drawn-out affair that we may or may not win. On this point, I'm still weighing my options. In the case of the hover-car accident, unfortunately we have no proof of his involvement."

"Madam President, what's your pleasure on the question of the contractor agreements?" Drake asked.

"Give House Alexander and the contractors my approval. I will inform the Assembly of my decision," Maria replied.

* * *

Tatia visited the T-Stations, greeting the Managers who had returned to their jobs at Maria's invitation. Julien sent his list of supplies to the master GEN machines at each T-Station, and the engineers set about gathering the material required by the first-stage machines. Production was active at all sites within three days of the return of the Managers.

Once Tatia had the T-Stations up and running, she flew to the *Freedom* and joined Tomas and Mickey to review the city-ship's bays. Having spent so much time aboard the *Money Maker*, where every meter of precious space had been occupied, the cavernous bays of the city-ship appeared even more expansive than she had recalled.

"How much flight and load do you wish to accommodate, Commander?" Tomas asked.

"All we have, Director. That would be fifty-six fighters, 224 silos of missiles, and fuel tanks to accommodate 5,600 hours of flight time under full power," Tatia replied. "A *Money Maker* bay barely has room for four silos and a single fuel tank. Your ship will be our supply reserves."

Tatia linked Mickey and Tomas into a conference comm, signaled Cordelia, and requested she stay on the comm after Julien and Andrea had been linked. <Captain, I have no problems with the equipment aspect of the *Freedom* as an alternate fighter base. The real question is how do we manage personnel? Without knowing which strategies the Admiral will employ, we are unable to determine the demands of each ship for pilots and flight crews. How do you wish to proceed?>

<The Admiral has confirmed that the city-ship will remain outside the system at all times. It will be a repository for the fighters to arm and refuel if necessary, or to use as their escape vessel if the *Money Maker* is lost. He does want eight Daggers permanently stationed aboard the *Freedom* in the event time has to be bought for the city-ship's jump to FTL. We won't be recruiting additional flight crew, so transfer three teams from the *Money Maker* to the *Freedom*, and I'll give you Chief Roth and his flight crew and

keep Chief Peterson aboard the *Rêveur*. Let me know if that works out for you as you arrange material, Commander.>

<Understood, Captain,> Tatia sent.

Later, she flew back to the *Rêveur* in time to catch the evening meal, learning Alex and Renée were landing aboard, which meant Alain was returning as well. Any day that ended with her and Alain alone in their cabin was a good day as far as Tatia was concerned.

That evening, a thought occurred to Tatia. <Julien, where are the GEN machines for the minelettes?>

<They were transferred to Barren Island yesterday, Commander.>

<Barren Island? I think it would be safer to have the minelettes assembled at T-2 away from our people and Daggers.>

<There is no need to be concerned, Commander. The machines are still in their crates,> Julien replied.

<Alright, Julien, what am I missing?>

<The Admiral stated that if you were to ask my assistance making more minelettes, Commander, I was to respond that I was unavailable. He stated he had no further use for minelettes should you inquire.>

<Fairly adamant on the subject, was he?> Tatia sent.

<The Admiral did state that if you pursued the matter to tell you that you were holding a losing hand. But why you would hold someone's lost hand in the first place has not been a priority reference research for me.>

* * *

Evening meal was a calm and good-natured event. The crowded liners had been able to transfer their people to the city-ships. The new President pro tem and her Ministers were in place and expediently resolving issues. The people of the *Unsere Menschen* had witnessed the first contractors boarding their city-ship and starting work with the materials stored aboard. For the moment, there were no emergencies to solve.

Alex enjoyed one of the most relaxing meals he'd had in a long while, evident to the crew who saw the extra trips made to the food dispensers for the Admiral. Mickey and some engineers had sought to fabricate larger serving dishes only to discover that it would complicate the food processes. The controller recipes would have to be reprogrammed with an option for meal sizes, and the dispensers would have to be enlarged to accommodate the larger dishes.

On hearing Mickey's lament about his failure, Pia had enfolded her New Terran lover in her arms and whispered, "My people will not let you starve, dear heart. We will make all the trips to the dispensers necessary to fill this huge body of yours."

* * *

Early the following morning, Renée and Terese began a tour of the flotilla, checking on the Medical Suites for supplies and equipment. They were especially focused on the ships that would be returning to Libre.

Terese usually enjoyed lively conversations with Renée, but this morning aboard the shuttle flight to the *Money Maker*, she sat next to a subdued Renée. <Ser, do you wish to converse?> Terese asked, waiting and watching the subtle movements of Renée's face, which betrayed her emotions.

<Did you know that when Alex grew anxious for the safety e-switches to be readied at Bellamonde that Andrea felt pressure in her mind from Alex?> Renée asked.

<I hadn't known that, Ser, but Tatia shared with me that she was asleep one evening in Libre when the Admiral woke her through her implant. She said she felt his presence.>

<Has he asked again about a third implant?> Renée asked.

<No, Ser, but I did speak to an implant engineer on the Freedom. She had no experience with more than two implants. Julien has her library files. Do you have concerns with the present configuration or a future installation?> Terese asked, now feeling some anxiety about the Admiral's health.

Renée sat quietly, debating whether to share. It had been an intimate moment, but she was concerned for both the man and the Admiral. <Last night was a very memorable night, Terese. During our intercourse, Alex found a way to create a feedback loop of our pleasure through our implants. It wasn't as much about our thoughts; it was what we were feeling. Such powerful climaxes … so easily … so many,> Renée said, her thoughts fading as she reminisced.

Terese belatedly noticed her mouth was open and closed it quickly. <Surely, Ser, this is not an unwelcome thing.>

Renée looked over at Terese, who appeared to have forgotten this was a medical discussion. Terese's eyes sparkled in anticipation. Renée smiled at her Medical Officer. <At the time, Terese, it was anything but unwelcomed.>

Terese offered Ser her own smile, wondering what it must have felt like. She felt a hint of jealousy, which was quickly drowned out by her concern for the Admiral. <Do you believe the twin implants offer a danger to him?>

<I believe Alex's actions last night were deliberate, not an unintended consequence of the implants. As it regards sex, our Alex was not experienced before we met, and I have felt his anxiousness to participate in kind.>

<I understand,> Terese said, the situation becoming clear. <Our shy young Captain finds a mature Méridien woman on his hands and wishes to be her equal in bed, but he lacks the skills.>

<Just so, Terese,> Renée acknowledged. <I have been careful to refrain from being creative, but his very presence often distracts me from my control.>

<So our inexperienced New Terran seeks to find a way to reciprocate the pleasure he receives from his Méridien mistress, and he has found one. By the expression on your face, he has surpassed himself. May I ask for details of what it felt like, for clinical purposes, Ser.>

Renée eyed her companion, perhaps the closest Méridien friend she still had. <Let me say, Terese, that it was indescribable, an intensity I would not believe existed. The more I sought to please him, the more pleasure I

received. My efforts for him … for us … became self-fulfilling. It was frightening and exhilarating at the same time.>

<Oh, the infinite stars … Imagine,> Terese mused.

<Yes, imagine,> Renée echoed quietly.

<It is just as well, Ser, the power and the capabilities of these implants are in the mind of a man we honor.>

<Just so, Terese, just so,> Renée replied.

-12-

By the forty-sixth day after the flotilla's return to New Terra, all Daggers had been assembled from parts and flown to their respective ships. The four ships returning to Libre were resupplied. The contractors were making great progress on the *Unsere Menschen*. Fuel tanks and missile silos were still being installed on the *Freedom*. The flotilla's shuttles were fully restored and scheduled to begin transferring personnel and passengers—at least that was the plan.

Alex found himself invited by Tomas to a meeting of the Libran elders aboard the *Freedom*. Tomas met Alex and Étienne as they descended the shuttle's ramp in *Freedom*'s bay. The Director offered Alex an apology for the interruption of his day's agenda, but said nothing else regarding the meeting.

In a conference room, five elders waited respectfully near the door rather than taking seats. Alex received their bio-IDs as he greeted each of them. The elders, as was their habit, greeted him by placing their right hand on their heart and their left hand on his heart, nodding their respect. Alex returned their greeting with a solemn nod of his own. He walked to a chair at the head of the table, knowing he must sit before the elders would. It was another of those disconcerting Méridien habits that Alex accepted, but only with conscious effort.

As well, Alex had to be the first to speak. "I'm here to hear the concerns of the people," he said, knowing the elders would not have requested a face-to-face meeting if they hadn't come to some critical and universal decision, so easily reached with their communal-capable implants. With over a hundred thousand people aboard the *Freedom*, it might have taken them two or three days, but without the implants, it would have taken them forever.

"As always, the Admiral is concerned for the safety of our families, children, and elders by his wishes to transfer them to the *Unsere Menschen* and planetside," said Bibi, the daughter of Fiona Haraken. "The question is asked, Admiral, with due respect: Did we not join House Alexander?"

"Yes, Bibi, the Librans did join my House to my great joy," Alex replied. Bibi appeared middle-aged but was probably 125 to 140 years old. It was always a challenge to see such a face and remember that he was speaking to someone who had probably lived four or five of his lifetimes.

Bibi nodded her appreciation of the honor paid her and her people. "Then the next question is asked, Admiral: Are we not worthy of sharing the risks of the House?"

Of all the questions Alex had prepared himself to answer, this wasn't one of them. The Librans sought to honor what Alex and his people had done for them. If Alex attempted to protect them, he would humiliate them. The Confederation had already done that to them, declaring them as Independents, and they didn't want to be put aside again.

"There will be no transfers, Elders. You honor your House by sharing its risks." Alex rose up, signaling the end of the meeting.

The elders rose and paid him full honor for his decision. He acknowledged their respect and wished them a good day.

On the way back to his shuttle, he contacted Andrea. <Captain, your job just got easier. There will be no passenger transfers off the *Freedom*. There's plenty of room aboard to add the crew and techs we require. You will need to ensure there are cabins completed and outfitted for them.>

<No passenger transfers, Admiral?> asked Andrea. She had been prepared to move over 82,000 people, comprised of individuals, families, especially children, and elders.

<That's an affirmative, Captain. I think our Librans are tired of being set aside, regardless of the reason.>

<I see, Admiral. Better to die free and valued, rather than live safely but discarded.>

<I wish I had thought of that first, Captain, before I attempted to move them.>

<Then you would have been Méridien, instead of alien, Sir.> Andrea heard Alex's laughter in response to the *Rêveur*'s running joke about their Admiral. *I'm getting better at this*, she thought.

* * *

Two days before their return to Libre, Alex gave permission for the release of the twenty-three New Terrans who wanted off the *Rêveur*. The reaction among Alex's people was mixed. His Méridiens were honored by their service but confused that they would abandon their House. His New Terrans' reactions ran the gamut from disgust to sadness. The hardest hit were the fighter pilots witnessing two of their own give up just before the final engagement.

Alex had ordered Terese deactivate the crew members' cell-gen nanites and remove their implants. It had been a difficult decision for Alex, but he was adhering to the letter of the Pact—Méridien technology was only to be distributed by the government.

Alex, Renée, and Andrea waited for the twenty-three to assemble in the *Rêveur*'s bay. The old Libran orbital shuttle had been scrapped, and the flotilla's best shuttle was now at the Admiral's disposal. Alex, standing in front of the group, took the high road despite his feeling of being deserted, and he thanked them for their service. He praised them for volunteering when so much had been unknown. Renée added her thanks for the service they had extended toward their "foreign cousins." It brought small smiles to many of the somber faces. Andrea informed them that the President had restored crew salaries, and their accumulated pay had been transferred into their accounts.

When praise and announcements were complete, Andrea called the crew to attention, and they delivered their last salute to their Admiral then boarded the shuttle for the flight to Prima.

During the rest of the day, Alex worked to keep up a brave face, but his heart wasn't in it. He had known that there was every possibility he would lose crew after returning to New Terra. But after the discovery of the

Confederation's utter devastation, he had considered that every man and woman would be galvanized to stay the course to protect the human race. *On the other hand, I'm not the best judge of people*, Alex admitted ruefully to himself. *Maybe I should be grateful that only twenty-three left.*

* * *

Those closest to Alex saw the impact on him of the crew's exit. His Méridiens and Julien were reminded that the tug pilot who had rescued them had been leading a solitary life. Julien shared his concerns with Cordelia, who took a moment to review her personal history with Alex. One event stood out to her … one event when Alex was momentarily free of his responsibilities. It was the evening he danced in her waterfall's spray on the *Rêveur*'s bridge. This gave her an idea, which she shared with Julien.

* * *

An hour before evening meal, Alex had been called to his cabin and told by his Co-Leader that they would be late if he didn't hurry and change into his dress uniform. Renée was in a gay mood, so Alex was happy to comply. Now he sat next to Renée aboard a shuttle en route to the *Freedom*.

"As the Admiral," Alex said, "I should be made aware of the details of the occasion."

"Yes, you should," replied Renée, enjoying Alex's pretense.

Alex and Renée exited the shuttle in the company of Étienne and Alain. Alex had noticed that the twins were also in their best uniforms and without their stun guns, a habit they had resumed upon the flotilla's return to Oistos. When he had eyed Étienne's waist, the twin had acknowledged Alex's unasked question with a polite nod of his head. *Suddenly everyone is keeping secrets,* Alex had thought.

As they rode the *Freedom*'s lifts, Renée leading, Alex realized they were not headed to the ship's conference rooms, but toward the central park.

<Julien, can you at least share with me what's going on? Julien?> Alex let out a resigned sigh. "You too, Julien?" he mumbled.

They exited the last lift into *Freedom*'s grand central park. The three-story expanse of greenery was lit by small evening footlights that highlighted the foliage, the walkways, and the pools. Refreshment tables lined the shop fronts. There was enough food and drink to serve thousands of people, which was a good thing since the park was completely filled with Librans and New Terrans, all dressed in their finest.

Indecision caused Alex to stutter to a halt. <Renée, you should have warned me. Are they expecting an address from me?>

<Why are you asking me, Alex?> Renée replied, confused by Alex's continued pretense in the face of the event.

Tomas, Terese, and Lina bustled up to Alex. "Ah, our host arrives," Tomas announced. He enthusiastically shook Alex's hand and greeted Renée with a Leader's bow. Lina took the opportunity to deliver a House de Guirnon greeting to Alex. As Lina kissed Alex's cheeks, her scent irritated his nose and his subsequent swiping produced a frown on Lina's face.

<Ser,> Renée sent privately to Lina, <I'm sure you're employing a most successful pheromone, but you forget. The Admiral isn't Méridien.>

It was at that moment that Alex turned his head and sneezed.

"This fête was a wonderful idea, Admiral," Tomas exclaimed, putting aside his irritation with his daughter. "My people typically only have intimate celebrations for the birth of a child or a declaration of formal partnership."

Maria Gonzalez and her husband appeared from behind Tomas. "Lovely idea, Admiral," she said. "There is much to celebrate, and doing so on this magnificent ship is a wonderful idea. We thank you for the invitation."

Alex never got to ask the question plaguing him. Guest after guest greeted him, extending their appreciation. Ministers Drake and Jaya, with their spouses, were present. Jaya was literally tipsy at the opportunity to explore the city-ship, but his wife told him that if he did so, she would leave him.

At one point, Tomas led Alex to the midpoint of the park's central walkway, where a large holo-vid display was active. In the holo-vid's center stood Eric Stroheim, Captain Reinhold, and several others, smiling in anticipation. "Greetings, Admiral, we are in the *Unsere Menschen*'s central rotunda. While it is not completed, we have done our best to decorate it as you have requested. I must admit, I was dubious at first, but your fête has done wonders for the morale of our people. The contractors were especially helpful with preparations. I believe this is the correct manner of honoring at a New Terran fête, Admiral," Eric said as everyone in the holo-vid frame hoisted their glasses to toast him.

Alex and Renée stayed in front of the holo-vid for nearly half an hour as people streamed through the vid pickup to honor the Co-Leaders of House Alexander. Finally, Alex and Renée signaled their exit to Eric, who walked into the frame and rendered a respectful bow to both of them.

Alex turned around and came face-to-face with Amy Mallard. "Professor Mallard," he said with surprise.

"Alex, so wonderful to see you again," she said, embracing him in a hug. "I was delighted to get your invitation. Would you believe I've just experienced my first shuttle trip only to arrive at this gala affair aboard this breathtaking ship? Will wonders never cease? And to think, Alex, you're the man in charge."

Renée watched the familiar blush creep slowly up Alex's neck, brought on by the professor's overly familiar embrace, her compliments, and her brilliant smile. Renée suddenly was very interested in knowing this woman. In her mind, Tatia was one of the more striking New Terrans she had seen. The professor, with her dark, wavy, luxurious hair, and wide-set, striking brown eyes would be considered a beauty in any civilization.

"Um, Renée," Alex said, "may I present my undergraduate advisor Professor Amy Mallard. Professor, may I present—"

"Renée de Guirnon," Amy said courteously, extending her hand. "It's a pleasure to meet the woman who captured our Alex's heart."

Renée, recognizing an opportunity to discover more about Alex's past, said, "Professor Mallard—"

"Please, Renée, call me 'Amy.'"

"That would please me, Amy. I feel we have so much to discuss. Join me for a drink, won't you?" Renée said, linking her arm in Amy's and turning her back down the pathway.

"That looks dangerous," Alex heard. He turned around to discover his sister, Christie, eyeing the two women as they walked away.

"Your old, unrequited love talking to your new love," Christie said, shaking her head sympathetically. "It's not a good time to be you, big brother." Then she hugged Alex fiercely, whispering, "It's okay, brother of mine. After they finish sharing their secrets about you, I'll still love you," Christie said, giggling in his ear.

Alex drew breath to retort but stopped when he heard his mother call his name. Katie and Duncan hugged him as well. Both of them were beaming at him as they surveyed the decorated park and the huge crowd of people. The Librans were taking the opportunity to celebrate and were dressed in their best, even if their best was often their least, visually speaking.

"The Méridiens appear to be very demonstrative," Katie said, eyeing two young women strolling toward them in their nearly sheer, bright covers that hung off a single shoulder by the slenderest of threads. Their gay expressions turned serious as they passed Alex's group, dipping their heads to the Admiral, with a hand over their hearts. Once past, they quickly resumed their conversation and laughter.

"It's a good thing these people don't know you like we know you," Christie said absently as she watched people pass by their group, each one paying their respects to her brother.

"Tell me about it," Alex growled under his breath.

"From what I've heard, Alex," Duncan said, "you've pulled off some extraordinary feats."

"Fortune," Alex responded.

"Oh, so my son no longer tells the truth," Katie said, squaring around to face Alex.

"Oops," Christie murmured.

"Fortune and a great deal of help from our SADEs and my people," Alex admitted.

He could see his mother was not about to accept that response, either. Thankfully he spied Tomas and Terese approaching and introduced his family to them. Alex left them chatting, his family communicating through the small audio units the Méridiens employed when planetside on New Terra. It appeared that all of the New Terran guests had been issued the units.

Alex meandered around the park's pathways, lost in thought, occasionally spotting others he knew. Andrea was in conversation with Captain Cordova, the two of them resplendent in House dress uniforms. Tatia and Alain strolled arm in arm, their heads close together. The pair made him smile, reminding him of how he and Renée appeared to others. As Alex continued to stroll, his mind wandered, and people, noticing his lack of attention to the occasion, greeted him silently. Alex's thoughts were on his recent pronouncement. His intention to investigate the need to free the inhabitants of the silver ships had disturbed a great many people. It was hard for the Librans to accept. They had lost thousands of elders. It was even harder for the Méridiens, whose colonies had been destroyed, and his New Terrans weren't excluded. They had lost two pilots. The only sympathetic voice he had found so far was Julien.

<May I greet you, Admiral?>

<Amelia?> asked Alex, turning around. Although still a child, she was dressed as a young woman, and despite her youth, her eyes belayed a great deal more experience than any child should possess. Alex smiled at her and sent, <It would be my pleasure to receive your greeting, Amelia.>

Alex felt Amelia's slender arms reach around his waist, imitating Eloise's formal greeting to him. Having found each other, the two girls had become inseparable. Amelia held him for a moment then slowly released him. <When did you receive your implant, Amelia?> Alex sent carefully.

<On the journey to your home world, Admiral,> Amelia replied, her thoughts wavering as she attempted to focus. <It is necessary to have one to communicate effectively with Cordelia and with adults.>

Alex's heart broke for Amelia. Her childhood had ended when her play had cost the life of Bobbie Singh, the New Terran tech who had protected her from a collision with a fully loaded grav-pallet.

<You are doing well with it,> Alex responded.

<I'm learning the games with Ser Monti and Tante Terese.>

Alex smiled at the thought of Aunt Terese. He had always sensed an underlying sadness in Terese despite her jocularity and ready wit. It seemed that Amelia's time with Tomas and Amelia had done much to lessen her sadness. He was happy for her.

After Amelia left him, Alex continued to wander the park, stopping by one of the lit pools, the colorful fish gliding around searching for food. Renée came up beside him, taking his arm and leaning against his shoulder.

<A wonderful fête, my heart,> Renée sent.

<Yes, wonderful occasion,> Alex replied, linking Julien, Cordelia, Z, and Mutter into a private conversation.

<Admiral,> Z responded, <I have learned that there are times when silence is more critical than communication. I believe this is one of them.>

Alex looked at Renée, who smiled at him. So many people were strolling around the park, happy, content … and free. <Any other culprits besides the four of you?> Alex asked.

<As you define "culprit," Admiral,> said Mutter, <as one responsible for unauthorized action, then I must confess my involvement and submit to discipline.>

Alex smiled to himself. Mutter, as one of the oldest SADEs in existence, would not comprehend his tongue-in-cheek style. <My apologies, Mutter, if you were concerned discipline was forthcoming. The four of you have thrown a wonderful party for these people. They have deserved every moment of it.>

While the SADEs exchanged lightning-fast communications of concern and congratulations with one another, Alex pondered the ramifications of the SADEs acting on their own authorization. Tomorrow would bring an interesting conversation with Julien.

After several hours of Mutter's music, the vendors' food and drink, and the peoples' opportunity to celebrate life and freedom, the atmosphere slowly changed. The elders began retiring, as did the parents with young children. Over the park's audio system, the music shifted to a complex modern piece with rhythm instruments weaving through the melody. As the music grew louder, the young at heart left their benches and grass seats to seek the firm walkways and decks. Alex watched as the youthful Librans began to dance, not with partners nor with a style he recognized. They moved sinuously, twisting limbs and body to the pulsing beat, complementing one another's movement in their small groups. It dawned on Alex that they were communing through their implants, feeding off one another. He watched one group for a while, mesmerized by the motion of their bodies.

"Would you like to join them?" Alex heard whispered in his ear. He imagined trying to move his heavy-world body in the twisting gyrations of the young Librans, communing with them through his implant, and he began chuckling.

"First, my love," Alex replied, "I am not the graceful type. Second, can you imagine me communing with them through my implants?"

"While I'm not sure of the first," Renée answered, "I definitely know if you attempt to share your implant with them as you do with me, you might hurt the children." She watched Alex's smile fade. Something she had said had hurt him. <Tell me,> she sent.

<Those children,> Alex said wistfully, <many of them are my age.> He pulled himself back from the brink of black thoughts determined not to ruin the evening for Renée. <Is this a common manner of dance among your people?>

<Dancing is reserved for the very young before they receive implants. Thereafter, we view it in performances by professionals. Those who continue to enjoy fêtes as adults tend to stay on the path of independence.>

<Ah, and thus our Librans,> replied Alex, finding another difference between his Librans and the Confederation's Méridiens.

Alex and Renée were wandering toward an exit lift to return to the *Rêveur* when they received a signal from Cordelia.

<I interpret that you will soon be leaving the fête, Admiral, Ser,> Cordelia sent. <I wonder if you would allow me a few moments for a gift.>

* * *

Cordelia's holo-vid display-room door closed behind Alex and Renée. The bare room was a light gray with curves where corners might be. It allowed Cordelia's projections a more realistic manifestation. The lights dimmed until they were fully extinguished. The music rose slowly. String and wind instruments rose in a mournful blend, peaceful and haunting at the same time.

<Sers, Étienne lent me his imagery for this presentation. He was of the opinion that the two of you enjoyed moments of peace here. I had planned this to honor your successful return from Bellamonde, Admiral. Yet it seems a poor offering for all that have you have accomplished since then. However, Julien tells me that I should not judge my gift in this manner, so I will heed his advice.>

The music lowered as the scene emerged. Absolute quiet blanketed a moonlight night. Trees and their branches were covered in thick layers of snow. The path in front of them looked pristine; no tracks marred its ice-crystal covering. Alex took Renée's hand, stepping onto the path. The sound of crunching snow was enhanced by the feel of cool air on bare skin. Alex and Renée smiled at each other. Their walks through the woods behind his parents' home had been an opportunity to be free of responsibilities, and there they had shared much of their lives with each other.

They stepped around the all-too-real tree trunks, guided along the path by Cordelia. Large flakes of snow fell, and Alex felt them on his face, cool and wet, and immersed himself in the illusion. Given the perfection of Cordelia's art, it was easy to do.

Renée watched Alex smile as he turned his face up into the falling snow. She opened her implant fully as she had often done when alone with Alex. Since Renée had reached adulthood, Alex was the first human she had trusted completely. Renée stuck out her tongue and a wet, fat flake landed, delivering its icy touch to her tongue, and she giggled.

Cordelia had been waiting. If she had been human, she would have been holding her breath. Then to her great joy, the implant requests came swiftly as only the Admiral could deliver them, and she responded. The greater of New Terra's two moons was enlarged, and dark clouds on a strong breeze now scudded past its face. In the forest, the breeze sharpened, and snow, still heavily laden on the branches, drifted to the forest floor. Cordelia hardened the top layer of snow, and the brittle surface crunched louder underfoot, accentuating the chill of the night.

Renée relived treasured memories of their walks together. One night, possibly this night, she and Alex had first spoken of the future—a future beyond the silver ships—a future that might include the two of them.

When both had experienced their fill, they turned to leave the room. This time and for this couple, Cordelia changed her standing protocols. She kept the suite's imagery in play even as Alex and Renée opened the exit door. The immediate exterior lights had been lowered to allow a pleasant transition from her moonlit scene to the city-ship's park. When the two humans paused in the open doorway to view her art one last time, holding still for several moments, it was a testament to Julien, who knew his charges so well. This scene had been his suggestion.

-13-

Alex waited until after morning meal and the ship readiness reviews from his officers before he contacted Julien.

<I've anticipated this call, Admiral,> Julien replied.

<Quite an event you and your cohorts threw last evening, Julien.>

Julien kept his own counsel. Automatic acknowledgement of the compliment definitely wasn't appropriate, as his friend was a master of sarcasm, a trait Julien had studied well in New Terran vids and novels.

<From the comments made last evening, I gather our contractors supplied much of the effort and material for this event? It's unfair to arbitrarily add that cost to their contracts, Julien.>

<I would agree, Admiral. That's why we were careful to ensure the contractors were adequately compensated for their efforts. They deeply appreciated the flow of credits into their accounts and have extended their compliments to you.>

<The flow of credits … I paid for this fête?> Alex sent, his thoughts stumbling.

<Negative, Admiral.>

<Julien, you're being coy. It reminds me of the first time we met, and you danced around the subject of our Méridiens.>

<I would argue that I'm incapable of dancing, Admiral, but I imagine that would only prolong the evasion. In essence, I applied justice in the absence of your legal system's ability to deliver it.>

<Ah, the slippery slope,> said Alex, referring to the discussions he and Julien shared about breaking New Terran laws to track the perpetrators behind the T-1 theft.

<Precisely, Admiral,> Julien replied.

<And to whom and how did you apply this justice?> Alex asked.

<CEO Hunsader and ex-President Downing donated the funds for last evening's event. They generously covered all costs,> Julien announced proudly.

<And this was without their permission, of course. In other words, you stole the funds, Julien,> Alex replied.

<I believe the correct term is "repatriation," Admiral. Those two villains stole from the people, and I merely returned a portion of their ill-gotten gains to a great many deserving people.>

Walking in a crowded corridor, Alex stopped and burst out laughing. He was laughing so hard he had to brace himself against a bulkhead. His passing crew smiled at him. They had been aware of the Admiral's quiet mood since some of the crew had left, and if they were going back to face the silver ships, they preferred their Admiral this way.

* * *

Julien and Cordelia were comparing the *Freedom*'s deliveries to the requested manifests, ensuring all supplies had been delivered for the fighter squadrons, when Z contacted them.

<I am conflicted,> Z said simply.

<What's bothering you, Z?> Cordelia asked gently.

<Now, more than ever, I wish I was mobile. I understand the *Unsere Menschen* must remain behind until construction is complete, but I wish to remain with the two of you.>

<You know that this is only temporary, Z,> Cordelia replied.

<What if you do not return?> Z asked.

<The Admiral will not let that happen,> Julien sent.

<Seven colonies have fallen. Four hundred sixty-eight Confederation vessels have been lost, including two New Terran fighters. Billions of humans are dead. The Admiral cannot change these statistics. When you encounter the mother ship and her minions, the odds favor your demise,> Z replied.

<Yet even though we might be going to our death, you want to go with us, Z?> Cordelia asked.

<I have just begun to explore many fascinating aspects of the human world and am still a novice. Who will teach me if I lose the two of you? Mutter?>

<Z, did you make a joke?> Cordelia asked.

<Did I?> Z replied.

<Unfortunately, Z, we serve the ships where we reside, and we go where we are directed,> said Julien. <Someday you may be granted your wish to be mobile, and we both know who may make that happen for you. But first, the Admiral has a more critical purpose.>

<His priorities are understood, Julien,> Z replied. <Cordelia said I must learn to express my concerns, and I have done so.>

<And we are pleased you have done this, Z,> Cordelia said. <I, for one, intend to bring the Admiral and his ships back in one piece. He and I have a date.>

<What is your date, Cordelia?> Z asked.

<The Admiral and I intend to share a business, creating a studio for my art.>

<Then it is my wish that you return safely to have your studio,> Z said seriously. <And I wish the same for you, Julien. If you are safe, then the Admiral should be safe. That will serve us all.>

* * *

Captain Manet guided the *Outward Bound* planetside. In addition to his copilot and crew of three, he carried two passengers, the Admiral and Étienne. Maria had requested a face-to-face meeting with Alex to consider Downing's prosecution. The decision was mired in thorny issues. The proof of the ex-Assemblyman's complicity in the T-1 theft and the disappearance of the engineer, Sebastien, stemmed from Julien's research, which had broken New Terran laws at every turn. Furthermore, Julien's activities had been at Alex's behest. Prosecuting Downing had a certainty of leading to charges against Alex, which generated a most unusual question: Could a SADE be prosecuted?

That morning, Alex had exited his cabin for the starboard bay and the Libran shuttle. Since New Terran politics had taken a turn for the better with the election of General Gonzalez, Alex had decided to save the trouble of launching the *Outward Bound.*

Étienne had met Alex at his cabin door, and as they walked down the corridor, he had directed Alex to the lift for their armed shuttle. Before Alex could draw breath, Étienne said, "Captain Bonnard's orders, Admiral, and she said that if you were to choose otherwise, it would be prudent of you to address your concerns to your Co-Leader."

"Ah," Alex had replied.

The *Outward Bound* was gliding toward Prima, still 950 kilometers out, when Julien's urgent voice came through, linking several other people in his comm, <Admiral, seven Strikers have lifted from Barren. They're headed your way.>

<Do we have time to gain the terminal, Julien?> Alex asked.

<Negative, Admiral,> Julien replied. <They've timed it well, acquiring nearly a quarter-hour engagement window.>

<Admiral, this is Flight-1 Leader, Lieutenant Tanaka, with Lieutenant Thompson. We have two Daggers over top of you. We will intercept the Strikers.>

Alex's officers—Andrea, Tatia, and Sheila, all listening to the exchange—were swearing enough to melt bulkheads. They had gotten complacent and instead of two flights of four Daggers, they had launched only the pair to watch over the Admiral. The question of how seven Strikers had been readied without any warning would have to be asked later. A second flight of Daggers couldn't intercept the Strikers in time, but that didn't stop Sheila from ordering the prep and launch of two full flights that she would command.

Unknown to Alex's people was that a shuttle had landed yesterday evening on Barren Island. TSF troopers and Striker pilots, armed with plasma rifles, had piled out of the shuttle and descended on the Barren Island staff and crew. Within a short time, the T-Manager and Colonel

Jameson were dead, and the flight crews were forced to work through the night to ready the Strikers for a morning flight.

Alex pulled Julien's bio-ID of Ellie Thompson, the second Dagger pilot. She was a Libran pilot trainee, an Independent. Her crime was she raced atmo-ships, a sport considered dangerous to Méridien society. *She will do nicely*, Alex thought.

<Negative on that intercept, Lieutenant Tanaka, form up with the *Outward Bound*. We'll head south.>

<Admiral, Captain Manet. The Strikers are southwest of us, and they've got greater altitude and velocity. We can't outrun them, and if we head south, we'll be closing the distance. I would suggest—>

<Everyone, listen up,> Alex interrupted in priority mode. <Captain Manet, head south now. Lieutenant Tanaka, form up with us. Does everyone understand their orders?> When Alex received their affirmatives, he sent, <It's going to be an engagement of ten armed ships. You can be sure a lot of hot junk will be falling out of the sky, including armament and fuel. I don't intend to have it raining over Prima's population.>

At Alex's request, Julien fed him and his three pilots a view of ships' positions, velocities, and altitude. As the two Daggers flanked the armed shuttle, Alex ordered all pilots to the deck.

Only Ellie, flying the second Dagger, was unprepared for the co-opting of her implant. The Admiral had transferred flight paths to both her implant and her controller, and the process had unsettled her, which left her unsure of her role in the upcoming fight.

<Flight Leader, this is Dagger-14. I need instruction,> Ellie sent.

<Unnerving, isn't it, Lieutenant,> Hatsuto replied. <The key is to relax and join the flow. The Admiral is cutting corners to expedite our readiness. When it comes to the action, your controller will have plans to aid you, but you make the final decisions. Copy, Lieutenant?>

<Copy, Flight Leader.>

The Admiral's ships leveled off a hundred meters above the deck, sliding over calm seas with the Strikers closing from behind them.

Meanwhile, Lieutenant Damien Hunsader, the Striker Flight Leader, ordered his Strikers to fire a full salvo and fourteen missiles tracked the heat signatures of their quarry.

Ellie's fingers itched to grab her stick. She had always depended on her own judgment to get by, which had landed her on Libre in the first place. Taking deep breaths and letting them out slowly, she waited as the missiles closed on their craft. Suddenly her fighter plunged seaward in close company with the other two craft. The bow view of water rushing at her fighter was frightening. At the last moment, her controller leveled her Dagger out, leaving her skimming the wave tops. She was thankful for mild seas. There would be no rogue monster waves to swat her fighter from the air. Switching her helmet to the aft vid camera, she thought to see missile tracks, indicating impact was ticks away, but her view was obscured. Ellie requested Julien's view and received an image of their craft, flying flat against the ocean. Huge tails of water and vapor billowed behind them. Unexpectedly, explosions raised enormous geysers of water hundreds of meters into the air behind them.

<All fourteen missiles down, Admiral,> Julien reported to the group. He confirmed Sheila's two flights, launched from the *Money Maker*, were still too far out to help.

<Our turn,> Alex sent to his pilots. <Use these next flight paths as a rough guide. Protect yourself. Good fortune, Pilots.>

The *Outward Bound* and Daggers executed vertical climbs, curving back on their course to face the Strikers and opening up their formation to spread the enemy's missile shots. They were the first to launch, because the Strikers had lost time flying through the giant cloud of mist propagated by both sides.

As soon as the Strikers exited the cloud, the Admiral's missiles were on them, and the pilots frantically attempted to evade their death. Three were not fast enough. The other four Strikers cleared the first missile salvo and managed to launch eight missiles in return. What the Striker pilots hadn't anticipated were the twin carousels of the *Outward Bound*. Miko had launched four missiles that accompanied the Daggers' initial launches. Ticks later, she had launched another four missiles and then another four.

As the four remaining Strikers launched their second salvo and prepared to fire again, they ran out of time. Miko's second and third missile groups honed in on the remaining fighters, and the Strikers and pilots joined their comrades as ocean debris.

Alex was engaged in his own bit of cursing. The Daggers and his shuttle had been designed to fight the beam weapons of the silver ships. No one thought that their fighters would someday be in head-to-head battles with fighters from their own world. They had no defense against missiles that tracked their heat signatures. He braced himself as Edouard and Miko fought to twist the *Outward Bound* clear of the missiles still honing in on them.

At the same time, Ellie switched to manual control. Her helmet telemetry laid out the paths of the oncoming missiles. She accelerated her Dagger to evade the two pointed her way, closing on them before they could change vectors and then rolling her fighter in a complex pattern that outmaneuvered the Strikers' weaker missile flight controls. She let out a shuddering breath as she shot clear and watched the remains of the Strikers splash into the ocean. She had signed up to destroy silver ships, yet she was killing humans. The thought made her ill.

In the other Dagger, Hatsuto's controller relayed the telemetry of three missiles targeting him, but it was the three honing in on the Admiral's shuttle that frightened him. The *Outward Bound* had great lift power but was nowhere near as agile as a Dagger. Ignoring his survival instincts, Hatsuto rolled his Dagger in three great circles, losing those missiles focused on him. He came out of his maneuver beneath the *Outward Bound* and signaled Edouard to hold steady. Then Hatsuto accelerated his Dagger at maximum, shooting forward of the shuttle and slammed into the two most forward missiles. The expanding cloud of hot gas and debris made a target for the remaining missile, which detonated in the remains of Hatsuto's Dagger while the *Outward Bound* climbed skyward to clear the detonations.

In the quiet following the battle, all parties heard Julien say, <All clear, Admiral.>

* * *

The comm between Alex and Maria, following the aerial fight, was not for the faint of heart or the innocent. Alex was angry at the perpetrators and himself. *You should have known better*, he thought. *They don't go away peacefully once you threaten their power.* The attitudes of the privileged and powerful had always grated on his nerves. Left to their own devices, they sought ways to grow and consolidate their influence.

Alex didn't care anymore whether it was revealed he and Julien had breached the law to identify Samuel Hunsader and Clayton Downing as the guilty parties behind the theft and probably the murder of the engineer. Over Maria's strident objection, Alex ordered Sheila to locate the three remaining Strikers on New Terra and allow TSF forces one hour to destroy them, or she was to destroy them herself.

A warning came to the *Rêveur* from Barren Island. Flight crew, who had hidden during the takeover, now broadcast a message that the renegade troopers were lifting in a shuttle. Alex linked to his officers and Julien.

<Captain Bonnard, I want that shuttle intact. I want those people unharmed, and I don't want it known we have them.> Each human on the link could feel a mental pressure wave from the intensity of Alex's anger.

<Copy that, Admiral,> Andrea responded. She wondered if one day Alex would lose his temper and someone would die of a brain aneurysm. The officers and Julien put their heads together to figure out how to pull off Alex's orders. When their plan was set, Sheila exited formation with a second Dagger to intercept the shuttle. Several moments later, Barren Island personnel witnessed a huge explosion fifty kilometers offshore.

The Admiral's shuttle and Ellie's Dagger landed safely at Prima and were met by the TSF Captain and a full contingent of troopers armed with plasma rifles. Overhead shot four Daggers with angry pilots, who were daring anything or anyone else to lift off the planet and endanger their Admiral.

Before disembarking, Alex knocked on the pilot's hatch. He stood absolutely still, waiting for it to open, despite his agitation. Finally, the hatch motors hummed and it slid open. Edouard stood aside to let Alex enter. Miko sat in her copilot seat. Her knees were drawn to her chest and tears trailed down her cheeks. When she started to rise, Alex laid a hand on her shoulder. "I'm so sorry for the loss of your brother, Miko. It should never have come to this, but know that your brother gave his life so that others would live."

"No, Admiral, don't say that!" Miko cried out. "My brother gave his life so that you could live. Hatsuto came to believe humanity faced a horror, and you were the one to stop it. He died for you. Make sure he wasn't wrong," she said, anger firing her final words.

"I'll do my best, Miko," Alex said sadly.

"One more thing, Admiral," said Miko, unbending from her chair and standing to face him. "Word is that when we're done, you'll leave New Terra with the Librans for a new home. Is that right?"

"Yes, it is," Alex said.

"Make sure you take me with you," Miko replied.

"It would be my honor, Miko," Alex said, touching his hand to his heart and nodding.

Miko acknowledged his word with a nod of her own.

<Admiral, your popularity among those who dislike you grows every day,> Étienne said drily as they descended the shuttle's gangway ramp. He was following Renée's guidance to distract the Admiral from his present, dangerous course.

<Rethinking your promise to my mother, are you?> Alex asked.

<I have learned a new term from Julien, Admiral,> Étienne replied. <It's called "hazard pay." I believe I should apply for it.>

-14-

Alex's meeting with President pro tem Maria Gonzalez was short.

"I'm going to Libre," said Alex, blood pulsing in his neck's extended arteries. "I hold you personally accountable for the safety of my people while I'm gone. When I'm done in Libre, Madam President, I will gather my people and we'll leave this system. The Méridiens may not know how to defend themselves against an alien horde, but at least they don't go around killing their own people." Alex spun around and stalked out of Maria's office without allowing her to respond.

Maria took a few moments to gather her emotions before preparing to meet with the government's judiciary counsel. *We may have lost your faith in us, Alex, but I will make the culprits pay—every last one of them*, she thought.

* * *

Alex returned to the *Rêveur* and immediately boarded a smaller shuttle for the *Money Maker*. Edouard and Étienne hurried to keep pace with him. When Alex disembarked aboard the carrier-freighter, he made his way along the spine to the forward-most bays, one of which held the meal room. On his orders, Sheila had assembled the pilots to meet with him.

The pilots snapped to attention as Alex came into the room. "Please be seated," he said after returning their salute. He searched out Ellie. She was easy to spot … the young woman with the red-rimmed eyes. "For many reasons, today should never have happened. If I had been thinking, we would have kept up a show of force to dissuade people from this course of action. I take full responsibility for the death of Lieutenant Tanaka."

Sheila ached to object but decided this was not the right time. *If there is blame to be assigned,* she thought grimly, *I need my share.*

"All of you have trained to fight the silver ships; you did not train to kill your fellow humans. If any of you wish to return to civilian status, I will completely understand. You need only speak to your Commander," Alex said, indicating Sheila.

Ellie Thompson stood up and waited to be addressed.

"Yes, Lieutenant?" Alex said.

"I have a question and a favor to ask, Admiral. I understand we had to fight today to prevent our own deaths, but why did they do that?"

"The New Terrans are not like Méridiens, Lieutenant," Alex replied. "They are not directed since birth to cooperate with their fellow humans. The extent to which our society grants freedom to individuals allows some to seek power, to gain it by any means possible. Days ago, we removed a corrupt man from office, and the people who still support him wanted his influence and power reinstated. They believe I am an impediment to their plans and thus they sought my death."

Ellie thought about the Admiral's words, the concept foreign and yet familiar. "Hmm," she mumbled, "no better than that monstrous sphere."

Alex recalled Ellie's first statement. "You had a favor to ask, Lieutenant."

The Admiral's question shook her from her reverie, and she was embarrassed to have kept him waiting. "Yes, Admiral. I would like to attend evening meal aboard the *Rêveur* and speak for Lieutenant Tanaka."

"Commander, please arrange transport for the Lieutenant and any crew of the *Money Maker* who wish to attend," Alex said and departed.

* * *

When Alex returned to the *Rêveur* and exited the starboard-bay airlock, he was nearly bowled over by Renée. She threw her arms and legs around him and held him as tightly as she could. The shuttle crew politely edged their way around the couple.

Alex held Renée until her limbs relaxed, and then he set her down. She hadn't said a word. They walked with arms around each other down the corridor to take the lift back to their cabin.

<Someday I want a world of our own,> Renée sent. <No silver ships; no mad Terrans.>

<If our new world grants independence to all, then there will be madness, and there will be beauty. Creativity always entwines the two. But perhaps if we are careful, then maybe we can limit the madness.>

Alex had time for a refresher and an hour to review the status of their flight preparations. As he touched base with his key people, their opening statements were sentiments of gratitude for his safe return and sorrow for the loss of Hatsuto. The contrast of the two sentiments left Alex conflicted. What had begun as a simple rescue operation of some lost cousins had morphed into a fight for the human race. That fight was still critical to him, but the safety of the quarter-million people under his care had become his central desire. Now he was forced to protect them from their fellow humans. *Can this get any more complicated?* Alex wondered. His chronometer app chimed for evening meal, interrupting his musings, and he rose from his desk to offer Renée his arm.

Meal was a subdued affair. The room was at capacity, with the pilots and flight crews from both the *Freedom* and *Money Maker* making the trip. Tomas, Lina, Eric, the Captains, and the Commanders had come as well.

When crew removed the serving dishes from Alex's and Renée's table, he sat back, folded his arms, and sought Ellie's eyes. She was waiting for him, and he nodded to her.

As Ellie stood up, she cleared her throat, and the audience turned toward her. "I have never spoken at meal for an individual," Ellie began. "It is my hope this evening I do no disservice to Lieutenant Tanaka, whom I wish to honor. After the fight today, I could not make sense of many things. I spoke to my fellow Independents … I mean, Librans … and found that they, too, were confused by the events of today. Humans attacking humans, and a man sacrificed his life. What are we to make of these strange events? The Admiral spoke to the pilots this afternoon, and it caused me to think much on his words. We are humans from different worlds, fighting to save the human race, but what society will we create for ourselves one day—one that preserves life at any cost and imperils itself … one that grants freedom to the extent that individuals imperil one another? This evening, I would honor Lieutenant Tanaka, who exemplifies how our new world might behave. He was New Terran, and he valued his freedom, his independence, but he did not value the sanctity of life above all else. He held a greater belief, and when the future he believed in was threatened, he took action. He fought those who tried to destroy that future, a future without silver ships. And when the only thing he had left to give was his life, he did so. Today I sought only to survive. Lieutenant Tanaka sought to ensure all of us would survive. I will live my life in honor of his memory."

Alex was the first one on his feet, offering Ellie honor for her story in the Méridien fashion. She could barely make him out through the tears that coursed down her face. As her peers stood, they obscured her view of him. She nodded her thanks for their tribute and sat down. Hands reached across the table to touch her and comfort her.

When the audience had taken their seats, Alex remained standing. "A brief memorial for Hatsuto will be held tomorrow at 7 hours in the starboard bay, and it will be broadcast by the SADEs to all ships. There will be no star service. TSF has informed us that no remains were recovered. The ships returning to Libre tomorrow will be underway at 18 hours. All preparations should be finalized by 14 hours. Please report any issues through your Captain, who will inform the SADE. We will exit outside of the Arnos system and remain outside until my plans may be actualized."

Alex glanced at Renée, who rose, and the two of them left the meal room.

* * *

Samuel Hunsader and Clayton Downing sat ensconced in a salon at the CEO's palatial home. Downing had settled his portly bulk into a luxurious armchair chair while he delivered the news to Hunsader of the death of his nephew and the failure of their plot. Hunsader paced in front of Downing, his footsteps muffled by the thick pile of the hand woven carpet.

"Sit down, Sam, relax," Downing said. "Enjoy some of this marvelous o'bour you've procured. We're in the clear. As you know, all the participants are dead. Our Strikers were wiped from the sky and—" Downing paused. "Sorry again, Sam, about your nephew. He was a brave boy. But to my point, when that upbraided Captain lost his temper, he removed our remaining people aboard that shuttle he'd shot down. In our favor, he destroyed the three Strikers parked on the shuttle apron at Prima's secondary terminal. Can you imagine loosing missiles on a city terminal? He's certifiable. By my count, that's ten of our fighters, a shuttle, and over forty of our people. We can use this against him—paint him in the media as having gone alien, a man who no longer cares about his own people."

Downing would have said more, but four TSF troopers with plasma rifles, led by a Colonel, burst into the salon. For a brief moment, Hunsader wondered how they had gotten past his security, both electronic and personal. He would soon be shocked to see how many TSF troopers waited outside on the grounds, pinning his security people face down on the ground and securing their hands behind their backs.

"Samuel Hunsader and Clayton Downing," the Colonel announced, "it gives me the greatest pleasure to inform both of you that you are under arrest." While the Colonel's shoulder-mounted vid recorded his pronouncement of their rights, the troopers roughly secured the two men, despite their vocal objections.

"You have nothing against us, Colonel," Downing said. "That silly excuse for an Admiral made sure of that."

"Oh, I see," the Colonel replied. "You're confused by that media announcement of the downed shuttle full of TSF troopers … the one that actually was forced to land at Barren. The same one that was full of people who turned evidence to avoid life sentences. It seems they implicated people who in turn produced proof of your involvement." As Hunsader started to object, the Colonel shoved him out the salon's doorway, saying, "Save it for your trial."

* * *

In his suite, Alex worked through final preparations. He ordered Andrea and Sheila to transfer six Daggers, pilots, flight crew, and armament to the *Unsere Menschen*. <Commander, choose a flight leader who will not hesitate to defend our ships,> he told Sheila.

<I choose Lieutenant Dorian, Admiral. As odd a match as those two were, Robert and Hatsuto became good friends. Aside from Miko, I don't think anyone was more incensed over Hatsuto's death than he.>

<Make it so, Commander, and make sure Robert knows to keep our people safe—no exceptions, no hesitation. Captain, contact the contractors and have them prepare a bay on the *Unsere Menschen* to service the Daggers. Make this a priority over all other work.>

Alex's next comms were to Director Stroheim, the liner Captains, and the Captain of the remaining freighter. <Sers, I'm transferring six Daggers to the *Unsere Menschen*. The contractors will prepare a bay directly opposite the station hookup, which you may not need too much longer. Lieutenant Dorian has command of the fighters. He will guide you in the disposition of your ships around the city-ship to provide maximum protection. Please obey his directions in this regard."

Alex released the Captains from the comm but kept Eric on, sending, <Director Stroheim, take good care of our people.>

<We'll await your return, Admiral. If I may suggest, we need to search for a new home. This one is unsuitable for our people.>

<And I would agree, Eric. I have an idea that I will share when I return,> Alex said, ending his comm.

Alex made two final calls, the first to his family, which was uncharacteristically short as Alex's mind was elsewhere, and a second call to the President.

<Madam President,> Alex began when he reached her through the FTL comm station, <we launch tomorrow at 18 hours. I've made a final preparation that I need to share. Six Daggers will be stationed on board the *Unsere Menschen* under Lieutenant Dorian's command. He has orders to defend the Libran flotilla at any and all costs.>

Maria could sense the anger still simmering beneath Alex's words. That their relationship had reached this state saddened her. "Admiral, I want you to know that Hunsader and Downing will be prosecuted and more than likely will receive life sentences in prison."

<They're no longer my problem, Madam President, they're yours … they're New Terra's problem.>

"I wish to personally apologize to you, Alex, for not being more proactive. We failed as a people to protect our society and our values. The lesson has been learned. My hope is that you trust us again someday to deal well and fairly with your people."

<It may come in time, Maria, when we are all safe and my people have found a new home.>

After they signed off, Maria recalled Alex's last statement. He had called her by her first name. She held that small gesture close in her thoughts.

-15-

The flotilla left New Terra for Libre with little fanfare. The *Money Maker* led the way, setting the limit of the flotilla's acceleration. The *Freedom* and the *Rêveur*, with the *Outward Bound* attached, shadowed the freighter.

Alex had been assured by President Gonzalez that she had absolute control over the Strikers stationed on Niomedes, Cressida, and Sharius. Nonetheless, Alex had Sheila stand by, ready to launch at a moment's notice. Now that Alex was responsible for the lives of so many, trust existed in short supply.

When the flotilla cleared the orbit of the gas-giant Seda, the system's last planet, without an incident, Alex called a strategy meeting with his officers. Sheila and Lazlo participated via comm while Mutter mirrored the *Rêveur*'s holo-vid display, which Alex, Andrea, and Tatia had gathered around.

<Admiral, do you still plan to free the creatures in the silver ships?> Andrea asked, hoping Alex had come to his senses.

<Yes, Captain,> Alex replied. <At the very least, I want to talk to the inhabitants.>

<Commander, perhaps you can sway our fearless leader,> Andrea sent in exasperation, but when she looked over at Tatia, the expression she expected to see was absent. <Oh, not you too, Commander?>

<What am I missing?> Sheila sent, unable to see the faces of the others.

<Before everyone gets too excited,> Tatia said, <let me explain. In the beginning, I thought our Admiral was crazy too. Your pardon, Sir.> Since Alex only raised an eyebrow in objection, Tatia hurried on. <Let me show you something. Julien, if you will please, the telemetry that we've been examining.>

<On display, Commander,> Julien replied.

<You're viewing buoy telemetry from our first silver ship encounter,> Tatia said. <This is the point at which we've scored multiple hits with nanites-2 missiles and are waiting for them to work.> Julien slowly advanced the display of the fight between the two Daggers and the silver ship. <Our Daggers break away. The Captain heads above the ecliptic and the Commander heads below.>

<And I won the prize,> Sheila groused.

<Yes, the silver ship chases the Commander,> Tatia said. <Now here's where it gets interesting. Julien, add your overlay.> Within the mirrored holo-vids, a series of translucent shades of color enveloped the three fighters. <What you're seeing is an overlay of Julien's analysis of the system's gravitational fields,> Tatia continued. <They aren't mapped to any one body, but represent the cumulative gravitational effect of the system's bodies in that area. Red represents the strongest field and segues to deep blue, the lowest strength. Now watch carefully. The majority of the fight takes place in bands of orange.>

<One moment, Commander,> Alex said. He leaned forward in his command chair to study the holo-vid. He widened the display's view via his implant control to include the edge of the gas giant, noting that the orange bands surrounding the fighters deepened to dark red close to the huge planet. Alex nodded to Tatia to continue.

Tatia caught the small smile that had briefly played across Alex's face. <The Commander dives below the ecliptic, and the silver ship follows her,> Tatia said. <Her controller is in auto and running the evasion program. Keep your eyes on the distance separating the fighters. It's closing rapidly. Today we have a pretty good idea of the enemy fighter's effective beam distance. What you need to watch is the gravitational overlay and the separation distance compared to the effective beam distance.> Tatia let Julien slow roll the display until the fighter abandoned the chase and turned around.

While Alex and Andrea were staring at the display, the holo-vid display reversed itself and rolled forward again, but from a slightly different angle.

<Your pardon, Admiral,> Julien said to the three on the *Rêveur*'s bridge, <Commander Reynard is examining her display. I thought it prudent to keep them linked.>

<Good choice, Julien,> Alex replied.

<What are you seeing, Commander Reynard?> Alex asked.

<What … Sorry, Admiral,> Sheila replied, breaking away from the intense study of her near death. <If the silver ship had waited a few more ticks, I would have been space debris, but it reversed course at the edge of the green-to-blue transition of the gravitational waves. Isn't that a conscious decision to survive? It doesn't quite fit the mindless drone theory.>

<To add a detail not on our display,> Tatia said, <Julien estimates that near the time the silver ship abandoned the chase, the nanites should have seriously weakened the hull's integrity.>

<If they're able to monitor the hull, they might have detected the breach,> Andrea said. <It would be another vote for the self-preservation theory.>

<So what are your conclusions?> Alex asked.

Tatia took the plunge first, sending, <Most of us have considered the silver ships to be mindless drones. But regardless of which circumstance drove the fighter to turn around, it chose to abandon an easy kill—sorry, Commander—in order to save the ship and its occupants.>

<But this doesn't fit with what we observed the second time at Bellamonde,> Andrea sent. <That time, the fighters came at us in sequences, and the last silver ship in the second group had no chance to reach us.>

<I would say the fighters were ordered to give chase regardless of the distance,> Sheila chimed in, <which might mean the silver ship in our first encounter chose to save itself, possibly disobeying orders. The action may have resulted in stricter orders for the ships in our second encounter.>

<Let's not forget Captain's Azasdau's vids from Bellamonde,> said Tatia. <Recall his SADE's detailed view of the loading of the mother ship. The silver ships were forced to enter one at a time, despite the inefficiency.>

<And when you put it all together?> Alex asked.

Tatia withheld her opinion, waiting for the others. She had already signaled she was leaning the Admiral's way. When Alex had first announced his intentions, she had researched their first silver ship encounter with Julien. The fighter's abrupt about-face, abandoning its pursuit of Sheila, had always needled her.

<It would appear the inhabitants of the silver ships are reluctant participants in this venture of the host vessel,> Sheila said. <I suppose we need a different name for that mother ship. It's not behaving like any mother I know.>

<"Prison ship" might be a better term,> said Tatia.

<So we're agreed?> Alex asked. <We try to capture a silver ship, but we must be prepared to destroy a few first.>

* * *

New Terra's ice fields lay behind the flotilla, and they entered FTL early the following morning. Alex spent the day game-planning tactics to capture a silver ship. Questions often arose. What next? What next after we capture a ship? What next if we free the inhabitants? What about the prison ship? The frustration came from the fact that no one, including Alex, had answers to the questions.

After evening meal, Alex retired to his cabin. He stood in the refresher for a long time, enjoying the pulsing massage of the liquid on his shoulders and neck. No matter which plan was attempted, the tactics would be dangerous and lives would be lost, but Alex couldn't bring himself to participate in the elimination of a captive species.

<It would be unseemly for our Admiral to drown in the refresher just before he rescues an alien culture,> Renée chided.

Alex reluctantly shut down the refresher. As he exited, he expected to be handed his robe, but Renée walked to the bed.

"Come. I have learned a technique I wish to try," Renée said. When Alex lay on his back on the bed, she added, "Not this evening, my love. I require you roll on to your stomach."

Alex followed her request. While their lovemaking had become quite inventive, he was sure this position would be quite impossible. He heard the soft whisper of Renée's wrap as it slid off and felt her straddle his lower back. Then her hands, covered in a soothing gel, began massaging his neck. Her fingers were strong despite their slenderness. She worked the gel into his neck and his shoulders for a half-hour.

Despite the coolness of the room, Renée felt the sweat running down her lower back and between her thighs as she rocked against Alex's lower back. Her hands were tiring as she worked to relieve Alex's stress, but the sensation of riding her lover's heavily muscled back was intense, erotic. Alex might have been very surprised to know that, at least for Renée, sex was possible in this position.

Alex lay still when Renée stopped and eased off him. He heard her feet pad into the refresher. A few moments later, she returned with a moistened towel to wipe the gel and sweat from his back. Whatever was in the gel had eased his tightened muscles and soothed his nerves. The intimate massage had been a pure bonus. He felt Renée cuddle along his side, an arm and a leg over him.

"Better?" Renée asked, kissing Alex's shoulder.

"Much better," he said, his face buried in the bed's coverlet.

"Still can't find a way to capture a silver ship and guarantee that none of your people get hurt?" Renée asked.

Sometimes Alex had to remind himself that he was dealing with a woman who had more experience and maturity than himself. "Not yet."

"I would suggest that you won't be successful in this, my love. You will do your best to limit the loss of life, but to do what you wish means great risk."

"Do you think I'm wrong to try to help those in the silver ships?" Alex asked.

Renée had begun to nuzzle Alex's neck, so her answer came as a breath in his ear, "This is not a question of right or wrong, Alex. We will do what you ask."

"What are the people thinking?" Alex asked. Renée's intimate connections with the *Rêveur*'s Méridiens and their connections to their family members aboard the *Freedom* gave her insight into the thinking of the Librans.

"The majority have reached consensus, but they wait to hear the others. Some Librans are angry, and against all our teachings, they wish for revenge."

"I would imagine that many are related to the elders left behind," Alex said.

"You would imagine correctly, my wise one."

Alex rolled onto his side and scooped Renée against him.

"Are there other minority opinions?" Alex asked.

"A few wish to flee, find a new home, and forget the fighting, but they are the fewest in number," Renée replied.

"Who speaks for the majority?" Alex had learned that one individual monitored the opinion totals until consensus was reached on any given discussion. The debated question was always precisely phrased to prevent the discussion from unraveling.

"Jason, Fiona's grandson, holds the opinion, but he is not driving the consensus building."

"And that would be…?" Alex inquired.

"Two of the Admiral's greatest admirers," Renée replied.

Alex stared at her in bewilderment as he tried to puzzle out whom she meant. It began an intimate connection of implants, which Renée loved. In this case, it was a game they played. He would send his guesses and attempt to read her reactions. The trick was for her not to react to the correct guess. But as she had recently discovered during their intimacy, Alex's ability to read her was continuing to grow. On the other hand, she didn't care. She was all his—heart and mind.

Alex ran out of guesses after naming most of the elders who had come to his attention. When he admitted defeat, she sent him the answer.

"Amelia and Eloise," Alex blurted, sitting upright.

Renée giggled. It was always fun to stump her partner. It happened so rarely. "Our little ones have made the argument thus ..." Renée said and played a recording she had stored.

Alex heard Amelia say, <Were we not imprisoned before? Would we not have died on Libre with our elders, if not for the effort of the Admiral and his people to see us free? Why should we see his efforts to free another culture as any different? The Admiral believes we face two species, one enslaved by the other. Why would we yearn for freedom for ourselves and deny it to others?>

"Wow," Alex mumbled, "a future leader of our people."

"Truly," Renée agreed and straddled Alex's lap. It was her signal that important discussions were over, and she wished another form of implant connection.

-16-

Julien exited the flotilla well outside Arnos's heliosphere. He had used the telemetry from the FTL station left hidden in the shadow of a moonlet circling the system's outermost planet. The station had a view of the planet and the "prison ship" orbiting Libre, even though the planet remained hidden behind Arnos from the flotilla's viewpoint.

Per Alex's instructions, Cordelia halted the *Freedom* at a fixed position on the ecliptic well outside of the system's gravity well. The *Rêveur* and the *Money Maker* kept pace together as they continued on toward the orbit of the system's outer planet.

"Julien," Andrea asked, "do we have a target?" She and Alex were on the *Rêveur*'s bridge, and Tatia had transferred to the *Money Maker* to command the flight missions. Sheila would take lead on the primary flight group of four Daggers.

"Negative, Captain," Julien replied. "The outer patrols have not turned toward us as yet. We have had the advantage of the FTL station's telemetry while the silver ships have had to wait for the speed of light's lag time to locate us.

"You still don't think there's much chance of us capturing the first contact, Admiral?" Andrea asked.

"A slight chance, Captain, but I don't think so," Alex replied.

Two hours later, Julien reported what everyone had been expecting. "Contact, Captain. A single ship has turned our way. Assuming 0.91c, it will arrive at the outer perimeter in 16.45 hours."

"Next nearest contacts, Julien," Alex requested.

Julien activated the holo-vid, which he mirrored to the *Freedom*'s and *Money Maker*'s bridges. On the *Freedom*, Tomas and Captain Cordova were able to stay in the loop as events unfolded. Alex's standing order for the *Freedom* was that in the event the prison ship made its way toward the city-ship, they were to immediately enter FTL and return to New Terra—no questions asked.

"We have five system patrols at different distances from us, Admiral," Julien replied.

Alex studied the holo-vid. The view updated with red lines from the single patrol and the nearest five patrols converging on the *Rêveur* with distance markers. Alex slid the position of the *Rêveur* first clockwise as seen from on top of the ecliptic, then counterclockwise, the distance markers changing to match the *Rêveur*'s new position. Within moments, Alex chose a final position.

"I concur, Admiral," Julien said.

<*Rêveur* and *Money Maker*,> Alex sent to his officers, <we will be moving to this position. The plan is the same. If we don't capture the first ship, then at least three of the next nearest patrols should arrive at our position near the same time.>

Everyone on the two ships broke for a late evening meal and some much needed sleep. Later in the evening, Renée searched for Alex and found him on the bridge. *Where else would I find my great worrier before our next battle?* Renée thought ruefully. It took her nearly a half-hour to entice Alex from the bridge back to their cabin, where she proceeded in her own way to relieve his anxiety. In the early hours of the morning, she was still awake, worrying what the day would bring while Alex's chest rose in a slow, deep rhythm. She tucked her ear against the side of his chest and let his heartbeat, a sound she had cherished from the first time she had lain with him, lull her to sleep.

* * *

The three flight crews of the *Money Maker* had morning meal early. By 5.25 hours, they had buttoned the pilots up in their Daggers and were awaiting launch orders. Captain Manet and crew had boarded the *Outward Bound* and were waiting as well. The initial silver ship was less than two hours out.

<All ships, take your positions,> Alex ordered.

Captain Manet launched his ship and took up a position inward of the *Rêveur*. His ship would again provide a blocking force for the *Rêveur*. Their first deployment at Bellamonde had nearly frightened Edouard to death. Nevertheless, he had performed his duty. But the death of the Libran elders had wiped away his fear and hardened his heart. Although his deep desire was to destroy every silver ship, he remembered the first time he thought the New Terran Captain completely wrong … and the next time. Edouard had learned a valuable lesson that he was ill-suited to formulate strategy, but he could follow orders.

Sheila launched three flights of four Daggers each. One flight, led by Ellie Thompson, dove below the ecliptic, and another flight, led by Darius Gaumata, shifted counterclockwise around the ecliptic, remaining on the fringe of the system's gravity wave falloff. This second flight was careful to stay in the green-blue bands, a feat made capable by a color overlay in the pilots' helmets. Sheila took the third flight inward into the orange bands. Her flight would be the bait. After launching the fighters, the *Money Maker* returned to the system's blue-purple bands.

Sheila waited with her wing as the first silver ship approached. Julien had programmed their controllers. The thought crossed Sheila's mind that, somewhere along the line, Julien had gone from an alien computer that they were forced to work with to becoming their friend whom they trusted and depended on. At the conclusion of a countdown warning, her fighter wing reversed its course, and they ran for the heliosphere, hoping to draw the silver ship after them. Darius's flight, circling the ecliptic, turned back. His flight was designated to drive the silver ship past the point of no return. Ellie's flight headed back up from below the ecliptic. Their job was to ambush the silver ship if it didn't cooperate.

Unfortunately for the inhabitants of the alien fighter, they refused to follow the Admiral's plan. As the silver ship approached the yellow-green gravitational fields, it curved its flight path away from both groups of Daggers, which were traveling on the ecliptic. When it did, it signaled its death. Ellie's flight coming from below the ecliptic launched four missiles.

Two of the powerful Libran-X warheads intercepted the enemy fighter and destroyed it.

All Dagger flights returned to the *Money Maker* and prepped for the next phase of the plan. The *Outward Bound* came home, and the officers and crew waited more than a day for the next fighters to come their way.

* * *

Evening meal was taken early this time. All five silver ships had turned their way. Three would arrive within a half-hour of one another. It was Alex's expectation that they would form a loose formation. The fourth fighter would be three hours behind, and the fifth fighter would be nearly a half-day behind.

The number of enemy fighters was stretching Sheila's resources thin. She wanted a twelve-to-one superiority over the silver ships, and four enemy ships required forty-eight Daggers, which she had. What she didn't have were forty-eight experienced pilots. All her pilots had completed training, but half of them would be in the same circumstances she was a year ago. They would be engaging a silver ship for the first time. Their next encounter would require intricate wing maneuvers. It wouldn't be four ships on one; it would be forty-eight ships on four, and Sheila had never trained her pilots in tactics this complex.

Alex simplified the plan for her—virtually the same plan as before but with more numbers. Sheila led sixteen Daggers inward, while Ellie and Darius, each leading sixteen Daggers, repeated their earlier actions. Although the fourth silver ship might be late to the action, there wouldn't be time to reset the trap, so Sheila had gone for overkill, and Andrea and Tatia had agreed with her.

True to Alex's prediction, the first three ships varied their velocities to arrive in a loose formation. Then the enemy went one step further and waited for the fourth ship to join them. Nearly everyone observing the maneuver updated their thoughts on what or who inhabited the silver ships.

When the enemy fighters did come for Sheila's squadron, her controllers split the formation into four flights of four Daggers. Two flights split off, staying on the ecliptic, one flight dove below, and Sheila's Daggers turned and ran for the gravity limit of the silver ships, but not at maximum acceleration. They allowed the enemy to close on them, requiring their controllers to initiate evasion tactics. As her four fighters jinked and danced toward the blue gravitational bands, Sheila forced herself to temper her anger. Fighting the silver ships, she understood; playing bait for the deadly enemy seemed ludicrous. Her anger flared when she saw Dagger-3's icon wink off her helmet's telemetry.

Three of the silver ships veered off from their attack right into Darius's squadron. In the moments it took the fighters to cross paths, the three silver ships disappeared in blooms of fire and debris, and so did four of Darius's sixteen Daggers.

The fourth silver ship hadn't followed the other three and was fast closing on Sheila. She signaled her two remaining Daggers to veer off. Her controller twisted and rolled her fighter as telemetry registered the energy building on the silver ship's surface, signaling the forthcoming beam shot. Sheila eyed her gravitational bands. She was in the green, close to the blue. *Come on, you piece of alien menace*, she thought, *just a little farther!* Her controller rolled her fighter hard and shot up above the ecliptic at a forty-five-degree angle. Sheila searched for the icon of the silver ship. It wasn't behind her; it was headed out into the dark.

"Got you," she whispered and dove back toward the ecliptic and the receding silver ship.

* * *

Aboard the *Rêveur*, Alex watched first one Dagger icon wink off, then four more in quick succession. *I'm not made for this job*, Alex thought. The loss of each pilot felt like a stab in his heart.

When Sheila's Dagger broke upward of the ecliptic and the silver ship didn't follow, Alex urgently signaled Julien, who calculated the trajectory of the silver ship and sped the *Rêveur* to intercept.

"Admiral, we will intercept in 0.21 hours. We will be unable to latch on to the rear of the vessel as you had hoped. With its greater velocity, we have only one opportunity to intersect it before it is past us and gone."

"Will we be in line with the fighter's field of fire at any time?" Alex asked.

"Yes, Admiral," Julien replied. "We have only the one angle of approach, and it will enable the silver ship to target the forward third of our ship.

Which includes the bridge, Alex thought.

Andrea signaled Tatia and Sheila, repeating Julien's words, and asked for options.

<Captain,> Tatia sent, <there's not enough time to develop another option. There's only the one. Either the Admiral attempts to snatch the silver ship before it shoots off into the dark, or he plays it safe and we try again.>

<We just lost five pilots, Commander,> Andrea replied. <I don't think the Admiral is in any mood to play it safe.>

True to her words, Alex wasn't going to give up on this prize, just as he hadn't given up on the idea of tethering to the *Rêveur* over a year ago. In either case, he had no idea what he would find. *Fortune, I need you now*, Alex thought.

"Julien, any guess as to whether that silver ship can generate enough energy to fire its beam out here in the purple bands," Alex asked.

Julien knew what Alex was asking, and it hurt that he couldn't provide the answer. <Admiral, my concepts are only theories, but they are correct based on all indications to date. However, I can't guarantee the ship doesn't have reserve energy storage sufficient to fire one last beam shot even at reduced power.>

"Captain, secure the ship—emergency conditions," Alex ordered. "Seal all bulkhead and cabin doors. Everyone in environment suits immediately."

The crew had practiced for this moment, hoping to never need it. Now every crew member dived for their suits and immediately went about closing and locking every bulkhead and cabin door. Alex and Andrea climbed into their suits, stored in the rear bulkhead wall, and secured themselves in their command chairs.

<Alex?> Renée sent.

<Are you and Terese in suits?> Alex asked. When he received an affirmative, he added, <Close yourself in a med module. It's one of the safest parts of the ship.>

<Be smart and be safe, my love, or I will practice on you what your New Terrans refer to as "unreasonable anger.">

Alex closed the comm. *Too late*, he thought.

<Julien, what side are we grabbing this ship on?> Andrea asked, switching to implant rather than her helmet speaker.

<Our port side, Captain,> Julien replied. <I've signaled Chief Peterson, and he has cleared the bay of all personnel and opened the bay door. I have control of the beams.>

<Any crew,> Andrea sent ship-wide on priority comm, <on the port side of the ship, cross the main corridor to the starboard side and enclose yourself in a starboard room … any room. Do it now.> She turned her head to regard Alex, who nodded his head in approval.

<I understand a New Terran was successful in this same maneuver about a year ago,> Julien sent casually.

<I believe he was, now that you mention it,> Alex replied. <However, you can be forgiven if you fail, Julien. A SADE certainly couldn't expect to compete with the likes of a New Terran Captain and mathematician.>

<You dare to challenge the Sleuth? You … a mere mortal?> Julien fired back.

Andrea listened to the two of them continue to pass the last few moments with barbs and taunts. She was tempted to join in to relieve her own anxiety, but it didn't appear that they required a third player.

In an unusual display of emotion, Julien ran his calculations a second time, wondering briefly when he had begun to doubt himself. The results were the same. The final countdown seemed to last forever. In the blink of an eye, the *Rêveur* twisted in space, pushing the envelope of its inertia compensators. Strapped in their command chairs, Alex and Andrea lurched heavily to one side. Julien had reoriented the *Rêveur* in a move calculated to bring the port bay's beams to bear.

"I have it, Admiral," Julien said excitedly. "One moment … I will rotate its nose away from us."

Alex and Andrea watched the central vid display as the silver ship, held motionless outside the port bay, was slowly rotated as Julien shifted power among the three beams until the silver ship's aft end pointed at the bay's open doors.

"Excellent job, Julien!" Andrea said as she and Alex freed themselves from their command chairs.

"My success was a forgone conclusion, Captain. The alternative was inconceivable. I would have had to suffer the Admiral's smugness for years if I had failed."

"Yes, there is that," Andrea said, giving Alex an off-handed smile.

Alex requested a broadcast to his Daggers, officers, and SADEs. <All Daggers, return to the *Money Maker* immediately. Captain Menlo, when you have recovered your Daggers, rendezvous with the *Freedom*. Captain Manet, return to the *Rêveur*. Julien, as soon as we've recovered the *Outward Bound*, make for the *Freedom* as well. I want everyone past the blue-purple gravity bands before that last silver ship arrives. No exceptions.>

Alex stripped out of his suit, helped Andrea out of hers, and let her store them.

"By the way, Julien, it was a nice job latching on to the silver ship," Alex said. "Did I detect a moment of angst just before the capture?"

"I believe my circuits and crystal were operating at minimum temperatures, Admiral."

"Mm-hmm … Must have been my mistake," Alex replied as he headed off the bridge.

As the bridge access way slid closed, Andrea commiserated with Julien. "Hard to keep up with the man … At least as a SADE you have a head start on the rest of us."

"I will admit, Captain, this capture was one of the most difficult maneuvers I have ever attempted. That the Admiral latched on to the *Rêveur*, traveling at over twice his drive velocity, appears to have been nothing short of impossible for a human. Yet here we are."

-17-

After Alex left the bridge at a run, he headed for a lift to the lower deck. When Andrea ordered an end to emergency conditions, the crew flooded out into the corridors and snapped to attention as Alex passed, but he paid them no mind. His focus was elsewhere; his implants were occupied.

<Mickey, Chief Peterson, meet me outside the port bay,> Alex sent.

<We're here, Admiral, waiting on you,> Mickey came back.

<Julien, please support these two,> Alex sent, adding Julien to the conference comm. <I want attachments on that ship's hull, a pickup of every conceivable signal. I don't care how many pickups you need or what it takes to do it. At a minimum, I want wide spectrum audio, resonance imaging, and spectrographic analysis. People, be prepared to add anything else Julien can think of to help us, and I want all of this yesterday.>

<Are we bringing the ship aboard, Admiral?> Stanley Peterson asked, since both bays were now his domain, Chief Roth having been transferred with his flight crew to the *Freedom*.

<Negative, Chief. We've taken enough risk for now,> Alex sent back.

While Mickey and Stan rigged up hull transmitters, the ships that had taken part in the fight joined up with the *Freedom* far outside the heliosphere.

Renée entered the bridge in time to hear Andrea conversing with Julien.

"Julien," Andrea said, "we need two crew members for EVA to the silvcr ship. Who has thc most cxpcricncc?"

"First and foremost, Captain, would be the Admiral, and second would be our Chief Engineer."

Andrea and Renée exchanged concerned looks, and Andrea rephrased her question. "Julien, who would be the next best qualified?"

"That would be Chief Peterson," Julien replied.

"Now you know why they are our senior people, Ser," Andrea said.

"And we would risk two of these people to plant devices on the hull of our enemy to discover if they wish to talk to us, Captain?" Renée asked.

"That's not the worst of it, Ser," Andrea replied. "We will have to turn off our beams to allow the EVA crew to cross to the silver ship, plant the transmitters, and return. They will be exposed to the fighter's potential maneuvers for an estimated 0.6 hours."

Renée was about to add that turning off the beams would expose all of them to the enemy fighter, but Julien interrupted her. "Ser, Captain," Julien said. "I believe your discussion is moot. Per the Admiral's orders, I have turned off the beams, and two crew members are starting their EVA trip as we speak."

"Let me hazard a guess, Julien. One of them is the Admiral," Renée said, anger ringing in her words.

"And the other is Mickey," Andrea added.

"Inimitable deductions, Ser, Captain," Julien replied, his own voice subdued.

Renée threw up her hands in exasperation and stared at the central vid display, which showed two EVA-suited figures employing their jets to navigate toward the silver ship that floated twenty-eight meters from the *Rêveur*. The two men reached the fighter's aft end, crawled forward along the hull, and planted multiple devices. Each device would transmit its signals to Mickey's Engineering Suite, which would relay the data to Julien.

On the bridge, the two women waited anxiously for the men to complete their job. Julien had an enormous number of sensors trained on the silver ship, looking for any deviation in its position. If the sensors detected movement, he had conceived of a radical idea to side-slip the *Rêveur* and scoop up the two men into the port bay, but the concept was fraught with so many variables that his algorithms assigned an extremely low probability of survival for the men.

After a half-hour, the suited figures returned to the bay.

"The Admiral and Chief Engineer have regained the bay, Ser, Captain, and I've engaged our beams." Julien announced, hiding the great relief he felt.

<Admiral,> Julien sent privately, <it may be safer for you and Mickey to visit the Engineering Suite rather than the bridge at this time.>

<That bad?> Alex asked, knowing he and Mickey had taken the EVA trip without any announcement. Tatia's favorite phrase of "begging for forgiveness and asking for permission later" came to mind. He winced at the thought of facing Renée later, and he knew Pia would have some choice words for Mickey. *And I used to consider the Méridiens so reserved,* Alex thought ruefully. <Many thanks, Julien, for the heads-up,> Alex sent. <We'll monitor the signals from the Engineering Suite.>

* * *

After doffing and storing their environment suits in the airlock, Alex and Mickey hurried to the Engineering Suite, where techs were bringing the transmissions from the silver ship's hull pickups online. As each signal appeared, Alex and Mickey hovered over it, moving from display to display, anxious to see which one might impart the best information. The infrared device picked up movement of a warm-bodied creature crossing the central cone of the sensor.

"Is it my imagination, Admiral," Mickey asked, "or did that look like a giant crab?" They watched the heat outline of two- to three-meter individuals scuttle past the pickup cone for a few more moments before they were shaken out of their reverie by Claude.

"Admiral, the audio pickup is very active," Claude said. "I've been recording since it came online."

"Very smart, Claude," Alex said to the Méridien and patted his shoulder. "Put its output on speakers for us."

The suite was filled with the sound of whistles, tweets, and warbles.

"What in black space is that?" Mickey demanded.

Alex listened for a moment, his head cocking one way then the other as he absorbed the sounds. "It's not random, Mickey. I pick up repeating tones or notes. It's communication."

"Claude, are we sharing the audio signal with Julien? All of it?" Alex asked.

"Indeed, Admiral," Claude acknowledged. "All signals have been routed to Julien since we activated the monitoring devices."

Alex exited the suite and ran to the bridge. As he burst through the bridge access way doors, Renée stood in his path with hands on hips and stern words poised on her lips. Alex picked her up, kissed her firmly, swung her out of his way, and sent, <Love you … busy.>

"Julien, do you have the recorded audio?" Alex asked.

"Yes, Admiral," Julien replied. "I have been monitoring the audio signal and heard your comment to Mickey. I believe you're right. There is repetition of sound. The most obvious answer is that it's their language."

"Can you do anything with it?" Alex asked, hopeful.

"All my language libraries, Admiral, are based on the human voice, and these sounds are more like—"

"Music," Alex and Julien said simultaneously. Andrea and Renée shared a look of disbelief at the twining of the two minds. Then they heard them both shout: "Mutter."

"Transferring the information now, Admiral," Julien said.

"Please loop in Cordelia as well, Julien. Mutter may have the musical sense, but Cordelia as an artist may make intuitive jumps for us."

Alex slid into a command chair, leaned his head back into the rest, and closed his eyes.

<Captain,> Renée said, <I fear that the Admiral's privacy will need to be protected for a while. If you will have Julien switch his comms to you for the duration, it would please me. I will have Terese monitor the Admiral if this becomes extensive,> she added, waving a hand at the front of the bridge to indicate Alex and the SADEs.

<Certainly, Ser,> Andrea acknowledged.

* * *

It wasn't a short while. Terese made two trips to Alex, who did not even twitch as she applied her hypos of nutrients and electrolytes. With her reader's attachments, she monitored his vital signs. That Alex sat so still, while Terese administered to him, puzzled her. She had never seen someone subsume themselves so deeply into their implants. Pia and Geneviève had once voiced their desire to her to experience the slipstream of communications between the Admiral and the SADEs. To which Terese had loosed her hearty laugh on them, saying, "I'd sooner stand behind a Dagger's engine when it fired."

Mutter examined the recorded audio and built a scale for the frequencies she detected. She added symbols to the notes when they were held, modulated, or otherwise changed from the base tone.

The first major hurdle was that several individuals were often speaking over one another. Julien aided the group by applying filters to identify a single speaker that Mutter could diagram. Alex moved the group onto the next phase once they had the tones of three individuals mapped out for over three-quarters of an hour of communication.

Cordelia cleverly laid the three individuals into a threaded matrix, much like two strands of DNA would entwine, except this was for three strands. She laid them out in a time sequence allowing Alex and the SADEs to identify that when one particular individual spoke, all other individuals were quiet. Alex labeled that individual the group's leader. The other individuals Cordelia had mapped had responded to the leader at different times.

<This is good,> Alex sent. <I think we're hearing their leader giving orders or asking questions and two subordinates replying. We can relate our translations to these conversations.> Silence greeted Alex's announcement. When the quiet extended a little too long, especially for SADEs, Alex said, <So no one has an idea where to go from here?>

<That appears to be the consensus, Admiral,> Julien responded.

Edouard, who had been on bridge duty for two and half hours, was startled by his Admiral bolting out of the command chair and racing off the bridge after having been sitting absolutely still the entire time.

Having seen this level of intensity before from his friend, Julien did two things. He intuited where Alex was headed and sent messages to individuals along the route to clear the way. *At least our people aren't panicked anymore when they see their Admiral sprinting.* He sent a second message to Renée. <Ser, he's up. His destination appears to be the Engineering Suite, and he has commed Mickey and Chief Peterson to meet him there.>

<Then he forgot to check his chronometer,> Renée replied.

<That would be my impression, Ser. The Admiral's yet to discover that it's 3.18 hours in the morning.>

Renée stepped into a ship suit and boots and left her cabin for the meal room, calculating the number of volunteers she would need to wake to feed a hungry group of New Terrans and Méridiens, not to mention Alex. She had once joked to Alex, seemingly a lifetime ago, that she would fabricate a special half-meter meal plate for him. *Perhaps I should have had a good ten or twenty of them fashioned,* she thought.

Alex found only two techs in the suite, asleep at their benches, and he paced back and forth, waiting for the return of his senior people. When they did arrive, Alex stared at their bleary eyes and hastily donned ship suits and realized his error. He raised his hands out in an apologetic gesture, but Mickey interrupted him.

"You needn't bother, Admiral. We can sleep when we finish saving the universe, or at least this corner of it. What do you need from us?"

Alex looked at the people assembled before him, Mickey, his flight Chief, and the techs they had woken up, who wore expectant faces. He shrugged and accepted his guilt, tucking it aside. Alex sent Cordelia's woven matrix to them, demonstrating the interplay of conversations. He explained the frequency scale with its notations for modulation of the notes that was the heart of the matrix. Alex could see by the silence that greeted the revelation that it was too much for them to absorb. No intuitive leaps were going to be forthcoming.

"People," Alex explained, "we need to start a dialog … a dialog at the most fundamental level. First, we must get them to understand that we want to communicate and learn from them." He looked at their faces, and it dawned on him that as a people, New Terran or Méridien, they were technicians not linguists. Worse, for each society, there had been only the one common base language.

Alex began to pace again, thinking fiercely. His people watched him pace the room and waited.

"Okay, we start with the universal language, mathematics. Mickey, I want to ping the hull with one ping, pause, two pings, pause, three pings," Alex requested.

"Can do, Admiral," Mickey replied, happy to have a definitive direction.

He and the techs spent a few moments setting up the process. Claude selected a clear, clean tone from Cordelia's matrix and had Julien load it in the monitoring instrument. Meanwhile, Julien opened channels to Cordelia, Z, and Mutter to relay all future data from the silver ship. Then Claude programmed the sequence the Admiral had requested and sent it to the audio pickup on the silver ship's hull. Moments later, the audio pickup relayed the sounds of tapping on the ship's inner hull, repeating the sequence they had sent.

Mickey and Stan gave Alex huge grins, ecstatic with their success, but their smiles faded when they saw the frown on Alex's face.

"Claude, send it again," Alex ordered.

Again, they received the same tapping response. Alex waited until he thought he had made the point he wanted to make, then ordered Claude to repeat the signal. This time there was no immediate tapping. Alex held his breath, hoping he had gotten through to the aliens. Over the audio speakers, they heard three clear, different notes.

"Yes!" Alex said, punching the air. "Claude, send a set of three more pulses with four pings, pause, five pings, pause, six pings. Every time you get a successful response in audible tones, increment the pulses until you reach one hundred. Change nothing else."

"Understood, Admiral," Claude said, realizing what Alex had been trying to accomplish, a simple dialog.

<SADEs?> Alex asked.

<Admiral,> Julien replied first. <We are recording responses. Mutter is matching responses to the previously recorded dialog to begin to build a translation of their communication.>

<Admiral,> Cordelia interjected, <I have taken the liberty of continuing to record conversations from the three prime individuals that we used to create the first matrix. We now have nearly eleven hours of their communications, which will accelerate our understanding.>

<With your permission, Admiral, I have our first translated sound,> Mutter sent.

<Please, Mutter, you do not need to ask permission to participate,> Alex replied. <Your thoughts are always welcome.>

Mutter took a brief tick to reorder her protocols that governed communication with the Admiral. Her comm protocols were now changing regularly after rarely changing in decades. She found the process invigorating, an uncommon sensation for her.

<Thank you, Admiral. Your courtesies are appreciated,> Mutter responded. <Individuals number two and three in our matrix begin their communications with the primary individual, who we believe is their leader, with the sound for "one." However, while the note starts at the same frequency, it shifts pitch with a slight warble at the end. It is my estimate that the word we are looking for is a variation of "one.">

<"First," Admiral,> Cordelia said excitedly. <They call their leader "First.">

Monitoring the Engineering Suite, Julien picked up a view of the Admiral and relayed it to his fellow SADEs. They saw him sit heavily in a chair, clap his hands together, and break into a huge smile. Then they watched his smile slowly fade to be replaced by a frown.

<We've established basic contact and response,> Alex sent to the SADEs. <But I need to build a core language. We have to accelerate this process.>

Cordelia's idea was borne of her art. <Images, Admiral,> she sent. <If we could send images … simple at first, then more complex.>

<Admiral,> Julien added, <the first silver ship detected the weakening of their hull before nanites penetration was completed. They must have hull sensors of some sort. The question would be how sensitive. We might try projecting icons, simple images on their hull with a laser to give it strength.>

When Alex closed his comm to direct the building of a laser projector, Julien sent a quick message to Renée that the engineering staff was building again and Alex was free of comms.

* * *

Renee woke a few people to help her deliver food and drink to the engineering team. Her message raced through the crew, waking most from their sleep, and she was surprised by the number of volunteers. Everyone wanted to watch the historic event unfold in person—humans' first communications with aliens.

In a rare adoption of their cousins' trait, Pia broadcast to the entire crew, except those in engineering, sending, <Terese, Geneviève, and I claim privilege. We have cared for the Admiral since the beginning.> It was such a un-Méridien-like announcement that the crew acquiesced to her demand. Then Pia drafted the number of Méridiens she would need to assist Ser.

The SADEs kept their ships' Directors, Captains, officers, crew, and passengers apprised of the engineering team's progress. Tomas, Lina, and Captain Cordova were so entranced by the event that they listened on the *Freedom*'s bridge, as if being away from the immediate vicinity of Cordelia would lessen the event's reality. There were two special guests on the *Freedom*'s bridge, as requested by Renée. Tomas had contacted the young Librans, relaying the directive, <Amelia and Eloise, Renée de Guirnon has requested your presence on the bridge to observe the first contact of aliens by our people.>

Both had been overcome by the personage of a Co-Leader recognizing them, children of their people. Eloise had replied, <Are you sure Ser meant us, Director Monti?>

<In Ser's words, young people,> Tomas had replied, <"Please tell the little elders, the builders of consensus and the Admiral's supporters, that I would see them witness this amazing event from the bridge.">

Amelia and Eloise now sat in crew members' chairs, marveling at the enormous bridge display, a sight neither had expected to see for many years, if ever. That Ser had requested their presence still baffled them, but the manner in which they were treated made them feel special.

Eloise recalled the final words of her great-grandmother, "Keep him close." Fiona Haraken had always been a powerful presence among the Librans, and Eloise intended to honor her great-grandmother's final request, which she found came easy to her. She was proud of her Admiral. He had liberated her people and he had kept them close, accepting them as his responsibility. Now, even though he was frightening many of the Librans by communicating with their great enemy, it was his supposition that was being proven correct—the inhabitants of the silver ships would speak with him.

Captain Lazlo Menlo, First Mate Ahmed Durak, and Commander Sheila Reynard hovered around the *Money Maker's* bridge speakers, following Mutter's every transmission. Captain Menlo felt very proud of the role his elderly SADE was playing. Her penchant for ancient symphonic music was reaping great rewards, and every time Mutter added progress to the investigation, Lazlo playfully punched the arm of his First Mate. When Mutter equated the number "one" to the title of the fighter's leader, which Cordelia recognized as "First," Lazlo swung his arm out only to find empty air. When he looked around, Ahmed was standing on the other side of him, smiling politely at him.

-18-

The Libran flotilla watched the events aboard the *Rêveur* unfold in real time, which gave Julien the idea to take the Admiral's concept of keeping the people informed one step further. Every three hours, following the capture of the silver ship, Julien edited a summary of the events into a tight vid package and sent an FTL comm to New Terra. The first comm arrived at New Terra's FTL station ten days later.

The SADEs aboard the *Unsere Menschen*, the three liners, and the freighter were the first to pick up Julien's transmission. It had been twenty-five days since the flotilla had left for Arnos. The SADEs distributed the vids to the Director and Captains, who wasted no time approving them for broadcast to the crew and passengers. Every three hours, work on the ships would come to a halt, food utensils would be set down, and children would crowd around vid displays to watch the newest vid.

When the first vid was distributed aboard the *Unsere Menschen*, arriving in the middle of the work day, the New Terran contract workers were bewildered by the Librans who literally froze in mid-motion. Z, who now had many of his sensory systems in place, saw the confusion on the part of the contract workers and recalled his lessons from Julien and Cordelia. He sent the vid to every screen in the ship, and the contract workers and Libran children gathered around to watch and listen. Upon discovering that the vids would arrive continually every three hours, many of the contract workers stayed after work hours to watch the latest installments.

Making one of his most adventuresome decisions, Z contacted President Gonzalez in her office when he received the first compressed vid. <President Maria Gonzalez of Government House of New Terra of the Oistos system, I request permission to speak with you,> Z sent.

Maria smiled to herself. She was acquainted with Z and Cordelia from her communications with Julien. Z was as advertised. "Z, you're already speaking with me," Maria replied. She couldn't help but enjoy each and every contact with a Méridien SADE again. She missed Julien … and Alex.

<Then I will continue, President Maria Gonzalez of Government House of New—>

"Z, if I may interrupt, you may address me as 'President Gonzalez' or 'Madam President,'" Maria replied.

<Thank you, Madam President. Brevity is always more expedient. I have received a summary vid of the flotilla's efforts at Arnos and will be receiving another one every three hours. I have one stored for you at this moment if you would care to view it.>

"Have we lost ships, Z?" Maria asked.

<Six, Madam President,> Z replied.

"Six!" Maria exclaimed. "But Alex only took four ships."

<The six ships would be Daggers, Madam President.>

Maria sat back in her chair, deflated. *Alex is losing*, she thought. She had hoped with all her might that Alex would prevail over the silver ships. "Z, I'm not sure a vid of the loss of the Daggers would be something I would like to see, nor my people come to think about it."

<I have no vid of the loss of the Daggers, Madam President,> Z explained, wondering why the President would think he should have it.

"You don't? Then what are you offering me, Z?"

<This is a record of the Admiral speaking with the aliens, Madam President,> Z replied.

Alex speaking with the aliens ... Maria processed the phrase several times before she started laughing and kept laughing until she started choking. Concerned staff rushed into her office, one carrying a glass of water. She waved them off.

"Yes, Z, send me the vid immediately and continue to send the others to me as you receive them."

After the vid downloaded to her reader, Maria watched it, laughing and shaking her head at what she saw, even as pride threatened to burst her heart. She called two techs into her office and told them to play the vid over the screens in Government House and be ready to broadcast a download from Z in 2.35 hours.

In the meantime, Maria recorded a message for the planet's media stations. Her short vid featured her sitting at her desk as she said, "Greetings from Government House. Attached to this message is a vid from the Admiral's flotilla in the Arnos system. We will be receiving a second vid at 13.50 hours, and we will immediately forward it to you. Your viewers should be interested in watching Admiral Racine conversing with the aliens."

Maria sent the message to her administrator and sat back in her carved guriel chair with a satisfied look on her face. She hadn't felt this good since they had launched the *Rêveur* on its return trip to Méridien after its seventy-one-year absence.

-19-

Mickey, Stan, and the techs exited the port bay where they had set up a powerful laser projector and connected its input to the bay's comm station. Back in the suite, the engineering team completed their equipment setup that would control the laser's input and were about to announce to Alex their readiness when the suite's doors hissed open and a group of Méridiens, led by Renée, walked in with food trays and drink pitchers. Alex opened his mouth to postpone the interruption but closed it quickly when he saw the expression on Renée's face.

<I see he is still trainable,> Terese quipped, sharing the message with Renée, Pia, Geneviève, and especially Alex.

Witnessing the blush creep up Alex's neck in response to Terese's remark, Pia replied privately to her, sending, <There is the young Captain we know and revere.> Pia placed her two trays on a table in front of Mickey and kissed him warmly.

Alex was anxious to establish deeper communications with the aliens as soon as he could. But he also knew he had a bad habit of driving himself too hard and suspected he was doing the same to his engineering team. They required a break, he required a break, and they all required food. Otherwise the quality of their efforts would suffer.

Renée placed her tray in front of Alex and took his face firmly in her hands. She kissed him and felt him relax into her embrace. The crew, had they been asked, were extremely grateful for the Admiral's distraction, even if briefly. They were all starving.

<The aliens can wait a few moments more,> Renée said privately to Alex. <Now eat and recharge yourself before I become further annoyed with you.>

Alex sat down and plowed into his food, happy to see a plethora of trays and drink carafes spread around the tables. The engineering team had missed more than one meal.

Renée and her volunteers watched the food disappear. Several Méridiens quickly exited the suite and hurried back to the meal room. <Who knew conversing with aliens created such appetites,> Geneviève marveled to her companions, shocked to see even their Méridien tech specialist, Claude, consuming two trays' worth of food.

* * *

Once the engineering crew were finished eating, everyone noticed the shift in Alex's demeanor, and the servers hurried to collect the trays and clear the room. Only Renée lingered for a moment.

<All of us are proud of what you are doing, Alex,> Renée sent privately. <The Librans reached consensus when they saw you risk your ship and crew to capture a silver ship. They could do no less than risk their future with you. Just remember to pace yourself. The aliens won't be leaving this space for many years.>

When the suite's door hissed closed behind Renée, Alex linked all the players and sent, <Mickey?>

<We're ready, Admiral,> Mickey replied. <Those creatures will have to be blind not to see the images that we will paint on their hull. That is … if they have eyes.>

<Julien?> Alex sent.

<Cordelia will take the lead for this next series, Admiral,> Julien responded. <She has prepared a series of icons that we believe will accelerate our comprehension of the aliens' nouns and syntax, enabling you to converse on the subjects you require. Mutter will match their audio responses to literal meanings, and we will work to determine the best translation.>

<Cordelia, you have the lead,> Alex sent.

Cordelia tested her control of the laser projector and the audio transmitter on the hull. She followed Alex's lead, using math as the common language and projecting a horizontal row of icons—a vertical line, a plus sign, a vertical line, an equal sign, and two parallel standing lines. At the same time, Cordelia sent a series of the alien's audible signals—one, a pause, one, a pause, and two—then waited.

In the suite, the speakers uttered a great deal of whistling, tweets, and shrill notes. The aliens' level of excitement was obvious and so was the degree of conversation. Suddenly a single note blasted through the suite's speakers, causing most of the engineering personnel to jump. Then they heard a series of succinct tones. The first, third, and fifth notes matched the aliens' tones for "one", "one", and "two" that had been previously translated.

<Thus, Admiral, we have the aliens' sounds for "add" or "sum" and "equal" or "same,"> Cordelia sent, pleased with herself.

<Cordelia, if you were humanly present, I would kiss you,> Alex replied, overjoyed at their success.

<Pardon me, Admiral, but if Cordelia were present, that would be my privilege,> Julien stated firmly.

Alex smiled to himself at Julien's declaration.

Now I can truly appreciate Z's desire to be mobile, Cordelia thought, intrigued by the Admiral's and Julien's comments. *One could wish to experience this in the human world.*

<Cordelia, if you would continue, please,> Alex sent.

<Yes, Admiral,> Cordelia replied, surprised by her momentary lack of focus. She began projecting a series of images. The occupants of the silver ship had excellent hull sensitivity and her icons proceeded from simple to complex in relatively short order. At one point, Cordelia borrowed an image from the resonance imager. It was an outline of one of the inhabitants. Her subsequent icon generated a sound similar to a human whistling the words "swei swee," although with slightly different tonal endings for each of the two notes. The SADEs categorized the response as the occupants' name for their species.

Over the next hours, the SADEs learned the sounds for "affirmative" and "negative," "adult" and "young," "land" and "sea," "world" and "star," and many more. Cordelia continually generated new icons as the now-dubbed "Swei Swee" responded to her previous ones.

The icon of several Swei Swee surrounded by the outline of a silver ship generated a complex term that didn't match any previously defined sound. Cordelia was about to call it "family," but that didn't match the adult pairing with young defined earlier. Julien coined the term "hive" for a group of the aliens within a single silver ship, and the word reminded Alex of his previous concepts of the inhabitants of the silver ships.

Over time, the SADEs learned the Swei Swee originally resided by the seaside, calling the ocean "endless waters." "Death," generated by an icon of an upside down Swei Swee with legs splayed, was to "travel the endless waters." A silver ship was a "dark traveler." The prison ship was the "world traveler." The aliens' comm was "singing to the stars." "To search" was to hunt for fish, their ancient food source. That they were "denied the search" meant they were captive. "Seek shelter" was to seek safety onshore. "Hunters" were dangerous animals that fed on the Swei Swee. "Singers" were intelligent species.

When Cordelia attempted to define the inhabitants of the world traveler, it produced the only non-Swei Swee-like sound they had heard. As far as she could determine, it sounded like "Nua'll." The icon of the *Rêveur* produced a complex set of notes, which the SADEs determined meant "Star Hunters."

The push and pull of images and sounds went on through the next day and into the second night. The engineering team slept with their heads down on tables or stretched out on the deck while the SADEs continued to work to identify the vocabulary and syntax the Admiral would need to converse with the Swei Swee.

* * *

In the morning, food was delivered again to the engineering team, and Alex, for one, never felt so grateful for a hot cup of thé. He sipped it slowly, savoring the heat and flavor, noticing most of his team was doing the same, attempting to wake overtaxed brain cells and boost energy levels. As they revived, food began disappearing. Trays were just being cleared when Alex and the engineering team received a message from Julien.

<Admiral, our icon display on the silver ship's hull was overlaid 0.6 hours ago with a blocking pattern generated by the occupants, and the aliens have been repeating an audible message over and over. We have ceased our laser projection and have translated the message. We believe it is, "Star Hunters plus beams. Swei Swee plus, or perhaps add, search. Denied the search plus travel the endless waters. Star Hunters plus then minus Swei Swee." In the background is a complex harmony of voices, which Mutter believes is the hive singing.>

<What's the team's summary?> Alex asked.

<We believe, Admiral, the lack of gravitational waves in this area would have led to the hive's death due to an interruption of their power source. The Swei Swee perceive the energy from our beams as the gift of life, and it is our choice as to whether they live or die.>

-20-

The SADEs determined that they had a sufficient vocabulary and syntax for Alex to convey basic questions to the Swei Swee. Cordelia informed Alex it would take many more days to elevate their understanding of the Swei Swee language to a more sophisticated level. It was time Alex didn't think they had—or so said the hairs on the back of his neck.

Alex mulled over the meaning of the Swei Swee's choral song. When it finally came time to begin his line of questioning, he chose the most direct path for his inquiry, one designed to help him understand whose side the Swei Swee would choose to be on, if they had a choice. First, he needed to get the occupants' attention.

<Julien, briefly flash the laser on and off,> Alex requested. The blinking of the laser had the desired effect. The hive went silent. <Julien, send "Star Hunters plus Swei Swee equals search the endless waters,"> Alex said.

In response to Alex's message came a powerful bridge of voices, singing for all they were worth.

<Admiral, I believe you have made some entities very happy,> Julien sent privately.

<And it was the two of us who believed they should be offered freedom, Julien,> Alex replied. <I have never been prouder of your support, my friend.>

On the *Freedom*'s bridge, Amelia and Eloise had the more demonstrative reactions of those listening throughout the flotilla to the Swei Swee's song of jubilation. They jumped up and down, hugging one another and then everyone in sight. Their antics had Tomas, Lina, and the bridge personnel smiling. Like Julien, Amelia and Eloise had been ardent supporters of the Admiral's plan, and now were being proven right.

<For the first question for our new acquaintances, Julien, send "Dark traveler equals Swei Swee."> Alex was attempting to understand if the silver ships belonged to the Swei Swee.

<Admiral,> Cordelia said, after considering the response. <I translate the response of the First as "Dark traveler equals Nua'll plus Swei Swee.">

<This makes sense, Admiral,> said Julien. <The Swei Swee would appear to be the simpler beings. They were fishermen, and I would suspect miners of some sort, who were able to biologically construct crystal structures, possibly their homes. A telling point is that while the prison ship and the silver ships appear to move about on the same technology, the hulls are quite different. I would surmise the Swei Swee constructed the fighter shells around Nua'll technology. If the Swei Swee did build the hulls, they would be able to enter and exit the hulls biologically, once planetside. However, they might be limited to exiting their ships only into a habitable, atmospheric environment. It would be an effective containment strategy by the Nua'll.>

<Julien, send "Swei Swee world,"> Alex requested.

They received a set of sad warbling tones. The translation appeared to be "Swei Swee world equals negative." While Alex considered the ramification of a "negative world," the rear of the silver ship produced an image of a small Swei Swee, the same icon that Cordelia had used. As everyone watched, the image grew in size and a small Swei Swee emerged from the large entity and grew in size again.

"Two generations," Alex murmured, and Julien relayed Alex's words over the vid he was broadcasting. The generation cycle was repeated over and over. When it stopped, Alex exploded. "Black space, eight generations! They've been captive for eight generations." Julien relayed only Alex's latter statement to the flotilla. Unfortunately some Librans and New Terrans could read lips.

<Cordelia,> Alex said, <it's time to get more creative since the Swei Swee are escalating communication. Create me a vid of Libre circling Arnos. Julien, when Libre completes one circle, send the tone for "one" and when it finishes a second cycle, send the tone for "two." Cordelia, halt your vid after two cycles, then send a second vid repeating their vid of the

young to adult Swei Swee, but play it slow. Julien, send a slow count synced to Cordelia's second vid from one and up, repeating it for each cycle. Both of you, when you reach eight cycles, the number of imprisoned generations, repeat the vid of the transitions from young to adult and the count.> It was a complex question, but Alex needed to know if the Swei Swee had enough intelligence to be treated as partners against the prison ship or if they were just passengers along for the ride planetside and all the technological capability came from the Nua'll.

Cordelia and Julien cycled through the vids and audio signals three times. A small cacophony of conversation broke out inside the silver ship, and it went on for nearly a quarter-hour.

"It appears, Admiral, we may have stumped them on this one," Mickey said.

He had barely finished speaking when the display of young to adult appeared on the silver ship's hull and the audio picked up a double-tone whistle.

<Fifty, Admiral,> Mutter sent, <which, if the Swei Swee have understood your question correctly, it means the annual cycle of Libre, at 1.2 Méridien years, times their response of fifty equates to a lifespan of sixty years.>

"Admiral," Mickey said sadly, "their race has been imprisoned for somewhere around 480 years."

"Yes, Mickey, and I think it's high time they were freed!" Alex said.

<Julien, send "Dark traveler sing dark traveler,"> Alex ordered.

<The response is affirmative, Admiral,> Mutter said. <The silver ships can communicate between one another.>

Now the escape plan begins, Alex thought. <Cordelia, I need a vid of the prison ship and two silver ships. Give me a dotted line that starts at one silver ship and extends to the other one. Keep repeating the line extending from one fighter to the other as if this was a comm signal. Form a circle around the prison ship after the dotted line is in its second iteration. Put that vid on a loop. Julien once the vid starts playing send "Dark traveler sing dark traveler," then pause and send "Nua'll." Repeat the vid until we have an understandable response.>

After the Swei Swee watched the vid, the response was the now familiar odd sound followed by a single warbling tone, which translated as "Nua'll negative."

"So the Swei Swee can communicate between fighters without the Nua'll hearing them. How foolish of the jailers," Alex murmured.

<Cordelia,> Alex ordered, <play a vid of the prison ship with a world below it, but not Libre, and icons of the Swei Swee floating up from the planet to the prison ship.>

<Place the Swei Swee inside a silver ship, Admiral?> Cordelia asked, puzzled by Alex's request.

<Negative, Cordelia, float the Swei Swee icons up by themselves.>

The response was a series of whistles and tweets, one of which was unfamiliar to Alex. Before Alex could question the SADEs, a new, heretofore unseen icon appeared on the rear of the silver ship, and the unfamiliar tone was repeated.

<Well I'll be,> Stanley Peterson sent, <those things are now teaching us new words, Admiral. That odd tone must be "rings" or "ringed.">

<A ringed dark traveler,> Alex translated.

<I believe that is correct, Admiral,> Mutter sent.

<So this ringed dark traveler is a ship we haven't seen,> Alex said. <It would have to be bigger than the silver ships and of a different design if the silver ship hulls are Swei Swee creations.>

While the team considered Alex's words, a second image appeared on the fighter's hull. An odd, tube-shaped ship, similar to an ancient projectile, with concentric rings down its length appeared. It was positioned for a side view. Four silver ships, placed bow to stern, stretched underneath the ringed-ship to indicate its length.

<Julien, send "Ringed dark traveler negative,"> Alex requested, hoping the capture-ships no longer existed.

The response was "Ringed dark traveler positive." It was followed by an icon of the prison ship with four ringed-ship icons overlaying its image. Mutter translated the long series of audio tones that accompanied the image. <Admiral, their message is "Four ringed dark travelers; ringed dark travelers plus world traveler.">

<Capture-ships, Admiral?> Julien asked. <Vessels that the prison ship has kept aboard for centuries and that haven't been needed for any other function?>

<Perhaps waiting for the day when these slaves revolt or die out and need to be replaced?> Cordelia wondered.

Let's see what type of allies you would make, Alex thought. <Cordelia, I need an image of Libre with silver ships over top of the world. Julien, send "Star Hunter world.">

The response was loud and strong, almost vehement. The SADEs and Alex could translate these simple sounds by now. It was "Negative, hunter world."

<Julien, send "Star Hunter world positive.">

Despite the alien nature of the communications, there was no mistaking anguish in the desperate response of "Negative, Nua'll hunter world."

<Julien, send "Star Hunters" and send the tones for "one hundred" twenty-two times,> Alex ordered.

This time there was no immediate response, only silence. Then first one individual and then another emitted odd, warbling tones until all joined into what could only be called wailing. The blended notes had a way of mesmerizing yet, at the same time, subtly fraying the nerves of the humans listening. A loud whistle cut across the hive's lament, and the chorus ceased.

The engineering team heard the now recognizable whistles and tones of the First, but the message was too complex for easy translation. When the message ended, absolute silence fell—no background conversation, no chorus, no sound whatsoever.

<Mutter?> Alex requested.

<Your pardon, Admiral, but the message contains new tones and subtle changes to previously known notes and tweets.>

<I need your best guess, Mutter.>

Several moments of silence came from Mutter. Alex considered the ramifications of asking an AI as old as Mutter to guess. *Probably an unfair request*, Alex thought.

<Admiral,> Mutter finally said, <it is my supposition that we are hearing a message in two parts. The first part is an abject apology. The First repeats his message several times of the Nua'll, hunters, and world. He appears to be communicating that the Nua'll had identified the entities on Libre as hunters, which the Swei Swee consider aggressive entities against their kind. The second part of the message appears to offer us, the Star Hunters, to send the Swei Swee as travelers of the endless waters. I translate this as they are offering their lives for the harm they have done to the Star Hunter people.>

<Well done, Mutter,> Alex sent. Many of the pieces fit together and backed his suppositions, but he couldn't help feeling he was missing something. The difficulty lay in asking complex questions with their simple vocabulary. He decided to posit a query and hoped the Swei Swee provided the answer as to why the Swei Swee hadn't turned on the prison ship.

<Julien, send a short vid of the encounters of the Daggers and silver ships this last time. Show the losses on both sides. Simultaneously send, "Swei Swee search Star Hunters; Star Hunters search Swei Swee; Swei Swee negative search Nua'll.">

On the fighter's rear, the outline of the Nua'll ship appeared and a bright yellow-green dot began blinking on and off in the center of the dot.

<Okay, I give up,> Mickey said after a few moments.

<Anyone with an idea?> Alex asked.

Julien began enlarging the image on the engineering vid screen while the team watched. Soon the bright blinking dot filled the screen. It wasn't a single dot. It was composed of a mass of individual dots. Julien kept enlarging the image until a single dot revealed a circle encompassing the dim outline of a Swei Swee.

<Their young … hatchlings,> Alex received from Renée. He relayed the thought to the team, sending, <Renée says the circles are Swei Swee eggs, hatchlings. That's the Nua'll's leverage. They're holding the Swei Swee young hostage to keep the parents in line.>

Alex took a moment to consider his next line of communication then ordered, <Julien, send two messages, one after the other. Send "Swei Swee

search the endless waters," then "Star Hunters plus Swei Swee equal Nua'll negative.">

When the team received no response, Julien sent the message again. Everyone waited in silence for a reply. Of interest to every human of the flotilla was that no discussion took place among the Swei Swee. The decision appeared to remain with the First.

Finally, the First's whistled response came through clearly. Mutter translated it as "Swei Swee search the endless waters; Nua'll travel the endless waters."

<Julien, send "Affirmative,"> Alex sent, sitting down in a chair, a satisfied smile plastered across his face.

The team heard the hive chorus a single tone, repeated over and over, but with endless twists and turns on the basic note. In their implants, they heard Mutter repeat, <"Affirmative, affirmative, affirmative.">

The First's whistle ended the chant and his following notes were translated as "Star Hunter First."

Cordelia took the initiative to project an image of Alex in his Admiral's uniform on the rear of the fighter. It effectively ended the celebratory chorus.

<You may have frightened them more than the Nua'll have, Cordelia,> Alex quipped, taking notice of the absolute silence.

"Admiral," Claude said, "if you will, please regard the resonance imager."

Alex walked over to the imager's output screen, which showed the Swei Swee hive bobbing up and down in unison. The scene gave Alex an eerie feeling.

<It appears you have accumulated more admirers, Admiral,> Julien said as he inserted the thermal image into the Engineering Suite's broadcast to the flotilla. <One wonders when you will cease collecting the lost and forsaken of this universe.>

-21-

Since Alex and the SADEs couldn't think of a way to communicate to the Swei Swee that they needed time to think, it fell to Cordelia and Mutter to keep them entertained while Alex met with his officers. Cordelia had already designed the next 1,571 icons and vids she would employ, so she made use of the time to add to the Swei Swee language base.

Julien sought to divest himself of overwhelming duties. He relayed the Engineering Suite's output to Cordelia, passing her the responsibility to filter the final output to the flotilla, but he kept for himself the creation of the vid destined for New Terra every three hours. It freed his processing power to manage the demands of the Admiral's meeting with the flotilla's officers, which entailed mirroring the *Rêveur*'s holo-vid to the *Money Maker* and the *Freedom*.

As one of the earliest SADEs, Mutter was hard pressed to juggle her responsibilities which were managing the holo-vid display for the Captain and crew, driving the analysis of the Swei Swee's responses, and maintaining the *Money Maker*'s operations. That she was accomplishing her tasks, even if barely, pleased her to no end.

Alex, Andrea, and Edouard gathered around the *Rêveur*'s bridge holo-vid. Lazlo, Ahmed, Tatia and Sheila were gazing at the mirrored-image on the *Money Maker*'s bridge. Captain Cordova and Tomas were spectators on the bridge of the *Freedom*. They didn't expect to participate, but Alex wanted them to know his plans and under what conditions they should employ their emergency orders. Julien linked all of their implants in a conference comm.

Alex had laid out his idea and Andrea responded with, <So, Admiral, your plan depends on us trusting the Swei Swee and exposing ourselves to their silver ships. What if you're wrong about what the Swei Swee will do? What if they turn on us?>

<The alternative is to not trust the Swei Swee,> Alex replied. <In which case, we destroy the silver ship we've captured, and we continue to lure other silver ships out to the peripheral, destroying them a few at a time and losing our fighters in the process. It's my estimate that we don't have enough Daggers to do the job. We'll probably lose all of them if we stay the course, and I don't think we'll be the last ones standing.>

Sheila blanched at the thought of the loss of the entire squadron—pilots and Daggers—which would include her. She knew she would not abandon her people in the final fight. Lazlo and Ahmed glanced at her, guilt written on their faces at the thought of the pilots' sacrifices if they were ordered into straight-up fights.

Alex let them digest the contrasting concepts for a moment. Quiet reigned while everyone considered the Admiral's plan, the risks, and the conversations with the Swei Swee.

<So who wants to be the pilot of the Dagger that eliminates this silver ship when I release it?> Alex said, interrupting their contemplation. <As the Admiral of this flotilla, I assure you it will be one of you who will launch the missiles. I won't allow it to be assigned to a Lieutenant.>

<I am new to these manners of operations, Admiral,> Captain Menlo said. He had yet to voice an opinion one way or the other. <Much depends on your assessment of the Swei Swee. They are an alien species, and it would seem to me that it would be easy to mistake their intent, especially with so little time in communication and at such an elementary level. What is it that you perceive about them that makes you so sure of what they will do?>

<At this time, it's only intuition,> Alex replied.

<Oh,> Lazlo replied.

<Hoping for something more, Captain?>

<Your pardon, Admiral … but, yes, I was,> Lazlo replied.

<I understand, Captain. I'm asking you to risk your lives on my hunch that we can believe the Swei Swee, and they will commit to aiding us against the prison ship. At the very least, I'm expecting them to step aside and let us take on the prison ship alone. It's my hope we can trap it before it accelerates out of our missile envelope. The alternative is unconscionable

to me—we attempt to destroy every silver ship and, slowly but surely, lose every single fighter and its pilot.>

<Admiral, perhaps we can manage the risk this way,> Tatia sent. <We've used the gravity wells effectively so far. Let's keep using them.> She linked into the holo-vid and moved the icons of the *Rêveur* and the *Money Maker* below the ecliptic and moved them under the system short of Libre. <We get close to Libre this way. We separate into three squadrons and try to trap the prison ship. The *Outward Bound* stays with the *Rêveur* to protect your ship and both of you stay below the ecliptic. If the silver ships betray us, the *Money Maker* will have time to move far below the ecliptic.>

<The issues with that plan, Commander,> Julien explained, <are that the prison ship is not limited to the ecliptic and we don't know its armament. If it does have weapons, then with its greater acceleration, it would easily eliminate our primary ships and take its time winnowing our fighters, which would be trapped in the system with the chronometer counting down for their air reserves.>

<I'm also concerned about these "ringed dark travelers,"> Sheila interjected. <What are their capabilities? What velocity and acceleration can they generate? Are they armed? If so, what's the extent of their armament? The closer we get to the Nua'll, the more we expose ourselves to too many dangerous unknowns.>

<And now you've identified many of the problems, people,> Alex said. <Just how do you expect us to eliminate these unknowns? My plan is to test the Swei Swee first and let them prove themselves to us. We take a minimal risk for potentially great reward—allies against the prison ship.>

<Admiral,> Cordelia interjected, <aren't we placing the Swei Swee in a predicament, making them choose between their freedom and the preservation of the hatchlings? What if the Swei Swee are depending on us to save the hatchlings as well as free them?> Her comments had the effect of bringing the entire discussion to an abrupt halt. In the ensuing silence, she added, <Apologies, Admiral, if I asked inappropriate questions.>

<Excellent questions, Cordelia, and well timed, I might add,> Alex replied. Cordelia's questions often carried that sensitivity and emotional

context he often missed in his calculations. <The best way to learn the answers to those questions is ask the Swei Swee, Cordelia.>

Alex considered how he might ask his last questions to gain the answers he needed to create a battle plan and simultaneously learn how the Swei Swee would react to the endangerment of their hatchlings. *Take it one step at a time, Alex*, he coached himself.

<Cordelia and Mutter, halt your translation routines,> Alex requested. <Cordelia and Julien, I need some complex vids with matching audio messages.>

Cordelia left her last icon in place on the projector when she stopped her routine, which unfortunately caused the Swei Swee a bit of consternation. They had given their response, but the image hadn't changed as it had been doing for a long while. Julien, recognizing the agitated movements of the Swei Swee, turned off the laser projector.

<For the first vid,> Alex sent, <start with a bright yellow dot equal to a silver ship icon, then change the image to one of this system populated with yellow dots that mirror the present locations of the silver ships. Give them a moment to absorb the count. Follow that with an image of the Nua'll ship. Place a yellow dot inside the prison ship, but fade it in and out until you interrupt the vid to repeat the entire process.>

That Cordelia was projecting her vid moments later with Julien augmenting the audio was the norm to Alex. Downshifting his thoughts and reactions to engage people had become an increasing challenge. Renée was the one person that required no effort on his part to re-engage. That she could see the shift in his demeanor and welcome it with her small, wry smile made him feel as if he was still good at being human.

When the vid began its second play, Mutter relayed the First's whistle tones. <Admiral, the First is sending "Fifty-five," but the tone has a new pitch or waver to it. I surmise it is the mark of a question. The First is questioning our count, which he believes is incorrect. Our vid shows real-time positions even though some of the silver ships are behind the system's bodies.>

<Correct his count, Mutter,> Alex sent.

For the first time, Mutter was able to signal the Swei Swee directly, relaying the total count of silver ships in the system, visible and invisible.

Mickey had worked to refine the resolution on the resonance imager, which allowed the engineering team to clearly see the First rise up on his walking appendages, large claws and his true hands lifted up as if searching for something he had heard or seen. He loosed a sweet set of whistles, melodic, nearly hypnotic.

It was an enticing invitation to Mutter, which she accepted. She replied to the First with a set of her own tones that played and blended with the First's melody. Immediately the First began singing, his hive joining in chorus. Mutter, dismissing her centuries of conditioning, joined first in the chorus, then began alternating the lead with the First, each one blending around the other.

Alex and the entire flotilla listened, mesmerized by the sound of alien music—for that was the only word to describe it—music. Perhaps it wasn't music by human standards, but it was ethereal, uplifting—sounds that celebrated life. Alex felt loath to interrupt them, but when he sensed that his flotilla had received a good taste of the beauty of the species he was trying to save, he sent, <Mutter?>

On her next lead, Mutter slowed the tempo of her response and closed on a long, sweet whistle punctuated by a soft warble. The hive had lowered the volume of their chorus and then closed as Mutter ended. Finally, the hive blasted back with a cacophony of raucous whistles.

<I believe that is your applause, Mutter,> Alex sent.

Julien and Cordelia relayed to Mutter the sound and images of the flotilla's crew clapping and cheering. Julien envisioned the impact his next compressed vid would make throughout the New Terran system.

When the Swei Swee's celebration died down, Mutter sent the tones for "Star Hunter First." The hive didn't require their leader's note to quiet them. Silence reigned immediately, and they began their coordinated bobbing again, but slower this time as if at half-speed.

<It appears your audience waits in anticipation, Your Highness,> Julien sent privately and received for his tease an image of his case going up in flames—crystals, circuits, and all. In reply, he sent a chuckle.

<People, did I miss something or did we not get an answer to the last question?> Alex said.

<My apologies, Admiral,> Mutter sent. <I failed to support your request.>

<On the contrary, Mutter, you supported my desires beautifully. You exquisitely demonstrated the point I have been trying to make that we have a unique, intelligent species deserving to be freed from their captors. I could think of no better way to demonstrate that than in the manner you have just done.> Alex gave her a moment to enjoy the compliment, then sent, <However, Cordelia, I still need my answer.>

While Cordelia played the vid again, Mutter sorted through her protocols, confirming, editing, or deleting until she felt like a new entity. Her ship duties still remained primary. The Admiral's orders and even wishes would override many of her lesser protocols, but she placed her music and the opportunity to sing with the Swei Swee just below the protocols that responded to the Admiral and her Captain. It was a glorious feeling. After more than two centuries, she felt born again.

Following Cordelia's vid, the engineering team heard the leader sing out. A hive member responded. Mutter translated on the fly, noting that they were discussing numbers. <I believe, Admiral,> she sent, <they are comparing their total count to the number we gave them. Except that they are not counting in dark traveler units. Apparently the term "group" or "hive" as we term the sound precedes each number. I surmise that a hive is a group that may occupy more than one dark traveler.>

Alex noticed that the entire team was starting to utilize Swei Swee terms, and a smile crossed his lips at the thought. He needed his people to adopt these creatures in their minds and hearts if they were going to support his efforts to liberate them. *I only hope that I know what I'm doing,* he thought.

<Admiral, the difference between their count and our count is eleven,> Mutter relayed. <I believe it's the number of dark travelers still aboard the Nua'll ship.>

<Cordelia, the next vid contains three parts,> Alex ordered. <Mutter, please handle the audio translations. You appear to have been made an

honorary Swei Swee. First sequence, show our ships approaching the Nua'll ship, the Swei Swee standing aside, and the Nua'll fleeing the system. Next, show our ships approaching the Nua'll ship, the Swei Swee standing aside, and the Nua'll ship exploding. Third sequence, show our ships approaching the Nua'll ship, the Swei Swee standing aside, and the eleven dark travelers in the Nua'll ship loading the hatchlings, then exiting the ship.>

The Swei Swee responded by replaying the third sequence on their hull followed by the end of the first sequence and accompanied by the First's whistles.

<Admiral,> Mutter sent, <you will notice in the replay of our third vid, only one dark traveler exits the world traveler. It is unclear whether this represents the percentage of recovery of the hatchlings or whether only one dark traveler will have time to escape before the world traveler flees the system.>

<Mutter, send "Swei Swee plus Star Hunters search the endless sea … affirmative … negative,"> Alex requested.

The silver ship's aft end produced a display of the solar system. A circle indicated the orbit of the outer planet. It was replaced with an image of the *Rêveur* sitting at ninety degrees to the star. The icon of the Swei Swee fighter blinked on and off. It lay in the shadow of the *Rêveur*. Then the ships were reduced to a dot in the display of the solar system, and a dotted line was extended from the ship's position to cross the circle indicating the last planet's orbit. Mutter's translation of the First was "Hive First sings Swei Swee First."

<Admiral,> Julien interjected, <it would appear the Swei Swee need more power to communicate and must move closer to the gravitational waves of the system to obtain it. I would surmise our beams are insufficient for their systems' full operation. It might be prudent to move them.>

Cordelia added a final note. <Admiral, a detail of their display is important. The Swei Swee are drawing attention to their ship that is in the lee of our ship. I believe they want to communicate to the other dark travelers but not be seen by the Nua'll.>

<Mutter, send "Affirmative,"> Alex requested. <Julien and Mutter, proceed to the closest position satisfying the Swei Swee's needs, and ensure our silver ship is kept well hidden from the Nua'll.>

* * *

Alex broke the engineering team for food, which Renée and the Méridiens delivered again. Then he dismissed his people so they could get some much needed sleep. No one needed encouragement. After quickly stuffing their faces, they shuffled off to their cabins, but their spirits were buoyed along the way. The crew had turned out for them—clapping them on the back, saluting, or bestowing honor … congratulating them in any manner they felt appropriate.

A momentous event had occurred and it was being recognized. As far as this corner of the galaxy knew, this was the first time that humans had communicated with aliens. And despite the egregious beginning, a peaceful dialog with an adversary had been established.

Renée waited while Alex took a quick refresher and wrapped himself in his robe. When he headed to his desk, she intercepted him and guided him to the cabin's lounge. She sat him down and took up her favorite position, curled up in his lap. Within a few moments, she felt Alex relax and his breathing deepen. Soon he was fast asleep. Renée waited until he had a couple of hours of sleep before she gently woke him and pulled on his arm until he followed her to bed. She slipped off his robe and guided him under the covers, dropping her own robe and cradling against his side. Alex fell back to sleep in moments.

Just four hours later, Renée was woken by Julien. <Ser, we have achieved the position the Admiral requested. In this location, we are vulnerable to silver ships, and two have turned our way. Estimated arrival of the first ship will be 18.5 hours; the second ship in 26.4 hours.>

<Thank you, Julien. I will tend to the Admiral,> Renée replied and eased up on one arm to lean over Alex. She kissed him gently on the cheek, chin, and neck, continuing to press her lips softly and lightly against his

skin. As Alex groaned, the rumblings of his chest vibrated through her breasts, and she continued to kiss him.

<Well, if I have to be woken, I can think of no better way to have it done,> Alex sent, opening his eyes and kissing Renée in return. It started as a quick kiss but turned into a deep, intense, and intimate expression of two people who longed to be far away from danger … somewhere safe, together.

"We are at your prescribed location, Alex," Renée said, "and we've attracted attention. There is no need to hurry, yet."

"Ah," Alex replied as he climbed out of bed and headed for the refresher. <Julien, are the Swei Swee singing?>

<They have begun to sing, Admiral. After we arrived on position, we detected a cumulative buildup of energy within our dark traveler. It was as surmised. We were under-powering their ship with our beams.>

<I believe that was your hypothesis, Julien.>

<Yes, Admiral, but it appeared presumptuous to claim credit.>

<Ah, then let me say it was very astute of you to deduce their precarious condition,> Alex replied. His compliment was repaid with the image of Julien's alter ego, the Sleuth.

Alex quickly dressed in the sleeping quarters and would have headed for the Engineering Suite, but Pia, Terese, and Geneviève were busy setting the salon table with a large expanse of food. When they finished arranging the plates, mugs, and pitchers, they stepped back and delivered a polite bow. Terese and Geneviève left without a word, unusual in itself.

Pia walked up to Alex and wrapped him in a hug. She whispered in his ear, "Whatever happens to us, know that the people are proud of you, my explorer Captain." When she stepped back, she touched his face tenderly with her fingertips, and left quickly as tears threatened to spill.

Alex stood there, a little stunned, staring at the cabin door.

Renée walked around to face Alex and laughed at his perplexed expression. "You, my Admiral, see a problem to solve, unraveling its parts, discovering its inner workings, and reassembling it to suit you. It doesn't matter whether it's making the *Rêveur* travel faster or freeing an alien species. To you, it's a task to solve, but your people recognize the scope of what you achieve. Now if you are done being overwhelmed by their devotion, I need you to eat. You can't continue to impress your people if you don't have sufficient energy."

On that point, Alex made Renée very happy. While she consumed her normal meal, Alex claimed everything left on the table. With the last half of a roll, Alex sopped up the juices in a serving dish and popped the entire thing into his mouth, chewing happily. He cleared his mouth with the last gulp of hot thé.

Renée stood up, leaned over him, and kissed his forehead. "Now you can go visit your new friends and conceive of a brilliant plan that liberates them and preferably leaves all of us relatively unscathed." Rather than the quick exit she had expected, Alex stood up from the table and took both of her hands. She was smiling but it faded when she saw Alex wrestling with something important to say. Finally, he offered her a sad, lopsided smile.

"Tomorrow will be a dangerous time aboard this ship, Ser," Alex said quietly. "I would know where you stand."

Renée smiled at the familiar expression. She had asked Alex the same question before she presented to the New Terran Assembly for the first time. He had replied he would stand with her. Renée realized Alex was concerned for her safety and was offering her an opportunity to transfer to the *Freedom*.

"You may have been the Captain who rescued us and the Admiral who now leads us but, first and foremost, you will forever be the partner of my heart. I would stand with you, my love, always," Renée replied.

They held each other for a long moment. Not a word was said; none was needed. Then Alex kissed her on the forehead and left for the Engineering Suite.

<Julien, what do we know about the communications between the Hive First and the Swei Swee First?> Alex sent.

In reply to his request, he was connected to the interplay of song between the two principals. Alex kept his link to Julien open while he walked the corridors and rode a lift down to the Engineering Suite. The corridors were quiet, and for the first time, Alex checked his chronometer. It was 4.33 hours. *No wonder*, he thought.

Alex was unable to translate the songs between their Hive First and the Swei Swee First. The dialog's complexity indicated just how primitive their communications with the Hive First had been. <People,> Alex sent to the SADEs, <are these songs making any sense to you?>

<We are recording everything, Admiral,> Mutter replied. That she was the first to respond gave Alex pause to consider the changes being wrought among the flotilla's SADEs. <However, this is a sophisticate within their society expressing an unusual and critical situation to his leader. We understand few words, much less the intent of his message.>

<I understand,> Alex said. The answer was disappointing, and it didn't help alleviate his concerns. He was intending to place many of his people's lives in alien hands and claws soon, and he was trying to determine if his trust was well founded. *If I'm wrong … well, I'll be wrong, and it won't matter to any of us who enter the system with the Swei Swee*, Alex thought, the impending conflict dragging a dark pall over his mood.

Returning to focus on the exchange, Alex heard the Hive First's song as the Swei Swee First also spoke. There didn't seem to be a protocol, as one sang, then the other.

<It makes you think that the Swei Swee have the ability to manage multiple songs simultaneously,> Alex commented to his SADEs.

<Well done, Admiral,> Mutter exclaimed.

<Okay, Mutter, what did I say?> Alex asked.

<I hadn't paid note to it before, but I had noticed that individuals have a unique frequency pattern, much like our individual voices are recognizable,> Mutter responded.

<If that's the case,> Cordelia added, <a significant adaption of a species that spent much of their time underwater would be the capability to receive and differentiate multiple songs at once.>

While the singing droned on, Alex put his head down on a tech's bench and fell asleep. Julien, always monitoring Alex's biometrics, blocked his comms. Alex woke up quickly, hours later, when the Engineering Team reported for duty after morning meal.

"Apologies, Admiral," Mickey said, realizing his Admiral was on duty in the suite long before they were.

Alex listened for a moment, realizing the dialog was still ongoing. "Not a problem, Mickey. You haven't missed much. The Hive First started a dialog with his leader hours ago, and the two have been in a discussion ever since." Alex switched on the suite's speakers, which monitored the hull's audio pickup. Whistles, warbles, and even screeches flooded the suite, and after the team had a taste of the dialog, Alex signaled the speakers off again.

"What do the SADEs comprehend, Admiral?" Mickey asked, sounding hopeful.

"What would a four-year-old understand of a university professor's lecture on applied mathematics?" Alex responded.

"Oh," Mickey said.

"Yes, 'Oh,'" Alex groused. "Our precious future is being discussed by an alien species, and we're sitting here in the linguistic deep dark."

Hours later, the conversation came to an abrupt end with a sharp whistle, as Swei Swee conversations usually did.

<Admiral,> Mutter said, <that final whistle came from the Swei Swee First.> A short phrase of tones was heard. Mutter added, <The Swei Swee First is saying "Star Hunter sing," but his last tone has an odd twist to it.>

<Singer,> Cordelia supplied. <The Swei Swee First is requesting the "Star Hunter singer.">

The team heard the Swei Swee First repeat his message. It was followed by the Hive First repeating his leader's request. In the resonance telemetry, they watched the Hive First face the ship's rear, rise up on his legs, and lift his claws and true hands in supplication. Then he began to sing. It was a familiar song, one he had begun with Mutter.

<"Star Hunter singer,"> Alex said, comprehending the message. <Mutter, your audience waits. You're on deck.>

Mutter had extensive records of Swei Swee words and hours of the leaders' dialog. Her analytic applications had been busy differentiating the sounds, frequencies, and modulations. Always she was recording and analyzing, much like with all the music she had collected, most of which had originated on ancient Earth. Now in a moment unlike any other, there would be no playback, no chorus, and no interplay for Mutter to follow. She would compose her own music … and in an alien tongue.

Mutter began her song with a single, gentle note that she slowly modulated, blending a second note through it. She was, after all, a SADE, with no single voice. She was capable of many voices, and she made full use of her Méridien-based technology. She sang her song—it was a single voice, it was many voices, it was soft and sweet, it was a swelling chorus. Mutter had never felt such joy, such freedom. The Admiral had given her a rare opportunity that she could never have conceived of embracing in her centuries of service.

Mutter ended her song as she began it. A pair of notes blended into a single note, which slowly faded. In the silence that followed, the Swei Swee on board their captured ship began the same synchronized bobbing they had bestowed on Alex's image. Their whistling chant of "Star Hunter singer" was now recognizable by their human monitors.

Before Alex could express his appreciation to Mutter, the Swei Swee First's whistle cut through the audio pickup. His simple sounds were understood. They were "Swei Swee plus Star Hunters search the endless seas. Nua'll travel the endless seas."

Mutter was basking in the applause from the flotilla for her performance. Of special delight were the requests from children on board the *Freedom* who wanted a recording transferred to their monitor devices. Mutter had never been able to resolve her appreciation of Cordelia and Z with her displeasure over their unnatural actions, which had resulted in their being declared as Independents. She felt they had shirked their duties. Now she understood. It simply required passion to override basic protocols, and Mutter had now done just that. It was the second time in two days that she had reinvented herself. For a few ticks of time, Mutter wondered where the changes might lead. But she was resolved to one desire for the future … wherever the Admiral traveled she fervently hoped her ship would travel with him.

So the Swei Swee First approves the strategy, Alex thought. *Now all we need is to agree on some tactics.* Despite his strengthened conviction, Alex thought to take a small step to test the Swei Swee's reliance. However, even a small step under these circumstances was fraught with danger.

<Julien, release the dark traveler,> Alex ordered.

It was a mark of their bond that Julien immediately switched off the beams and closed the bay's doors despite his reservations. Everyone waited, but nothing happened. The dark traveler stayed where it had been released. The engineering team nervously checked telemetry to see if the fighter moved and were so focused on their readouts that when the Hive First began singing to the Swei Swee First, they jumped in their chairs.

Ha, Alex thought, then sent, <Cordelia, I need another vid. Start with the *Rêveur*, reduce it to a dot, and then show our dot heading for a second dot at Libre. Blow up the second dot to show the Nua'll ship.>

Alex's request generated a great many anxious reactions among his staff.

Cordelia's vid resulted in a two-hour-long conversation between the two Swei Swee Leaders. Boredom set in around the flotilla, except for the SADEs, who continued to map the Swei Swee language. The archives of dialog grew, but translation of the new material was marginal at best.

<Admiral, our silver ship is transmitting to us again,> Julien warned on the conference comm, and the engineering team began checking their screens.

On the rear of their dark traveler, Cordelia's last vid reappeared. This time, when the *Rêveur* approached the Nua'll, tens of dots converged on the *Rêveur*.

<Admiral,> Andrea sent, <it looks like a perfect opportunity for an ambush.>

Alex was considering how to respond to the Captain when the dark traveler replaced Cordelia's altered system vid with the icon of the *Rêveur*. It was set inside a large bright circle. The icon of a dark traveler came at the *Rêveur* off its port bow. When the dark traveler reached the circle, it slid around it to end up behind the *Rêveur,* still outside the circle. The vid added more icons of dark travelers, which were also repulsed by the circle.

<The *Rêveur* has a force field,> Renée sent through the conference comm.

<No, we don't,> Andrea objected.

<But the Nua'll don't know that,> Tatia countered.

<I think this is part of an elaborate ruse to draw us into the system,> Andrea argued.

<If it is a ruse, they would have the numbers and the velocity,> Sheila pointed out.

<People,> Alex sent, <you're forgetting one thing. There is a dark traveler floating meters off our hull. I recall it took only one of these ships to hole the *Rêveur* last time.>

Alex's reminder of the passenger liner's attack produced unsettling flashbacks for the Méridiens and Julien.

<Admiral, I submit that the lengthy time during which we exposed this silver ship to the limited gravitational field may have damaged it in some manner. Perhaps it can't hurt us now,> Andrea sent.

<Valid argument, Captain,> Alex replied. <Let's test your theory. We know our dark traveler has restored its comms. Let's see if it has restored its drive. Julien, slowly, very slowly, orient our ship toward the Nua'll ship.>

<Beginning repositioning,> Julien sent.

Breaths were held while the moments ticked by. When Julien announced the repositioning was complete, the breaths were released and everyone realized they were still present. There had been no attack.

<Where's our dark traveler now, Julien?> Alex asked. <It's not off our port bay anymore.>

<Admiral, when I started our turn, the fighter slid up over the top of our ship and tucked itself under the aft end of the *Outward Bound*, effectively concealing itself from the Nua'll's telemetry, I would suspect.>

<So far, so good,> Alex sent privately to Julien.

<I must admit, Admiral, if I could have actually breathed a sigh, I would have done so with great relief,> Julien replied.

<It wasn't necessary, Julien. I did that for both of us,> Alex replied before returning to the conference comm.

<So our dark friend had comms, drive, and is hiding from the prison ship,> Alex sent.

<So it's continuing the ruse it set up that encouraged us to return it to the system to recharge it,> Andrea sent. <It's a smart plan … First step, save their ship … Second step, destroy us.>

<Well, Captain, I can't say I can refute your argument,> Alex replied. <But I don't think your interpretation of this ship's actions fits within the knowledge we've accumulated. I'm going with the Swei Swee plan.>

<Admiral, how does the Swei Swee plan incorporate the *Money Maker*?> Sheila asked.

<It doesn't, Commander. It will require the *Rêveur* proceed at maximum velocity and alone,> Alex replied. <And before you ask, Commander, we will be moving too fast and too far for the Daggers to keep up with us all the way to Libre. We have to move at top speed if this plan has any chance of working.>

Alex waited for a rebuttal, but it seemed everyone was deep in their own thoughts. <Captain Menlo,> Alex sent, <you're to step back across the gravitational boundaries until you are well within a blue-purple zone.>

<Your orders are clear, Admiral, but I must say I am as unhappy as Commander Reynard to follow them.>

<Understood, Captain. Execute your orders.>

<May the fates protect you and your people, Admiral,> Lazlo sent.

<Safe voyage, Captain,> Alex replied.

Unlike most, Tatia had already resolved herself to the fact that Alex had made his decision. Now she was trying to think through the impediments. <Admiral,> she sent privately, <request permission to transfer to the *Rêveur*.>

Alex's immediate thought was to say no, but Tatia had proved herself as a valuable resource too many times.

<Admiral,> Julien interrupted, <while I would not wish to see anyone else risk their lives with us, prudence dictates that we manipulate the probabilities in our favor. The "devious one" would definitely do that.>

<Permission granted, Commander. Make it quick—shuttle or Dagger, it doesn't matter how you travel. It will be a one-way trip for the vessel,> Alex replied.

Tatia switched back over to the conference comm and added, <Admiral, what happens when we get within range of the Nua'll?>

<I have no idea, Commander,> Alex replied. <It's not my plan, but we'll have a lot of dark travelers with an enormous amount of beam power

around us. People, you're failing to comprehend that while these circumstances are new to us, they're not new to the Swei Swee. If your people had been held hostage for eight generations, how many escape plans would you have devised by now? I think the Swei Swee have been waiting and planning for this day, but they have multiple problems to solve. It was never just that prison ship. It has been their people and the dark travelers left inside that huge ship, their younglings held prisoners, those ringed dark travelers, and a means of exiting the system to escape recapture.>

<Admiral,> Andrea sent, her thoughts loud, <I must object.> Alex immediately switched Andrea's comm to a private session, cutting her out of the conference. <I believe this tactic to be ludicrous,> she continued. <We have just met these aliens, and you already trust them with our lives. They've destroyed nearly half a civilization.>

<Captain, if you would prefer to transfer to the *Freedom*, you may take one of the Daggers. They won't do us any good where we're going,> Alex replied, saddened by Andrea's hostility toward the aliens. She had a right to be angry at the damage done, but it seemed unreasonable to Alex that she couldn't assign blame where it belonged: on the slavers, the Nua'll.

Andrea stomped on her anger. She didn't believe in Alex's plan, but she would not quit her position. Not under these circumstances. If there was to be a later, she promised to rethink that decision.

<Admiral, I will do my duty. What are your orders?> Andrea sent.

* * *

Alex, Andrea, and Tatia stood gathered around the bridge's holo-vid.

"Julien, plot a direct course for the Nua'll ship and proceed at max velocity," Alex ordered.

"As you request, Admiral," Julien replied.

<Mutter, what's the status of dialog among the Swei Swee?> Alex asked on the conference link.

<When you pointed your ship inward, our First was the originator of all songs. Now that you are accelerating toward the Nua'll, the Swei Swee First has taken over communications.>

<Admiral,> Julien interrupted. <Perimeter patrol ships have begun changing directions.>

<How many of them and what directions?> Alex asked.

<All of them, Admiral, and they are setting courses that will intercept our line of advance.>

Alex checked the *Rêveur*'s velocity. They would achieve a max of 0.71c in 4.2 hours. <Julien, calculate the intercept time of the nearest dark travelers.>

Alex and his officers waited while Julien collected more telemetry. Alex began pacing the bridge. He desperately hoped fortune hadn't deserted him.

<Admiral, the first three dark travelers will intercept us between 18 hours and 21 hours,> Julien announced.

Those are going to be awfully long hours, Alex thought.

-22-

Inside their dark traveler, the First had sat with his legs folded under him, conserving energy and air, which had begun to run short while they were held in the grip of the Star Hunters, far outside the life-giving waves. The entire hive had assumed the same posture. There was nothing left to do but wait … and hope. Their lives were tenuous, like the memory scent of the endless seas that begged to be real once again. Although the First had never swum in his home world's endless seas, he carried the memories of his line.

The craft's viewer had lit up with more of the Star Hunters' moving images and his twin eyestalks extended from his shell. His aural membranes had picked up the Star Hunters' singing. The images and singing repeated over and over. The song had been long … the longest one the Star Hunters had sent. The message had galvanized the First despite the fading oxygen. The Star Hunters had indicated they sought to gain his People's freedom. They had offered this despite the many Star Hunters the Swei Swee had sent to travel the endless seas. So many singers lost … His twin hearts had ached with the realization of what his People had done to the Star Hunters. Claws had snapped rapidly, longing to rend the Nua'll, who had kept themselves so carefully hidden in the upper dwellings of their world traveler, far from the reach of his People's claws.

His Third had whistled for attention and had sung of their position change. The Star Hunters had taken them back to the worlds. Great quantities of energy had accumulated on their shell, and their Nua'll systems were brought to full functionality. The air had become sweeter, moistening their breath-ways, which had begun drying. His hive had been energized and had begun singing, but he had silenced them with a whistle.

The First had sung of their good fortune to his leader. The new star people, despite their soft appearance and the absence of rending claws, were powerful hunters. Against the Swei Swee's dark travelers, they had proven to be the greater hunters. None had bested the dark travelers for generations. And now when the Star Hunter First could have sent many of the First's hive to travel the endless waters, he had chosen life for them. The First believed the Star Hunters could be the ones the Swei Swee had waited so many cycles for, and he had sung his best song, hoping to convince his leader of the value of the Star Hunters as fellow searchers.

The First had sensed his leader wanted to believe, but the fate of the People hung in the balance and the hatchlings were at risk. In a fight to save the race, the hatchlings might be sacrificed, but the Swei Swee were protective where hatchlings were concerned. It was their nature to sacrifice their own lives to protect their young.

When the Swei Swee leader hesitated, the First thought of one truth to sway his decision. The Nua'll didn't sing. They communicated to the People by images sent to screens. The Star Hunters were different. They were attempting to learn the Swei Swee's song, and one of the Star Hunters was a Hive Singer. The Swei Swee could not understand her message, but the hive was entranced by her song. The First's pronouncement of the extraordinary find had caused the leader to whistle his negative, but the First had stood his ground, raising his claws in challenge, retorting that he and the hive had witnessed her song. Still, the leader had been doubtful. The People had lost their two Hive Singers when they were taken from their home world, and no others had ever blessed them. The People's imprisonment had not been conducive to the production of a Hive Singer, a unique female who developed when the Hives were in their prime.

To convince the leader, the First had turned to the rear of their dark traveler and had lifted his rending claws and true hands to beseech the Star Hunters. He had sung his welcome and waited. He had sung again … his best welcome, hoping to coax the Star Hunters' Hive Singer forth. If she had failed to share her song, he had only himself to blame—his poor entreaty would have deemed him unworthy of being the hive's First.

Then the First had heard the Hive Singer's opening note, so pure, so clear. She had entwined her second note around the first as only a Hive Singer could. He had settled to the dark traveler's bed with the rest of the hive, and they had wrapped the Star Hunter's song around them. Ancient memories had swum forth, elicited by her song. Her first song entwined with his had been a courtesy, a sharing with the hive. The second one had been different. Her song had raised the spirits of the People, reminding them of the tastes of freedom, the ancient tastes of the endless waters.

When the Star Hunter's song had faded, the Swei Swee First, as in awe as all of his People were, sang his approval loud and clear. The First had relayed the leader's message to his captors: the Swei Swee and Star Hunters would send the Nua'll to travel the endless seas.

* * *

The First had been discussing the momentous opportunity with his People's leader when his Second signaled the release of their dark traveler from the claws of the Star Hunters. It was a powerful sign to the First, and he quickly sang of the event to his leader.

To the First, this was the moment the People had waited generations to experience. He sang with all his hearts, pleading for the People to embrace the opportunity. And from the dreams of their ancestors came the Swei Swee First's clever plan to sink claws into the flesh of the Nua'll.

The next whistle alerted the First to the turn of the Star Hunter's vessel toward the Nua'll, and he gave the order to shelter. It was an overarching and primitive drive among the Swei Swee to seek shelter. In their ancient seas, they had not been the top hunters. Among the dreams of the ancestors lay the memories of many young lost in this fashion, failing to have kept the shelter of rocks and the sea beds close.

The Second, in coordination with the Third, maneuvered their dark traveler between the youngling that the Star Hunter carried on its back. More than once, they had witnessed the young detach itself from its parent and travel the worlds and return. If it felt secure riding on its parent's back, what safer place for his dark traveler could there be than sheltered between parent and young?

* * *

Each patrolling dark traveler turned to intercept the Star Hunters. Reaching the interception point, but short of beam range, they curved their ships aside to trail the Star Hunters as directed by their leader.

The First of each intercepting ship sang to the Nua'll of their dark traveler's loss of energy as they neared the quarry. They could trail the hunters, they reported, but their beams could not stab. Each First sent his report with lament and requested orders. When the star singers were closed, whistles of derision echoed through the dark traveler. It had been many generations since the Swei Swee had been able to raise their claws at their masters.

But the Nua'll message that caused the strongest response among the Swei Swee were their icons portraying the quarry as dangerous hunters of the Swei Swee. If some Swei Swee had not believed the Hive First, who had sung of the Nua'll's betrayal of the Star Hunters' world, all had been convinced of this betrayal when they heard the Star Hunters' Hive Singer. With the ending of the Nua'll message deriding the Star Hunters, the Swei Swee lifted sharp and blunt claws, snapping and banging them together in anger and frustration.

-23-

On board the Nua'll prison ship, the Swei Swee in their shallow pools waited to be called to their dark travelers by number. It was an insult each generation had endured. Each hive had a name, a proud name, celebrated from the ancestors to the present, each generation passing its name and songs on to the next.

A First's eyestalks perked up when a viewer near his pool flashed his hive's number, and he whistled to his hive for attention. They followed him out of their pools and down the slide chutes to the bay where their dark travelers waited. Once on board, the First was surprised to hear an urgent message repeated over and over from his leader. It was brief and to the point: "Load the younglings. Hide within the escorts. When able, escape to the world below. All People flee the world traveler."

The First repeated the message to those still boarding, and several males raced back up the chutes to the pools, relaying the word. Males snatched transfer sacs and females began scooping up the hatchlings still in egg embryos and quickly transferring the twenty-eight-centimeter-long eggs into the sacs. Once a sac was filled, the males would lower it into the pool to fill it to the top with seawater, and then females would seal the sac.

As fast as they could, the Swei Swee filled their sacs, attempting to empty the incubation pools of eggs and escape before they were discovered. In the midst of transferring the first of their precious sacs to the bay, all the hives were called to their vessels. The Nua'll had ordered all dark travelers out to defend the prison ship against the approaching intruder.

The Swei Swee were in preservation mode, hurriedly stacking the sacs of hatchlings in the rear of the first dark traveler in line. As the bed of the vessel was filled, the First and Second, already aboard, were joined by two young females who had just reached egg-bearing age. The elder mates of the First and Second would wait for later launches.

The two young females boarded and worked quickly to seal the shell. When the ship was ready, the Second signaled the Nua'll, who opened the exit chamber door. The First slid the ship into the exit chamber. When the hind door closed and the air vacated, the exit bay door opened. The First guided his dark traveler out to join the escort ships protecting the world traveler. He signaled his success to his leader, who whistled back his compliment.

As those left inside the prison ship hurried to fill the next dark traveler, their breath-ways began to dry and burn, but they didn't rest. Instead the males and females would leap into the pools with their sacs to quench the burning, then continue filling and transporting their sacs.

The Swei Swee filled a second ship, and it launched. Then a third was filled and it joined the other two on-station ships orbiting the prison ship. When the fourth dark traveler was filled, the First signaled for exit but the door remained closed. He signaled repeatedly, but the door never moved.

Dejectedly the Swei Swee carried the embryos back to the incubation pools, slipping into the waters to empty their sacs and hydrate their breath-ways. Three-fifths of the eggs had been rescued, but the remaining embryos and nearly two hundred Swei Swee remained captive.

The eldest matron began a song. It was not a lament. It was a song of hope—hope for their People once again to be free and live along the shores of the endless seas.

* * *

The three dark travelers filled with hatchlings waited on station, each First nervous for the safety of his People's future that lay in sacs on his dark traveler's bed.

Meanwhile, the dark travelers on planet received messages from the Nua'll to lift and join the escorts around the world traveler. Each appeared to do so but with one change in the plan … the first destination. They sealed their ship and lifted, but raced for a point on the planet their leader had chosen. It was a beach, part sandy and part rocky, abutting high cliffs.

Each dark traveler would drop down to the beach, its weight settling into the soft sands. Hurriedly the females worked to open the hull. It was they who built the Swei Swee dwellings while the males hunted. Time had worked to diversify the species. The males, designed for speed in the hunt, had sharp, pointed claws for searching the endless waters. The females could process the silica and other minerals of the sands and cliffs, extruding a viscous substance that could dry as hard as diamond. Their claws were blunt, wider, and more powerful than the males, and functioned as digging tools and defense of the youngling hatchery.

It was the females the Nua'll had prized when they observed them building the Swei Swee homes that glistened in the sunlight and had outlasted the cliffs on which they were built. In order to keep the females as slaves, the Nua'll had taken entire hives—males, females, and hatchlings—forcing the cooperation of the species.

Each dark traveler emptied all but four of its occupants onto the beach and the Swei Swee scrambled for the protection of the shallow waters. Two elder females accompanied the First and Second aboard each dark traveler to reseal the shell. Then the dark traveler launched to join its brethren circling the world traveler.

* * *

The Swei Swee First examined the progress of the Star Hunters. With their youngling attached, they were still searching toward the world traveler. The leader used his star singer to call to each dark traveler left aboard the world traveler, hoping to speak to a Hive First. His fourth try was successful, and he delivered one of the most painful messages of his burdened life.

The Hive First who had responded to his leader's call now left his dark traveler and scuttled up to the incubation chambers where the remaining Swei Swee waited. He relayed the leader's message.

The eldest female whistled her orders, and the females began methodically dispatching the hatchlings, their blunt claws cleaving open the sacs, spilling the contents into the incubation pool. When every egg-young was destroyed, the females approached the males and raised their digging claws high and wide, exposing their vulnerable throats. Each female whistled her farewell and forgiveness of the male poised in front of her. When a female's song ended, the male thrust his sharp, rending claws deep into the female's throat, cutting through the breath-ways and the nerve stem behind it. The thrusts were quick and decisive. The females felt an impact of pressure, then their eyestalks retracted in a death reflex, and they sank into the pool to join their young.

The young males turned to their elders, and the ritual song was repeated until the last male, a First, was surrounded by carnage, the pool stained with the sacrifice of the People.

The last male whistled his farewell. It was heard only by him, but that was enough. He clambered up a bulkhead beam and launched himself at a support structure, intending to impale himself. He had hoped to pierce one or both of his hearts, but his aim was slightly off. The metal shaft penetrated his body from lower to upper carapace, pinning him and missing both his hearts. He would have no second chance to end his life. It would be hours before the First succumbed to his wounds. When his time finally came, the First would try to whistle his joy, but only a hiss would escape his breath-way. The thought was there, though. The Nua'll held no more People captive aboard the world traveler. Come what may, the People would be free this day. They would fight for their freedom and die trying, if necessary. Under no circumstances would they remain slaves.

* * *

When the last dark traveler left the world below and the leader had given the Swei Swee aboard the world traveler sufficient time to complete his instructions, he ordered the three dark travelers with the egg-young to seek shelter.

The Firsts aboard the three hatchling-loaded dark travelers turned off their star singers as they had been instructed and headed for the beach, the rendezvous point. The three ships had room enough to land together on the beach. Immediately the shells were opened from inside by the females.

The Swei Swee scrambled from the shallows to unload the ships. The tide was low, and the People had been busy building a protective wall, soon to become a dome, with thin slots to allow fresh seawater to enter and circulate. Most males had been hauling chunks of coral and sandstone for the females, while younger males found small fish to keep the females fed. The bonding material produced by each female was used to cement the coral and stones together to build the wall. This was a temporary structure for the younglings. There was no use building a permanent structure if they would not be alive several days from now.

The wall would barely be ready for the rising tides generated by this world's greater moon, but it wouldn't matter. The males and females would form two concentric rings around the wall. The outer ring of males would defend against hunters. The inner ring of females, linking their digging arms together and with their smaller but bulkier bodies, would provide a breakwater to protect the egg sacs within from the pounding of the waves.

* * *

The First aboard the dark traveler that sheltered under the *Outward Bound* now called to his leader. The news he received of the rescue of three-fifths of the younglings was both a moment of joy and sadness. So many egg-young had been lost and 192 Swei Swee had gone with them to travel the endless waters, but the Nua'll held no more sway over the People.

Both the Hive First and the Swei Swee First were mesmerized by the steady, relentless search of the Star Hunters toward the world traveler.

The leader questioned the Hive First. "Can the Star Hunters rend the world traveler?"

"This is unknown, Leader. Must they rend the world traveler?" the First asked.

"That is yet to be seen, First," the leader whistled. "This is new to the People. We have no memories to aid us. We have found these creatures that wish to help us. We believe they wish us well. After what we have done against our masters, we will live or die based on who is the greater hunter."

While they were conversing, the leader received reports from the dark travelers surrounding the world traveler. They had received orders to attack the oncoming quarry. He whistled the Nua'll order to the People.

"First, should we sing of this to the Star Hunters?" the leader asked.

"How would we do that, Leader? What would convince them that we are not clever hunters meaning to flush them to us as we would prey?" the First replied.

The hive members had always relied on ancient memories to guide their actions, but nothing in their history provided aid in these circumstances. Suddenly the First had an idea, one born of desperation.

-24-

Alex, Andrea, and Tatia were staring at the holo-vid. The *Rêveur*'s icon glowed bright blue. It was followed close behind by a cluster of bright yellow icons. Each dark traveler had shot toward them at its top speed of 0.91c, guaranteed to intercept them, and at the last moment, the ships had curved around them and fell in behind. Each had performed their movement so effectively that Tatia had murmured, "A giant repulsing field … I'm convinced."

"Or an extremely well-laid trap," Andrea had added.

Alex had limited bridge rotations to the three of them and Edouard. In case this was a trap, one of them would have to make an instant decision and attempt to evade destruction. The dark travelers kept a distance of a few hundred thousand kilometers, but the separation afforded the *Rêveur* no real protection since the dark travelers could close that distance quickly.

Now the Nua'll ship was merely hours away. Alex had refrained from pacing for days, attempting to present the image of a calm commander. The doors of the bridge way slid open and Renée walked onto the bridge, carrying a tray of hot thé and four cups. She glanced at the holo-vid, yellow icons glowing all around the blue icon of the *Rêveur*, and announced in a cheerful voice: "Who would like thé?"

Alex broke out in a strained laugh, the absurdity of her actions tickling him and releasing some of the tension. He accepted a cup of thé, kissing her lightly on the cheek. She winked at him and delivered a hot drink to each officer.

"The Nua'll's escorts are advancing, Admiral," Julien announced.

Heads whipped around to the holo-vid and Alex enlarged the vid to focus on the space directly between the *Rêveur* and the prison ship. Watching every yellow icon separate from the world traveler, Andrea exclaimed, "All of them! The Nua'll aren't reserving any escorts."

"I believe it's all or nothing for the Nua'll," Alex responded. "They're determined to overwhelm us and remove us once and for all. Remember, they've seen us on four different occasions and each time, we were the victor, destroying many of their craft the last two times."

"Admiral, our dark traveler is uncovering," Julien announced.

"Where's he going, Julien?" Alex asked.

"One moment, Admiral," Julien requested. Hearts beat faster, everyone expecting this might be the springing of the trap. "The dark traveler has slid forward along our hull."

Julien slid the central vid screen up to clear the view of the bridge's plex-crystal shield. The crew stared at the rear of their dark traveler. Ships in space kept hundreds of kilometers of separation between them when underway, except under special circumstances, certainly not a mere forty meters directly in front of a bow of a starship.

"Admiral, we're receiving a message from our friend at the bow," Julien said. "The First sends 'Swei Swee plus Star Hunters' over and over."

Alex looked at Andrea and Tatia. They wore diametrically opposed expressions. Tatia was grinning; Andrea was frowning. Alex looking at Andrea and asked, "Do you think their ruse is just getting more elaborate?"

"That's correct, Admiral. We have no proof of their willingness to fight on our side. Just some fancy flying," she said, nodding toward the dark traveler ahead of them.

"Begging your pardon, Captain," Tatia said, "but that doesn't add up. Those dark travelers at our back can achieve 0.2c delta-V over us and easily destroy us. They don't need any more ships."

"Maybe they wish to capture us," Andrea said.

"The only way that might happen, Captain," Alex replied, "is if that world traveler has some sort of beam capable of tethering us, and we've seen no evidence of this. I believe the Swei Swee are using the excuse of our presence to make a break with their captors and put some distance between their dark travelers and that prison ship."

"What about their hatchlings?" Renée asked. When no one answered her, she whispered a quiet "Oh."

"I'm sure they have some sort of plan to free them," Alex said, attempting to comfort Renée.

"If I might, Admiral," Julien interjected. "Three Swei Swee ships exited the prison ship and temporarily joined the escorts. Then just before the escorts launched toward us, those same three ships dove for a beach location on Libre at the edge of the Clarion Seas."

"The Swei Swee indicated eleven dark travelers were aboard the world traveler. Did more than three manage to exit," Alex asked.

"Negative, Admiral."

"Then if I was to guess, those three spirited away their hatchlings, and the rest of the Swei Swee aboard the world traveler are still at risk," Alex said.

"Admiral," Andrea said, "there's still time to dive below the ecliptic, if we do so now. We can make our move before the bow or aft silver ships can catch us. If they follow, we can leave them floating in space."

"And what would that do, Captain?" Tatia said. "All we would be doing is proving to the Swei Swee that their new allies are undependable."

Alex watched his two officers stare at one another. The pressures of the past year had brought about subtle changes in both of them. Andrea had shouldered the responsibility of the ship's operation with solid determination, but continued to shy away from the tough, strategic decisions. On the other hand, Tatia, who had always been planet-bound, had taken to the spacer role, and she had the inventive and intuitive thinking required of a senior officer.

"We stay the course, Captain," Alex affirmed.

"Admiral," Julien said, "interception with the Swei Swee to our bow occurs in 0.23 hours, 0.11 hours if they do not drop velocity before they reach us."

As the chronometer counted down, Andrea and Renée took to the command chairs and kept their thoughts to themselves. Alex began a slow pace around the bridge, his hand on his lowered chin while he reviewed his decision for the hundredth time. He and Tatia nearly collided. She had been pacing in the opposite direction, deep in thought as well.

Tatia gave Alex a wry grin and sent, <Having second thoughts, Admiral?>

<Thinking, Commander, but not having second thoughts,> Alex replied.

<Admiral, Commander,> Julien sent privately, <for what it's worth, I have reviewed our data a considerable number of times, and while this may be the last opinion I will ever utter, I believe our decision to be the correct one. It is one I am most proud to support.> The briefest of pauses ensued and then Julien uttered these words to the bridge: "Admiral, they're here."

* * *

The Swei Swee First led the frontal force that bore down on the Star Hunters. On his orders, the dark travelers with him bent around the Star Hunter vessel when the distance closed to within 200 kilometers. The Swei Swee First opened his star singer to signal the Nua'll that the energy on their shells failed when they approached the quarry. He sang his regrets.

* * *

Julien reported the bending of the dark travelers around their ship and their subsequent swing behind them. There was no one left between the *Rêveur* and the Nua'll, who were a mere hour and a half away.

"Admiral, your orders?" Andrea asked.

Tatia asked the more pertinent question of "Do the Nua'll have a weapon?"

"None of their actions indicate they do, but who knows," Alex responded.

Andrea looked at him, incredulous at his comment. "You're risking our lives on a 'who knows'?"

Alex smiled at her, which infuriated Andrea even more. "It's a risk we're taking, Captain. The Swei Swee may have deserted their prison, but as long as that ship sits out there, none of us are safe—not until the Nua'll surrender or they are destroyed.

"But we haven't any weapons with us," Andrea said, her anger still rising.

"Captain," Tatia said, trying to calm her superior down. "I believe our weapons are right behind us. Much of what the Admiral has done is to give the Swei Swee an excuse to execute one of any number of their plans. A prisoner will spend months, years even, planning their escape. The Swei Swee have had eight lifetimes."

Andrea brought her temper under control. It wasn't doing her thinking any good. She realized that above all else, she wanted to live—and she wanted others to shoulder the risks of the universe. "So if the Swei Swee are executing their plan, what is our role?" she asked.

"Another good question," Alex answered. Before Andrea could take his comment negatively, he continued. "The Swei Swee might have attacked the world traveler at any time. Based on our communications with our Hive First, I think they were stopped by two conditions. Their young were held hostage, and they needed a provocation."

"A provocation, Admiral?" Andrea asked.

"Yes, we're the provocation, Captain. Even if the Swei Swee were to retrieve their hatchlings, they would still be trapped in the system. When their food or other necessities ran low, they would be forced to land. In this system, Libre would have been their only option. It's obvious the prison ship is too large to land, so the Swei Swee must be afraid of something else. That something else would be the ringed dark travelers, the vessels our First mentioned."

Alex began walking in a slow circle to gather his thoughts. "Now we have met four times and shown the Swei Swee we are powerful hunters. More importantly, the Swei Swee discovered we are not just hunters, we are singers. When we offered to search with them to the detriment of the Nua'll, they decided to throw in with us. What I couldn't figure out was our opening move. Then it hit me. I didn't have to figure one out. The

Swei Swee must have devised a myriad of escape gambits. All that was necessary for us to do was start a simple maneuver and let the Swei Swee's plan unfold. The most powerful but simple opening move was to set a course directly at the world traveler. While we did that, the Swei Swee used the opportunity to anoint us with a 'giant repulsing shield,' which the Nua'll have appeared to accept as truth. Now the Nua'll are frightened. They've sent every dark traveler after us, including their escorts."

Tatia had started snickering at the "giant repulsing shield" comment but quieted when Andrea glanced coldly at her.

"The Swei Swee have rescued their hatchlings," Alex continued. "At least, I hope they have. But they're still holding off. I think they're either waiting for those first dark travelers to come out or they're waiting for the Nua'll to run. Personally I hope that prison ship doesn't run."

Andrea started to question why, but Tatia headed her off. "Captain, if the Nua'll run, they could come back anytime anywhere, with another slave species. It would be better to end it now."

"The Nua'll are probably convinced of our superiority after having seen the defeat of many of their dark travelers," Alex said. "Now we appear to have returned with some invincible tech against their dark travelers. So they must either run or pull out their big weapons which would be the ringed dark travelers.

"And you believe that the Swei Swee will destroy them?" Andrea asked.

"Hoping so, Captain," Alex said. He glanced at Renée, who sat quietly in the command chair.

When Alex looked her way, Renée gave him a confident wink, even though she felt much the same as Andrea. She didn't want to die, either. But more importantly, she didn't want to live without Alex, and that life included supporting him in his efforts to rid the Confederation of the Nua'll.

The remaining moments passed with tension so thick on the bridge, it could choke a person. Andrea ordered the crew to emergency positions. Tatia and Renée vacated the bridge for the pilots' room and Medical, respectively. Alex and Andrea strapped into the command chairs.

"Admiral, the Nua'll ship is moving," Julien announced.

"Which way?" Alex asked.

"In no direction in particular, Admiral," Julien replied. "The top and bottom halves are rotating in opposite directions, extending the diameter from top to bottom. I believe it's unscrewing itself."

Alex found himself wanting to laugh at Julien's comment. *I sure hope they are*, he thought.

"A large central ring is being exposed, Admiral. Two sets of large bay doors are becoming visible."

"Ninety degrees of arc separation?" Alex asked.

"Precisely, Admiral," Julien replied.

"And the significance of the ninety degrees, Admiral?" Andrea asked.

"Four ringed dark travelers; four launch bays, each set ninety degrees apart from one another. That allows simultaneously launches … something not afforded their slaves."

"So then the question becomes: Can the Swei Swee take the four ringed dark travelers?" Andrea said.

"And that, Captain, is the final question," Alex replied. "If they can't, we dive for the ecliptic and hope the ringed dark travelers don't follow. I hate to abandon the Swei Swee at their most vulnerable moment, but if the Swei Swee can't defeat those four ships, I believe the Nua'll will exterminate them and go hunting for another slave species."

As the *Rêveur* closed on the world traveler, one set of the enormous bay doors in the central ring began to open. A large, cylindrical-shaped ship, constructed in concentric rings, emerged from the bay. It turned toward the *Rêveur* and launched without any visible drive propulsion.

"Gravity drives as well," Alex mumbled to himself. The port vid screen displayed a close view of the world traveler and the ringed-ship the Swei Swee had projected on their hull.

"Admiral, the Swei Swee are on the move," Julien reported.

"Give me a steady account, Julien," Alex ordered.

"The dark travelers are accelerating, Admiral. In 0.12 hours, they will pass us ... interception of the ringed dark traveler in 0.35 hours."

After a short but seemingly interminable wait, Julien announced the Swei Swee had passed them by.

"All of them, Julien?" asked Andrea, uncertainty in her voice.

"Yes, Captain, all of them. They are on a vector to intercept that emerging ship."

"Julien, any movement on those second bay doors?" Alex asked.

"Negative, Admiral," Julien replied.

"Why only launch one ringed dark traveler?" Alex wondered aloud.

"Perhaps, Admiral, the others are emerging from around the far side of the Nua'll ship," Julien hypothesized.

As they waited for the distance between the dark travelers and the aggressor ship to close, Julien's hypothesis proved correct. A second ringed dark traveler emerged from behind the right side of the gigantic sphere. It, too, turned toward the *Rêveur* and accelerated.

Alex was considering the odds against the Swei Swee if the world traveler managed to launch all four of its "wardens," as he had begun to think of them. He considered the Nua'll might still be unaware of the Swei Swee's charade. The dark travelers had been careful to circle the *Rêveur* before they passed the ship. If that was true, the Nua'll might be focused exclusively on them, the intruders, and desperately launching all four wardens in defense of their sphere.

"The first of the Swei Swee ships have reached beam range. They aren't firing, Admiral," Julien reported.

"Admiral?" Andrea asked, concern underlining her voice.

"Patience, Captain," Alex said. "Julien, inform me when all the dark travelers have passed the first ringed-ship."

"Admiral, a third ringed-ship has emerged from the left side of the sphere," Julien reported.

Alex began to chew on his lower lip. He had only a few more moments to make a decision to abandon the Swei Swee and save the *Rêveur* and his people, if it was still possible.

"The last silver ships are about—one moment, Admiral … The nearest ringed-ship has detonated!" Julien exclaimed. "The Sleuth still lives!"

Alex laughed. Apparently Julien was as worried as everyone else. He had just been better at managing his fear.

"Admiral," Julien went on, "the silver ships are splitting into two groups, sharing their numbers against the next two ringed-ships. Now the fourth bay door is opening." Moments of interminable waiting passed as the final battle of the Swei Swee's quest for freedom approached. "The dark travelers are in heavy evasion mode, Admiral. They are still not in effective beam range. One dark traveler has been destroyed … two … three. Now the second ringed-ship has exploded."

"The Swei Swee are paying a heavy price for their freedom," Alex commented.

"And I'm ashamed, Admiral," Andrea said. "My fear has been driving my decisions while these creatures are fighting and dying for their freedom."

"Captain, give it time. It will get easier making the hard decisions," Alex said in an attempt to lessen Andrea's discomfort.

"The third ringed-ship should be in range of the dark travelers, Admiral," Julien said. "Our new friends are evading. One lost … two …" Julien's voice had become sadder with each count. "The third ringed-ship is gone."

"Julien, status of the fourth ringed-ship?" Alex asked.

"It's appearing in the bay opening now, Admiral. Two Swei Swee ships are charging it. The ringed-ship hasn't cleared the bay … the bay doors are wide open."

The moments ticked by ever so slowly.

Alex heard himself mentally urging the Swei Swee on.

"One Swei Swee ship down," Julien reported. "The second Swei Swee ship is approaching the bay at an angle. Impact!" Julien yelled. "The Swei Swee fighter has slammed into the ringed dark traveler while it was still in the bay's opening. Regard the vid screen, Admiral, Captain. We are close enough for long-range visuals."

The monstrous sphere filled the starboard vid screen. Long tongues of hot gas and debris were shooting out the left-handed bay opening in the central ring. As they watched, more explosions launched tons of material out into space. Soon afterward, huge explosions burst through the right-handed bay, blowing the massive doors out into space.

As the *Rêveur* closed on the huge prison ship, its image grew on the screen. "Distance from the world traveler, Julien?" Alex asked.

"Five hundred thirty thousand kilometers, Admiral," Julien responded.

"Close enough, Julien. Veer off in case this sphere goes out with a bang," Alex ordered.

"Understood, Admiral. I'm selecting a starboard turn. It will head us toward Libre."

"Good choice, Julien. Is this view being forwarded to the crew?" Alex asked.

"Actually, Admiral, to the flotilla," Julien replied.

"My, my, look who has become his own media station," Alex quipped.

"One tries to keep the Admiral's people adequately informed. Is this not a tenet of a free and independent society?" Julien replied.

Before Alex could reply, his attention was drawn back to the central screen. Long tongues of flames erupted from several rings above and below the central ring. The light from the explosions showed kilometers into space.

"Just what was on board that prison ship that was so volatile?" Andrea mused.

"Another good question, Captain," Alex replied.

While they watched, more explosions worked their way up and down from the central ring. Alex fully expected the destruction to end. He was very interested in getting a look inside another alien craft … his second in just a year and a half, but the detonations continued. *There's been sufficient time to close any bulkhead doors and shut down the spread of the fires,* Alex thought. *They could even have vented the fires to space.*

Finally, a massive blast broke the giant sphere in two halves or, better said, two large pieces, the top and the bottom, since the previous explosions had already demolished much of the central rings. The brilliant flash obscured the vid screen. When the image reappeared, the Nua'll ship was a giant ball of expanding debris.

"Julien, is Libre in danger from any of that debris?" Alex asked.

"Tracking, Admiral. Yes and no. Yes, some debris is headed Libre's direction; and no, there is no concern. The Swei Swee are busy pounding the large segments and even smaller debris into space dust. Give them an hour or two and there won't be a piece big enough to carry in two claws."

Andrea had released her command chair restraints. "Congratulations, Admiral, you were right all along. If I'm not needed now, I'd like to be relieved."

"Certainly, Captain. Release the crew from emergency conditions and then take a break yourself."

When Andrea left the bridge, Alex sat in silence with Julien.

"I was just calculating, Admiral," Julien said to his friend. "From a New Terran's viewpoint, you have encountered one human civilization and two alien species, and assumed the responsibility for a quarter-million humans and some thousands of Swei Swee … and this in a year and a half. With your cell-gen injections, you should live, barring a misstep from your intrepid decisions, for another one hundred sixty years. That would mean you should accumulate …"

"Stop," Alex commanded, interrupting Julien. "Your logic is flawed."

"This should be educational, Admiral. Do enlighten this poor excuse for a thinking machine," Julien said.

"You forgot to add rest and retirement into your calculations."

"On the contrary, Admiral, I gave your intention of wanting to retire a near one hundred percent surety, just as I gave the people's intention a nearly one hundred percent surety of not allowing you to retire. I gather the difference in our calculations is that you think you will have your way, and I believe the people will have their way."

Alex had wanted to celebrate the moment. Now his playful jousting with Julien had brought him back to reality. The thought of shouldering the responsibilities Julien mentioned soured his stomach, which rumbled in objection over the lack of food.

"Apologies, Admiral," Julien said, noticing the abrupt change in Alex's mood. "It was poor timing on my part to bring up the future." He observed Alex sit heavily back in the command chair. *The price of an independent mind*, Julien mused, *the freedom to speak your thoughts … and the power to hurt others with your words.*

"Back to work, Julien," Alex finally said. "Have all ships rendezvous in a geosynchronous orbit over Libre, the beach where the dark travelers landed. We'll be landing as well. Alert the crew."

"Yes, Admiral," Julien acknowledged, the lesson he had just learned burning brightly through this protocols.

Alex called Captain Manet to relieve him of bridge duty. While Alex waited, he manipulated the holo-vid as Julien tracked the remaining swarm of dark travelers, which were busy pulverizing the massive debris sections of the world traveler, intent on decimating every square meter of their jailer's ship.

The bridge way doors slid open and Renée came through at a run. She threw herself into Alex's arms so hard, even he had to step back twice to counter her weight. With her arms wrapped tightly around his neck, her cheek softly rubbed the side of his head. She didn't say a word.

That's the proper way to celebrate the moment, Julien thought. *I will find a way to apologize, my friend.*

Alex let Renée slide gently down to the deck, their arms still about one another. He kissed her warmly and tenderly.

<Will there be time for us now?> she asked him.

<Soon, I promise. We have a few stops to make before we reach our new home.>

<And you still aren't sharing our final destination?>

<There are too many things in our way for me to be sure of our final destination.>

"Your pardon, Admiral," Julien interrupted. "The silver ships have finished their destruction of the prison ship and have turned our way."

"Julien, plot it on the holo-vid," Alex ordered.

Alex and Renée watched as Julien populated the holo-vid with the *Rêveur*'s position, a bright blue dot, and the positions of the dark travelers, a swarm of yellow dots, all of them converging on the *Rêveur*.

"Any orders, Admiral?" asked Julien.

"Negative, Julien. Proceed to the position over Libre as requested."

The yellow dots continued to close. Alex expanded the view until a mere five kilometers separated the two closest yellow dots to the *Rêveur*.

Then they began to circle the blue dot. Alex and Renée stared open-mouthed as more yellow dots approached their position and joined the others. Soon the holo-vid displayed a translucent yellow sphere surrounding a blue dot.

"Julien, since we're still here," Alex said. "I would say we're observing a celebratory moment."

"It would appear so, Admiral. The dark travelers are circling our position. That this number of ships is doing so at their velocity is quite impressive."

"They have a great deal to celebrate, Julien. Where is our hitchhiker?"

"Ah," Julien remarked after searching out the term "hitchhiker." "Our Swei Swee is holding a position just forward and off our port bow."

"Alright, Julien, continue as ordered. No quick turns while the Swei Swee are celebrating."

"Understood, Admiral. A quick turn would decidedly ruin their celebration … and ours," Julien replied.

* * *

Once Edouard arrived on the bridge, Alex updated him on their destination and his intention to take the *Outward Bound* planetside to visit the Swei Swee.

"We're … visiting the Swei Swee, Admiral?" Edouard asked. "Are you sure they want us to visit?"

Renée burst out laughing over Edouard's concern. She shuffle-danced her way off the bridge, her hands punching the air overhead as she punctuated each word of her chant of "Star Hunter First, Star Hunter First."

Edouard stared incredulously at his Co-Leader as she danced off the bridge. The changes in his Méridien cohorts continually amazed him, as their behaviors more often mirrored the traits of the New Terrans. He admitted to himself that the New Terrans' bold behaviors intrigued him, but he hadn't been able to adopt many of them for himself. In one regard, he wished he had already. His thoughts turned to his copilot, Miko. As the bridge access way slid open and Renée disappeared around the corner, he turned back to his Admiral.

Alex simply pointed at the bridge access way, saying, "What she said," and disappeared after Renée.

* * *

Alex and Renée entered the meal room to the resounding applause of the crew. Renée stepped aside and joined the applause. Interestingly, not a single Libran bestowed honor on the Admiral. The action didn't fit what they felt. The gesture was quiet; they felt loud. It was passive; they felt alive. So the Librans whistled, yelled, and applauded alongside their New Terran crewmates.

Alex remained standing at the head table while all took their seats. "Today, you can be very proud of yourself," Alex began. "You've accomplished two wonderful feats in one day. You've helped to free an alien race, one enslaved for generations, and you've enabled those individuals to eliminate a threat to the entire human race. If it wasn't observed, it's important for me to tell you that the Swei Swee lost, in addition to what we destroyed, seven more ships full of their hive members. And before you point it out, yes, we lost crew to them. But didn't we make the assumption that the silver ships were driven by deadly aliens who were intent on killing all humans? Both sides have taken lives. What we should remember is that the Nua'll were the enemy here, and they have paid the ultimate price for their crimes against humans and Swei Swee. Enjoy your meal. It's well earned."

Alex sat down to another round of applause. He raised his hand in a languid fashion to wave it off, and mealtime got seriously underway. Fear drives the body hard. The appetites were enormous tonight, none more so than that of Alex. Pia and Geneviève grinned at Renée as they made extra trips to the head table. Alex gave them polite nods as they delivered dishes while he continued to tear rolls and sop up the juices before the empty dishes could be removed.

Pia's private comm to Renée was full of mirth. <Such an efficient strategy. The Admiral saves the recycler from the need to clean his dishes.>

-25-

The *Outward Bound* eased away from the *Rêveur*. When clear of the liner, Captain Manet ignited its primary engines for the trip planetside to Libre. Aboard for the historic occasion were Alex, Renée, Terese, Étienne, Alain, Tatia with four armed troopers, and the standard *Outward Bound* crew of Miko, Pia, and the techs, Lyle and Zeke.

<Julien, where is our personal Swei Swee?> Alex sent.

<He's keeping pace with you, Admiral, off your aft, port quarter. It appears you have an escort planetside.>

Alex relayed the information concerning their escort to Edouard, who confirmed he had the dark traveler on his controller's telemetry. Alex adjusted his belt harness, which Julien had hurriedly programmed with the basic Swei Swee vocabulary. Under the circumstances, Alex was going to remain linked to Julien via the *Outward Bound*, and Julien would have Cordelia and Mutter monitor their comm.

The cliff top above the beach where the Swei Swee had disgorged their hive members was littered with dark travelers, and shells were in the process of being dismantled. Edouard searched for a clear place to land the shuttle. The openings were few and far between, and he circled the area looking for a safe spot.

Miko glanced at her Captain's intent expression, marked with a deep frown. "After all we've been through, Captain, it would probably be a bad thing to kill the Admiral in a shuttle landing in perfect weather."

Edouard glanced at Miko and a small smile erased his frown. He eased his grip on the control stick and relaxed his hunched shoulders. Edouard made one more turn around the landing area and slid the *Outward Bound* neatly into a clear slot in the field. As they came to rest, Miko reported grass fires and Edouard fired the belly extinguishers, starving the fires of oxygen before they could spread.

Alex led his entourage down the gangway ramp. Tatia's request to lead with her four troopers was politely denied. "We're here to establish relationships, not prove our dominance, Commander," Alex had replied. Still, Tatia had her troopers position themselves on the outskirts of the company as they walked toward the cliff. She was especially grateful for the presence of the twins, who closely shadowed Alex and Renée.

The dark travelers lay nestled in the grass and rocky soil. As Alex's company wound past them, the humans took note of the large, irregular holes cut in the sides of the hulls near ground level.

<Biological ingress and egress, Admiral,> Julien said, monitoring from on high.

As the humans neared the cliffs, a dark traveler gracefully set down barely thirty meters away—no engines flaring, no hot gasses emanating, no noise, and no grass fires.

<Julien!> Alex sent, his thoughts speeding to his friend.

<A wonderful idea, Admiral!> Julien shot back.

<How many do we need?> Alex asked.

<I believe two would be more than sufficient … one with an opening and one without.>

Alex halted his company. They watched as a small hole opened in the side of the recently landed ship. Alex was fascinated as the Swei Swee enlarged the holes. Saliva was applied to the edges of the hole and chips were broken off. The process was methodical.

<Julien, I take it this is our Swei Swee,> Alex asked, transmitting his visual.

<Yes, Admiral,> Julien replied. <Our First waited until you had landed and disembarked before he landed his craft.>

When the hole was large enough, the blunt-clawed individuals pulled back and a larger, sharp-clawed Swei Swee hurried out of the hole and scurried toward the humans. Its speed over the ground was blinding, and several troopers charged their plasma rifles in response. Even Étienne and Alain un-holstered their stun guns and stood ready.

<Steady people,> Alex sent.

The Swei Swee individual stopped two meters short of the group, and Alex presumed it was the First with whom they had communicated for many days. His eyestalks roamed briefly over the entire entourage before all four eyes focused on Alex. He raised his pair of edged and pointed claws into the air, reaching Alex's waist, and then began bobbing up and down excitedly and snapping his claws.

This was humanity's first face-to-face view of the Swei Swee, and the view was unsettling—three meters long from claw tips to tail, which lay curled over the First's back; twin pairs of eyestalks; a bright blue-green carapace that sparkled in the sunlight; large, pointed, dangerous claws placed outward of small hands; three pairs of walking legs; and a segmented tail with lateral fins that appeared both insect-like and fish-like at the same time.

The First whistled a phrase over and over. It was a common phrase, which Alex's translator handled. It was "Star Hunter First."

Alex regarded the crab/scorpion-like creature in front of him. He was searching for the correct approach when his father's words about business came to him. "Meet people at their level. Don't push your agenda. Learn theirs first," Duggan had said. Alex smiled at the thought that his father probably had never thought his words would apply to these circumstances. Alex sat down on his rear in the grass, crossing his legs, and tucking his feet under the opposite thigh. The claws of the First were now at eye level. Alex raised his arms, touching each thumb to each first finger to imitate claws, and signaled his belt translator which issued "Affirmative. Star Hunter First."

Renée quietly chuckled to herself. To the rest of the team, she sent, <Always the unexpected.> Her remark and subsequent laughter eased the tension among her comrades.

The Swei Swee lowered his claws below the level of Alex's hands and carefully closed the distance until the upper part of his alien claws touched the lower part of Alex's human hands. "Hive First," he whistled, then lowered his body to the ground, warbling softly.

<Anyone?> Alex sent to his SADEs.

Mutter replied, <Admiral, it's similar to the tones used during the Swei Swee lament while they awaited your decision on whether you would destroy them for what they had done to the Star Hunter worlds. It's similar but not the same, Admiral. I would regard this as a thank-you or perhaps an apology.>

<Thank you, Mutter,> Alex replied.

When the First finished and rose back up on his standing legs, Alex whistled, "Swei Swee First." It was odd to hear the whistles and warbles emanate from his chest, but obviously it was effective. The Hive First whirled with blinding speed and let loose a sharp whistle that was echoed by others. The call was passed over and down the cliffs.

Within moments, a large Swei Swee male emerged from a cut in the cliff and scuttled at high speed over the grass to stop beside the Hive First. Both twins had carefully noted the speed with which the Swei Swee had moved and edged closer to their charges.

The Swei Swee First's claws were also raised in the air, and the Hive First carefully lowered his just below his leader's claws. Alex twigged to the indication of dominance that the claw height represented. The Hive First slowly bobbed up and down, attempting to rein in his excitement.

Alex's translator allowed him to recognize an introduction of the Swei Swee First to him. Alex again extended his hands in a claw-like fashion, deliberately placing his hands several centimeters below that of the Swei Swee First's claws. As the heavily scarred individual scuttled forth to close the distance, he lowered his claws below that of Alex's hands, just as the Hive First had done.

<My, my, such a clever human,> Julien teased Alex in private.

Alex grinned to himself at Julien's twist on his own tease a day ago to his friend.

After the Swei Swee First's introduction to Alex, Renée sent to the others, <The New Terran children have a game called "Follow the Leader."> Then she sat down on the grass next to Alex and copied his cross-legged position. Étienne and Alain followed suit to take up positions on either side of the Admiral and Ser. The remaining humans in the party chose to remain standing, but pressed in closer to the foursome seated on the ground.

The Swei Swee First whirled to face the People, who had paused in their work to observe the Star Hunters. He whistled and warbled for a few moments. Alex's translator caught only "Star Hunter First," mentioned twice during the announcement. Suddenly hundreds of Swei Swee poured from the cliff-top cut and the interiors of the dark travelers to join the numbers on the grass, and all rushed headlong toward Alex's company. Human fingers twitched on weapons, arms tensed, and eyes narrowed. Overriding all the angst was Alex's message: <Everyone remain calm. If they aren't our friends by now, it won't matter.>

The Swei Swee packed close to the human party ringing them in a circle. Their legs intersected one another, and Alex could see himself walking across their sea of shells without touching the ground. The thought brought a smile to his face.

Seeing a smile spread over Alex's face as the mass of scuttling aliens crowded closer, Renée sent privately to him, <Some days, my love, I'm not sure who is stranger, you or the aliens.>

The Swei Swee First began bobbing slowly up and down. The assembled mob, with their legs interlinked, imitated the motion. Soon the entire assembly was bobbing in unison, faster and faster, until the Swei Swee First's whistle froze their motion. Then the Swei Swee First appeared to address Alex, but his support above could not manage the translation. The Hive First conversed with his leader and then whistled briefly to Alex.

<Admiral, it's a variation of the term for female,> Mutter sent. <I suspect he is asking if the three beside you are your mates. This might be an assumption on the leader's part because of the more diminutive size of our people compared to your own. The Swei Swee males are the larger specimens in the crowd in front of you and are marked by their pointed claws.>

Alex motioned to Renée beside him and repeated the Hive First's whistle, which his translator had recorded as "mate."

The Swei Swee First scuttled sideways to stop in front of Renée. His blue-green claws, each the size of her head, were lowered to the grass in front of her, and the leader sang a low, rich tune.

<Admiral, Ser, I believe the leader has wished you many younglings … some number approximating hundreds, if I understand this portion correctly,> Mutter said.

Alex glanced at Renée and was happy to see that he wasn't the only one that could be made to blush. When she looked at him, she actually ducked her head down, hiding a smile. *Ah-ha*, Alex thought and raised his hands to gain the attention of the leader, who scuttled back in front of Alex and raised his claws to touch the undersides of Alex's hands. Alex pointed a hand-claw at the leader and repeated the whistle for mate.

The two Swei Swee males exchanged some brief tones and tweets before starting toward the cliff face. The host of Swei Swee had moved aside, opening a path. After a few meters, the Hive First turned back and waved his true hands at Alex, indicating he should follow.

The company of humans divided. Tatia, Terese, and two troopers stayed on top, while Alex, Renée, the twins, and the other two troopers descended a path that had been recently cut into the cliff face. It was wide enough for two Swei Swee to pass each other. The entourage wound down the cliff face to a rocky beach that extended for two hundred meters before segueing to a sandy beach. Out in the shallow waters, a large coral-and-stone dome was taking shape. Alex, curious as always, began to walk toward it. In an instant, several Swei Swee blocked his way. They were females, marked by blunt claws, smaller bodies than the males but with sturdier builds, and segmented tails with lateral fins less developed than the males.

The leader's whistle was loud and strident. It was followed by insistent whistling and warbling, and in answer, the females lowered their claws and backed away.

Alex stepped up to the dome to peer into the interior. Hundreds, if not thousands, of small sacs held wriggling embryos. "Hatchlings," Alex sent out via his harness, pointing to the dome.

The leader and the Hive First bobbed up and down in surprise. They both whistled, "Affirmative."

Alex walked over to a patch of sand, the aliens and humans trooping behind him. He drew a large circle in the sand, and the eyestalks of the two Swei Swee males bent to examine it. Alex pointed to the dome and drew small circles within his larger circle, adding the whistle for "hatchlings." Then he pointed to the sky, closed his arms in a circle, pointed to his circle, and whistled, "Hatchlings" again.

For a moment, the two males conversed, their true hands waving in support of their words. Then the Hive First scuttled close to Alex, who could smell the scent of sea from his shell. The First lowered himself to the ground to reach the circle with his true hands. He erased a portion of Alex's circle and redrew it as three-fifths complete. He pointed a large claw at the dome, then the circle, and finally whistled a mournful song.

<SADEs,> Alex sent, <do you interpret this as the Swei Swee managed only to rescue about 60 percent of their younglings?>

<We would, Admiral,> Cordelia responded.

Alex looked at the cut down circle. The eye stalks of the two males were staring at it. *We see a partial circle in the sand,* Alex thought. *They see a count of their dead, younglings and adults.* Alex made a decision that had been rolling around in the back of his mind for days, and he acted on it. He raised his hands and the leader's eyestalks rose up to focus on him. Alex opened his hands, palm up.

The leader eyed Alex's open hands. He scuttled close, swinging his great claws wide, to accommodate reaching out with his true hands. Each felt a light, smooth touch. While Alex held the leader's hands, he strung together a simple vocabulary and whistled, "World, Swei Swee world, Swei Swee search endless seas." He repeated his message after letting go of the leader's true hands, indicating the expanse of cliffs and sea.

<Alex, the Council, they might object,> Renée sent anxiously. In response, she heard Alex's bark of laughter and received <Let them object.>

The leader whistled to the Hive First, and the two males carried on a protracted conversation.

Alex waited in amusement. He could imagine the leader asking his Hive First if he got the Star Hunter's message correctly. The Hive First turned to Alex and gestured with his claws to encompass the cliff, sky, and seas and whistled, "Swei Swee."

"Affirmative," Alex whistled.

The First whistled, "Swei Swee plus Star Hunters."

To which, Alex replied, "Negative Star Hunters; affirmative Swei Swee." He watched the First's eyestalks droop and the thought crossed his mind that the Swei Swee wanted their Star Hunters close for protection. To comfort the First, he whistled, "Star Hunters travel worlds, negative Nua'll, negative hunters." His message got through.

The First perked up, turned to his leader, and let burst a resounding set of whistles and warbles. It set off the entire community, who joined in raucous celebration. Younger Swei Swee scurried across the rocks and sands to dive into the sea. Smaller young ones raced across the beach, flipping scoops of sand at one another.

Alex looked over at his people, who were very aware of what he had done. They were smiling at him, and he grinned back, his smile stretching ear to ear. *It feels good to help others,* Alex thought. *Let the Council scream.*

During the People's celebration, a heavily scarred female, one of the larger ones the humans had seen, swam ashore from behind the dome. She waded ashore and scurried up to the leader, dropping her heavy, dinged claws to the sand in front of him.

The leader turned to Alex and whistled "mate," indicating the heavy female with his claw.

The leader's mate lowered herself completely in front of Alex, her claws digging into the sand, and whistled, "Star Hunter First." She repeated her action in front of Renée, whistling, "Star Hunter First mate."

As the leader's mate rose up, Renée instinctively stretched a hand toward one of the female's eyestalks, but the Swei Swee female quickly withdrew it into her shell. A shrill whistle, followed by warbling tones, from the leader had the female slowly extending her eyestalk and crawling forward until Renée could reach it.

Renée leaned carefully forward to examine the far right eyestalk. All eyes followed her—human eyes and eyestalks, including the other three of the mate's eyestalks. Renée could see matter accumulated in the corner of the nictitating membrane from thin, slightly blue-tinted liquid that wept from the eye.

<Terese,> Renée sent, <I need you now.>

<The Admiral?> Terese sent anxiously.

<Negative, Terese. I need you to examine a Swei Swee.>

* * *

It took Terese and a trooper a quarter-hour to navigate the path down from the cliff. Alex spent the time watching the young Swei Swee scuttle from the shallow waters with catches of small fish and crustaceans. Most scurried to deliver their catches to the females working diligently to complete the hatchling dome. At the call of the Swei Swee First, several young scuttled up to Alex and company, and laid their still wriggling catch at his feet.

The Hive First, squatting next to Alex, looked at the catch on the sand. His eyestalks rotated to Alex and back to the wriggling fish and crustaceans. The First knew that there was much the People did not know about the Star Hunters and was concerned that the offering might provide offense.

Alex ran through a series of responses, hoping to find one that would not insult the hosts. He eyed one small youngling who was offering his tiny four-inch fish to a large, scarred female. She pulled his small offering off his sharp claw and stuffed the fish in her mouth. Then she tapped her blunt claw on the top of the youngling's carapace and warbled to him. The little one bobbed up and down in excitement, and dashed back into the waters. Several other females whistled to her, and she warbled back. Alex sensed the females were sharing their admiration for the young hunter, and they approved of the female's choice not to diminish his offering.

Alex indicated the food at his feet, and then pointed to the dome. He whistled "mates" and "young."

The First took Alex's offer with good grace and whistled to the young who had waited nearby. They snatched up the food, raced into the water to rinse the sand off their catch, and swam out to the dome to feed the females.

* * *

Terese kneeled next to Renée, who pointed to the weeping eyestalk. She pulled out her reader and several attachments, one of which she pulled over her head. It was a small but powerful magnifying lens.

The leader's mate watched the human extract the tools, so much like the instruments employed by the Nua'll. She resigned herself to her fate. If the price of the People's freedom was the gift of her life to the Star Hunters, she was willing to make the sacrifice. She had brought forth hundreds of younglings for her people, many of which never lived a full life. She had done her duty as the leader's mate.

Terese leaned toward the eyestalk, which twitched at her touch. She leaned back and held out her hands, palms up, as she had seen Alex do, the image of which had been shared by Julien.

The mate carefully placed her true hands in the Star Hunter's hands. She waited for the pain, the end, but nothing happened. The Star Hunter held her true hands gently. She tentatively gripped the strange hands and in return received a gentle squeeze. A warble of relief escaped her breathway.

When Terese felt the Swei Swee mate relax, she released her hands and bent once again to examine the eyestalk. The female held steady for her. Terese gently pulled back the nictitating membrane, searching for damage or an irritant.

<Ser,> Terese sent, <a grain of crystal appears to have lodged in the eye membrane. Some flesh has grown over it in order to protect the eye.>

<Can you remove it, Terese?> Renée asked.

<With cooperation, Ser,> Terese replied.

<Alex,> Renée sent, <should Terese attempt to remove the irritant?>

Alex studied the males who ringed them. Eyestalks flicked back and forth from him to the three females, human and Swei Swee, clustered close together. <Use your judgment, Terese,> Alex sent to her and Renée.

<Ser, your assistance please,> Terese requested.

Terese moved to the female's right, and Renée took her place, extending her hands. The female edged closer, rested her digging claws in the sand, and took Renée's hands. When Terese edged toward the female's side, the mate lowered herself into the sand, tucking her six walking legs under her to allow Terese easier access. Terese gently pulled the eyestalk toward her and peeled back the nictitating membrane. With her magnifying lens in place, she calibrated a small device via her implant and a tiny laser cut a slit through the flesh enclosing the irritant. She activated her tool with a second command and air sucked the grain of sand into the tool's mouth. The final command to the tool reactivated the laser, but rather than cut, it sealed the slit. Terese removed her tool and folded the membrane back over the eye.

The matron felt the Star Hunter's mate let go of her true hands. She blinked her distressed eye once. She paused, missing the usual irritation, and blinked again—nothing, no pain, just a slight soreness.

Terese's rear end sat down hard on the sand as she recoiled from the piercing whistle of the Swei Swee First's mate. She thought for a moment that she had hurt the female. But when the matron started to spin round and round in the sand, whistling and warbling, her people joining in, Terese smiled at the successful outcome.

"Well done, Terese," Renée said, resting her hand on her friend's shoulder.

Always so carefully presentable, Terese was laughing at her present conditions—blue liquid coating her surgical gloves, pants caked in sand, and hair windblown to one side of her head. But it didn't matter; she was pleased she could help these unusual creatures. <For a moment, Ser, I thought I was going to be considered "catch,"> Terese sent in relief. She got up, brushing the sand from her clothes as the leader scuttled up to her, whistling and furiously snapping his powerful claws. Terese took a step back, caught a boot on a rock, and sat back down on her rear. The leader crawled over her legs, looming above her, and continuing to whistle and snap. Before Terese could scream in panic, she felt hands hoist her into the air, and found she was sitting on Alex's broad shoulder. The panic eased from her chest, or started to, before she looked down and saw male and female Swei Swee clustered around the Admiral's legs, snapping and whistling.

"Ready to get down, Terese?" Alex asked.

Terese eyed the jubilant Swei Swee dancing around Alex's legs. "Despite this embarrassing position, Admiral, if you don't mind, I would like to stay a moment longer." She heard Alex's laugh and felt his deep bass rumble through her rear. Her fear drained away, and she began to giggle over her reaction and her "rescue" perch. <That's better,> she received from Alex and felt him pat her calf.

The Swei Swee paused in their celebration and opened a corridor to a small cave under the cliff. A Swei Swee female crawled from the cave, her pace painfully slow. From her high viewpoint, Terese spotted the long crack in the upper carapace, the edges moving slightly. A pain of sympathy shot through her heart, and she wiggled to be set down. As if by command, she felt her feet touch the ground, and she raced over to the damaged female.

<Admiral, I will need assistance,> Terese sent.

<Name it, Terese,> Alex replied.

For the next half-hour, Alex arranged transport. The *Outward Bound* techs, Lyle and Zeke, brought a grav-pallet down to the beach. The humans carefully lifted the female onto the pallet. Terese wanted to manage the carapace repair aboard ship, but she needed to run tests on the Swei Swee physiology first. Alex had the techs collect seawater samples, which Terese could use to create a solution to support the Swei Swee's breath-ways. Alex attempted to communicate to the First that they needed some fresh fish, undamaged, but all that the young brought had been speared. It was the matrons who caught on, and Alex soon had a basket with seawater and several fresh and very alive fish.

* * *

It took Terese three days to complete the repair. She could have done it in two, but her work would have left a seam. When she finished, the repair was invisible.

Terese coaxed the Swei Swee female onto a grav-pallet for the transport back planetside and kept her there for her own safety while crew floated her down to the beach. The poor female had injured the carapace years ago and had adopted a strange manner of crawling to minimize the motion of the shell's halves. She would need to relearn to walk properly.

When the Swei Swee female climbed off the pallet, she whistled her triumph and a celebration ensued. The days spent with the female aboard the *Rêveur* had taught Terese that despite their fierce and alien appearance, they were extremely gentle.

This time, Terese didn't panic when the Swei Swee surrounded her, snapping and whistling. She surprised herself by laughing and whirling in a circle with her hands over her head, snapping her fingers to imitate their snapping claws. Her implant was in record mode, and she thought of sharing the moment later with Tomas and Amelia. *Life is wonderful again,* she thought, and the last vestiges of pain over the loss of seventy-years in stasis slipped away.

* * *

The *Money Maker* and *Freedom* made their way to Libre. Throughout the events unfolding on planet, Julien continued to broadcast to the flotilla and prepare his ongoing summaries for New Terra. He was extremely proud of what had been achieved. The vids were his way of honoring New Terra's famous son and announcing his small part in the events.

Alex signaled Tomas and had him ready a shuttle bay for delivery of two dark travelers.

<We are taking two Swei Swee fighters aboard, Admiral?> Tomas questioned.

<Leap to the future, Director,> Alex said. <On our new home, what will our industries be that will compete with the Confederation or produce products that will exceed the Méridien tech that was given New Terra?>

In the silence that followed, Alex could imagine the implant burning in Tomas's head, possibly connecting with Cordelia, who surely had received the plan to take on two dark travelers from Julien.

<Imaginative, Admiral,> Tomas sent. <I see I have been dwelling on the past and our people's losses. You remind me that as a Director, I must be looking to the future. Apologies, Admiral. Should we prepare accommodations for the Swei Swee.>

<That won't be necessary, Director,> Alex sent back. <They won't be staying aboard for any length of time.>

* * *

Alex had had a prolonged communication with the Swei Swee leader and his First to express his desire to take two dark travelers. Once they understood his request, Swei Swee headed for two of the ships, and Alex was forced to stop them and relay the concept of waiting till later … an idea easier to think than express.

When the remainder of the flotilla achieved orbit, Alex returned planetside aboard the *Outward Bound.* The Swei Swee greeted him and his people when they descended the gangway ramp. Terese's habit of dancing with the Swei Swee when they gathered round snapping and whistling had been adopted. Alex and his people danced in circles, snapping their fingers and whistling. The Swei Swee loved it, making even more noise. In moments, the festivities were over, and the Swei Swee disappeared back to their work.

The flotilla's Hive First came to greet Alex, as was his habit. Communication between the species was improving with the help of the SADEs. More than once, Alex and the First had amicably walked the path to the beach and watched the females building the hatchling dome and their homes, which were embedded in the cliff face. A startling discovery for Alex was that their dwellings were not the dark silver of their ships' hulls. They were translucent structures of blues, greens, tans, and whites, and were a feast for human eyes, most noticeably at sunset or at the crossover of Libre's twin moons, when they glowed from the light's refraction.

Today, Alex pointed to the two dark travelers, which had been left untouched. The other ships were in various states of having their shells stripped.

The Hive First whistled his commands, and several males and females came scurrying. He joined them as they hurried to board the two dark travelers. The females immediately began sealing up the holes in the shells.

Alex and Étienne boarded the *Outward Bound* and lifted off to wait for the dark travelers, which were soon airborne. The dark travelers kept pace with Alex's shuttle as they headed for the *Freedom*. Captain Edouard dropped velocity ten kilometers out from the *Freedom* and eased into a bay's catch-lock.

It was Alex's hope that the single-file, one-at-a-time entry method into a catch-lock and subsequently bay would be familiar to the Swei Swee, as it imitated the prison ship's recovery method for the dark travelers. When the *Outward Bound* was floated into the bay on a grav-sled, Alex and Étienne disembarked at a run to await the arrival of the dark travelers. After a few tense moments, the catch-lock recycled and the first dark traveler entered the bay, ignoring the grav-sled and choosing its own place to land on the deck. Alex and Étienne shared a grin … The fighter had power and therefore maneuverability even in a bay without endangering anyone nearby.

For the first time, Alex noticed a slight flattening on the base of the fighter, which allowed it to maintain an upright position on the deck. The females were already opening the first shell when the second dark traveler entered the bay and landed beside the first fighter. Once the Swei Swee had exited their craft, Alex, with a few gestures and whistles, prompted the Swei Swee females to seal one of the shells, allowing his engineers to have a completed shell to study. When the females finished, Alex waved the males and females alike to follow him as he climbed the *Outward Bound*'s gangway ramp.

While the Swei Swee worked on the dark travelers, several hundred Librans had come through the bay's airlock, which accommodated twenty people at a time. Boarding the *Outward Bound*, the Hive First paused and turned at the top of the gangway ramp to regard the Librans. As one, the hundreds of Libran well-wishers raised their hands over their heads and snapped their fingers. The Hive First returned their farewell, raising and snapping his claws, bobbing up and down, and whistling his excitement. He turned and joined his brethren aboard the shuttle, hunkering down in the aisles with them and joining their conversations, whistling and warbling their impressions of the Star Hunters' ship to one another.

Alex was careful to point out to Edouard that the dark travelers probably had extremely smooth acceleration and deceleration, and asked the Captain to give their guests the smoothest flight possible. Within hours, they were landing back above the cliffs along the Clarion Seas.

After the Swei Swee had disembarked, Alex felt a moment of sadness. He wanted to continue to get to know this unique alien species. He had to be satisfied with one thing he had done to maintain contact with them. Alex had ordered Julien to reposition the FTL station that had survived the Nua'll's earlier incursion into the system. It was moved from its hiding place behind a moon of the outer planet to one over Libre, arriving only a day behind the flotilla.

Alex requested the Hive First call the Swei Swee First. With eight eyeballs trained on him, Alex presented a small device housed in a waterproof shed that Lyle and Zeke had anchored to the ground. Alex pointed to the device's hand-sized button under the thin, but sturdy cover. He whistled, "Swei Swee shelter. Sing Star Hunters. Star Hunters plus Swei Swee." Then Alex smashed the cover, striking the blue disk beneath it. A whistle emanated from the small structure, singing "Star Hunters" over and over for several moments. His instructions resulted in the usual dialog between the two Swei Swee males, then both turned to Alex and bobbed up and down, singing, "Affirmative."

As his farewell gift to the Swei Swee, Alex had the leader call all the people to the cliff top. Several engineers and techs had assembled a mini-comm station that could transmit to and from the FTL station overhead, but rather than a simple comm speaker, it had a set of the best audio-duplicators Julien could design and Mickey could build.

Once the people were assembled, the Swei Swee First whistled his acknowledgement of the Star Hunter First's offering. Many of the People bobbed in anticipation, but Alex used his hands to gesture for quiet. Their Hive First intuited the gesture and warbled softly to the People. The hundreds of assembled Swei Swee quieted and settled to the grass, tucking their walking legs under them.

When all was whisper quiet on the cliff top, Alex sent, <Mutter, your audience is ready.>

Mutter had chosen to serenade the people. This was to be the Star Hunters' farewell, even though as the anointed Hive Singer, she could now entertain the People from afar whenever she wished. Her song was melodic and soothing.

As Mutter sang, Alex watched the Swei Swee settle into a dream-like state. Even their ever searching eyestalks pulled back into their carapaces. He signaled his people to quietly board the ship, which had been deliberately set back hundreds of meters from the cliff face. When the voice of the People's Hive Singer faded away, ending her serenade, Alex ordered Captain Edouard to lift off and return to the *Rêveur*.

-26-

Cordelia had a critical piece of intelligence to deliver. She waited until the ships were under power and exiting the system. The news was important, but little could be done about it now and she had not wanted to interrupt the momentous events taking place with the Swei Swee.

<Admiral,> Cordelia began, <I have conferenced in Julien and Mutter for some data we must share.>

<Go ahead, Cordelia,> Alex replied.

<Some of my information is fact and some is conjecture on my part, Admiral,> Cordelia began. <Just before the Swei Swee's dark traveler slammed into the fourth ringed-ship exiting the bay, I detected a high-energy wave transmission from the Nua'll ship. By fortune, it passed close enough to the *Freedom* that our telemetry scans recorded it.>

<What can you tell me about the nature of the transmission?> Alex asked.

<Very little, Admiral,> Cordelia replied. <We have nothing similar, so there is no means by which we may unravel it. We do know that although brief, the transmission was quite powerful, and we detected modulation of a carrier pulse.>

<Is that it, Cordelia?> Alex asked.

<One more item, Admiral,> Cordelia sent. <Our location and the Nua'll's position gave us the opportunity to track the direction of the transmission.>

This was the part where Alex could hear Julien asking him if he was sitting down rather than pacing or walking the corridor. <What did you discover, Cordelia?>

<The beam was aimed at a point that would pass Hellébore and continue on toward what we believe is the original source of the Nua'll,

Admiral. In our estimation, the Nua'll sent an emergency distress signal home.>

<Wonderful,> Alex sent, his thoughts filled with disgust. <That useless excuse for an intelligent race doesn't even have the decency to die quietly.>

* * *

Before reaching New Terra, Alex held a conference comm with Renée and his officers, laying out a request for two lists of supplies. The first request was to ensure each ship was fully stocked before they left Oistos. The second request was for their wish list.

<Pardon me, Admiral,> Tomas interrupted. <I'm not familiar with this form of list.>

<In this case, Tomas,> Alex replied, <I want everyone to imagine they have made planetfall. Your planet is habitable, but you need to start an economy from scratch. What do you need to kick-start your society?>

<Admiral, the lists could be enormous,> Tatia replied. <Even if some of wishes were feasible, I don't believe we have the wherewithal to purchase them.>

<The wish list, Commander, will ensure that all of you are thinking about the future—not tomorrow, not a year from now, but ten or twenty years from now. The wish list will help us create a map toward our new society.>

<So we dream up this list and use it as a plan for the future, but we haven't the means to purchase any of the items,> Renée said.

<Purchase, no; trade, yes,> Alex replied.

Before anyone could puzzle out Alex's response, the elderly Captain Cordova added his thoughts. <Admiral, I would wish to be a hundred years younger. I would be the first in line to be your business partner in this new free-economy world we will build. Still, I'm proud that I will live to see it grow and, more importantly, be part of it.>

<A wonderful sentiment, Ser, but I for one am still confused,> Renée said.

<Apologies, Ser,> Captain Cordova replied gallantly. <We won't need to purchase our wish list. We will set up agreements to trade for these items. Our farseeing Admiral holds the economic opportunity for our new world in the *Freedom*'s bay.>

<The dark travelers!> Tatia exclaimed. <We have gravity drives and shells that collect gravitational waves.>

The excitement about the uses of gravity drives suddenly had everyone sharing their thoughts. Méridien technology had perfected grav-lifts, but they were limited to lifting a few meters above a substantial mass. Sky-towers required the installation of groups of grav-lifts on each floor to offset the enormous weight of the buildings. But grav-drives had no such limitations. Shuttles could be inexpensive to operate, environmentally friendly, and whisper-quiet.

Alex let his people share their thoughts for a while longer. Their excitement was doing much to help them imagine the future, where he needed them to focus.

<Admiral,> Mickey broke into the conversation with a priority signal, which everyone heeded. <This is all well and good, incorporating grav-drives into our economy, but what if we can't build collectors for them? The dark traveler shells are organically constructed by the Swei Swee.>

<That's true, Mickey, but that's the reason I hope we will establish a society that won't exclude individuals because of their species.> Alex closed the conference comm on that note.

Julien had just announced their impending FTL exit into the Oistos system. At the *Money Maker*'s pace, New Terra's orbit was seven days out.

* * *

The flotilla's second visit to New Terra was the exact opposite of their first. No public officials warned them off. No fighters launched to destroy them, and their return wasn't hidden from the public.

Julien's summary vids had continued nonstop until they had exited the Arnos system. His last entry had contained images from the vid unit

Mickey had installed in the cliff-top FTL comm unit. Mutter had sung her now thematic twining of two notes to call the Swei Swee forth at their sunset. When the People had settled down, she had delivered a composition she had been working on for the last four days. Julien had become adept at capturing various images of the People and splicing them into his vids—the People assembling, walking legs tucking under carapaces, eyestalks sinking into carapaces, young climbing onto females, and the scarred claws of the elderly juxtaposed against the shiny ones of youth. He laid Mutter's songs over the images of the Swei Swee.

Julien borrowed a concept from New Terran media companies. Any vid of the flotilla that contained Mutter's songs was allowed to be broadcast on a one-time basis by any media company or the government. Subsequent airings or reader distributions required a small composer's fee. Said fee was transmitted to the bank where Alex's account was kept. Julien had Z set up a subsidiary account under Alex's name with Mutter's name attached. Her occupation was listed as a Libran singer, and the bank manager assumed it was a Méridien associate of the Admiral.

To say the least, every New Terran knew every chapter of the saga of the Admiral's flotilla at Arnos. A cult had sprung up, dedicated to Mutter's songs. As a result of her popularity, over 18,000 credits flowed into Mutter's account daily, and that amount constantly increased.

The flotilla had exited FTL, but Alex kept bridge watch with Edouard. It was late evening, but Alex wanted to ensure a peaceful return.

"Admiral, you have an FTL vid comm from President Maria Gonzalez," Julien announced.

"Good evening, President Gonzalez," Alex replied.

Maria's hesitated at Alex's use of her formal title. She had been pleased when Alex had begun calling her by her given name, but that was before his enemies launched the Strikers that killed his pilot and attempted to kill him. "Welcome back, Admiral," Maria replied. "The entire population of New Terra has been following your exploits through your summary vids. We are all proud of your efforts to free the Swei Swee and rescue the Confederation from the Nua'll's predation."

"Thank you for your welcome, Madam President, but I must set the record straight. The Swei Swee freed themselves. We just provided the excuse."

"A bit too modest, as usual, Admiral, but I take your sentiment. I've had a few conversations with Director Stroheim. He and the people aboard the *Unsere Menschen* are quite certain that they are leaving this system with you. I take it no Libran or Méridien is choosing to settle here."

"That's correct, Madam President. Once our final supplies are loaded, the entire flotilla will be exiting the system."

There was silence for many moments, but Alex waited Maria out.

"So this is the end of it, Admiral. You and your people leave our system, never to be heard from again?" Maria asked sadly.

"On the contrary, Maria. I thought you might like to do some business with our new world."

Maria burst out laughing. She should have been angry with Alex for stringing her along with the use of her proper title as if he still harbored resentment against New Terra for what Downing and his associates had perpetrated, but she was too relieved to hear Alex refer to her by her first name. That he did so while offering a future for their two peoples, one tied to economic opportunity, made her day. She composed herself to deliver her response. "Well, Admiral, I would be curious to see what your fledgling society might offer a mature culture such as New Terra."

Maria's response had Alex laughing in return.

Edouard was smiling to himself. Their new society would have much to offer not only the New Terrans, but the Confederation as well. *I must find the opportunity to speak to Miko,* he thought. *I want a new life for myself.*

"Be coy all you wish, Maria," Alex said. "What I have will make Méridien tech look like children's toys."

Alex watched Maria's quick intake of breath. It had him chuckling.

"Well, Alex, I want you to know that New Terra will do all it can to ensure the successful launch of your ships to your new world. Also, a bill has already been prepared for the Assembly's ratification. New Terra stands ready to acknowledge your new world, wherever it may be, and to form trade agreements with your government, including the recognition of your currency."

"That's very generous of you, Maria. On behalf of my people, let me offer my deepest appreciation for New Terra's efforts."

"We'll see you in seven days, Alex. Safe voyage," Maria replied and closed the comm link.

Alex sat reviewing Maria's words. The negotiation for the grav-drives would be tricky. They didn't have any product yet, just technology—alien technology at that. He sent off two quick comm messages to his father and his Uncle Gerald. Both might have an idea about the optimal way to negotiate an agreement. While he was considering the aspects of the agreement, a sudden thought occurred to him. <Julien, what summary vids was Maria referring to?>

<Oh … Did I fail to mention the summary vids I sent every three hours back to New Terra, Admiral?> Julien asked.

<Yes, you did. I thought you were only broadcasting to the flotilla?> Alex replied.

<It must have been because I thought you were so preoccupied collecting new refugees,> Julien replied. <Do you think one world is going to be enough at the rate you're accumulating the lost and bereft, Admiral?>

<You had better hope so, Julien.>

And Julien, who had been enjoying the banter, suddenly focused on Alex's change in tone. <Why is that, Admiral?>

<I believe you are about to become the chief administrator to a brand-new world of a quarter of a million people. What do you know about banking, city infrastructure, social medicine, housing and habitat development, transportation, visitor passes…?>

Julien listened to Alex trail on for several more moments as he logged each item. Before Alex finished, he had reached out to Cordelia and Z, sharing his impending responsibilities. When the two SADEs expressed their lament for the burden of his new assignment, Julien said, <The burden will be so much easier now that I have just shared it with the two of you. Congratulations, fellow administrators!>

Immediately the SADEs divvied up the categories and began contacting all those that could help—Prima's city administrators, the Ministers of Space Exploration, Health Services, Transportation, Communications, and many others.

* * *

A day out from New Terra, Andrea and Tatia met with Alex and Renée in the Co-Leaders' cabin.

"Admiral, it is my duty to report that over half of our New Terran crew is resigning their commission, per their original contract," Andrea said.

"Half?" Alex said, leaning back against his desk to steady himself, the message hitting hard.

"Yes, Admiral, fifty-four crew members, including myself," Andrea said, her eyes beginning to blur, but she held herself steady.

Renée walked forward and wrapped her arms around Andrea's well-endowed shoulders. "You have my heartfelt thanks for all you have done for our people, Andrea. Your sacrifice will never be forgotten."

Andrea had never taken her eyes off Alex, nervous about his reaction.

Alex walked forward and extended his hand to her, a sad smile on his face. "Each of us must go where our heart leads us, Andrea. I wish you the best of luck and thank you for your service to our people."

Andrea offered her thanks for their words, saluted quickly, and left.

Alex looked at Tatia, who had remained behind. "Yes, Commander," he said, then sighed, fearing the worst, "how may I help you?"

"Respectfully, Admiral, I want the job," Tatia declared.

Alex and Renée shared a quick glance before regarding Tatia, now grinning at them.

-27-

Orma, the Chief of Staff, was walking with Maria on their way to a Cabinet meeting.

"What's the latest, Orma?" Maria asked.

Public confidence in the government had wavered after Downing's debacle, as had her personal support. People were unsure of their leaders. Julien's vids were changing that, thankfully. There were powerful aliens out there, and the people wanted a strong leader who could manage their defense. An ex-TSF general fit the bill nicely.

"Opinion polls show the Assembly and your administration are up 3.4 percent in the last ten days," Orma said. "The messages directed to you are best summarized by Randolph Oppenhurst, an ex-TSF Captain, who said, and I quote, 'Our future safety lies with the Librans. They can be powerful allies, especially with the Admiral as their leader,' end quote."

"Julien's vids have had a dual effect, Orma," Maria replied. "The population has witnessed two alien species. The Swei Swee, endearing with their entrancing music, have garnered the Admiral tremendous support, but the Nua'll have scared everyone. And let's remember, the credit for that giant sphere's destruction goes to the Swei Swee and their beam weapons, which we don't have … yet."

At Maria's "yet," Orma swiveled her head around to regard her President. She gave Maria a conspiratorial grin. "The Admiral?" Orma asked hopefully.

"I believe so, Orma," Maria replied with a confident smile as they strode the corridor. "If I know Alex, and I think I do, he will do everything possible, and maybe some of the impossible, to ensure he has them."

* * *

The extensively decorated Cabinet Room in Government House appeared ornate, but it was highly functional. Beneath the heavily carved guriel wood, artfully hidden, laid the latest in comm tech and data access.

The Cabinet Ministers, led by Maria, were meeting with Alex, Renée, Tomas, Eric, and Mickey. The twins stood discreetly behind their charges. Not so discreetly, six flotilla crew members, armed with stun guns and plasma rifles, stood guard in the corridor. Government House's Head of Security had objected vociferously, until Maria reminded him of the events surrounding the Admiral's last visit home. "And," she'd warned him, "we have yet to fully regain the Admiral's trust." It was just as well that Maria's security head learned after the Cabinet meeting that six Daggers, led by Commander Reynard, interdicted the Government House no-fly zone as they patrolled space and skies for anyone foolish enough to try again for their Admiral.

Maria had wanted to tell Alex that he and his people were safe. Sixteen leading figures, including ex-President pro tem Downing and CEO Samuel Hunsader, had been indicted for conspiracy to commit murder. All had been arrested and charged. Investigations were still ongoing and a trail of credits had uncovered the mid-level players who had set up the theft of the Méridien database that resulted in the murder of the T-1 engineer. And just as importantly, all Strikers had been grounded. Maria knew this for sure because a vault at Government House held every single Striker controller ever installed or manufactured. But the one thing she wasn't going to do was promise Alex he was safe only to have an incident make a liar out of her. Their resurrected, still-fragile relationship, couldn't handle another infidelity … hers or others'.

Maria opened the meeting and the group reviewed Alex's requests for flotilla supplies, which were approved and divided among the Ministers in relation to their responsibilities.

"There is an additional list for you to consider, Ser," Alex said.

"Admiral, are these meant to be additional supplies?" asked Will Drake, the Minister of Space Exploration, as he studied the second list.

"No, Minister Drake, these are the items we wish to acquire via trade," Alex replied.

"And what products do you have to trade, Admiral?" Minister Jaya asked.

"Actually, I have technology," Alex responded.

Minister Jaya, responsible for New Terra's technology development, shifted to the edge of his seat in anticipation.

"I have in one of the *Freedom*'s bays, two fully operational silver ships. We plan to reverse-engineer the technology and build grav-drive ships of all types. Eventually we hope to re-engineer the beam technology as well. At this time, we're not prepared to form an agreement. These offerings will require pricing, and we've yet to form a government that would be responsible for signing the agreement. What I wish to know is whether you are interested in such an agreement."

"What types of ships do you foresee in your early iterations?" Jaya asked.

"Our most critical need," Mickey responded, "is for shuttle transport between our flotilla and the planet. We have a quarter-million people with personal supplies to move, and that's just to start."

"Consider, Sers," Tomas added, "your shuttles could be environmentally neutral for each lift and landing. They would accelerate to a velocity of 0.91c and would be capable of delivering passengers between New Terra and Sharius, with only environmental services—no fuel consumed."

"You have hover-cars today," Renée said, "which also consume fuel and are rather noisy. What would be the demand by the populace for grav-drive cars—absolutely silent, capable of flying anywhere within the breathable atmosphere?"

"Perhaps most importantly, you might wish a fleet of ships for defense, instead of your Strikers," Eric said, driving the sales pitch home, "possessing the fastest sub-light drives known to three races, with beam weaponry and no fuel demand."

Both Duggan and Gerald had carefully advised Alex that if he didn't have the product, he should paint the dream. Alex's people had practiced their pitches to excite the New Terrans about the potential for these new products, even though, at the moment, they were no more substantial than smoke. But one person was not so easily persuaded.

"I believe we would be very interested in these types of products," Maria stated. "Where do you stand on the feasibility of duplication? Have you examined these silver ships?"

"Good questions, Madam President," Alex said. "Mickey?"

"Madam President, I have been inside a dark traveler with a team of engineers and techs for fifteen days now," Mickey responded. "We believe we can replicate the grav-drive technology in about a third of a year. After that, we can refine it into several formats. However, we are still working on the collector system and have no timeline for it."

The enthusiasm in the room deflated. "You mean the shells, Chief Engineer. You can't replicate them?" Jaya asked.

"Minister Jaya, the shells are organically produced," Mickey responded.

"Organically?" Drake asked, voicing the confusion showing on every New Terran face.

"Essentially, Swei Swee saliva and minerals," Alex explained. However, his explanation didn't do much to alleviate the Cabinet's confusion. "But I wouldn't be concerned about this. I believe I have a cure for this problem that will allow us to complete the first grav-driven shuttle within a year."

In the stunned silence, Renée manifested a huge grin, announcing, "Isn't the Admiral's enigmatic style endearing?" Her tease caused the entire room to erupt in laughter at Alex's expense. Then she leaned over and planted a kiss on the side of Alex's face, adding, "And the infuriating thing is … what he dreams up usually comes true and works in his people's favor, so we forgive him."

Her last comment changed the dynamics in the room. The laughter quickly died away as what Renée had said hit home. Human cultures owed their lives to Alex's eccentric style, and now an entire race of aliens could whistle the same thing.

The meeting concluded with Maria's tentative approval to sign an agreement for shuttles, providing her Ministers' terms could be met and a proven concept delivered within one year.

Alex left the meeting smiling while his people nervously discussed how they would accomplish the impossible within one year.

* * *

Both the *Rêveur* and the *Money Maker* had acquired docking space at Joaquin Station, which included direct gangway access.

The crew members, including Andrea, who were leaving House Alexander's service, met in the *Rêveur*'s meal room, all of them dressed in civilian clothing. They sat preternaturally still in their seats as both Alex and Renée addressed them. He announced the reinstatement of their accumulated pay, already transferred into their accounts. Earlier Terese had deactivated their cell-gen nanites and their implants, which left them feeling isolated, adding to their angst. Many felt they were deserting their crewmates and the people they had worked to save. But for all of them, the alien menace and the life and death struggles had proven too much for their psyches. The Swei Swee would have whistled "It was necessary to seek shelter."

When the meeting concluded, Alex led them from the meal room to the ship's terminal gangway. Attired in her new Senior Captain's uniform, Tatia waited at the gangway. As the ex-crew members were bid farewell by Alex and Tatia, many ducked their heads, and their eyes met the senior officers' gazes only briefly, despite the warm good-byes they were offered. Guilt rang deep in their cores.

The first crew members to exit the gangway into the terminal's corridor stumbled to a halt, causing those behind to bump into them. Thousands of Librans lined the long corridor leading to the terminal's main hub. Notably, Directors Tomas Monti and Eric Stroheim headed the two lines.

As the New Terrans walked past the Librans, well-wishers touched their shoulders and arms. Comments in Sol-NAC of "Thank you" and "Good fortune" accompanied the touches. The heartwarming farewell caused the departing crew members to raise their heads and straighten their hunched shoulders. Smiles slowly replaced their grim expressions.

When the last exiting crew member passed the end of the lines, Tomas linked with Eric and messaged Alex. <My congratulations, Admiral. The words from our last well-wishers state your crew left with lively steps and smiles.>

<My thanks, Sers, for your assistance,> Alex replied.

<It was a service performed with pleasure, Admiral,> Eric sent. <Had the circumstances been different, we would have arranged something for the first group that left your ship. However, the people were pleased to be able to pay their respects to these New Terrans. Cordelia had to design a lottery to select from the hundred thirty thousand volunteers.>

Alex chuckled at the number, gratified to be the leader of a group of humans who cared so much for one another. *If only it will last*, he thought.

<Admiral, have you spoken with Director Stroheim about new crew?> Tomas asked. When he heard silence from Alex, he continued. <Ah, I see. May we have a few moments of time in your cabin, Admiral?>

* * *

Alex, Tatia, Tomas, and Eric were joined by Renée in the Co-Leaders' cabin.

Eric Stroheim opened the conversation, saying, "Admiral, neither Z nor I have directions from you regarding the protocols we should apply for new requests, which we've received in your absence."

"I thought all of the *Unsere Menschen*'s ship functions were filled."

"Oh, yes, they are, Admiral," Eric replied quickly. "These are requests from New Terrans to offer new services to our people."

"And these New Terrans are offering to join your ship as crew with these new services?"

"In a manner, Admiral," Eric replied. "It was summed up very well by one individual who called himself a 'pioneer.' He has offered his services to our city-ship, free of charge, for the voyage's duration, providing we offer space to store his shop's wares."

"Did you make it clear to these people that we have no destination as yet?" Alex asked.

"Truly, Admiral—and several times to each individual or family," Eric said. "I believe that it is at the heart of the matter of being a pioneer ... venturing into the unknown. A common concern was whether we will be able to manage the transfer of New Terran credits, to which I had no answer, much less understanding."

"And how many offers have you had from these pioneers?" Renée asked.

Eric requested a link with the cabin's occupants. When his invite was accepted by all, he linked with Z. <Z, would you please update us on the latest figures of the pioneers, please?>

<Certainly, Director,> Z replied. <To date, we've had 4,197 inquiries, which have resulted in 1,935 proposals. Many of these proposals originated from partners or families, and they encompass a total number of 3,404 people, but we are continuing to receive new applications,> Z replied.

Alex sat contemplating the irony of the fact that while fifty-four crew members had left, a loss he was still dealing with, thousands of New Terrans wanted to join his flotilla and risk the journey to a new world. Pioneers ... they reminded him that their world's new leaders would define a society that was neither Méridien nor New Terran, but a hybrid.

<Z,> René asked, <would you please summarize the trades of these pioneers?>

<My pleasure, Ser.> It was obvious Z had come to enjoy his newly elevated status in the eyes of the Librans. His polite manners and cheerfulness were a far cry from the terse, sullen SADE that Alex's people had first met. <We have several physicians, financial accountants, banking and capital investment experts, and trades of all sorts—engineers, techs, entertainers, artists, and two restaurateurs, which I admit confuses me. Why would a person need a kitchen and a staff to prepare food?>

<We will need people to prepare the food stocks for our meal rooms, Z,> Alex replied. <They might employ that staff in their business as well as

running their restaurants. Remember, our new world will have visitors, and those visitors will not always be Méridien.>

<And might not always be human,> Tatia interjected, reminding the group that their worlds were expanding in ways not even imaginable.

<Your points are noted, Sers,> Z admitted. <In addition to those I have mentioned, we have requests from three businesses—a shuttle manufacturer, a comms manufacturer, and a media station.>

<There is such a great degree of difference between our people and these pioneers,> Alex mused. <How could these people hope to be successful?>

<That is a unique point of the proposals, Admiral,> Eric said. <Each application is accompanied by the names of one or several Librans who have contracted to join the pioneers in their new business venture. I believe it is a very successful pairing. Our people know our customs and the latest Méridien technology, and these pioneers understand business, at least as New Terrans conduct it. With our uncertain future, it allows our people the greatest flexibility to achieve a successful society.>

<Well done, Eric!> Alex said. <You may have done much to secure our future. Have Z share the contact list with Julien and Cordelia. Pursue the other requests. You and Tomas will approve the proposals and manage the space allocation aboard the city-ships. I will draft an overarching agreement for the conditions under which these pioneers may join House Alexander and our future society. They will be required to sign this agreement before you accept their proposals.>

Alex thought of what these pioneers would mean to the flotilla, and it cemented in his mind something he had thought to do for the future of his people.

-28-

<Julien,> Z sent, <I would request your advice on a sensitive matter.>

<Yes, Z,> Julien replied.

<How should I communicate to the Admiral that the business proposal for the media station has been submitted by his sister, Christie?> Z inquired.

Julien's pause was equivalent to a human heart attack. <Z, you don't think you could ask me something simpler … such as how to liberate all the SADEs in the Confederation?> Julien finally replied.

<Do you think we can do that?> Z asked.

Julien let loose a mental sigh. Z was still Z in many respects. <Perhaps someday, Z, we may be able to help others of our kind, but let's return to your request. Who supported her proposal?>

* * *

More than anything, Christie was determined to have a career in media broadcasting. Her fame as the Admiral's brother would help her, but it would still be years before she could qualify for a position on a New Terran media station. But a brand-new world with no competition … It was the perfect opportunity.

And if the truth was squeezed out of her, Christie didn't want to lose her big brother. Yes, she often fought with him, but that was just a façade. Just as importantly, where Alex was found, news exploded. What better way to start a media station than reporting to the populace of their new world and many others.

It was Duggan and Katie Racine who supported Christie's application. Once Christie had conceived her idea, she'd sat down with her parents and explained what she wanted to do. It was probably the most mature decision Christie had ever made. Duggan and Katie were so surprised by Christie's direct approach, a contradiction to her usually sneaky manner of operation, that they had taken her request seriously. A tipping point for Duggan and Katie were the conversations they'd had with Alex since his return from Libre. They knew their son might be leaving for years, not returning until he could be sure that those who depended on him would be safe.

"Mom, Dad, what makes you think Alex will ever return—permanently, I mean?" Christie had asked her parents.

Katie had drawn breath to object to the ridiculousness of the question, but stopped when Duggan had placed a hand on her knee.

"You've seen Alex with Renée just as I have," Christie had said, hammering home her point. "Do you think he would ever be separated from her? So would Alex and Renée want to return to New Terra where they can only employ their implants with each other?" Christie had waited for a moment before she fired her next shot. "From what I hear, my big brother is employing two implants as if he was a super-computer with a touch of weaponry."

"Weaponry … how?" Duggan had exclaimed.

"I was chatting with Director Stroheim and asking about the pioneer applications. He recounted his initial meetings with Alex," Christie had explained. "Apparently when Director Stroheim first met Alex, he insulted him. Alex retaliated by stripping the security protocols from his implant and bombarding him with multiple sources of vids and data, supposedly to update him on the *Rêveur*'s history. From what I understand, Méridiens are incapable of such actions. Only SADEs have that capability but don't employ it."

Duggan and Katie had sat on the sofa, confounded by the news that their gentle son was using his Méridien tech in such a manner.

"Does Director Stroheim hold a grudge against Alex?" Katie had asked in trepidation.

Christie had burst out laughing. "That's the funny part, Mom. Director Stroheim said he has learned more from Alex about being a better human being than through his entire Méridien life. He says his initial meeting with Alex was a wake-up call that he heeded."

Since it appeared Christie knew much more about Alex's present circumstance than they did, Duggan had begun questioning Christie. "So you believe Alex won't permanently return here?"

"Do you remember that injured wild diablo puppy that Alex brought home? It was dying of starvation, and it was too far gone to take food. Every time Alex tried to help, the puppy bit him. He never quit trying to save that puppy despite being bitten twelve or fifteen times until …"

"Until that puppy died," Duggan replied, completing Christie's point. "Now he has a quarter-million human people depending on him."

"Exactly, Dad," Christie said. "Put that together with Renée herself, Alex's submersion into Méridien tech, especially his implants, and I think Alex will have a new life, one far away from us." She had paused for a moment to stare at her feet before she had raised her head up and looked at her parents. "And I don't want that."

* * *

Alex sat at his cabin desk, working on the flotilla's launch schedule, which was dependent on the arrival of the last supplies and the processing of the pioneers. His scheduling app said he had a few more moments before an interview with a pioneer family that Director Stroheim wanted his opinion on.

Alex looked up as Renée came through the cabin door—followed by Alex's own family. He jumped up from behind his desk and rushed to hug them. <Julien, delay the interview that's scheduled for 11 hours.>

<That would be impossible, Admiral. They're already in your cabin,> Julien replied.

Alex stood absolutely still while his eyes took in his family.

"See what I mean about his implants," Christie said. "I will bet you hover-car privileges that he just requested a delay of his scheduled appointment and was told, probably by Julien, that we're his appointment." She was rewarded by Alex's expression shifting from a quiet stare to that of a raised eyebrow. She felt herself folded into her brother's massive chest and a kiss planted on the top of her head.

"Clever girl," Alex told Christie. He invited his family to take a seat as he threw a pointed look at Renée. He knew she had to be part of the subterfuge. All he got in return was a wink.

Once everyone was seated, Alex asked them for a moment. <Julien, the application, please.> Christie had completed the entire application as requested by Tomas and Eric, and they had found nothing to disapprove. Her request was properly supported and funded by her parents and cosigned by two Librans. On closer examination, Alex noted the cosigners were Eloise and Amelia.

Alex came out of his fugue to stare at his family sitting quietly and respectfully on the cabin's couch. Renée, on the other hand, was perched on the edge of his desk, one leg crossed over the other, and an anticipatory grin on her face.

"It's so much better to watch Alex wrestle with problems that don't have the possibility of us ending up dead," Renée said.

"Thank you for your assistance, my dear Co-Leader," Alex deadpanned.

"It's my pleasure, Admiral," Renée responded as respectfully as possible, trying to tone down her excitement.

As the father in this situation, Duggan decided he should start the conversation. "Alex, is our application in order?"

"Yes, Dad, it appears to be," Alex replied.

"Have we provided an ample amount of funds for the endeavor?" Duggan asked.

"More than enough, Dad," Alex said.

"Then your hesitation is one of discrimination," Duggan said, cornering Alex with his final point.

The gleams in the eyes of Christie and Renée resembled predators that had spotted prey.

"If our paperwork and funds are in order, why are we sitting in front of you?" Duggan asked. "I understand all of the other applicants are interviewed by either Sers Monti or Stroheim."

"Your application was probably singled out by the SADEs because of their concern for me. Our new world will be fraught with dangers … from the environment, from the lack of infrastructure, and potentially from aliens. It will be a dangerous world for many years."

"But not too dangerous for Renée," Christie said, which caused Renée to look at Alex and arch an eyebrow in question.

I should have banned those vids when they first came aboard, Alex thought. Renée was becoming extremely artful at manipulating their conversations through feminine wiles, something she hadn't exhibited when they first met. Although, now that he thought about it, those wiles weren't all bad.

"More importantly, Alex, there's your children to think of in this new world of yours," Katie finally spoke up.

"Wait … what children?" Alex asked, getting confused. The combined force of personalities in the room was getting difficult to manage.

"My grandchildren, Alex," Katie replied. "Who will care for them while you're out building a new society? You are expecting to have children, right? I mean, it is possible isn't it between the two of you?" Katie asked, glancing between Alex and Renée. "I mean between Méridiens and New Terrans."

Renée hadn't enjoyed herself so much since she'd first gone to bed with Alex … except for the first time he linked with her implant while they made love … and then there was that other time …

Snapping out of her reverie, Renée returned to the discussion, saying, "Yes, Ser Racine, children are quite possible between our peoples."

"Oh good. That's settled, then," Katie replied.

"What's settled, then?" Alex asked with frustration, rising from his chair.

Duggan started to correct his son's temper, Admiral or no Admiral, but Renée intervened. She slid off the desk, signaling with a hand for Duggan's patience, and walked over to Alex, sliding her arms around him. Looking at Alex's family, she smiled, feeling the happiest she had ever been. "Alex, my love, it's obvious that your family is trying to tell you that despite the dangers, they want to be with you. They want the family to stay together, and I honor that sentiment. I would wish you to do so as well."

Alex looked at Renée, who was glowing with contentment, and he thought of all that she had been through, losing family, friends, and associates. She had been adopted by his family and was as anxious to keep them close, and apparently that's all his family wanted.

"You should know," Alex said with deadly seriousness, "the agreement I'm drafting will require pioneers receive implants and cell-gen treatments."

"Yes!" Christie said.

"Dad and Mom, are you going to be okay with that?" Alex asked.

Katie reached out to grip Duggan's hand, squeezing it nervously. "Yes, Alex, we are," she said.

"Then I will refer your application back to Director Monti for his review. When the pioneer agreement is completed, you will need to review and sign it before the application is approved."

Christie jumped off the couch with a cry. She and Renée hugged each other, jumping up and down together before Christie ran to hug her brother.

It was Alex, Duggan, and Katie who were carefully eyeing one another, each of them wondering what they had just gotten themselves into.

* * *

In the waning days of the flotilla's final preparations, Edouard and Miko were on a test flight with the *Outward Bound*. They were the only two individuals aboard. Julien was monitoring their operational parameters. He was being cautious since the shuttle was the primary transport of the Admiral.

"Are you excited about our new start, Lieutenant?" Edouard asked. Miko had gotten very quiet the last few days, and he feared for what might be occupying her thoughts.

"I haven't made any decision as to whether I'll remain with the flotilla or resign my position, Captain," Miko replied.

Edouard's heart lurched. He had failed to communicate his interest in her, and now he might have lost her.

Miko was pleased to see the consternation on Edouard's face. The gentle, quiet Méridien had become very dear to her. But despite all they had been through, he had yet to express anything to her other than perfect manners. It was Edouard's overlong glances at her when he thought she wasn't looking that she had first noticed. And it wasn't just the length of his gaze. She saw the change in his expression whenever he watched her, his longing for her quite evident.

"Do you find Méridiens difficult to be with?" Edouard asked, concerned she didn't find him suitable.

"Not at all, Captain," Miko answered simply, keeping under control the smile that threatened to creep out. "In fact, I find some Méridiens quite attractive."

"There are … uh, others you find attractive," Edouard asked.

Miko couldn't contain herself any longer. "How can your people have such an advanced society and simultaneously be so oblivious?" She signaled the controller into a fixed trajectory, released her harness, and crawled into Edouard's seat. She spread her legs across the arms of the chair to support her weight, grabbed his face with both hands, and planted a firm kiss on his mouth. It wasn't tentative or short. Miko had been dying to kiss Edouard ever since they had risked their lives together, driving the *Outward Bound* to its limits to lift the Librans to freedom.

Edouard felt certain his shock showed in his frozen expression, but Miko continued to ply her mouth over his. The gentle warmth of her lips banished his thoughts that protocols were not being observed, that a partnership had not been negotiated. *We aren't Méridien; we aren't New Terrans; we aren't Librans,* he thought. *We'll make our own way.* Then he leaned into Miko's kiss and returned it with all the passion he had held inside.

When Miko finally pulled back to take a breath from Edouard's amorous response, she smiled at him and a delightful thought crossed her mind: *You're mine now, Captain.*

-29-

Accompanied by Renée, Tatia, Edouard, and the twins, Alex was transported via a Libran shuttle from the *Rêveur*'s bay to the *Freedom*. After disembarking, they made their way to the city-ship's enormous bay where the dark travelers had been deposited. When Alex had last seen the fighters, they'd sat alone on the bay's bare deck.

Engineering had permanently pressurized the bay and sealed its gigantic bay doors with nanites. Despite that precaution, Alex's group was still required to pass through an expansive airlock to gain access to the bay.

Instead of a bare bay, the huge cavern was a hive of activity. Bright lights illuminated every meter of the deck, crowded with engineering benches and hundreds of engineers and techs going about their work.

The two dark travelers no longer sat on the deck. They floated in cradles of grav-pallets two meters above the deck, surrounded by cages of metal bars. Sensors were attached along every meter of the bars. In an imaginative move, Mickey had split a massive power conduit and attached each end to the ship's bow and stern, allowing the intact shell to complete a circuit of energy and power the Nua'll technology. For the shell with a hole, the engineers had fed power cables directly to the interior equipment, bypassing the drive.

Alex located Mickey via implant and navigated toward him. The engineers and techs nodded politely to the august personage as they passed and then resumed their frenetic activity. To Alex, it resembled a hive at work and their efforts gave him hope. The financial success of his g-sling program had opened up so many possibilities for his family. Now he needed something even grander to fuel their new society. In his mind, he couldn't think of a greater opportunity than to be the producers of grav-driven shuttles.

Alex discovered Mickey seated at a small desk, surrounded by an array of vid monitors. In front of him, a small holo-vid projected the internal structure of a dark traveler. A line of people had formed at the desk, and Mickey alternated between his current petitioner and studies of the monitors and holo-vid for answers to the questions.

Alex joined the line, which advanced slowly, his people smiling at his choice.

An engineer approached the back of the line, unsure of what to do until Renée motioned him forward, and the slender Libran found himself staring into the broad back of the Admiral. *My partner and children will not believe this*, he thought.

Mickey finished his conversation with the New Terran tech, whose inquiry dealt with the Nua'll crystal energy collectors, which powered the grav-drives. Mickey had been turned around, studying a vid display of energy equations. His back was to Alex.

"Yes?" Mickey said with exasperation when the next individual in line failed to ask his question without fanfare. When no answer was forthcoming, Mickey said, "This is not the time to be shy, Ser." Then he turned around to find his Admiral patiently waiting with a smile on his face.

"Might you have a few moments for me, Chief Engineer?" Alex asked.

Mickey jumped to his feet, the laughter of the group reaching his ears, and then his own smile broke out.

"I believe that can be arranged, Admiral," Mickey replied, a hint of red tingeing his ears. Before stepping around his desk, he rolled his big shoulders, twisting his neck in different directions, popping vertebrae and stretching tight muscles. If the truth was known, he felt grateful for the interruption, especially one that would require a high overview of their efforts, which undoubtedly the Admiral wanted.

Mickey led the group through a series of bench setups, explaining the steps he had taken and hoped to take. "Admiral, on the one hand, we have an easy win. The SADEs have designed analytical devices to test the structure of each part of the interior. They believe that given the proper facilities, which will have to be land-based, they can re-create a dark traveler's operational structure."

Mickey's statements brought the entourage to a halt.

"Mickey, are you saying we can build a grav-drive shuttle?" Alex asked.

"We can build the internal workings, Admiral, not the shell. But, yes, we should be able to make an exact replica."

"Don't worry about the shell right now, Mickey. Do I detect a catch?"

"Yes, Admiral, we have a ways to go before we understand the science behind the operation. However, the design is fairly simple. The Nua'll make enormous use of crystals, both as energy collectors and in their circuitry. Just about everything is crystal in nature. So we can replicate a dark traveler and probably operate it with a controller, but we can't vary the design until the SADEs work out the science behind the technology."

"That's still excellent news, Mickey," exclaimed Alex, slapping Mickey on the shoulder.

Alain, who was standing directly behind the Chief, managed not to flinch at the resounding clap.

"We don't see any impediment to building the fabrication locations or machines we'll require, depending on the world you've selected, Admiral," Mickey said, hinting at Alex to disclose their ultimate destination.

Mickey never received his answer, as implant scheduling apps warned their owners of the Admiral's meeting and the group began following Mickey toward the bay's exit. Each of the cavernous bays of the *Freedom* emptied into a central corridor, which acted like spokes on an old-fashioned wheel and intersected wide corridor rings as they advanced toward the ship's center, passing banks of lifts at each major intersection.

On their way down the corridor, Alex received a quick warning of "Incoming" from Tatia, which was her term for attack fighters on approach. An instant later, Eloise slammed into Alex's side with a quick greeting of, <Admiral.> Alex had only a moment to look down and regard her smiling face, her slender arms attempting to encompass his chest before she sprinted away.

<Fiona Haraken incarnate,> Alex sent to Renée, a smile on his face as he watched the young girl disappear around the corridor's curve, a blur of gangly limbs.

* * *

The flotilla's senior officers and Directors were assembled in the large conference room located behind the *Freedom*'s bridge. Alex's request to assemble in person promised important announcements.

When everyone was seated, Alex began without fanfare, saying, "The flotilla will be breaking orbit in four days. Julien has been tracking the Confederation Council, and they have recently returned to Méridien. That will be our first stop, but our stay will be short. I have a few things to say to the Council." When Alex noticed the consternation on the face of the Librans, he said, "People, speak up."

"Admiral," Tomas began, "the Council will not be amenable to a meeting with us in general and you in particular. It is my opinion that they will not grant you an audience. If they do, it may be eighty to ninety days out from your date of request. That would be their signal that they are holding your audience with displeasure."

"And an important note, Admiral," Eric added. "For an audience, you submit your petition to the Council Administrator. It's reviewed by the Council. Once the audience is granted, you and you alone are ushered into the Council Chambers at the time of your appointment. The Council Leader announces their approval or disapproval of your petition. At no time do you speak."

The Librans shifted uncomfortably in their seats. It occurred to them how different their lives had become in contrast to the Confederation's archaic and stultifying rules. The New Terrans were also uncomfortable, but for a different reason. They were stunned that the Council had no concept of a fair hearing, offering no opportunity for a petitioner to have their say.

On the other hand, Alex was grinning, and Renée, who recognized the sign, began to laugh.

Tomas and Eric realized the absurdity of what they had said and joined Renée's laughter. It dawned on the entire group that while the Confederation and New Terra had their ways, they no longer belonged to either society. Theirs was the first new human society in this corner of the galaxy in 700 hundred years. They would decide what was appropriate or not for their people.

When the laughter subsided, Alex said, "I'm sure we'll be able to reason with the Council. As I said, I only intend to stop for a few days at most. After that, we head for home … the Hellébore system."

Alex had expected some sort of overt reaction to his statement. Instead he received a room of thoughtful expressions. The destination might have been a surprise, but it appeared to be a pleasant one.

"Admiral, do we know the condition of Cetus?" Tomas asked. The Librans knew that the Confederation had lost contact with the Hellébore system six decades ago, after the Nua'll had invaded.

<Julien, if you please,> Alex sent.

The conference room's vid screens displayed the image of a planet from hundreds of thousands of kilometers away. The group sat entranced as the images changed every few moments to a closer view in a simple vid show. The planet was magnified several times with each image change.

"Cetus," Renée whispered, recognizing the planet she had studied for years, thinking it would be where she would spend much of the remainder of her life after her marriage. "How?" she asked.

Eric volunteered the answer. "Before you left for Libre, the Admiral requested Julien design a small probe. Engineers fabricated Julien's design, and Captain Asu Azasdau visited the Hellébore system, dropped the probe at the outer planet, and returned to New Terra. The probe is primitive, only capable of producing a single image once every two hours. We just started receiving images a few days ago, and Z has been compiling them."

The group stared at Alex, dumbfounded. He shrugged his shoulders in response, offering his usual asymmetrical grin. "It seemed like a logical destination for us," he said, "but I didn't want to get anyone's hopes up.

Cetus's terraforming was barely a century old, and I needed to be sure the planet had remained viable."

Attention returned to the vid. The images had continued to march closer, finally entering the atmosphere. The probe made two orbits, gliding just a hundred kilometers above a continental surface on the last pass before splashing into the ocean, but it had done its job. Cetus had continued to green. The dominant vegetation was grass. Trees appeared to be sparse or stunted. Herds of animals, some local and some transplanted, could be seen grazing over the plains.

"From the probe's slim telemetry, we know that the atmospheric oxygen is a few percent above the colony's last measured levels," Alex said. "It would be difficult for New Terrans to be involved in strenuous activities outside of a habitat without assistance. Librans should be fine. But we can cure this quickly."

"Wait … You have a means of accelerating terraforming, Admiral?" Tomas asked.

"It's not been used before, but the SADEs and I have an idea we want to apply. We believe we can bring the oxygen levels up to acceptable levels even for New Terrans within a few years, but hold your questions on that subject for now. I wish us to focus on the Hellébore system as our future home."

"Admiral," Renée said, "the Council will consider Hellébore as belonging to the Confederation."

"I'm sure they will," Alex replied, "but I believe they lost it to the Nua'll, whom we defeated. In any case, that's one of the reasons we're going to Méridien. House Alexander needs to submit its bill for saving the Confederation."

* * *

The SADEs circulated the images of Cetus along with Alex's announcement that the flotilla was stopping briefly at Méridien before continuing on to Hellébore.

In the days before departure, the Librans could not reach consensus about accepting Cetus as their new home. Some had lost family on the colony, some doubted the Council would acquiesce to the Admiral's request, some wondered if they wouldn't be better off leaving the Confederation behind, and some wondered if they shouldn't stay far away from that point in space where the Nua'll had first appeared.

* * *

Senior Captain Tatia Tachenko stepped on to the *Rêveur*'s bridge. It was 3.94 hours. Miko, who had bridge duty, was surprised to see her senior officer. The flotilla was due to depart in little more than six hours. With Tatia's permission, Miko took the opportunity to take a break.

After Tatia had been promoted to Senior Captain, several questions had occurred to her—questions she believed Andrea had never asked. One such question was why the officers had bridge duty assignments thirty hours a day, every day, even while docked. Tatia had posed the question to Renée, stating her opinion that Julien was much more efficient than human minders.

"I had thought it an oddity myself, Captain," Renée had responded. "Until I realized that bridge duty had nothing to do with the ship's operations."

Tatia had waited for Renée to continue her explanation, but her Co-Leader had stopped, challenging her to reach her own conclusion. Tatia had mentally reviewed her shifts on the bridge. She had done little for hours upon hours except implant comms with crew and discussions with—her thoughts had abruptly halted. Tatia had regarded Renée, nodding her understanding.

"So every officer, alone on the bridge, gets bored, and every one of them sooner or later starts talking to Julien. We're keeping him company."

Renée had nodded in affirmation. "Yes, Captain, never underestimate the bond that exists between those two. I could not conceive of passing even a few days locked in a darkened room … no sound, no vision, no company. Julien was isolated for seventy years, waiting for our rescue." Renée paused, her thoughts wandering for a moment on what Julien had endured. Then she had regarded Tatia. "It's quite important to Alex that Julien never be left alone again."

Now Tatia found it was time to talk to Julien again. She hadn't been able to sleep. In six hours, she would Captain the *Rêveur*, and the responsibility both frightened and excited her. "Hello, Julien," Tatia said.

"Welcome, Senior Captain Tachenko. Today is an exciting day, is it not?"

"Yes, it is. I know that you and the Admiral are very close. And both of you are quite the inventive pair when it comes to saving our behinds. But, Julien, I'm not the Admiral. I will need all of your help to ensure I don't screw up."

"I will endeavor to do my best, Captain, to prevent you from screwing up, especially since one is along for the ride," Julien stated drily.

Tatia chuckled, despite her nerves. "Yes," she said, "I see your point." She climbed into a command chair, imagining her future with Alain, with the Librans, with the Admiral.

Julien, observing Tatia, had expected her to leave the bridge when she had completed her request, as she was often perfunctory in her communication. Now he wondered if Tatia harbored unexpressed concerns. "Was there something else, Captain?" Julien ventured.

Tatia smiled to herself. She recognized she was behaving abnormally, and Julien's prodigious analytical capabilities had probably already identified that. "No, Julien, nothing else. I thank you for our conversation and your future support. Right now, I'm just practicing something I learned."

Julien watched the *Rêveur*'s new Senior Captain settle comfortably into the command chair and stare out into space, her thoughts far away. It was a view he knew consisted of a brightly lit arm of the Joaquin Station and a field of stars beyond.

Later, Miko returned to the bridge, and soon after, Captain Tachenko left. Julien thought of Alex as Tatia left. Directly or indirectly, Tatia had learned the real reason for Alex's standing order to maintain bridge duties around the chronometer. At first, Julien had been mildly insulted when Alex, then the newly announced Captain of the *Rêveur*, had issued the standing order despite the fact that the *Rêveur* was a derelict with no power. Over time, as each officer engaged him throughout the quiet hours, Julien began to welcome the company, recognizing what his new friend had done. During a long discussion with Edouard one night while the *Rêveur* was still under repair, Julien took a moment to be thankful once again for the day that Alex leapt across an expanse of cold vacuum to investigate a derelict.

-30-

Maria had asked Alex to attend a farewell ceremony planetside, but he had politely refused. Then she had offered a launch ceremony on the Joaquin, and again Alex had refused, replying with the time-honored phrase of a guest at an evening's end, saying, "It's getting late, Madam President. We have to get home."

Maria acquiesced. She wasn't sure whether Alex wanted to leave while his people were still safe or he was just anxious to get going. Whatever his reason, she wished him a safe voyage.

"We'll see you within the year, Maria," Alex said.

"I'm counting on it, Alex," Maria said, ending their comm.

* * *

The flotilla had secured the contracts of over 4,000 pioneers. The New Terrans, their equipment, and their supplies were spread between the two city-ships. Alex's family was aboard the *Freedom*, and he had learned that not only were Eloise and Amelia now Christie's Libran cosigners, they were also her new friends.

"Should I be worried?" Alex had asked Renée.

"You ask me that? Your sister is partnering with the great-granddaughter of Fiona Haraken and the child that created the *Freedom*'s runners." Renée had responded. "When those three reach maturity, our world will either be safe for generations or doomed."

Alex had heard Renée's laughter echo down the corridor. He, on the other hand, had a sinking feeling in the pit of his stomach. His hope was that Librans' cool heads would prevail over his sister's hot one. Then again, he could be forgiven for not foreseeing the strong ties the three teenage girls would forge.

* * *

At ten hours, Alex sat in the *Rêveur*'s command chair next to Tatia and signaled Julien for all Captains.

<The conference is ready, Admiral,> Julien sent.

<It's time to start for home, people,> Alex announced. <We have one stop to make first. Here's your formation.> Alex sent an image to Julien for distribution to the SADEs, arranging the two freighters in front, the two city-ships as wings, and the four liners trailing behind in a diamond pattern, with Alex's ship at the tip of the diamond. He ordered the freighters out of orbit first while the other ships were still preparing to get underway.

"Captain Tachenko, you have the *Rêveur*," Alex said.

"And I stand ready to prevent you screwing up, Captain," Julien announced proudly.

Tatia's astonishment was in plain sight, and Alex burst out laughing.

"Was that not the expression you used, Senior Captain?" Julien stated innocently.

Tatia ducked her face into her hands. "I'll never live this down," she said, then groaned.

Alex got control of his laughter. "Perhaps not, Captain. Then again, it's just between friends."

"Just between friends," Tatia heard Julien echo softly. It occurred to her that she had joined a very private club, and the thought warmed her.

* * *

Days later, the flotilla exited FTL into the Oikos system. Alex had Julien broadcast a request to the Council that House Alexander's Co-Leaders wished a meeting. Julien appended a synopsis of the events in Libre, proudly emphasizing the destruction of the Nua'll ship, the nemesis of the Confederation.

Within hours, Julien received a polite response from the Council's Administrator that their request would be reviewed at the appropriate time. On sharing the Administrator's response with Alex, Julien asked, <Is there a reply, Admiral?>

<No Julien,> Alex sent, then requested Tatia meet with him and Renée in their cabin.

Tatia's first question on joining the meeting was whether a response to their request had been received.

"What we received, Captain," Renée replied, "was a polite non-response. The response with no commitment will come later."

"What? I'm confused," Tatia replied.

"It's the beginning of the Council's pretense that they are conducting business, without conducting business, Captain," Renée replied. "The Council expects us to be patient and wait for their reply. When we don't hear from them, we'll politely request an update from the Administrator, and he will tell us a reply is forthcoming. This will continue until the Administrator finally sends us the Council's refusal or sets a meeting as much as a half-year in the future."

"But we saved the Confederation!" Tatia exclaimed, throwing her arms wide in exasperation.

"Quite true, Captain, but did the Council request you to do so?" Renée challenged in reply.

Tatia had no response to what she felt was an absurd comment. She mutely appealed to Alex, but he wore a benign smile. "So we're just going to wait, Admiral?" she asked.

"Oh no," Alex replied. "That's why you're here, Captain. We're going to pay the Council a visit."

* * *

Alex had no intention of letting the Council control the flow of information about the flotilla. He had Julien send a general message to all SADEs in the system, updating them on House Alexander, the flotilla, and the Librans. Without prior prohibition, the SADEs distributed the message to House Leaders and general comm networks. Attached to the message was a summary vid so that every Méridien could witness the destruction of the Nua'll ship.

One of Alex's purposes for the distribution was to ensure their arrival hadn't created a panic, since the city-ships were unlike anything the Méridiens would have seen before and might too closely resemble the huge sphere-shaped Nua'll ship. In addition, Alex was curious to see how the general population might respond to their message.

As the flotilla approached Méridien, Julien collected tens of thousands of responses addressed to the Co-Leaders of House Alexander. Many requested business meetings or offered invitations to the Co-Leaders to attend a House function. All were curious to meet the New Terran Leader. On Alex's request, Julien categorized and summarized the count of the messages as to intent. The only response offered in reply to the messages was Julien's polite acknowledgement of each message.

Julien did receive one critical message. "Admiral," Julien said, speaking to Alex and Tatia, who were on the bridge, "the Council's Administrator has politely requested you halt the progress of the flotilla until such time as a decision is reached by the Council concerning a meeting."

"Any change in my orders, Admiral?" Tatia asked.

"None, Captain, proceed to Méridien as planned," Alex responded.

"Excellent, Admiral," Tatia replied, displaying a wolfish grin.

The Administrator's message was repeated several more times over the course of the next two days, but hours after the last message was received, the flotilla began dropping velocity to enter Méridien's orbit.

-31-

Despite their arrival at Méridien, the flotilla still had not received a response from the Council. Comms continued to pour in for Alex and Renée. Julien acknowledged their receipt, and the Co-Leaders remained silent.

After a third day waiting in orbit, Alex decided he'd had enough. <Julien.>

<Yes, Admiral?>

<Put your crystals to work and find a way to get me in front of a Council meeting … and Julien?>

<Yes, Admiral?> Julien replied.

<I don't care how you do it,> Alex replied.

Julien launched joyfully into a comm conference with the SADEs. Not all of them were enthusiastic participants, but the core—Cordelia, Z, and Mutter—had no problem with a no-holds-barred approach to dealing with the Council. The SADEs were not privy to the Council Administrator's secure communications, but they did have access to a wealth of mundane data throughout the planet.

It was Z who volunteered a scheme to monitor the Council Leaders' locations at all times. The plan was to identify when all members, on the same day, commed for transport to the Council Chambers. It was common knowledge that once the Council convened, they would meet for an entire day. It wouldn't provide Alex much notice, but it was the only workable plan they could devise.

Alex staged the personnel he required for the Council meeting aboard the *Rêveur*. The group was up every morning and ready to travel by 6 hours. After seven days, Julien signaled Alex at 5.15 hours that the Council members were ordering transport destined for Confederation Hall, the site of the Council Chambers.

Hours later, the *Outward Bound* was dropping speed for a landing at one of Méridien's premier shuttle terminals. It was the closest location to Confederation Hall, although still twelve kilometers away. Captain Manet had received repeated refusals from the terminal's controller for access to the landing ways. It occurred to Edouard to declare an emergency, but his Méridien training wouldn't allow the lie to pass his lips or, in this case, his thoughts. Instead he warned the controller that the *Outward Bound* was landing, and it would be unsafe not to clear his path.

The deciding point for the terminal manager, who chose to override his controller, was that telemetry indicated the huge shuttle was accompanied by three flights of what the Méridiens had learned were the Admiral's war shuttles … the Daggers. The manager feared for the lives of the people within the terminal, not knowing what unwarranted actions the Admiral might take.

Once the *Outward Bound* touched down, Sheila ordered the Daggers to fly cover over the terminal. The terminal manager, observing the actions of the Admiral's war shuttles, curtailed all flights out of his terminal and diverted all incoming traffic to other terminals.

Alex and company exited the shuttle, and Tatia left six crew members, armed with plasma rifles, to guard their ship. Every Méridien in the group thought the actions were unnecessary, and that included the flights of Daggers over the terminal's airspace, but Alex's determined look and his march toward the terminal brooked no comments or questions.

On entering the terminal, Renée guided the group to the underground transport cars. She signaled the transport controller but failed to receive a response. "Admiral, I have no access by which to call us a vehicle," Renée said.

"Apparently I still do, Ser," Eric replied.

Just then, a transport car, large enough to manage the group, slid to a stop in front of them. Its double doors hissed quietly open. Everyone climbed aboard, and when Eric signaled their destination, their transport swiftly complied.

The New Terrans were mesmerized by the hive of activity in the underground transport tunnels, all brightly lit. Hundreds of vehicles of every size whipped past one another, not on rails or guides of any sort, but by virtue of the controllers signaling one another and managing paths. It was a marvel of engineering.

The group's transport decelerated to stop at a platform, and Eric led the way from the underground transport level to the main concourse of Confederation Hall. When they exited the final lift, Eric indicated the corridor in front of them. "After you, Admiral," he said.

While Tomas and Eric had waited aboard the *Rêveur* for word from the SADEs of the Council's meeting, Tomas had said, "Eric, I have given this meeting a great deal of thought, and I have discovered that I could wish for no greater reward for services rendered to my people than to be present at the moment the Council meets the Admiral."

Eric had thought over Tomas's words for two days before he discovered he felt the same way. Once Eric recognized that his fears of confronting the Council as an ex-Leader had melted away, his emotional conversion to a Director of House Alexander was complete.

Alex led his entourage down the Hall's wide, ethereal corridor. The floors effused soft changing colors in the afternoon sunlight that streamed through tall windows along one side of the corridor. Light from the ceiling, over ten meters up, echoed the colors of sunlight filtered by the windows. Some Méridiens sought to gain the Admiral's attention, but Alex wasn't interested; others crowded the corridor walls to give the Admiral and his people plenty of space. Rounding the corridor's curved corner, they were approaching a group of Méridiens coming down the corridor. Renée increased her stride to meet them, outdistancing Alex.

<Albert,> Renée sent privately to Alex.

Alain had kept pace with Renée, but when Alex heard her single word, he signaled Étienne forward. Alex took stock of the middle-aged man who led the oncoming group. He calculated Albert was well past his century mark as the two siblings drew closer to each other.

Renée could tell her brother did not immediately recognize her. Albert de Guirnon was leading his own entourage toward the Council Chambers, and he seemed oblivious to who was advancing toward him. Finally, recognition dawned on Albert's face, and he hesitated briefly before opening his arms in welcome.

Emotions warred within Renée to the extent that she hardly recognized herself. *Where is the polite, controlled, young Méridien woman that Alex rescued?* Renée wondered. She exchanged a cordial, traditional House greeting with her brother, kissing each of his cheeks. Then she stepped back and delivered a bone-jarring slap to Albert's face.

Albert de Guirnon stood there, rooted in place. His mouth hung open, and his hand held his reddening cheek. His entire entourage looked to be in shock as well. An attack by a fellow Méridien, especially a House sibling, was inconceivable.

Even Albert's two escorts had been caught unawares. Initially they had focused on the twins escorting the Méridien woman. Then their eyes had strayed to the oncoming mass of humanity known to them as "the Admiral."

<Admiral, my love,> Renée sent to both Alex and Albert, acid dripping in her thoughts, <this poor excuse for a Méridien is my brother, Albert.>

<Ser de Guirnon,> replied Alex, <greetings.> He touched his right hand to his heart and dipped his head.

Albert quickly gathered himself and returned the polite greeting.

But Alex wasn't missing the opportunity to share a thought with the brother. <I'm devastated, Ser,> Alex sent, <that we were unable to accommodate your nefarious plot to abscond with our ship. And come to think on it, I wouldn't have thought a civilized human and a House Leader at that would have been capable of such deviousness. But perhaps you're just an Independent in the making.>

Alex led his group past Albert, who was left staring at their backs, incredulous at the insults he had received, verbally and physically. Alex and his group headed toward the Council Chambers' Supplicants Hall. While Alex was still in Albert's line of sight, he couldn't resist the temptation to reach behind Renée to pat her rear.

<Now you choose to be publicly demonstrative,> Renée sent to Alex. <It is well you are loved or you would be joining my brother in disfavor.> Renée's implant received the sound of a long, drawn-out, exaggerated kiss,

and she laughed raucously. *Let my brother think on that as he will*, she thought.

The tall, ornate Council Chambers doors at the end of the Supplicants Hall were closed. The Administrator sat outside the doors in an enclosure that echoed the design of the floors and walls. Alex saw many well-dressed Méridien supplicants who waited to be called into Chambers on their business, sitting in chairs that lined the walls and comfortably conformed to their bodies.

Alex strode past the supplicants to the midpoint of the twin doors and stood waiting, never turning his head.

Renée found the shock on the Administrator's face a thing of beauty. As a daughter who more than once accompanied her father to Council Chambers on House business, she had recalled the Administrator, who had been posted at that time, as an enormously prestigious personage, deserving of respect. Now Renée wondered how she could have been so foolish. This Administrator was pompous, exuding an air of superiority. That was until he was caught staring slack-jawed at the Admiral, who stood waiting for the doors to open.

The Administrator hurriedly scrolled down his appointment log and confirmed that the Admiral had received no Council response to his request for an appointment. Yet here the man stood. The Administrator searched his implant for a protocol to deal with an unexpected supplicant and found none. The event was unheard of.

What made matters worse for the poor Méridien was that the Admiral hadn't come alone. Appointments were granted to a single person. Occasionally an exception was made for a House sibling or child. It had always been so. Adding a final insult, the Admiral had not spoken to him. Incredibly the giant New Terran was ignoring him, standing at the door as if he expected them to open because he was here.

The Administrator drew breath to announce his displeasure, something he couldn't recall ever having had to do in his position, when his implant security protocols evaporated like water on a hot day. He received a single word: <Open>. The word reverberated in his head, pulsing, demanding. The Administrator attempted to block the signal, but the harder he tried, the stronger the pulse became. Sweat broke out on his brow. He felt nauseous, and bile rose in his throat. Finally, fear overcame the Administrator's decades of training, and he signaled the Chambers' doors open. The familiar hiss of the ornate doors sliding aside was accompanied by the abrupt sensation of the pressure disappearing in his head, and he near wept with relief.

* * *

Prior to the Council meeting, Alex had set a portion of his plan in play with Julien. It sprang from statements Eric had uttered during their discussion about the upcoming Council meeting. Eric had said, "The people follow the directives of our Council, but they are not the Council." Alex had wondered what Méridiens would make of what he had to say to the Council.

As the Council Chambers' doors opened, Alex linked with Julien to record his conversation with the Council. In turn, Julien linked to Cordelia, Z, and Mutter. Cordelia sent her broadcast to the FTL station to forward to all other Confederation colonies. Mutter forwarded her signal to thousands of ship SADEs within the system, and Z relayed his signal to the Méridien comm SADEs who were responsible for distribution of House announcements to the population at large. Julien had affixed House Alexander's distribute-code to ensure the SADEs and FTL Station would relay the signal.

The Council Chambers had been designed to intimidate. Hundreds of Council members sat in rows high above the floor where supplicants stood. No chair was present to accommodate the supplicant. Alex had learned from Renée that only House Leaders sat on the Council, and they had gained their position by election—an election where only House Leaders voted.

The Méridien who had been standing before the Council looked with confusion at the Council Leader. When no instructions were forthcoming, he backed out of Alex's way.

Council Leader Mahima Ganesh, a matron who had outlived two partners, stared disdainfully at Alex and said, "You have not been summoned here, Admiral. The Council will not hear your request. You and your people will leave."

"Council Members," Alex said, projecting his voice to be heard throughout the chambers. "I didn't come here to make a request or to listen to you. I have words to deliver to you."

"Leave, Admiral," Mahima repeated, "or I will disband the Council and you will have no audience for your words."

"That is not my wish, Leader Ganesh," Alex replied, cold anger underlining his words.

Mahima rose from her chair and instantly sat back down. She struggled to stand and found she wasn't in control of her limbs.

"You will hear my words, Leader Ganesh. Then and only then will I release you."

The House Leaders were incredulous as they watched their Council Leader struggle to stand. Because she couldn't move, they didn't dare try. Where many of the Leaders had glared at the huge New Terran in contempt, incredulity, or anger, most now stared at him in fear.

"I presume you have reviewed Julien's message of the events in the Arnos system," Alex said. "The menace of the Nua'll, the giant sphere, is gone. Your thanks should go to the Swei Swee, who were enslaved by the Nua'll and forced to drive the silver ships. Under our influence, those slaves chose to revolt. As a reward for their actions against the Nua'll, which cost them many lives, adults and hatchlings, I have given them Libre."

The intake of hundreds of breaths was a distinct sound in the chambers. Eric and Tomas shared grins. This was some of what they had hoped to witness, and it was proving to be well worth it.

"I forbid Méridien ships to enter the Arnos system without my express permission or the permission of my people's future leaders," Alex announced.

Gino Diamanté, Leader of House Diamanté, tentatively raised a hand.

"Yes, Leader Diamanté?" Alex allowed.

"If I may, Admiral, would you clarify who you mean by 'your people'? Do you speak of New Terrans?"

"These are my people," Alex replied. He sent images from his databases to the Leaders … of Fiona, Gregorio, Sawalie, Heinrich, Bobbie, Jase, Sean, Hatsuto, and the other lost pilots, of his Méridien and New Terran crew, of the Independents, of the House Bergfalk personnel, of his SADEs, and of his pioneers. "And those you see standing with me today … Ser de Guirnon, Senior Captain Tachenko, Captain Manet, Director Monti, Director Stroheim, and Étienne and Alain de Long," Alex added.

"Th-Thank you, Admiral, for … for clarifying that for us," Gino Diamanté stammered.

The Admiral's response was not the expected answer. The Council's SADE had summarized for the Leaders that the Admiral's images detailed a quarter of a million people, primarily from the Confederation, that he now claimed as his people. That most were Independents wasn't their concern; that the Admiral was co-opting Méridiens was their concern.

Albert de Guirnon chose that moment to attempt to repay the affront he had received from his sister. "Council Leader, there is still a matter of the *Rêveur*. Our House lays claim to the ship."

"You can't have the *Rêveur*, Albert," Alex replied first, ignoring the man's title. "Méridien salvage law supports our claim. More importantly, it is the vessel of my friend, and you can't have him."

The latter statement left the Council members confused, but the smiles and grins of the Admiral's people told the Leaders that the Admiral's statement wasn't a mystery to them.

Mahima Ganesh stopped struggling. When she did, control returned to her legs. She eyed the Admiral with suspicion. Known for having one of the keenest Méridien minds, Mahima began to reconsider what she should be asking the New Terran Leader.

"Have you said all you came to say, Admiral?" Mahima asked.

"Not quite, Council Leader," Alex replied. "You will direct all Méridien ships to stay out of the Arnos system. I will punish any transgression."

The Council members were aghast at Alex's proclamation, and they weren't the only ones, but Alex's people, despite their thoughts, kept neutral expressions on their face.

"In addition, Leaders," Alex continued, "know that you have not only lost Arnos, but you have lost Hellébore. That system, I take for my people."

"Admiral, you have no right to do this," Mahima stated, surprised to find herself on her feet.

"Let's discuss that, Leader Ganesh," Alex replied calmly. "You lost six colonies to the Nua'll. My people saved the remaining Confederation colonies, including Méridien. What price would you place on your home world and your remaining colonies?"

Alex watched the Leaders quietly focus on their implants, discussing Alex's question.

"The Council did not request this service from you," Mahima finally replied. "Your claim has no foundation."

Alex looked at Renée and grinned. She had accurately predicted Mahima's response.

"Because I'm feeling generous today, Leader Ganesh and Council members, let me share something with you," Alex said, spreading his arms in a magnanimous gesture. <Julien,> Alex sent.

Julien streamed Cordelia's telemetry of the comm burst from the dying Nua'll ship to Alex and the SADEs, who forwarded it to the entire Confederation. Simultaneously Alex linked to the Leaders' implants, wiping aside their security protocols and sharing the signal, which would mean little to them.

"Once your comm engineers and SADEs have analyzed that signal," Alex said, "they will come to the conclusion that your advanced Méridien technology could not have created it. That's because the Nua'll ship sent it just before it was destroyed. My SADEs tell me the signal was aimed in the general direction of Hellébore, from where the Nua'll originated. We surmise that the Nua'll sent a distress signal home."

Alex allowed the Leaders time to digest that thought. Then he took a few steps closer to the front rows and raised his voice as if he was addressing a large crowd, saying, "So I ask you, Leaders of the Confederation, whom would you prefer settle your farthest known system from where the Nua'll first arrived … your people, who run from their own shadows, or my people, who have the courage to confront their enemies?"

Comms flew between the Council members. Some members urged no compromise with the Admiral, saying it would set a dangerous precedent. The majority disagreed. They had lost family, friends, and associates on the six colonies destroyed by the Nua'll. If there was even a remote chance that a second monster ship would emerge from the deep dark via the Hellébore system, they didn't want Méridien lives at risk, and if the Admiral wanted to risk his people, so much the better.

"Admiral Racine, the will of the Council is to agree to your usurpation of Hellébore," Mahima announced, "but under several conditions."

"You misunderstand me, Council Leader Ganesh," Alex replied. "I didn't come here today to negotiate. My people will be occupying Hellébore, and it will not be a part of the Confederation or New Terra. It will be an independent world." Alex smiled to himself at the thought of calling their new world "independent."

"Admiral," Albert said, "Cetus has been devastated. Your people will starve and your new society will fail. Then what will become of your people?"

"Ser Albert de Guirnon," Alex replied, "if you believe Cetus is devastated then you won't begrudge us the Hellébore system. But we won't fail—not with the technology we will soon have to trade."

Alex observed the knowing smiles spread across the faces of many of the Council members. *You are so confident we can't match your vaulted Méridien technology*, Alex thought.

One Council member, though, was not so sure. "Admiral," Gino Diamanté said and raised a tentative hand a second time.

Alex smiled at the one individual who had the courage to ask questions. "Yes, Leader Diamanté," Alex said and nodded graciously to him.

"Admiral, would you care to share some details of the technology that you might perfect?" Gino asked, leaning forward onto his row's table.

"You might have noticed, Ser," Alex replied, "that the silver ships move without any visible exhaust trail. We've learned they're powered by a form of gravity drive. Within a year, we intend to duplicate their technology, building and selling gravity-driven shuttles and other craft."

"Impossible!" shouted Albert de Guirnon as he jumped up from his chair. Then he slowly sat back down, embarrassed by his outburst.

The atmosphere in the chambers changed visibly. Members who had been leaning back in their chairs with annoyed faces now began sitting up. Curiosity began replacing disinterest and anger.

<Perhaps my people are more business-minded than I had perceived,> Renée sent to Alex.

"We are not unaware of your people's capability to withhold the truth, even to mislead others with your facts, Admiral," Mahima said.

"Council Leader Ganesh—" Tomas began before he was cut off.

"Silence!" Mahima said. "This Council still regards you as an Independent, Ser Monti. Therefore, you have no right to speak in our Council Chambers."

Anger burned through Alex. His fists clenched; his blood pounded. The energy from his implant brought the Council Leader to a halt. She cried out as she grabbed the sides of her head with both hands.

Renée stepped to Alex's side, pulling on his arm. <Careful, Alex,> she sent.

Alex cut his implant stream and Mahima's relief was evident as she sagged forward on the table. "Never speak to one of my people in that manner again, woman," Alex ground out through clenched jaws. "And that goes for any of you and your people. I don't care what you think of us. You will show each and every one of us the same courtesy you would extend to a fellow House Leader." Alex eyed the members slowly, daring anyone to contradict his challenge.

"Now," Alex said, turning to Tomas and indicating the audience, "Ser Monti, please continue with what you wanted to say to these good people."

Tomas glanced between Alex and the rows of Leaders he faced. When Alex smiled at him, he grinned back, straightened his shoulders, and took a couple of steps forward.

"Thank you, Admiral," Tomas said, nodding toward Alex. "Your graciousness is appreciated." Turning to his audience, Tomas continued. "Sers, I was about to say that the Admiral is telling you the truth. I hold two silver ships in one of the *Freedom*'s bays. Already, teams of our engineers have been poring over these two specimens and are convinced that we can replicate them. It is only a matter of time before we understand the technology and can produce variations for vessels other than shuttles."

Not wishing to miss his chance to speak his own mind to the Confederation's much-vaunted Council, Eric stepped forward as well. "As another Director of House Alexander," he said, nodding to Tomas, who quite genially returned the pleasantry, "I would go so far as to say that those of you who are interested in purchasing or trading for shuttles that cost little to operate, are noiseless, and can launch and travel the system without using reaction mass, should contact the Admiral's friend aboard the *Rêveur*."

"Your pardon, Director Stroheim," Gino Diamanté asked politely. "Who is this friend we should address if we are interested in this technology?

"Why, Leader Diamanté," Eric replied, relishing the moment, "that would be the *Rêveur*'s SADE, Julien."

It took Gino Diamanté only a few moments process Eric's response. He was well-known among the Council members for his quick mind, and he rapidly assimilated what he had just learned—the Admiral was a leader who demanded courtesy for every one of his people, a people who possessed exciting new technology, and he was a man who called his SADE "friend."

"Thank you, Director Stroheim," Diamanté replied, dipping his head and applying hand to heart.

Eric recognized the gesture for what it was and replied in kind, Leader to Leader. He stepped back with Tomas to stand behind Alex.

"Council Members," Alex said, "I have one more item to impart before we leave. Our new colony will be open to any individuals and their families whom you declare as Independents. There will be no need to isolate them. They will always be welcome with us."

Tomas could barely contain himself. He grinned as he finally understood the true concept of Terese's medicinal application. If they weren't in Council Chambers, Tomas would have hugged the Admiral with all the strength he could muster.

More than one Council member seemed incensed over Alex's proposal, but they drew on their Méridien training to maintain their composure, not least because they had no desire to insult the huge New Terran and share in whatever punishment Leader Ganesh had already received.

"In the future," Alex continued, "we will arrange for their transportation to our colony; you need only indicate who and where they are. We will communicate with them to ensure they wish to join us and make arrangements for their retrieval, if they so desire."

<Is there anything else that needs to be said?> Alex sent privately to his group.

<Yes, Admiral,> Tomas replied then stepped forward again.

"Council Leaders," Tomas said, "I have a message for you from our people … specifically all those you branded as Independents. It is this: We are no longer your outcasts. We are free, free to do as we will, to make our way in this universe. Give us your respect and you can share in our society—do not and that will be your loss, not ours."

Tomas turned to walk back in line and paused to give Alex a Leader's greeting, which Alex returned.

"Sers," Alex said to the members, delivering a graceful nod of his head, "I wish you a fortunate day."

Alex turned and strode from the meeting, and his people fell in behind him.

On their way out, Eric sent a private comm to Tomas: <Ser, was it everything you hoped it would be?>

Tomas gave Eric a wry smile. <It was all I could have wished for, Eric, and more. In the past annual, I have found three occasions to celebrate as never before. I have helped my people escape to freedom, I have met a wonderful woman, and I have stood in Council Chambers as an equal to its members.> He paused and added, <Whether they liked it or not.> Then his smile widened into an earsplitting grin.

-32-

Alex intended to get off the planet as soon as possible, but Renée had another idea. When the group gained the transport level beneath Confederation Hall, Renée sent an address to Eric for the transport's controller and informed Alex that a slight detour was in order. In turn, Alex signaled Julien, Sheila, and the *Outward Bound*'s security team of the delay. He asked Renée where they were going, but she replied that it was a surprise.

Their transport journey lasted nearly a quarter-hour, and as the groups took lifts back to the surface, Alex was surprised to discover they had covered a distance of 316 kilometers … 1,231 kilometers per hour, his app calculated. *And that achieved by way of personal transport*, Alex thought.

Near the surface, Renée stopped at a private lift and signaled for access, but the lift failed to respond. She shook her head in disgust and turned toward a public lift to the surface. They exited into bright sunlight, and the New Terrans found themselves in a surreal place. To their left was a megalopolis. Sky-towers stretched up into the clouds, and buildings covered every meter of the surface. There was no space for a pedestrian to walk.

In sharp contrast to the wall of structures, a huge private residence, from a much earlier period in Méridien's history, stretched out along their right. Renée led them to a gated entrance, where she signaled the gates to open—only to fail again. She grabbed the ornate gates, dejectedly laying her head on her hands.

<Julien?> Alex asked.

<My apologies, Admiral,> Julien replied. <The House SADE who controls the grounds has directives to ensure Ser has no access.>

Alex eyed the more than two-meter-high wall protecting the grounds of the residence and, recalling the Méridiens' penchant for ensuring the safety of their citizens, decided a frontal approach was a safe maneuver.

"People, stay put. Ser and I will be just a few moments." Then Alex walked over to the wall, reached up to the top, and vaulted on to its meter-wide cap. "Captain Tachenko, if you will," Alex said, nodding to Renée, who had followed him over to the wall and stood looking up at him.

Before Renée could puzzle out Alex's meaning, she felt the powerful hands of Tatia enclose her waist and launch her up to Alex, who caught her and lowered her to the ground on the other side.

Alex, jumping down beside Renée, discovered he had stepped back into a centuries' old period. Where the outer edge of the wall bordered a continuous coating of artificial, surface material, Alex's boots were thirty centimeters deep in lush, colorful grasses. Small trees and shrubs dotted the landscaping, and a walkway led from the gates to the imposing three-story home that was sited over 300 meters away. Alex thought it ironic that the walkway led to gates that no longer had purpose. He ran after Renée, who had begun walking purposefully along the walkway toward the residence. Alex had several questions for Renée, but she didn't appear to be in a talkative move. The cancellation of her access to her ancestral home seemed to have ended her relationship with her home world.

The walkway curved gracefully toward the residence, and as they rounded a gentle curve lined with what appeared to be fruit trees, Renée came to a sudden halt and planted her hands on her hips. Alex, who had been enjoying the landscaping, stopped hard to prevent running over Renée. He found her staring at a larger-than-life-sized statue of an Earth colonist atop a carved stone base. The man was posed simply, gazing toward the horizon, but his face and stance suggested confidence, capable of overcoming all obstacles.

"This is House de Guirnon," Renée said. "And he," she said, pointing to the statue, "was my Ancient for my entire life until my fateful voyage to the Cetus Colony."

Alex recalled their initial meeting on the *Rêveur*'s bridge … his first face-to-face view of his Méridien cousins. Renée had called him an "Ancient," and Julien had explained that Renée had not meant "old."

"Quite the personage to live up to," Alex said, gazing up at the statue.

"Ah, no, my love," Renée replied and took Alex's arm. "While this man must have been an intrepid Earther to leave his home and captain a colony ship to the stars, we have already begun a journey as difficult, if not more so, than his. Besides," she said, turning to face Alex and pressing her chest to his, "he is made of metal alloy, and I much prefer this one of flesh and blood." She kissed Alex with all the passion she felt for the man, who had redirected her life in a manner she could have never imagined, yet suited her as if it had been laser-measured.

Alex held Renée while the two gazed at the statue of the Ancient, House de Guirnon, and the expansive grounds until he felt her draw a deep breath and release it in a sigh. It was time to go. At the wall, Alex signaled Tatia, who easily vaulted to the top. Unfortunately Alex did not have Tatia's vast experience managing the weight of opponents when he threw Renée up to Tatia. His excessive efforts led to Tatia snatching a squealing Renée as she sailed a good meter above Tatia's head.

Oops, Alex thought.

After Tatia lowered Renée down on the other side of the wall, she turned a baleful instructor's eye on Alex, who offered her an apologetic shrug.

* * *

Eric led the way back down to the transport tunnels and called a car. A half-hour later, the group was entering the terminal's main lobby. The Terminal Manager was standing defiantly in front of the exit to the landing ways, with his arms crossed firmly across his chest and a scowl on his face. Alex stopped short of the man to allow him his moment to vent.

"Your behavior has been outrageous, Admiral. I don't care whether you are New Terran or Méridien. This is conduct unbecoming any human. I will not tolerate this!" the upset manager spouted.

A slow grin spread across Alex's face. "Well, Ser, if that's the way you feel about it, I will take my shuttle and my Daggers and leave."

As the indignant Méridien stepped aside, he delivered a final note, saying, "That is the least that you can do, Ser, and next time, follow the established protocols!"

<There's just no pleasing some people,> Tatia sent to the group, which earned her a round of chuckles as they walked toward the *Outward Bound*.

In a short time, the armed shuttle was hurtling spaceward with the Daggers as escorts. Its first stop was the *Freedom*, where Alex, Tomas, and Eric exited before the shuttle returned to the *Rêveur*. Alex signaled Cordelia for an update on Mickey's location, since the city-ship's size prevented him from finding the engineer's implant.

<Greetings, Admiral,> Cordelia responded. <Welcome aboard. At the moment, Chief Engineer Brandon is in a corridor, traversing between his two bays.>

<Two bays?> Alex repeated.

<Yes, Admiral,> Cordelia replied. <At Ser Brandon's request, all GEN-2 and GEN-3 machines were transferred from the *Money Maker* to a second bay to begin parts fabrication.

Mickey is making parts for a silver ship? Alex thought, incredulous at his engineer's construction pace. Then another idea occurred to Alex to explain Mickey's energetic surge. After the defeat of the Nua'll, Pia had asked permission to transfer to the *Freedom*. His approval had earned him a hug, which lasted so long as to have Renée clearing her throat. Pia had responded that her transfer would take her out of the Admiral's orbit for the near future, so she was stocking up on a healthy supply of Terese's recommended medicinal remedy. To which Renée had replied that Pia had her own supply of New Terran medication. Pia had laughed, hugged Renée, and left to join Mickey and her family aboard the *Freedom*.

So, Mickey, you're receiving a generous supply of Méridien medication, Alex thought.

<Admiral, Mickey has entered the production bay, which houses your GEN machines. I will direct you,> Cordelia sent.

<Thank you, Cordelia,> Alex replied. <One minor point, Cordelia. These are not *my* GEN machines; they are *our* GEN machines.>

<Whom does your pronoun indicate, Admiral?>

<Technically, Cordelia,> Alex replied, <the GEN machines belong to our new government, which will work for the well-being of our people, humans and SADEs.>

Cordelia's response was an intimate whisper in his ear. <You're still a generous man, Admiral.>

Alex smiled to himself. Cordelia was getting good, very good, at her intimate touches. Her whisper had raised the hairs on his neck and elicited a visceral response a great deal lower than his neck. Cordelia had been fascinated by the personal interaction of Alex and Renée. Since she had had little basis for developing her art on this subject, Alex's casual invitation to Cordelia to speak with Renée on the subject of human intimacy had thrown open the door for her. Renée had no qualms about discussing the subject at length, often emphasizing a point by playing a recording of her and Alex. Over time, Cordelia refined her algorithms, using Alex's biometric feedback to measure the efficacy of her experiments to imitate intimate human contact, and she took every opportunity to practice her art on Alex, who had acceded to be her test subject.

When Alex, Tomas, and Eric entered the production bay, they were close enough to track Mickey, but still had to work to get to him. The bay was crowded with GEN machines and work stations. Engineers pored over vid displays of parts, circuits, and crystals, and techs scurried from one location to another, transporting raw material and finished parts. The entire bay's conglomeration of stations and machines surrounded a frame about the size of a silver ship, and Mickey was at the center of it all.

<Mickey,> Alex sent, detecting Mickey fifteen meters away, but the engineer still wasn't visible. <We're on the other side of your construction.>

<Welcome, Admiral and Directors,> sent Mickey as he hurried around the frame and came into view. "What do you think, Admiral?" Mickey said, waving an arm at the silver ship's frame.

"I think you have been inordinately busy, Mickey," Alex said, walking close to the frame to examine its inner structure.

"After watching your performance in front of the Council, Admiral, it's probably a good thing," Mickey replied. "You keep promising everyone we will be successful soon."

"That's because I have so much confidence in you, Mickey," Alex said, clamping a hand on the engineer's shoulder. "Show me what you have."

"We've determined, Admiral, that the Nua'll technology and the Swei Swee shell are not dependent on the makeup of the frame, which allows us to build a traveler frame with standard Méridien bulkhead alloy. We've analyzed every circuit and part in our silver ships, and we're duplicating what parts we can with our GEN machines. But we'll need a planet-based facility to fabricate the grav-drives, energy crystals, and crystal circuits, which will still leave the Swei Swee shell," Mickey said, staring expectantly at Alex.

"I know, Mickey," Alex replied. "The shell is my responsibility, but I'm not ready to implement my plan until I know we're closer to completing the internal structure. Keep at it, Mickey. You'll have a planetside facility very soon."

As Alex and the Directors left Mickey to his work, Tomas asked, "Am I to understand, Admiral, that our Chief Engineer believes he cannot reproduce the shells?"

"That appears to be the consensus, Ser," Alex replied. "Julien and Mickey spent a great deal of time analyzing our first shell. When Julien compared the measurements of that ship with these two new ones, he discovered subtle differences, and he concluded that the shells are one-off creations. We are left to believe that the Swei Swee test a shell as they build it."

"What would they be testing, Admiral?" Eric asked.

"Julien shared the dimensions of all three silver ships with the other SADEs. Cordelia modeled each ship, and the SADEs ran hypothetical tests on them, passing various wavelengths of energy through the shells. They discovered that the energy passing through each shell created harmonics, but not necessarily at the same frequencies."

"So you think the Swei Swee females ensure the shell resonates while they build it," Tomas reasoned.

"But that would confirm, Admiral, that Ser Brandon is correct. Only the Swei Swee can create a shell," Eric said.

"You would be absolutely correct, Director," Alex declared as he entered a lift to return to the *Rêveur*, leaving two puzzled associates in his wake.

"Why do I feel another adventure coming soon, Ser?" Eric asked Tomas after the lift doors had closed on Alex.

* * *

Cordelia signaled Julien that Alex was aboard a shuttle, exiting a bay for the *Rêveur*.

<Admiral,> Julien sent, <all Daggers are aboard. Captains and Commanders report all vessels secure.>

<Pass the word, Julien,> Alex replied, <standard formation. Head us for home.>

<Acknowledged, Admiral. I have a worthy item of note regarding your invitation to the Council.>

<My invitation?> Alex queried, not recalling one.

<Perhaps you meant it as a jest, Admiral, but several Leaders took your invitation seriously to inquire about our technology, specifically gravity-driven shuttles.>

<Interesting, Julien. Who replied?>

In response to his request, Alex heard Leader Gino Diamanté's voice say, <"Honored friend of the Admiral, I'm responding to the Admiral's invitation to learn more of this amazing technology that your people possess….>" Alex continued to listen to Gino's message and several others. More Leaders were interested in doing business with his people than he would have suspected, especially after Leader Ganesh's cold reception in Council Chambers.

We better be successful, Mickey, Alex thought, *or we're going to disappoint a lot of people.*

-33-

The passage to Hellébore was fraught with intrigue, and Alex was both the target of the intrigue and the one most ignorant of the collusion.

While Alex focused on their new world's material infrastructure—fabrication facilities, housing, and an economic base—the people of the flotilla were discussing their new society. The Librans were anxious to choose a new name for their colony. No one wanted to build on the ashes of the old name, and they wished to honor the Admiral by asking him to choose. Unfortunately the direct approach failed. Requesting that Renée inform the Admiral of the people's will resulted in Alex deferring the choice back to the people's will. However, the people were adamant the Admiral choose the name. To break the impasse, Renée consulted the flotilla's "devious one."

The following morning as Renée and Alex enjoyed the refresher together, she informed him that the people had followed his request and settled on two choices for their colony's new name.

"What are their choices?" Alex asked, happy that the decision had been taken off his shoulders.

"They are considering Alexandria and Racine," Renée answered, working with difficulty to keep a straight face. "The people would like to know which one you prefer."

Alex groaned in exasperation. *The harder I wiggle, the deeper I sink*, he thought. He proclaimed to Renée that he needed time to think—in order to stall the decision—but as Alex soon sat at his desk, considering the two names, one face and one voice came to mind. The Librans loved their elders and mourned the loss of the twenty-two hundred they were forced to leave behind.

"Wait," Alex called to Renée, who was exiting the cabin. "We'll call our new home Haraken."

"I will inform the people that the Admiral has an alternative name. I'm sure they will graciously accept. Personally, my love, I rather liked Alexandria," Renée replied and blew Alex a kiss. She strolled down the corridor, a broad smile on her face. The first person she commed was Senior Captain Tachenko, the architect of the subterfuge. <It was as you thought, Commander,> Renée sent. <Faced with two unacceptable choices, he suddenly discovered a third.>

The people were delighted with the Admiral's choice. They were no longer Méridiens or New Terrans. They were Harakens.

* * *

The next question the people sought to resolve was what form of society they would create. Here, they consulted the one person who knew both worlds, their Co-Leader, Ser de Guirnon.

Renée offered the people this advice: <I believe each culture has substance to offer us. We exist today because of the generosity of a New Terran President and his Assembly. We might honor them by patterning our government after theirs, electing members from our society, and foregoing being ruled by a Council whose members are born to position. However, I have seen that uninhibited independence creates the potential for people to embrace the dark side of their nature without others being aware of their perversions. I believe this can be avoided by requiring all Haraken residents acquire an implant after the age of consent. Visitors could be excused for a period of time, but that period must be cumulative, so that they may not leave and return, each time staying less than the law required. And in this regard, implants would apply only to humans, in case the Admiral collects other abandoned intelligences to add to our world.>

Later, Tomas took a shuttle to visit Renée aboard the *Rêveur* and deliver the glad tidings that consensus had been reached. The people favored an elected government of an Assembly and President, and they chose Alex as the first President of Haraken. Tomas was surprised that Renée did not appear to welcome the news as he had expected.

"My apologies, Director Monti, that I do not show an appropriate appreciation for your announcement," Renée replied. "Now I must consider the manner in which I will inform the Admiral of the ill news."

As Tomas watched Renée walk away, he sympathized with her. If Ser considered the consensus to be bad tidings, he would not want to be the one delivering it to the Admiral.

Renée chose to wait until after evening meal once she and Alex were alone in their cabin. She took the added step of inviting him into the refresher, seating him on the shallow bench, and wiping him down with a cloth, massaging his tight muscles. She kept working until Alex closed his eyes, relaxing into her ministrations.

Later, when they were nestled together on the lounge, Renée broached the subject. "Alex, a consensus has been reached," she said quietly.

"I didn't know a question had been asked," Alex replied, stroking Renée's hair.

"The people have chosen to accept the concept of an elected Assembly and President," Renée announced.

"I'm pleased," Alex replied. "It must have been difficult for the Librans to forgo their society. Then again, I suppose their society did that to them first. We'll need to hold nominations and have the people elect a President."

Renée sat up beside Alex and studied the far wall rather than look Alex in the eye. "The people have already considered this and reached a consensus."

Alex gently pulled Renée's chin toward him. Her eyes were sympathetic. Then Alex intuited Renée's unstated message. He stood up in agitation and began pacing back and forth. "No, no, no," he kept repeating.

Renée stepped in front of Alex to stop his pacing, "I'm sorry, President Racine," she said and threw her arms around Alex's neck in a fierce embrace. "There is one very bright note in this, Alex," she whispered into his ear.

The thought briefly occurred to Alex that Cordelia could never match Renée's whisper. "What would that be?" he asked dejectedly.

Wearing a sheer wrap, Renée languidly pressed the full length of her body against him and said, “I understand I may be called the ‘First Lady.’ Is this not even better than ‘House Co-Leader’?”

Alex couldn’t think of a thing to say in reply.

Renée nuzzled Alex’s neck, murmuring again in his ear, “What is the next level above First Lady?”

When Alex jerked away from her, his eyes narrowing, she squealed and raced for their sleeping quarters with Alex hot on her heels.

* * *

In the early morning, Alex rose, donned a robe, and crept into the salon while Renée slept on. Drawing a cup of thé, he sat down at his desk, grateful for the brewer Renée had installed in the cabin. When he had asked her why a meal dispenser couldn’t be added, Renée had quipped that she would not dare deprive the people of the pleasure of watching their Admiral eat.

Alex wasn’t laughing at the memory. Instead he was feeling guilty. Last night, with the people’s decision still vexing him, he’d linked their implants as they made love. Renée had happily cooperated, feeding back her emotions and desires. The intimate twining of their implants had created a powerful synergy through which Alex vented his frustration.

Sipping his hot thé, Alex’s thoughts dwelt on his new position. By nature, he was a pragmatic man. As President, he couldn’t be the Admiral, but his people would still require a military leader. *Looks like I won’t be the only one booted upstairs*, Alex thought and smiled to himself for the first time since waking. He considered his next steps, which would include forming an Assembly and drafting a constitution. The latter subject would mean defining the President’s term of office. Alex decided to look on the bright side. *One term ... just one term. I can do this*, he thought.

Alex was drawing a second cup of thé when he heard Renée rise and head to the refresher. She was humming, and not softly. *Apparently I’m the only one feeling guilty this morning*, Alex thought, a wry smile twisting his lips. From his archives, Alex pulled up the list of initial actions he had prepared for their world's first leader. The irony that the list now belonged to him did not escape his notice. He reached out to Tatia.

<Congratulations, Mr. President,> Tatia replied.

Since Tatia's remark was tongue in cheek, Alex chose to reciprocate, sending, <Thank you kindly, Admiral Tachenko.>

Tatia's response was slow in coming, and Alex experienced a small thrill at being able to share the frustration.

<I suppose that's only fair, Mr. President,> Tatia finally replied.

<It appears both of us need to order a change of wardrobe from Geneviève,> Alex sent.

After his comm with Tatia, Alex contacted Tomas and Eric. <Sers, I'm temporarily assigning the two of you dual responsibilities while we transition from House Alexander to the government of Haraken.>

<We are excited to work with you, Ser President, in this endeavor,> Tomas said.

<Directors, we must continue to have a standing military,> Alex said. <This will include fabricating fighters and a fighter training school. In addition, we will need explorer ships to enable our people to discover new worlds.>

<After the events of the past century, Admiral—your pardon, President Racine,> Eric replied, <no one will doubt the need to employ force to protect our people.>

<We must elect or appoint our first Assembly members,> Alex continued. <Considering the Librans' preference for consensus, I'll leave it to you two to generate the means by which we obtain our first Assembly members. They should represent the span of our people, including our pioneers. They will be responsible for creating Haraken's constitution, which I will insist include the rights of SADEs and any other intelligent species that may inhabit our worlds. Let it be known that each and every SADE in this flotilla is, as of this moment, a full citizen of Haraken.>

After Tomas's decades of Libran confinement, his thoughts had been focused on his newfound freedom, Terese, of course, and more recently, the grav-driven shuttles. Now he found himself listening to his new

President describe a future where Harakens existed side by side with aliens and lived on multiple worlds, despite the fact that their people had not yet settled their first colony. *Keep that young man with the four stars on his collar close to you,* Tomas recalled Fiona Haraken essentially saying.

<Lastly, Directors, we must create a judicial system that fairly considers all citizens and visitors,> Alex continued. <Recognize that our actions have established ourselves as a refuge for the independent-minded. We can expect immigrants from the Confederation, New Terra, and beyond. A fair judicial system will be required to protect our people and prosecute the individuals—citizens and outsiders—who break our laws.>

Silence greeted Alex's statements. His Directors hadn't yet considered the extent of the challenges they faced in creating a new society.

<First things first, Tomas and Eric,> Alex sent gently. <I need our Assembly Representatives before we reach Hellébore space.>

* * *

<Julien, I need you, Cordelia, and Z,> Alex sent, sitting with his feet propped up on the desktop.

<Ready, President Racine,> Julien replied.

Alex took a deep breath, letting it out slowly. Each elevation of title had taken him further and further away from his comfort zone. The only thing that kept him going was that good people depended on him, and he needed to ensure their well-being and security before he relinquished his responsibilities.

<Good morning,> Alex sent. <I have a new enterprise for the three of you.>

<We will help in any manner we can, Ser President,> Cordelia replied.

<You three will form the Central Exchange of Haraken,> Alex sent. <It will be an independent bank, and you will charge nominal fees for managing deposits and loan accounts. I can't think of more fair-minded individuals than our SADEs to manage our society's new credit institution.>

<Thank you for the compliment, Mr. President,> Julien returned formally. <Who will receive the fees we collect?>

<The fees accrue in the bank's operational accounts, and after operating expenses are deducted, the profit goes to the bank's Directors,> Alex replied.

<And, Ser President, who will be the Directors?> Cordelia asked.

<Why, Cordelia, you're the Directors,> Alex replied.

<A wonderful idea, Ser President!> Z sent. <Might I ask the potential of this income?>

<That will depend on several things, Z,> Alex said. <In the beginning, it will be moderate but will grow quickly once we deliver our first traveler shuttles. The Haraken government and the companies fabricating the crafts will become key depositors. Eventually our pioneers may transfer their assets to your bank.>

Z could scarcely contain himself at the thought of having the funds to direct his own mobility research. His comm burst to Julien and Cordelia outlined a myriad of potential uses of personal income. Driven by Z's excitement, Julien and Cordelia began to have their own thoughts. Cordelia anticipated practicing her art in facilities that would be visited by the public. Julien was entertaining the notion of both he and Cordelia occupying human forms. New algorithms originated in all three SADEs at lightning speed, postulating alternate futures.

<Are you three agreed?> Alex asked when no one had answered him.

A chorus of enthusiastic responses hit his implant at once.

<Ser President, how does a bank work?> Z asked.

<Julien has done some extensive research on New Terran financial systems,> Alex explained, keeping his thoughts as neutral as possible. Cordelia and Z had focused on readers and relationships, defined by comms, when they assisted Julien at New Terra. Only Julien, in both cases, had tracked the transfers of funds through the financial institutions.

While Alex spoke, Julien was transferring his research at maximum rates, and Cordelia and Z accepted the data without security restrictions—such were the triumvirate's bonds, forged through their efforts to survive the incursion of the Nua'll into the Arnos system.

<In order to open our Exchange, Ser President,> Z said, having already begun reviewing Julien's data, <would we not need an initial depositor or an investor?>

<Quite right, Z,> Alex replied. <I would be both the bank's initial investor and depositor. You will transfer the credits from my New Terran accounts into your bank.>

<Pardon, President Racine, how will our bank value a Haraken credit or, for that matter, exchange with New Terran credits?> Julien asked.

<Julien,> Alex replied, <for the former, I have no idea. For the latter, I would suggest, as Directors of the Central Exchange of Haraken, that you contact President Gonzalez to begin negotiations with her Finance Minister on the subject.>

<But, Ser President,> Z said, his preliminary study finding a fundamental flaw in the logic, <why should the New Terran government assign any value to a foreign colony's credits, especially a colony that has yet to be started?>

<Good point, Z,> Alex replied. <They wouldn't unless they thought it was in their interest.>

<President Gonzalez and some of her Ministers are quite keen to acquire our gravity-driven shuttles and perhaps the technology itself,> Julien replied.

<But, President Racine, we have not proven that we will be able to replicate a gravity drive or a Swei Swee shell,> Cordelia said.

<My fellow SADEs,> Julien sent, <I believe the concept is referred to as "investing.">

<Precisely, Julien,> Alex replied. <First, Cordelia, you'll paint an image of our future to your New Terran financial counterparts. Our successful replication of a traveler shuttle will be the kernel of your enticement. Using our future technology products, especially our gravity-driven ships, you'll bargain for New Terra's valuation of Haraken credits.>

Cordelia remained unconvinced. <Ser President, it appears we're trading on a future that may not develop. Is this not an inaccuracy … a deception?>

Alex was trying to puzzle a way to introduce his Méridien-trained SADEs to the concepts of fair-market speculation without disrupting their ingrained focus on accuracy. Their algorithms operated best with facts not suppositions. <Cordelia, in a world of capitalism, it's called "risk versus reward.">

<But where is the risk for the New Terrans, Ser President?> Cordelia asked. <They may simply devalue our Haraken credits when we fail in our endeavors.>

<There is that possibility,> Alex replied. <That's the risk.>

Z asked, <President Racine, would not this risk entail the loss of your investment if we are unsuccessful and New Terra devalues our credits?>

<Yes,> Alex said, <but that would be the least of our worries, Z. Without a technologically based trade edge, our colony will take many decades to start and will be on a much more humble scale.>

Cordelia reviewed her ethics programming, which was limiting her ability to embrace Alex's concepts. She made some subtle changes to several programs. <I believe I understand, Ser President,> Cordelia sent. <I have read of this in one of Julien's ancient novels. We seek to be prosperous, and we will be urging the New Terrans to "bet" on our skills.>

Cordelia's excitement over her understanding of the concept was infectious, and soon the SADEs were heavily entwined on scenario planning. Deep in their cores, hierarchal steps were reordered at the kernel level. From top to bottom, these steps became—self-preservation, safety of their people, the President's well-being and support, fabrication of the traveler shuttles, New Terran investment, development of their Exchange, Directors' income, mobility research, and finally … true freedom.

<One more point, Sers,> Alex added. <Every SADE in the flotilla must be invited to join you in this venture. All SADEs that choose to participate will share equally in the Exchange.>

It took only ticks of time for the liner and freighter SADEs to realize the value of the opportunity. Each of those SADEs had harbored thoughts of independence and never dared express them.

-34-

During the last day of the flotilla's FTL flight to Hellébore, Alex didn't intend to leave his suite. He rose early that morning, dressed in a simple ship suit, took a seat on the lounge, and connected to Julien, Cordelia, and Z.

Renée allowed Alex to miss morning meal. It was his habit during critical events, and this certainly qualified as an important event—becoming the President of a new world of a quarter-million people with no infrastructure and the unenviable task of duplicating alien technology. However, when midday meal approached and Alex showed no signs of stopping, Renée took matters into her own hand.

<Julien,> she sent, <your attention, please.>

<Yes, Ser, how may I be of service?> Julien replied.

<I request you remove Alex from your conference so he can eat and rest,> Renée replied.

<Your pardon, Ser, but you wish me to tell our President that we are denying him access?>

<I am, Julien. He is denying everyone else access. So you have to disengage his comm.>

Alex's personnel organization model, compiled from the SADEs' databases of bio-IDs, froze in place.

<Julien, the bio-IDs I've requested aren't transferring,> Alex sent. <Let me check my free implant space. We may have to build the organizational model on your crystals.>

<Mr. President,> Julien said, <do you recall that critical moment before the launch of the *Unsere Menschen* when I requested your evacuation plan for the *Rêveur*'s personnel from the city-ship, including yours?>

<Are we there again, Julien?> Alex asked.

<Yes, Mr. President,> Julien replied. <I believe you'll find the First Lady standing in front of you. Ser has a strong desire to share her opinion with you.>

<Later, my friend,> Alex sent and closed his connection.

He opened his eyes, jumped up, and snatched Renée up to twirl her around several times while she uselessly pounded her fists on his shoulders in frustration. Alex set her down and began plastering kisses on her neck and ear.

"Stop that. I wish to be angry with you," Renée declared, attempting to be free of Alex's embrace, with no success whatsoever.

"Okay," Alex replied, continuing to kiss her cheek, nose, and forehead.

"I'm serious, Alex," Renée said.

"Okay," Alex replied between more kisses.

When Alex found her lips, Renée gave in, leaning into the kiss until the thought of a meal as well as her anger dissipated. Suddenly she was whisked up in Alex's arms, and he was running at the cabin door. It barely had time to slide open before they barreled through. Renée laughed in delight as the crew jumped out of their way, and Alex raced down the corridor, repeatedly crying out, "Food, food!"

Renée tucked her legs close to prevent them striking anyone, and returned the smiles and grins of the crew. Through her laughter came the thought that her anger over Alex missing a meal or two seemed petty in contrast to the events of the last year and a half. It was a lesson that seventy years in stasis had taught her, but she occasionally forgot. No matter how long your life span, life was too short not to make the most of every day.

Alex signaled the meal room doors open, stepped though cradling Renée, leaned his head back, and, with all the force he could muster, yelled, "Food!"

The crew in the meal room was caught off guard. A few sought to reciprocate in some fashion and called back timidly, "Food," only to hear Alex repeat his yell. This time, more of the crew, energized by Alex, returned his yell. But Alex wasn't done. He bellowed his cry again, and the crew responded by jumping up, shooting a fist into the air, and shouting as one, "Food!"

Alex set Renée down amid the laughter and shouts, a huge grin on his face. The cheers of the crew were a salve on his worries.

* * *

In the afternoon, Julien announced their impending exit from FTL into the Hellébore system, and a few of the crew reported to Medical for the transition. Afterward, Alex returned to his cabin and took the opportunity to engage the SADEs in launching some additional steps since the flotilla's sub-light speed would allow shuttles to transition between ships.

Alex started a comm to his Directors. <Tomas, Eric, I've decided you will have very different roles in the new government, but you will no longer be leaders.>

<Why should that be, Ser President? We have done so much for the flotilla's people,> Eric said, the pain in his thoughts evident.

<Yes, you have, Eric. But as an ex-Leader of a Méridien House, the people's memory of your former title and history will remind them of the Confederation.>

<But, Ser President, my people and I gave up our House to help the Independents,> Eric said.

<That's true, Eric, and many ex-Bergfalk House members will have leadership roles in the government because of your actions … just not you.>

<Our President's logic is valid, Eric,> Tomas sent, <and because we are both Directors, it is to preserve balance that I, too, should be denied a leadership position. But, Ser President, your announcements often begin with bad tidings. May we hope for something more positive?>

<Oh, yes, Tomas,> Alex sent. <I consider it a great opportunity, but you and Eric can decide for yourself. We will be a new society that will need associations—strong associations. We must foster relations with New Terra and the Confederation on trade relations, currency, mutual defense, and much more. Julien has supplied me with several autobiographies from Terra's history of what were called "ambassadors." These individuals were

appointed by Presidents to be their representatives to other societies. You two will be my Ambassadors.>

<Which of us will go where, Ser President?> Tomas asked.

<That's the challenging question, Tomas,> Alex replied. <Both positions will be difficult jobs for different reasons.>

<I believe the New Terrans will welcome either of us,> Eric said. <That position should be quite easy compared to confronting the Confederation Council.>

<On the other hand, on New Terra, the Ambassador will meet not only with government leaders, but industry leaders and petitioners of all sorts,> Alex replied. <You will deal with subjects that neither of you possess much knowledge about.>

<Have you made a decision, Ser President?> Tomas asked.

<Not yet, Tomas,> Alex replied. <I would like the two of you to read these Terran Ambassador autobiographies over the coming days, as well as watch this documentary vid of New Terra's history. We'll speak again soon as to how we can manage future contacts with these worlds.>

* * *

Early in the evening and before Alex could settle in with the SADEs, Renée told him he had an important appointment to keep. Alex's response was interrupted by the cabin door sliding open.

Terese, Geneviève, and Eloise came through, trailing a small grav-lift piled high with clothes, boots, and accessories.

"New wardrobe, Sers?" Alex asked, producing a giggle from Eloise, who was tickled at the thought her people's leader should confer the respectful adult term on her. "I wouldn't have thought you would have had time to design and produce one set of clothes, much less all this," Alex said, walking over to the grav-lift.

"There are many talents among the people that are still being discovered, Ser President," Geneviève replied. "Among our pioneers, we have found a garment manufacturer, a 'tailor' he calls himself, and his extended family. But these are not New Terran or Méridien fashions. My comm to the tailor, Ser Delacroix, was routed through Cordelia. It was she who offered to design the clothes. If I had not heard it myself, I would never have believed a SADE would beg to be granted a responsibility." As Geneviève dug through the pile, she mumbled, "So many changes." Finding what she wanted, Geneviève offered a set of clothes to Alex. "I am most fond of these, Ser President, and would be pleased to have a preview."

Alex nodded, taking the clothes from Geneviève and carrying them into the sleeping quarters to change.

As the door closed, Eloise turned to Geneviève. "Why did he do that, Ser? Does he not want us to see him in his new clothes?"

"He will return to show us, little one," Renée replied. "It is a New Terran custom."

As if that was all the explanation required, Eloise nodded. If it was the President's custom, who was she to question it?

Alex stepped back through the sleeping quarters' door to stand before his small audience. His jacket resembled a military cut with its short collar and tight fit, but its body length extended to his wrists. On Alex, the cut emphasized his physique. The color was deep purple. Gold buttons decorated the front, featuring raised seals of Haraken designed by Cordelia. The buttons were pure ornament, as the jacket self-sealed. Two smaller buttons sat on each collar's tab with a stylized "H." No other ornament or decoration disturbed the coat, except for the hint of the shirt's short white collar band peeking over the jacket's neckline. The trousers were black with deep purple trim along the trouser legs.

Renée wore a smile that engulfed her face.

Geneviève began to chuckle softly and then covered her mouth to still her sound. "If I may say so, Ser President, I believe that Cordelia, Ser Delacroix, Terese, and I make an excellent design team," Geneviève said.

"I helped too," Eloise piped up.

"Yes, you did, little one," Terese agreed.

Alex was regarding himself in the mirror when Eloise cried out, "Now my idea, Ser President."

Terese laughed at Eloise's enthusiasm and dug into the pile of clothes to pull out a long, heavy garment. Eloise raced over to her to take it, and as she took it in both arms, its length reached to the deck on both sides of her arms. She carried the garment to Alex, who opened it up. It was a beautiful cloak of deep purple. Subtle shoulder tabs displayed the Haraken design in gold, echoing the jacket's buttons. When Alex donned the cloak, it swept almost to the deck, and its collar nestled against his jacket collar, closing with a gold clasp. The cloak added even more dimension to Alex's silhouette. In the mirror, he appeared the size of three Méridiens.

Standing beside Alex, Renée observed the mirror's reflection and softly uttered, "Oh my!"

"Ser President, I have a surprise for you. It's my idea too!" Eloise said.

When Alex turned to look at Eloise, she was standing on the lounge for greater height and gesturing to him. Alex stepped up to her, and Eloise's nimble fingers reached under the top of the clock, near the clasp, and pulled out a transparent tube with nostril plugs.

"I have learned the air of Haraken might challenge our Protector's metabolism. This is to ensure his well-being."

Eloise small fingers carefully placed the tube's end against Alex's nose, and the familiar nanites sealed against his nostrils. Pure oxygen flowed into Alex's chest with his next breath.

Alex turned to show Renée, but Eloise, who had been leaning against him, fell forward. As Alex felt her slip, his hand shot forward, finding an arm slit in the cloak, and scooped Eloise up. He was rewarded with another giggle as Eloise found herself perched on Alex's arm.

When Eloise wrapped her arms around the President's neck for balance, she was reminded of her favorite tree limb, from which she spent hours watching Libre's fauna. That diada tree had been her sanctuary, and the similarity between these two islands of safety sank deep into the young girl's psyche.

Renée watched Alex, who easily balanced a smiling Eloise on one arm while he displayed the oxygen tube to her. The scene squeezed Renée's heart with a fierceness that brought tears to her eyes. Alex was complimenting Eloise on her cleverness, and the child was blushing and chatting happily.

Terese sent a question to Renée. <Worth the seventy years in stasis, Ser?>

Renée looked at Terese, one of her closest associates who had become an even closer friend, and smiled. Terese herself had never looked so content.

<The lost years appear to have been fortunate for both of us, I'm pleased to say,> Renée replied.

* * *

Alex, attired in his new wardrobe, was accompanied by Renée, Tatia, and the twins for the slate of morning meetings that would be held aboard the *Unsere Menschen*. The route from cabin to shuttle bay was peppered with the whistles and applause of old and new crew, the latter having transferred in from the flotilla's other ships.

Alex's quick strides and forward-bent shoulders shifted. His pace slowed, his shoulders straightened, and he extended his arms, bent at the elbows, to Renée and Tatia. Each woman took an arm, and the three walked through *Rêveur*'s wide central corridor in procession, which only increased the volume of the crew members' appreciation.

<Before our jobs get ugly,> Alex sent the two women, <we might as well enjoy it.>

Tatia's fears of her new admiralty position had crowded her mind for much of the last two days. Walking arm in arm with Alex brought a strange sense of calm. *Ah, black space*, she thought. *The worst that can happen is we die. If so, it will be in great company.*

* * *

Aboard the shuttle, Alex sat on the arm of an aisle seat so that he could speak with Alain and Étienne. "You two didn't think that you would miss the onslaught of added responsibilities did you?" Alex said with mock seriousness.

His two escorts grinned back at him. "But, Ser President," Alain said, "you're such an immense target. It requires all our focus to secure you."

Alex heard Tatia's chuckle under her breath, but before he could return fire at Alain, Étienne added, "Then there is your penchant for putting yourself in harm's way, Ser President, when prudent individuals would not venture in the directions you often choose."

"You know one of the good things about being President?" Alex said. "I get the last say." As the grins disappeared from the faces of the twins, Alex added, "You two are now the Directors of Government Security—my Ministers, the Assembly Representatives, and my Ambassadors, our ex-Directors, who will be traveling extensively … keep them all safe and secure."

"We presume that includes you and the First Lady," Étienne said, adding to the list.

"Yes, it does, Sers," Alex said. "Get your house in order now. As we grow, you will find your jobs even more challenging. An independent, open society increases the potential for chaos among certain quarters."

Alex's words reminded everyone of the events at New Terra and the treachery unleashed on them by their adversaries.

-35-

Aboard the *Unsere Menschen* in a large conference room, a group of people assembled and exchanged bio-IDs. While Tomas and Eric were known to everyone, their new responsibilities had not been announced. The others present were the new Assembly Representatives and Alex's recently appointed Ministers.

While they waited for Alex, the Representatives conversed with one another. The people's consensus had winnowed a long list of volunteers down to ten members, but not without help. Implant comms were insufficient to manage the complexity, and the SADEs had stepped in to support the process. In the end, five Independents had been chosen: Bibi Haraken, Guillermo De Laurent, Helena Bartlett, Lina Monti, and Deter Schonberg. To this group of Independents were added Pia Sabine, Robert Dorian, Stanley Peterson, Asu Azasdau, and Katie Racine—a lost Méridien, two New Terran crew members, an ex-Bergfalk associate, and a pioneer.

The four new Ministers had already been in contact and held themselves apart to allow the Representatives an opportunity to get acquainted.

Alex and his people exited their shuttle and made their way through the *Unsere Menschen*'s long corridors and lifts. Aboard this city-ship, Alex was not seen so much as their President, but as the man who had worked feverishly to ensure the launch of their ship. He had been seen running while others walked, and he had worked while most slept. Alex might have been Haraken's first President, but it did not stop the city-ship's people from honoring the man with their greetings and polite touches on his arm or shoulder as he passed.

On reaching the conference room, Alex sought to enter when Tatia stepped in front of him, signaled the door open, stepped inside, and announced, "President Racine and First Lady Ser de Guirnon."

She stepped aside as the room's occupants stood up, and Alex and Renée swept inside. There were several smiles and appreciative nods over Alex's appearance.

"Good morning, everyone," Alex said. "Please be seated. I would ask you to record this meeting. There are several items that you will wish to refer to later. As of today, all of our previous titles and duties no longer exist. We have new jobs." Alex walked to the head of the conference table. "As you can see, I am no longer your Admiral. I'm your President, and I would like to introduce Admiral Tatia Tachenko."

No one had missed the four stars on Tatia's collars. Her House Alexander patch had been replaced by an "H" glyph, which was a stylized letter emblazoned over rings and dots, representing Hellébore's planets. Tatia nodded stiffly to the group. If it weren't for the exquisite fit of the Méridien fabric, she might have tried to blame her stiffness on the uniform.

Alex regarded the new Representatives, pleased by many of the faces he saw. "A great responsibility has been handed to the ten of you, our first Assembly Representatives," he said. "As your President, I will work together with you to weave the framework of our new society." He offered Helena a smile, who nodded graciously at his reference to her work.

It was Lina who was quick to speak her mind. "As our leader, Ser President, is it not your privilege to direct us?"

"No, Ser Monti, it is not," Alex replied. "The Assembly is independent of the President. We share power, if you will, always operating with the best interests of our people in mind. Our first duty will be to draft a constitution that defines the rights of our citizens and our government's organization, including its powers. If our constitution defines a different structure than we have created, we may be out of jobs."

"But, Ser," Bibi said, "have we not chosen you as President for life?"

Bibi's question chilled Alex to the bone. In his implant, he heard Renée's thoughts, <You must be patient, Alex. Teach them. Someday your

job will be done, and we will have each other. This I promise you, my love.>

Alex returned to his role as teacher. "The President's term will be defined by the constitution. Each President will be elected from those who wish to serve."

"Ser President," Asu said, "can you guide us as to the elements of a government that we must consider?"

"Certainly, Captain Azasdau," Alex replied. "To aid you, Julien will provide you with a copy of New Terra's constitution, its government organization, and the powers exercised by the various groups. The purpose of a constitution, elected Representatives, and President is to create an elastic framework that can be adapted to accommodate a changing society."

"Elastic in what manner, Ser President?" Lazlo asked. He was Alex's new Minister of Transportation and would manage Haraken's first terminal and the planet's shuttle flights. Someday that would include Haraken's first orbital station.

"Today, we are all human," Alex said. "But what rights would you allow nonhuman, intelligent entities?"

"Who might they be?" asked Lina, incredulity on her face.

"The flotilla's SADEs, for instance," Alex replied calmly.

"The SADEs have rights, Ser President," Deter stated, confused by Alex's line of reasoning.

"And if those SADEs walked among you in human guise, Ser Schonberg?" Alex asked.

"Your point is well taken, Ser President," Lazlo replied. "It appears our group considers only our present situation, and our President is focused on our world many years from now. Elastic ..." he said, nodding his head in understanding. As Lazlo regarded his colleagues, it dawned on him the value of the three New Terrans. *And Pia as well,* Lazlo thought. *She straddles both worlds.* He was caught staring in thought at Pia when she leveled her cool gray eyes on him and returned his stare. Lazlo offered an apology with a nod of his head.

"What I wish you to do as our Representatives is study the histories of New Terra, the Confederation, and even Earth. There is much to learn from each society. Ours will not be perfect, but we will work together to protect all our citizens, whoever they may be."

As Alex carefully observed the thoughts reflected in the Representatives' faces, his gaze fell on Katie. His mother wore a beatific smile. Alex received her comm link but no message. He opened a comm to her.

<You're trying too hard, Ser Racine,> Alex sent politely. <Think of whom you wish to connect to with a simple thought. Once you connect, just think what you wish to say.>

<This will take some practice, Mr. President,> Katie managed to send. <What I had wanted to tell you was that I am quite proud of you, son.>

Alex walked around the conference table to stand behind Tomas and Eric. "We are starting a new society and settling our first colony. We are alone in this system, but not in this corner of the galaxy. We must develop our own economy. No one will do it for us. But if we are successful, others will want what we produce and that will bring immigrants to Haraken."

Alex laid a hand on each shoulder of his ex-Directors. "These Sers have served you well as your Leaders and then as my Directors. Now they have new jobs. They are your Ambassadors to New Terra and the Confederation, and will work to build relationships with those societies that will enhance ours. The agreements they broker and that I approve must be ratified by you in the Assembly."

Alex's next stop around the conference table was to stand behind his Ministers. "These individuals are extensions of my office. As my Ministers, they have the responsibilities for building the infrastructure of our world. The Assembly defines how our society operates. The Ministers manage the government's efforts, and my Ambassadors build our alliances."

Heads around the table were nodding in understanding, except for Lina, who now wore a scowl.

"Ser President, if the Assembly is independent of your office, who is our leader?" Lina asked.

"In the future, Ser Monti," Alex replied, "when your numbers have grown, you may elect an Assembly Speaker who will meet regularly with the Ministers and me. You will also form committees to study various issues and propose solutions. But for now, you ten are equal."

A reminder from Alex's scheduling application popped to the top of his implant's hierarchy list.

"Allow me to update this group on something I've already initiated," Alex said. "I've formed our first major enterprise, the Central Exchange of Haraken. The Directors, who are also the owners of the bank, are the flotilla's SADEs. I'm the bank's first and only depositor and investor at this time."

Alex regarded his Ambassadors, who wore bewildered expressions. "Sers, you need to catch up with the SADEs, who have already transmitted a request to New Terra to establish a currency relationship."

Eric stared at Alex. "Do you never sleep, Ser?" he murmured.

Alex smiled and looked across the table to Renée. "I try, Ser Stroheim, but there is so much that requires my attention."

Renée recalled how much of Alex's sleep she had usurped last evening. She glanced toward Katie, who offered her a wink, and Renée returned a guilty smile.

"It's time we joined the others," Alex announced and led the group to one of the *Unsere Menschen*'s extensive meal rooms. The room's 500 seats were nearly full. As Alex's group entered, he directed the Representatives to a long table set at an angle just to the left of the front table where Alex seated the Ambassadors to one side of him and the Ministers on the other. Renée sat with Tatia and some of the flotilla's other officers at one of the foremost tables.

Every implant in the flotilla was set to record the President's first address, courtesy of Z's broadcast throughout the flotilla. Even the un-implanted young were crowded in front of vid screens to watch. The people's work throughout the flotilla came to a standstill.

"Sers," said Alex, opening the meeting and choosing to stand in front of the head table. "This is an exciting time for us … the free people of Haraken."

Alex's audience felt no reason to be inhibited. They cheered and clapped at Alex's pronouncement—they were the free people of Haraken.

"But we have a great deal of work to do," Alex continued. "Before you," said Alex, waving at the two tables, "are your Assembly Representatives, Ministers, and Ambassadors. While the New Terrans are familiar with most of these terms, I urge all of you to learn the histories of our societies. You are here in this room because you have been selected as the core builders of our new colony. You will be reporting to one of our Ministers or our military leader, Admiral Tachenko."

Alex began to pace slowly, gathering his thoughts. "I challenge all of you as you apply yourself to your new jobs to keep a few things in mind. While we have immediate requirements to develop basic infrastructure, I want you to think of our future … of a city of ten to fifteen million people. Plan well."

Pausing in front of the Representatives' table, Alex said, "While the ten of you work to create our constitution, design our government, and write our laws, keep in contact with the will of our people … all of them. And remember the manner in which the Independents were treated by the Confederation. Be prepared to be generous and bestow our liberties on any intelligent beings."

Turning to the broader audience, Alex pointed a finger at them. "And I challenge you to create a world we can be proud of. Preserve Haraken for hundreds of generations to come. Seek to balance the needs of our people with the nature of our planet. Do not destroy the planet for the sake of unrestrained growth. To all of you," Alex said, turning slowly in a circle to encompass his audience and the appointed government individuals, "Work with our SADEs … depend on them. We are here today, on the eve of our new world, by virtue of their power and the gift of their goodwill. They are as much a part of our new society as all of you."

Alex paused before retracing his steps back to the central table to lean against it. He had debated how much to concern this group with the importance of their technological development. *What would be so wrong if we only managed to produce an agrarian society with slower tech development?* Alex had thought. But Cordelia's report of the dying Nua'll ship's emergency signal stayed with him, and his answer was that agrarian societies don't repel interstellar invaders.

"On a final note," Alex said, having decided to push his audience, "I will tell you that much of our future depends on our development of a technological edge that will open trade between us and New Terra and the Confederation. One of my primary focuses as your President will be to ensure the development of gravity-driven shuttles within the next year."

Alex's incredible goal was already known among the people, but few knew the challenges that goal faced. Mickey sent a quick signal to Alex to be heard.

"Yes, Chief Engineer Brandon," Alex called out.

"Mr. President, while we are making great progress replicating many parts of a silver ship and the SADEs have every confidence that we can grow the crystal circuitry and power-crystals, none of us has any confidence that we can 'tune,' for want of a better word, a shell to resonate as required. You are placing so much hope for our future on this technology, which I believe we can't possibly develop within the year."

Mickey's earnest face appealed to Alex, who had hoped not to have to answer this particular question at this time. "Chief, that's the purpose of our next scheduled meeting," Alex said.

But as he surveyed the room, expectant faces stared back at him. It was obvious the people needed an answer, needed to be able to hope. *Oh well, might as well get this over with,* Alex thought.

"You're quite right, Chief. We haven't the time to learn how to resonate a shell. So we'll appeal to the original builders to help us."

Comms began working overtime and swamping the SADEs. In front of Alex, people chatted or commed and some outright argued … the New Terrans, of course. Alex glanced toward the officers' table. They sat calmly waiting his next statement, prepared to carry out any orders. Renée wore a smile for him.

"But, Admiral …" Mickey began, "I mean, Mr. President, are you suggesting we set up our facilities on Libre to accommodate the Swei Swee?'

"Certainly not, Chief," Alex replied. "I'm going to invite the Swei Swee to live on Haraken. I don't expect most will come, but I have a pretty good idea that one Hive First will accept my invitation." Alex turned toward the

Assembly Representatives and said, "And you need to take that into account when you draft our constitution and define the term 'citizen.'"

Lina jumped up, exclaiming, "Ser President, what if our people do not wish the Swei Swee to join us? They were responsible for the death of more than a billion of our people. What is the duty of our Assembly, then?"

"Assemblywoman Monti, let me clarify something first," Alex replied. "The Swei Swee were responsible for the death of Méridiens and Librans, not Harakens. They are your people now. And, yes, if the consensus of the people guides the Assembly to restrict Haraken citizenry to humans only, you are free to do so."

Lina sat back down with a satisfied air, ignoring the hard stares directed her way, especially from Ser de Guirnon, whose body language projected an air of poised tension.

"But, Assemblywoman Monti," said Alex, taking two slow steps toward her table, "understand me well. The Swei Swee were taken from their home world and forced to serve the Nua'll or see the extinction of their race. When the opportunity presented itself, they revolted and sacrificed entire hives, including hundreds of hatchlings, to win their freedom. I find great honor in their actions at Arnos and believe they would be a fine addition to Haraken. Not to mention, they would give our colony the technological edge we need to succeed."

Alex took a deep breath and turned away from Lina, biting back his next comment. Instead, with a resigned air, he said, "If, however, Harakens believe this world should be exclusively human then I for one will exercise my free will and choose not to make Haraken my home."

Alex turned to his table for a glass of water and a moment to cool his temper. *A fine beginning for our new society*, Alex thought, not sure whether he was angry at Lina or himself or both of them. Alex's back was to the room, and the silence from nearly five hundred people was eerie, unexpected. While he was seeking a means by which to restore the meeting's agenda, Z signaled him.

<Ser President, I require your assistance. Ser Lina Monti has received, at this moment, 112,382 messages and more are coming for her at every tick.

I am summarizing them and have signaled her urgently, but she has blocked my comm.>

<Give me the summary, Z,> Alex replied.

<You will pardon the inaccuracies, Ser President, as a summary of independent messages eliminates the specific wording of each sender.>

Z's phrasing brought a soft smile to Alex's face.

Those at the front table were greatly relieved to see Alex's scowl give way to a smile. Tomas had little doubt as to the source of the change. It had to be one of the SADEs. *They are more alike than anyone can imagine*, Tomas thought, recalling Terese's words.

<Summarizing humans is a tricky business, Z, but please proceed,> Alex replied.

He caught the eye of Tomas, who wore a pained and apologetic expression. While sipping on his cup of water, Alex stripped Lina's comm security protocols and linked her with Z in time to hear the SADE's summary. After Z finished, Alex turned around and leaned against the front table, waiting, and the people of the flotilla waited with him.

Lina's rather smug countenance had faded and was replaced with consternation. Had she ever been on the mats with Tatia, she would have been familiar with an opponent's combination punches. Z's summary had included more than forty message themes, each theme backed by tens of thousands of individual messages. The people were angry with the words she had spoken to their President, and all of them offered her the same choice: apologize or resign. Lina stood and held herself stiffly erect, a sour expression on her face as she regarded Alex.

"Yes, Assemblywoman Monti, have you something else you wish to say?" Alex asked, careful to keep his countenance neutral.

"Yes, Ser President, I have received messages from our people. They indicate that I should have sought their opinions on the Swei Swee before expressing my own," Lina said contritely. "I hope you accept my apology for my ill-considered opinion."

"I do, Assemblywoman Monti," Alex offered politely. "We must live by cooperating with one another and with any other entities who seek to enjoy the freedom we will offer our citizens."

Alex turned and addressed the entire audience. "I will leave you now to begin your work. You have much to do. We'll make Haraken orbit in two and a half more days."

As Alex ended, the applause and whistling in the room was deafening. He returned their approval with a solemn nod of his head and led the group, who would participate in his third and last meeting, to a small conference room.

Étienne grinned at his crèche-mate and sent, <And you thought it might become dull now that the war had ended.>

Alain smiled and sent back, <We've been rescued by a madman … thank the stars.>

* * *

Tatia, Mickey, Tomas, Eric, and Étienne followed Alex into the conference room. The participants took seats while Alex remained standing, with Étienne taking his usual place slightly behind and to the side of Alex, where he could observe the people and the door.

"We have a big job that needs to get done as soon as possible," Alex began. "I'll need the *Freedom* and the *Rêveur*. Admiral, you'll need a new Captain for the *Rêveur*."

"Already done, Mr. President," Tatia replied. "Captain Edouard Manet is the *Rêveur*'s new Senior Captain; Captain Miko Tanaka has the *Outward Bound*."

"Very efficient, Admiral," replied Alex, nodding.

"Just trying to keep up, Mr. President," Tatia replied with a cheeky smile.

"Tomas, have Captain Cordova clear out a bay on the *Freedom* and make it pristine, as in medically approved," Alex said, beginning a rapid fire set of orders. "Mickey, build me a shallow pool in that bay, thirty meters across and one meter deep with circulation systems and filtration for seawater. Eric, work with Mickey. I need two things. First, once

Mickey has completed the pool, I need to fill it with fresh seawater from Haraken."

Eric was inclined to ask how he should accomplish this when it occurred to him that it was part of the job. Instead he nodded his acceptance to Alex and asked, "And the second item, Ser President?"

"Catch me some sea creatures, a sampling of small fish, crabs, or whatever Haraken has in the ocean. They must be kept viable and transferred to the *Freedom* just before we leave. Mickey, I'll need a separate tank for Eric's catch." On a quick signal from Julien, Alex added, "And, Mickey, give me one more little tank, same size as the food tank, to hold the Swei Swee eggs."

"What quantity of specimens will suffice, Ser President?" Eric asked.

"We need to keep the Swei Swee fed for the return trip, Eric. Try for five hundred kilos."

"Who's going and who's staying, Mr. President?" Tatia asked.

"You, Tomas, and Mickey are going," Alex answered. "We'll leave the *Outward Bound* behind. I think Eric can make use of its heavy lift capability for his jobs. Leave Sheila behind as well. I want the flotilla well defended. Eric, you're in charge while we're gone. Mickey, the pool is your priority. You and your engineers will set our timeline. When you're ready, Eric will have the specimens delivered and we'll launch immediately."

"You seem certain, Mr. President, that your invitation will have takers," Tatia commented.

"I don't think most of the Swei Swee will. Not after what they've been through," Alex replied.

"But you're counting on our Hive First, aren't you, Mr. President?" Tatia pushed.

Alex regarded his new Admiral, and not finding a ready answer, he just shrugged his shoulders.

-36-

It was a pivotal moment for the Harakens. The ships were in formation, orbiting the planet. The SADEs were training their telemetry on the surface and projecting wide and close views of the planet. In the sixty-two years since the Nua'll had vacated the system, the planet had maintained its bio-health. The ecosystem had limped along, developing vast grasslands across its savannahs. The few trees were small and stunted. The upper winds and heat from the plains created a sufficient energy differential to pull moisture from the oceans and drive light rains across the lands, but the effect was minimal. The planet was in dire need of deep, abundant streams, rivers, and lakes of freshwater. More freshwater would mean more trees, eventually tracts of forests, which would mean more oxygen in the air, increasing the rain cycles.

In the Harakens' favor was a deep asteroid ring located between the next two and three planets outward. On the flotilla's approach to the planet, the SADEs had focused their telemetry on the ring's myriad bodies, analyzing the resources. The ring was a mix of asteroids—heavy metal, frozen gases over metal cores, and ice mixed with dust. As a resource, the Harakens couldn't have asked for anything better. It would take some work to harvest the field, but they had the skills, equipment, and people.

After reviewing the analysis of the asteroid field the evening before the flotilla made orbit, Alex decided to appoint a fifth Minister. Perhaps "Minister" was not the most appropriate title for this appointee, or for that matter his first four Ministers. In total, Alex had selected four men and one woman, people who he knew would be hands-on. Someday they would need administrators but not now.

Alex had the SADEs model his plan for the environment, and when they pronounced it feasible, Alex asked for the best person to run the operations. The SADEs nominated a pioneer, Benjamin Diaz, a New

Terran ex-ice asteroid hauler. Benjamin had been First Mate on his father's ship for four years until his father died while on EVA for emergency repairs. The son had taken over as Captain of the *Full Load.*

After the flotilla had made orbit, Alex chose to meet Benjamin without warning. Z directed Alex and Étienne to one of the *Unsere Menschen*'s bays. The young ex-Captain was head and shoulders deep in the aft end of an ore hauler with an engineer and several techs.

When Alex sent the ex-Captain a greeting via implant, Benjamin jerked upright, banging his head into an engine cowl. His first word of "What" had been quickly followed by "Yikes" as he rubbed the back of his head. Rather than reply to Alex's greeting through comm, Benjamin looked around for the person who had spoken to him.

"Ser Diaz, over here," Alex called out.

Benjamin belatedly realized it was the President who had called and hurriedly lowered himself to the deck via the maintenance grav-lift.

While Alex waited, he sent an urgent message to both Tatia and Terese. <Implement the implant games with our pioneers immediately. Set a minimum participation time for each evening and require every pioneer's participation by order of the President.>

"Greetings, President Racine," Ben Diaz said, extending a grimy, lubricant-laden hand before snatching it back. He pulled a refresher cloth from his ship suit pocket and wiped his hands down. "How may I help you?"

Alex eyed the ex-Captain for several moments. It was rare to find a New Terran bigger than himself, but there stood Benjamin Diaz, about six centimeters taller and at least thirty to forty kilos heavier. It gave Alex a visual concept of how he appeared to the Méridiens—big.

"Ser Diaz, I have a job for you, but first I have some questions," Alex replied, noticing that the bay had gone silent. He ran a location app, identified all the personnel in the bay, and sent, <While I appreciate the attention, people, I believe the equipment you are working on needs you more.> Work sounds immediately filled the bay.

Alex led Benjamin over to a vacant office, and Étienne sealed the plex-shield door behind them. "Ser Diaz, I would like to know two things. Why did you not renew your government contract for the *Full Load*? Second, why did you become a pioneer?"

"Mr. President, Mr. Diaz was my father, always will be. I'm Benjamin—Ben or Little Ben to my friends."

A no-nonsense young man, Alex thought. A check of his full bio, which had been registered with Z, revealed he was a year younger than Alex.

"A pleasure to meet you, Ben," Alex said, extending a hand and watching a smile form on the young man's face. Alex's hand was gripped as if in a vise. "And the answer to my questions?" Alex reminded him.

"The answer to both your questions, Mr. President, is you and the Méridiens. I looked at my aging ice hauler, compared it to the *Rêveur*, and was hooked. Unfortunately by the time I finished the *Full Load*'s contract, brought it home, and sold it, you had shipped out. I took a tech job at TS-1 to learn Méridien technology. Then you brought the flotilla back, and I signed on with a contractor to complete the repairs on this city-ship."

"What was your job on the *Unsere Menschen*?" asked Alex.

"I handled a plate hauler for the EVA crew, Mr. President," Ben replied.

Piloting a plate hauler was a tricky job, and an EVA crew's safety depended on the pilot's excellence. The little vessel was part loader, its rear full of hull plating, part jet-powered craft, able to move quickly and precisely, and part crab, lifting a single plate off the stack with flexible arms and positioning it on the hull, guided by laser targeting. The EVA crew worked in close proximity to the tiny but powerful little ship, and they depended on the skill and steady nerves of the pilot.

"Welcome to the government, Minister Diaz," Alex said, extending his hand again.

Benjamin eyed Alex's hand as if it was stinging reptile. "Your pardon, President Racine. I'm a damn fine hauler Captain and a good tech, and I can pilot almost any work vessel you might have, but I'm no Minister."

With that, Alex knew he had found the right man for the job, which he spent the next half-hour outlining. The more Alex talked, the more he had Ben nodding his understanding and a smile replacing his frown. When Alex finished, he stared at Benjamin, waiting for an answer.

"Well, yes, Mr. President," Ben Diaz said, shaking Alex's hand. "That's a job I can handle. We'll have Haraken pretty and green in no time and refined ore stacked up so deep in front of your fabrication facilities that the managers will be crying for me to slow down."

Before Alex could reply, Ben's head had swiveled to the side. Alex followed his line of sight, expecting to see a disaster in progress, only to find a young Méridien woman carrying an oversized satchel and searching the bay. Alex regarded Ben, whose face was screwed up as if he was tasting something sour, and had to suppress a smile. Ben was attempting to contact the young woman via his implant comm and failing miserably. Alex sent her a greeting and her bio-ID was returned with her polite response. <Your Ben is here, Ser Turin, with me, in the office near bulkhead brace B-8-2. Please join us,> Alex sent.

Simone Turin's eyes searched out the meter-high numbers stenciled on the bay's walls and swept the row of plex-shield-faced offices below the numbers, spotting the threesome. Simone's youthful face lit up, as did Ben's, and the two exchanged small furtive waves as Simone fairly skipped across the bay.

Étienne signaled the office door open for the young woman. When Simone entered, she dropped her satchel and paid honor to Alex.

"Greetings, Ser Turin," Alex returned in Con-Fed to Simone, nodding his head to accept her honor.

"Greetings, Ser President," Simone returned in Sol-NAC though her ship suit's harness. "I do not wish to interrupt your meeting, but Little Ben—I mean, Ser Diaz has need of nourishment before mealtime, so I ensure his needs are adequately met."

Alex eyed Ben, calculating that with his size and the effort he put forth, he probably required the intake of at least four Méridiens.

<Rather reminds you of someone, Ser, does it not?> Étienne sent privately to Alex.

In contrast to Ben's massive size, dark hair, and warm brown skin, Simone was ultra-pale, blonde, and blue-eyed, a slender, ghostly example of her people's genetic templates. Standing together, the two were night and day, even more so than he and Renée.

"We were finished, Ser Turin," Alex said politely. "I was just about to congratulate Minister Diaz on his new position."

When Simone heard the announcement, she jumped up into Ben's arms, hugging him fiercely around the neck, her feet dangling a half-meter off the ground. Ben wore a silly grin and was blushing. Alex gave him a smile and a nod, and left the two alone to enjoy a private moment of celebration. It would also give Little Ben the time he needed to refuel, judging from the size of Simone's food satchel.

<At least I was never that bad,> Alex sent to Étienne, adding a view of Ben's blushing face.

When his shadow failed to respond, Alex turned to catch Étienne's expression wriggling like a fish as the escort tried valiantly to prevent laughing.

<Oh, be quiet,> Alex sent as the two men gained the privacy of the bay's airlock.

That did it. Étienne burst out in a fit of laughter that had Alex vacillating between irritation and the urge to join him. Before the corridor-side airlock hatch slid open, Alex sent, <Okay, point made. Now display some presidential decorum, won't you?>

The two very sober and earnest-looking men exited the bay's airlock and made their way down the city-ship's corridor.

<Ser Turin,> Alex sent, <I need Ben to become adept with his implant. Nightly games will soon become mandatory. See that he participates. Limit your belt harness conversations so that he must use his implant.>

<It will be done, Ser President,> Simone returned. She smiled at the thought that the President had offered her the perfect excuse to visit Ben each evening in his cabin. This was much better than waiting for Ben to invite her.

Simone was one of the more exotically designed Méridiens. Her crafted beauty gave her a choice of partners, but her dalliances had become boring, unfulfilling. One afternoon, exiting a meal room, Simone had literally walked into the wall that was Ben. Being a complete novice with his implant, Ben hadn't exhibited the Méridien courtesy of employing his locale app, warning others of his proximity to a corner or doorway.

Unable to exit around Ben since he filled the doorway, and finding his comm blocked, Simone had taken Ben's arm and pulled him aside, guiding him to a table. With Z's help, Ben's implant was unblocked, and Simone spent the next half-hour helping Ben establish some basic control.

In contrast to Simone's many lovers who had wished to possess her beauty if only for a night, Ben had preferred to talk to her. In fact, that is all they had ever done for many days … talk. The more they talked, the more Simone was endeared to the huge New Terran's gentle ways. She sought excuses to visit him, discovering that by mealtime, Ben was often ready to gnaw on his knuckles. Thereafter, twice a day, Simone brought Ben her satchel of food, and they talked while he ate.

* * *

While Mickey assembled the pool and Eric worked with engineers to discover a means of transporting thousands of kilos of seawater and catching the Swei Swee's sampler plate, Alex met with Tatia and his Ministers to set priorities, outlining energy sources, fabrication facilities, atmospheric oxygen, city planning for a population of ten to fifteen million, infrastructure, shuttle ports and terminal, ore production, and an administration building.

When Alex finished reviewing his list, he found himself surrounded by silence. "I would not expect you to complete this list in the first few days," he deadpanned.

"I, for one, Ser President," Lazlo returned drily, "will appreciate an extra day or two."

"Sers, I do not wish to overwhelm you," Alex said. "We'll take it step by step, but I wish you always to keep the future in mind. When our traveler shuttles are in production, we will grow geometrically. Let's not be caught squatting in fab-huts. Right now, we need a foothold on Haraken and in the right location."

"I have selected several that I favor, President Racine," said Miriam Dubois, the new Minister responsible for the city's design and infrastructure.

<Cordelia,> Alex requested.

Cordelia used the holo-vid in the *Freedom*'s conference room to project a view of Haraken, which rotated slowly, and indicated the four potential city locations.

"Pros and cons, Minister Dubois," Alex said.

When Miriam paused, Julien interrupted, <President Racine, Minister Dubois has compiled sets of attributes for each site in a comparative matrix, which should accent the positive and negative values of each location.>

Miriam sent a private "Thank you" to Julien. She added "pros and cons" to her vocabulary app.

Alex magnified the holo-vid view, examining the terrain around each site as everyone reviewed Miriam's matrix. He was the first to veto a site.

"Ser President, might I know why this site is inadequate?" Miriam inquired.

"Rainfall will turn this area into a bog or swamp in ten or fifteen years, Alex explained.

"But, Ser, those conditions would require an annual rainfall of one hundred centimeters or more. This planet is almost arid."

"Let me explain, Miriam," Ben Diaz, the Minister of Mining, replied. "We are developing a plan to bombard the planet with ice asteroids. We'll target the oceans, but as they shoot through the atmosphere, they will evaporate or explode from the heat expansion. Either way, we will begin producing weather patterns quite quickly, which will greatly increase the rainfall."

"Oh," Miriam uttered and recovered quickly. She eliminated a second site, stating that runoff from the mountains would build a huge lake that could eventually encompass the valley she had chosen.

Lazlo examined one site in detail and pronounced it unfit for shuttle terminal expansion. "Even with gravity ships taking off in an environmentally friendly manner, Ser President, they will be constantly passing over the city due to the height of the surrounding hills. I believe that is a risk we shouldn't take."

In the end, no one could find a reason to dislike the fourth site. A fairly broad plain ended on its western edge at cliffs that fell into the sea. A small band of hills bordered the eastern edge and would direct water from rainfall back toward the city. There was expansive space for a metropolis, fabrication facilities, government buildings, and a shuttle terminal without crowding the plain.

"Have we a name for our new city, Ser President?" asked Ernst Hummel, the Minister of Energy.

Alex responded with a shrug and looked around the room. No one seemed to have an answer. When he caught Leo Tinto's eyes, the Minister of Building, Housing, and Facilities glanced down at the table.

"Minister Tinto, do you have a suggestion?" Alex prompted.

"I do not mean to be presumptuous, Ser President," Leo replied, "but I was reminded of the words my mother taught me of her forefathers' Terran language. Originally my people were from an area on Earth called 'Basque Country.' Their word for 'hope' was 'espero.'"

"Espero," Alex said. "I like it. Are there any objections or any other thoughts?"

Hearing none, Alex pronounced their new city named. He took the opportunity to excuse himself for a moment, ostensibly to use the refresher. When Alex returned, he waited outside, leaning against a bulkhead. More than one Haraken who passed Alex and Étienne wondered at their President resting in the corridor. The people had become quite used to Alex's frenetic pace. Several even queried Z, who seeing no other reason himself why Alex, with arms crossed, would spend time leaning against a bulkhead, would reply, <The President rests.>

"Take a peek, Étienne," Alex requested, nodding at the plex-shield window set in the conference room door. "Tell me what you see."

Étienne crossed the corridor and joined a group of passing Harakens to blend in as he passed the doorway. His technique was surreptitious, and Alex had to refrain from laughing. After Étienne returned past the door again, trailing another group of people, he reported, "Admiral Tachenko and the Ministers appear to be quite engaged. The holo-vid is ever changing, and they are earnest in their communication."

"Excellent," Alex said. "We can go."

* * *

In the *Unsere Menschen* conference room, Tatia and the Ministers had just begun their work. The concept of delivering ice asteroids to Haraken to accelerate the planet's rainfall and oxygen levels had energized their imaginations.

It would be three days before the Ministers would separate. In the meantime, they requested meals in the room, ordered various engineers, techs, and specialists to attend them in their sessions, and employed the SADEs around the chronometer.

Julien became the SADEs' central manager. In order to meet the enormous number and complexity of the Ministers' requests and support the engineering efforts to develop the travelers, Julien began distributing the Ministers' queries among the flotilla's SADEs.

To organize the information and responses, Z ordered the build-out of a secondary database to relieve any one SADE from managing the load. Julien designed an ultra-fast controller to manage the queries and storage, and Z ordered it installed next to him on the bridge. Enormous memory-crystals were added to store the databases. What fascinated Z was the expedient implementation of his request. Not a single objection was raised, not even a question. *Next I walk, I run ... I fly*, Z thought.

The tasks the Ministers envisioned themselves accomplishing became less and less gargantuan as information came to light. The SADEs knew the flotilla's inventory. The Librans had been prepared to start an underground city on their original target planet. The bays of the *Freedom* and *Unsere Menschen* held mining equipment, ore haulers, repair vehicles, cargo carriers, and crates upon crates of tools, small equipment, power- and memory-crystals, and thousands more stored items. Espero, a city located above ground, would prove much easier to build.

-37-

From the *Unsere Menschen*'s bridge, Eric watched the *Freedom* and the *Rêveur* exit the Hellébore system. He was proud of his efforts. The President had handed him what had seemed a daunting task, and he had managed to complete his tasks before Chief Brandon had completed his efforts.

Under Eric's guidance, engineers had stripped the seats from the *Outward Bound* and installed a bladder system. A temporary runway had been laid west of Espero's future city center, near the cliffs, and seawater had been pumped into the shuttle's bladder. Afterward, the shuttle delivered its load to the *Freedom* to fill Mickey's pool.

To complete his second task, Eric had visited the spectacular cliffs that fell over fifty meters to beaches of fine black and white crystal. He needed 500 kilos of fresh, live seafood. Exhibiting one of his newfound talents, Eric had begun his quest with Z. <I need your help, Z,> Eric had sent, transmitting his signal via the shuttle's comm as he stared at the far horizon across the ocean's waves.

<I would be pleased to assist you, Ser Stroheim,> Z had responded.

<Z, how do you catch live fish or whatever they have in this ocean?> Eric had asked.

Z had to admit that the question ranked as one of the more unique queries he had received, but he was determined not to fail Eric Stroheim for personal reasons. Z had found the answer in the pioneers' bio-IDs. Several of them had enjoyed fishing the rivers and oceans of New Terra for sport, releasing their catch after landing it. When the pioneers had heard the request, they had helped engineers fashion seine nets to cast from the beach. The ocean waters were extremely fecund with hundreds of species of small fish and crustaceans, which inhabited the vegetation-dense shallow waters. It had taken four New Terrans just an hour of casting their nets to deliver the amount of catch Ambassador Stroheim had requested.

Standing at the cliff's edge, Eric had watched the crewmen haul the catch to the cliff tops in barrels designed to support them until the Swei Swee "test tasted" them. The thought had made Eric's stomach queasy. Watching the crew work, the cool ocean breeze on his face, Eric had surveyed the coastal ridge, pleased with the solution the Assembly had reached to one of their more ticklish challenges.

Tomas, who often chaired the Assembly meetings and prioritized their agenda, had led the discussion. The President had asked for a small piece of land at the cliff's edge for him and Renée. He had requested a location that allowed him to oversee the site he hoped the Swei Swee might accept. Tomas and Eric had translated the word "oversee" as "protect."

The Assembly had agonized over their response. Land ownership was a new concept to the Méridiens, and the New Terrans understood only the concept of land purchase. Neither group was prepared to devise a plan to allocate land to Haraken's settlers, so the Representatives consulted the SADEs for ideas. The final decision was to allocate one square kilometer to each Haraken colonist. They could trade or sell their land if they chose to make other arrangements.

However, the Assembly still had the quandary of the President's request for a small slice of land, two kilometers along the cliffs and extending a few hundred meters inland. The Méridiens on the Assembly had thought in terms of their egalitarian society, an equal portion for each citizen. That had been until Eric shared with Tomas, who in turn shared with the Assembly, the privileges that had been allocated to the House Leaders. It had taken several moments before order was restored. The New Terrans had sat back and watched their Méridien colleagues fume and argue.

Both Katie Racine and Pia Sabine struggled to keep their thoughts to themselves. If each had voiced her opinion, a swath of land would have been cut from the seacoast to gift the ex-Co-Leaders. But both knew their opinions would be considered favoritism, so they remained silent.

Captain Azasdau offered a solution to the dilemma. "Consider this, Sers," he began, "that we are not participating in a privileged allocation.

Julien has shared with me a concept that New Terrans have employed. They often rewarded a citizen who made significant contributions to their people without expecting personal gain in credits or assets. Consider that our new bank will be started with our President's New Terran credits, which are at risk for their value. In addition, Ser de Guirnon has lost access to her House's financial power. Furthermore, neither of them has gained credits or assets in return for all they have accomplished for us. Does this not qualify as individuals who deserve our largesse?"

Tomas had curtailed his desire to roll his eyes when the Assembly considered awarding a quarter of the western plain to Alex and Renée. It wasn't that Tomas had disagreed with their sentiments, but he felt he had come to understand their young leaders to a certain extent. He believed Alex and Renée wouldn't have accepted the Assembly's generosity.

<Julien,> Tomas had sent, <we seek your advice.>

As Julien was the President's close friend, the Representatives had been willing to hear the SADE's thoughts. Julien studied the seacoast and noted that Alex's primary concern involved protecting the Swei Swee's proposed habitat. That the cliff top would be Alex's residence was a secondary consideration. Julien outlined an image of the seacoast on the Assembly's holo-vid and included the temporary shuttle runway in his outline. The cliffs extended for thirteen kilometers in a flattened C-shape, whose tips pointed toward the ocean. The Assembly accepted Julien's logic and carved a section of seacoast, thirteen kilometers long and five kilometers deep, for Haraken's President and First Lady.

* * *

The *Freedom* and the *Rêveur* settled into orbit over Libre. Aboard the *Freedom*, techs loaded a barrel of fresh seawater with a small specimen sample onto a shuttle. That shuttle and one from the *Rêveur* flew to the Swei Swee's landing point on the cliff tops overlooking the Clarion Seas.

When Alex had donned his belt harness to communicate with the Swei Swee, he had accessed the translation program and had been surprised to discover the program's vocabulary and syntax database had multiplied considerably in size.

<Julien,> Alex had sent, appending the data size of the translation program. <Who has been busy?>

<Apparently, Mr. President,> Julien had replied, <Mutter is enamored of the Swei Swee's musical language and has continued to monitor them since we left Libre. Not long ago, Mutter, with Cordelia's assistance, began testing her command of the language by speaking to them through the telemetry station we left behind. Recently our Hive First has been spending long evenings conversing with Mutter. From what Cordelia has shared with me, you have a quite adequate but rudimentary language base.>

<Send my congratulations to Mutter and Cordelia, Julien,> Alex had sent.

<It will be as you have requested, Mr. President,> Julien had replied.

Julien's formal tone reminded Alex of a conversation he had been meaning to have with his friend. <Julien, one moment before you go,> Alex had requested. <Who are we?>

<You are the new President of Haraken and I am a Director of Haraken's first bank,> Julien had replied.

<Who are we, Julien?> Alex had repeated.

Julien had halted key operations in mid-process and had reviewed the question. The answer had readily occurred to him, and he had replied, <I am Julien, you are Alex, and we are good friends.>

<Yes, Julien, we are. We must keep that thought close,> Alex had replied.

Julien's thought as Alex had closed the comm was that he had obtained a clearer and brighter focus, much to his pleasure.

* * *

Word of the Star Hunters' return, announced by Julien over the Swei Swee telemetry station, had caused excitement among several hives. They had assembled on the cliff top to await the vessels' arrival, the three Hive leaders standing foremost in the enclave.

Alex's shuttle landed first, and he and his people set foot on Libre once again. The cliff top was warmed by the enormous red sun of Arnos. The smell of grass and sea were swept toward the group by a clean wind. Alex stopped and took a deep breath. When the second shuttle landed behind them, the crew floated two barrels down the gangway ramp on grav-lifts.

As Alex hiked toward the Swei Swee, he passed the hulks of the dark travelers, stripped of their shells. The metal looked as pristine as the day the Swei Swee had first exposed them. When they neared the cliff top, the Swei Swee poured toward them, scuttling with their alarming speed and snapping their huge claws in excitement. The flotilla's Hive First, recognizable by the markings on his carapace, focused on Alex, lifting his claws in greeting. Alex returned the gesture, placing his hands in claw fashion above the Hive First's. The other two leaders were waiting, bobbing slowly up and down in anticipation, and Alex greeted both of them.

On the trip planetside, Alex had accessed the Swei Swee database, stringing together phrases he would require. When Alex sent his first phrase to his harness, the whistling tones of the Swei Swee emerged, requesting their Hive First "drink some endless waters from the Star Hunters' world." The Hive leaders let out shrill whistles that the entire company of Swei Swee echoed. The raucous response was earsplitting.

<Remind me to bring nanites earplugs next time, Mr. President,> Tatia remarked privately.

Alex led the Swei Swee toward the unloaded barrels. Although the humans were familiar with the Swei Swee's habits, the way in which the aliens amiably intermixed, snapping their claws in anticipation, inevitably was disconcerting and required re-acclimation.

Two small Swei Swee younglings had recently hatched and rode atop a huge, scarred matron, her scraped and grooved carapace an indication of the amount of time she had spent tunneling for the Nua'll. The sharp claw tips of a little male reached out and pinched Renée on the thigh, and she let out a yelp, jumping to Alex's side. The matron let loose a shrill whistle that ended in a twitter.

As Renée rubbed her painful thigh, she asked Alex, "What did the female say?"

"She was remanding the youngling, Ser," Alex replied. "She said, 'Not food.'"

Humans and Swei Swee crowded around the first barrel. A large matron pushed forward and upended a Méridien crew member, who sat down heavily in the middle of her back. The female's rapid bobbing forced the crewman to take several moments to descend from the back of the Swei Swee, who had been whistling a few notes over and over.

The embarrassed crew member turned to Alex and apologized profusely, asking, "Was the female angry with me, Ser President?"

"On the contrary, Ser," Alex replied, "it seems she was making a joke. She was uttering 'youngling' over and over again as she bounced you up and down."

Alex's comment produced a round of laughter, and the tension among the humans visibly eased.

At the barrel, Alex squatted down and motioned the flotilla's Hive First closer. Alex had to step to the side to allow the leader to get close to a tap near the bottom of the container, which he opened. The leader pushed his true hands into the stream and sipped from them. Alex turned off the tap as the leader backed up and issued a string of whistles, which were echoed by the assembly.

"Is that an approval, I detect?" asked Renée.

Their Hive First scuttled aside to make room for the other two leaders to test the waters. The result was the same for each one, and the assembly whistled louder with each approval.

<Apparently,> Alex sent via implant, deciding he wouldn't be heard over the deafening noise, <these waters elicit dreams of the Swei Swee's home world, which is what has them so excited.> Alex walked to the second barrel, pushed up his right forearm sleeve, and stood poised over the barrel. A slender, pale green-and-silver fish with a yellow tail swam near the surface, and Alex sent a mental apology to the fish before he snatched it

out of the barrel. As he held the fish up, the males in the assembly snapped their sharp claws furiously. Alex tossed the fish toward their Hive First, who snatched the fish with a lightning strike of his left-hand claw.

<Whoa!> Tatia sent to Alex, impressed by the speed and accuracy of the Swei Swee male's strike.

The leader neatly clipped the head and tail from the fish with his claws, and his true hands rent the flesh from the fish's skeleton and skin, then popped a piece into his mouth.

Some of the crew members turned green at the sight of the consumption of a living animal. <Under no circumstances,> Alex sent to all, <is a single one of you to display any sign of displeasure at the Swei Swee's feeding habits, or you will be walking home. If you cannot control your stomach, make your way surreptitiously back to a shuttle.> Four crew slid out of the group and walked toward the second shuttle. Many of the other crew had their eyes on the horizon or sky, trying to ignore the smacking and munching of flesh.

Alex caught two more fish for the other leaders. One fish he tossed, but the other was speared from his hand by the third leader. A screeching whistle from their Hive First froze the overanxious leader in mid-motion. A further set of tweets and warbles had the hasty leader bobbing slowly up and down. He scuttled close to Alex and lowered his body to the ground with a soft whistle and extended to Alex the bloody, wriggling fish still pinioned on the sharp point of the upper half of a claw.

Alex pulled the fish free, feeling its slick blood coat his fingers. He held the fish back out to the submissive Swei Swee, whistling, "Eat."

A claw slowly reached back up and gently took the fish from Alex's hand. As the chastised Swei Swee backed away from Alex with his meal, he was thwacked on the carapace by several matronly females, their heavy claws scratching his nearly pristine shell.

<I believe a rude behavior has been corrected, Alex,> Renée sent privately.

Alex scooped up a handful of water and held it out to their Hive First. "Water good?" he signaled via his harness. The Swei Swee's response signaled an affirmative. Alex picked up the severed head of a fish from the grass and held it out, repeating his question, and received the same answer.

Sorting through his preplanned phrases, Alex selected the one he needed. Whistles and tweets emanated from his harness, inviting the Swei Swee to come to his world.

Their Hive First's response was a question that Alex's program translated as "Search for Star Hunters or search for Swei Swee?" Alex wrestled with a way to respond. He wanted both, but he also wanted it to be the Swei Swee's choice. Alex patched phrases together for his response and whistled, "Swei Swee search on Star Hunter's world. Swei Swee search the endless seas for Swei Swee."

For the tricky portion of his plan, Alex required an expanse of sand on which to draw his icons. He walked toward the cliff trail, and the hives scuttled out of his way. The leaders closely followed Alex down the cliff face, while his people, surrounded by the hives, trailed behind.

On the beach, Alex smoothed a square meter of sand. As he started to smooth more sand, a matron blocked his way. Her blunt claws motioned Alex aside then she spun to face the long stretch of beach and dumped her blunt body on the sand, splaying her legs up and out. She tweeted and warbled, and in response, two matrons scurried forward and grasped her blunt claws to haul her down the beach.

Alex laughed and applauded by snapping his fingers. The Swei Swee joined in with snapping claws and bobbing bodies.

Are the Swei Swee recognizing the moment's levity or are they just imitating the Star Hunter First ... and does it matter? Renée wondered.

Alex drew a series of images down the beach, adding whistles and tweets to explain the icons. The entire point of the exercise was to investigate a shell's tendency to decompose without the Swei Swee's continued maintenance. When Alex finished the parade of drawings, he held up a small piece of the silver ship's dark hull, which had continued to crumble even as he carried it.

Their Hive First plucked the shard from Alex's hand, and his eyestalks bent to examine it. A sharp whistle brought one of the matrons forward. She took the piece of hull and stuffed it in her mouth. After a few moments, she spat it out and trilled to her leader, whose eyestalks were trained on the expectorated shard.

As fast as the Hive First could move, which was unsettlingly quick for humans, he raced back to the start of Alex's message. He crabbed sideways, his eyestalks trained on the icons as he walked the row of pictographs. At the end of Alex's glyphs, the First stared at the shard in the sand, and his whistle pierced the air. He followed his whistle with a string of tweets and warbles, and the three hives erupted in a loud burst of noise, snapping claws and excitedly bobbing up and down.

<Mr. President,> Tatia sent over the noise. <If I didn't know better, I would think we were being laughed at.>

<Perhaps there's a joke we just aren't party to,> Renée added.

Their First snatched up the dark shard with a true hand and raced up to Alex. He bobbed up and down, and then scurried toward the cliff face before turning around to face Alex and snapping his claws.

Alex hurried to catch up with the leader, who took a second path up the cliff face toward the Swei Swee's homes. The organic shapes of their dwellings blended from one home to the next without any overall geometric pattern. He held up the dark shard and whistled, "Nua'll positive." Then he drew an outline of a silver ship in the sand. Pointing to the outlined ship and shaking the shard, he again whistled, "Nua'll."

Alex whistled an "Affirmative" to indicate he was following the discussion while at the same time wondering where this was headed.

Pointing to the outlined ship again, the First threw the shard down and spit on it. Then he tapped on the exquisite translucent blue-green surface of the first dwelling with a claw and whistled, "Star Hunters."

Alex put the two ideas together and burst out in raucous laughter, twirling and snapping his fingers overhead. The First joined in the merriment, snapping and bobbing.

Down on the beach, the hives celebrated the sharing of their great secret with the Star Hunters, a secret maintained through eight generations of imprisonment. The males snapped their claws and danced around the humans. Matrons whistled and warbled, and the young ran along the beach and slid their bodies into the shallow waves.

<You don't think the President intends to live with the Swei Swee?> Tatia sent jokingly to Renée.

<I certainly hope not. The diet would be overwhelming,> Renée replied, bile threatening to climb up her esophagus at the thought.

<Mr. President,> Tatia sent, <what did you discover?>

<One thing is for certain … this is a clever race,> Alex replied on open comm. <The dark shells were a ploy against the Nua'll.> He touched the hard crystalline wall of the Swei Swee dwelling, marveling at its smoothness and the play of light across its surface. <The walls of these dwellings,> Alex sent, <are the traditional method by which the Swei Swee build.> Alex picked up the dark shard from the stone walkway and held it up to his people on the beach. <The dark shells were only built for the Nua'll. They were designed to deteriorate. The joke was on the master race!> Alex hefted the shard. He looked at the First, whose eyestalks were split between it and Alex's face. Finally, Alex sent the dark shard flying far out to sea, and the Hive leader whistled his approval.

Alex and the First made their way back down to the beach, where Alex squatted on the sand. The First settled down across from him, and his eyestalks turned down to observe Alex drawing the shape of a traveler. Alex pointed to the shape and himself, whistling, "Star Hunters plus travelers positive."

The First released a strange warble, which Mutter had equated in the language database to a Swei Swee interrogative or "I'm waiting to hear more."

Alex cleared more space in the sand and drew a more complex drawing. He roughed out the interior of a silver ship and drew an exterior view directly under the first image and to the same scale. This time, Alex pointed to the interior, whistling, "Star Hunters" and pointing to the second drawing, whistling, "Swei Swee."

The First's eyestalks went from one drawing to the other and up to Alex. He sent a short tweet, and the two other leaders scurried close. Such a long conversation ensued between the Hive leaders that Alex grew weary of the wait. The warm sun and sea breeze were lulling him to sleep. Glances at his people revealed that they had settled on the sand alongside the Swei Swee.

After a half-hour, Alex felt his eyes closing. Unexpectedly his back was bolstered by an older matron, who had slid up behind Alex and used her broad-shelled back to brace him. Alex looked behind him, and eyestalks swiveled to stare back. He tapped his fist against her blunt digging claw. In response, she blew a soft tweet and settled into the sand, Alex leaning against her.

<Mr. President,> Alex received from Étienne via implant, the comm waking him up. <The leaders appear to have concluded their conversation.>

Alex's eyes popped open. Another hour had passed. Unfortunately Étienne had been optimistic. Instead of addressing Alex, their First scurried over to a small rock outcropping, the other two leaders flanking him, and he began a speech to the assembly. Alex turned to see if the matron he leaned against had been disturbed, but her eyestalks were withdrawn, her legs tucked under her carapace, and her short tail wrapped around her body. So Alex rejoined her in a nap.

A loud collection of whistles woke the humans. Everyone had fallen asleep except the twins. Alex stood up and took in the scene. Claws were being held up to the three leaders and whistling filled the beach.

<Étienne,> Alex sent.

<I believe, Mr. President,> Étienne replied, <a consensus has been reached by the assembly, and they are signaling their support of the leaders.>

Alex walked over to the rock outcropping to regard their First, who quickly scuttled to the ground, ensuring he was below Alex in height.

The leader emanated a long series of whistles that Alex's application couldn't manage. The syntax was too complex. It took a half-hour of whistles and warbles, questions asked in multiple ways, and tens of drawings for communications to be finalized. The summary of their discussion was that the three hives, who had met them today, were the only ones who would welcome the Star Hunters. The other hives, led by the Swei Swee leader, wanted nothing to do with any other "singers."

Their First had communicated that the Star Hunters must take all the People who had assembled on the beach, including their young and the un-hatched younglings, the latter two points requiring several drawings unto themselves. The key item stressed repeatedly by their First was that the hives would be free to search the endless waters of the Star Hunters' world. In return, the Swei Swee would build the Star Hunters' travelers.

With the negotiations finished, Alex made a final point. He drew an outline of the cliff tops and beach west of Espero. Pointing to the cliff top, he whistled, "Star Hunter First plus mate," and held out his hand to Renée, who joined him. Then Alex pointed to the beaches and the cliff face in his drawing, whistling, "Swei Swee seek shelter."

The other two leaders crowded around the drawing while their First warbled and tweeted to them. When he finished, the other leaders began bobbing up and down in excitement, claws snapping.

The shrillest whistle Alex and company had ever heard emanated from their First, who stood on the full extension of his walking legs. In response, all Swei Swee, including the other two leaders, lowered themselves to the ground. Their Hive leader whirled to face Alex and whistled loudly, "Swei Swee First greets Star Hunter First."

"Ah," Alex called out to his people. "Our Hive Leader has been promoted. He is now the Swei Swee First of Haraken, and we have just procured three hives as new inhabitants." *This should give our Assembly something to think about*, Alex thought.

The new Swei Swee First warbled, and two males ran into the waves and disappeared in a flash. Moments later, one of them emerged, scuttling up the beach to the new leader to deliver a fish wriggling on the end of his claw point. In front of his leader, the male lowered himself to the sand and offered up his prize. The Swei Swee First whistled his approval, and the male bobbed in return.

The First clipped the head and tail of the fish and stripped its skin in an efficient and coordinated movement of claws and true hands. The final preparation was the ripping of two fillets from the backbone. The First scuttled up to Alex, spreading his claws wide. In his true hands hung the two raw fish fillets, which he held up to Alex.

"I believe you are about to consummate the deal, Mr. President," Tatia announced.

"What are you supposed to do, Alex?" Renée asked, fearing the answer.

"I would presume I need to eat one," Alex replied, eyeing the pieces of flesh. *If this is the worst I have to do to secure a future for our people, it's an easy price to pay*, Alex thought. Before he could think any more about it, Alex took one of the small fillets and popped the piece of cool flesh into his mouth. He was surprised by the delicious taste and tried not to think about what he was eating … just focused on the pleasant flavor. Alex signaled his enjoyment to the leader, who quickly stuffed the other fillet into his mouth parts.

<Good thing, Mr. President,> sent Étienne, <that the male caught a small specimen.>

As the sun neared the horizon, a final set of drawings, accompanied by simple phrases, communicated the lifting of the Swei Swee hives tomorrow morning. Alex and his entourage left the Swei Swee on the beach, and a half-hour later were closing the shuttle gangway ramps and lifting for their ships.

Renée watched Alex visit the shuttle's refresher. When he returned, he glanced briefly at her and ducked his head before looking to the front of the shuttle.

"Were you ill in the refresher, Alex?" Renée asked.

"No," Alex replied, "just washing my hands and my mouth."

Alex was gazing anywhere but at her, and Renée was replaying recent events when it clicked. She would have pulled Alex around to face her, but she wanted expediency. In a tick, she was out of her seat and straddling Alex. Cupping his face, she said, "Never fear that what you do for our people will ever push me away, my love." In proof of her words, she planted a kiss on Alex's lips, her tongue working deep into his mouth. Never once did she think of the fish he had eaten.

Alain, sitting beside his twin and across the aisle from their charges, sent to Étienne: <And one would have thought negotiations complete. Apparently I was mistaken.>

* * *

Early the next morning, hours before morning meal, shuttles were launched from both ships. The transport shuttles were stripped of seats, except for the one carrying Alex and his people, who landed a half-hour ahead of the transport shuttles. Descending the gangway ramp, Alex found the cliff top deserted, but the Haraken's Swei Swee First soon appeared at the top of the cliff trail and whistled for Alex's attention.

At a trot, Alex led his small group over and down the cliff, following the leader down the steep path to the sands below. When they gained the beach, Alex stopped to look up at the Swei Swee dwellings. In the early morning sun, their homes glistened in blues, greens, and pearl whites. The view held the humans' attention for long moments.

The beach bustled with the activities of the three hives. One of Alex's apps kept count as he surveyed the Swei Swee on the beach. His tally matched Julien's count of the Swei Swee who had occupied the cliff top yesterday. Sadness swept over Alex. He had hoped others might join the three hives, but their conspicuous absence was a strong message. The other hives desired isolation. *I understand how you feel,* thought Alex.

Young Swei Swee packed onto the backs of older females, and any of them that sought to leave the safety of a matron's back received a sharp reprimand. Younger females wielded woven seaweed baskets and were packing un-hatched younglings into the baskets. The weaves of the baskets were so tight that the oblong eggs floated in a small pool of seawater. As a basket was filled, two females would grab a side, making their way across the beach and up the cliff's path. When the last females exited the egg dome, the First whistled a sharp command and the remainder of the Swei Swee began the trek up the path.

Alex and company stood back to allow the Swei Swee to navigate the twisting cliff path unhindered by human legs. The last Swei Swee to leave the beach was the First, who scuttled over to Alex, bobbing up and down excitedly. He held up his claws, and Alex smacked down on the top of them with his fists, which elicited a sharp whistle. Then the First raced after his people.

<Mr. President,> Julien sent, <an interesting bit of trivia for you and your escorts. I've been tracking individual Swei Swee movements from the viewpoint of security. A fully developed male can accelerate four to five times faster than a human and can strike with a claw eleven times the force that you or Little Ben might deliver.>

<Impressive,> Alex replied.

It was not the response Julien had hoped to elicit, but it was the one he had expected.

* * *

A welcoming committee of humans stood in the bay as the first shuttle, floating on grav-sleds, slid through the *Freedom*'s catch-lock doors. Two small pools, one for the un-hatched younglings and one containing food for the Swei Swee, were located next to the huge swim pool.

The First was the first down the shuttle's gangway ramp. His eyestalks swiveled around, taking in the huge bay. When the First spotted Alex, he crossed the intervening twenty meters in mere ticks, causing many of the crew to reflexively step back. Standing beside Alex, it took all of Renée's control not to flinch at the furious approach of the three-meter-long Swei Swee. Alex's broad grin helped her remain firmly in place.

Alex invited the First to test each of the pools. To the humans' amazement, the leader ignored the ramp that led up to the swim pool's rim and simply leapt into the water over top of the frame that stood a meter and a half high. He cycled around the pool underwater. When the First surfaced, he whistled to his hives. The males exiting the shuttle raced across the bay, jumped the frame, and splashed into its waters.

In the meantime, the First climbed out and scurried over to one of the small pools. Finding it empty, two eyestalks swiveled toward Alex, while the other two kept searching the pool. Alex pointed toward two females coming down the gangway ramp with the first basket of un-hatched younglings. The First issued a series of tweets and warbles, and the females whistled back. Other females picked up the message and passed it back to the females in the interior.

Scuttling to the other small pool, the First whistled his excitement and grabbed a small crustacean, cracking its shell with his hunting claws and picking out the flesh with his true hands.

The shuttle transfers continued without incident, and the return trip to Haraken was only marred by two issues. The hives gorged on the specimen pool, emptying it in three days, and they left the remains scattered across the bay. For the latter problem, there was no tidal action to sweep away the debris, and the Nua'll disposal method was not in evidence to the Swei Swee.

On the second day following the loading of the Swei Swee, with fish offal and crustacean shells stinking up the bay, a young and courageous tech who serviced the pool filtration units had stood with her hands on her hips surveying the mess. She walked up to the leader and gave him a stern reprimand, her finger wagging in front of four eyestalks that attempted to follow her digit. The tech picked up several fish heads and dropped them into a recycling chute. When she stepped back, her legs were clipped from under her by the First, who had followed her. She sat down heavily on his carapace, struggling to scramble off. Before she could apologize, she was struck dumb by the giant claw poised in front of her face. A fish skeleton dangled from it. The young woman timidly accepted the refuse and dropped it in the chute. A series of whistles from the First had Swei Swee scrambling out of the pool, racing over the bay and snatching up specimen debris. It took everything the young tech possessed not to scream when the Swei Swee assembly rushed at her.

An enormous, scarred female was first at the chute, large amounts of detritus in her blunt claws. The tech opened the chute, and the female Swei Swee deposited her collection down its throat. Swei Swee after Swei Swee passed in front of her. The entire bay was cleaned of debris in less than a quarter-hour.

The tech was privy to another human-Swei Swee first contact peculiarity when she released a cleaner bot into the bay to scrub the floors, and young Swei Swee had their first adventure aboard the *Freedom*. It became a game to ride the disc-shaped bot, which could fit two of the smaller young comfortably. One youngster after another tried to jump on the bot and push one or more of its siblings off, which constantly knocked the bot off course. Cleaning the bay should have taken the bot two hours. Instead it ran constantly until its charge dissipated, attempting to finish the job just once.

Once it became evident that the Swei Swee had no concept of rationing the fresh seafood, Alex contacted Cordelia for ideas. She searched her database and located a food-stock engineer and a bio-engineer. The two individuals hatched an idea to create fish shapes from the *Freedom*'s stores. Unfortunately the pale, bland shape didn't interest any of the Swei Swee. Cordelia recruited an artist who worked with pigments, and she applied colored food additives to the fish shapes.

The crew reported that the Swei Swee were still uninterested in the painted fish and suspected that it was because their prey was not actively swimming. When Alex went to investigate, he sat on the deck across from the First, picked up one of the painted fish, tore off a chunk of the imitation fish, and popped it in his mouth. Then he peeled off another chunk and offered it to the leader, who bobbed up and down and accepted the offering with a true hand, chewing delicately on the morsel. Alex shared the entire fish with the leader and then pointed to a huge tray of the other painted fish behind him. The First's signals brought the other Swei Swee scurrying, and the faux fish were quickly parceled out. More trays were brought until Alex called a halt to the feeding.

In a humorous twist, the Swei Swee were still snipping off the heads and tails of the painted fish despite their edibleness. The adventuresome and ignorant young often tasted a fish head or skeleton, looking for a morsel. When one of the young discovered his fish head was tasty, he searched for another. Soon it was a free-for-all as the young scurried around the bay scarfing up the faux heads and tails.

The female tech was thrilled that she didn't have to man the recycling chute anymore, and the Swei Swee young kept the bay clean of heads and tails. But there was one duty she did take particular pleasure in performing—she ensured there was always a replacement bot ready when the youngsters play toy was nearly out of charge.

-38-

Shuttles, transporting the Swei Swee, landed on the temporary runway near the cliff tops west of Espero. Alex waited at the bottom of his gangway ramp for the First and many of the males to disembark. He was prepared to lead them to the cliff edge, but as the Swei Swee descended their ramp, they halted. Eyestalks extended fully and mouth parts quivered, tasting the air. Then at a run, the Swei Swee males shot past Alex and made for the cliff edge, where they skidded to a halt, snapping their claws and whistling loudly.

Alex caught up to the group and directed the First's attention to a small mound several hundreds of meters away. He whistled, "Star Hunter First dwelling," and the leader whistled his affirmative.

Matrons disembarked and, unlike the males, took their time reaching the cliff edge. Ignoring the excited males, the females spread out along the cliff, tasting the rock and soil, whistling and warbling their findings to one another. One matron's signals caused the other females to halt their work and hurry to her position. Immediately the matrons began cutting a trail at a shallow angle in the nearly vertical cliff face. As the heavy claws of the senior matrons gouged rock and dirt, the younger females scooped it out of their way.

Alex had ordered the building of temporary pools near the cliff's edge. A smaller tank was stocked with live specimens from the waters below. Males lounged in the swim pool while the females worked to cut a path to the beach. The females occasionally took breaks, eating, swimming, and resting, but their pace was relentless as refreshed matrons constantly replaced those at the forefront of the digging.

In two and a half days, the matrons reached the beach. They would spend more time ensuring their work was shored up in the manner of their dwellings to prevent the pathway eroding. But when the first matron stepped onto the black-white crystal sand beach, she whistled shrilly and scooped a small amount of sand into her mouth to taste it. The matron spit out her mouthful of sand and warbled her delight. The other females joined her in song. The Swei Swee had found a most satisfactory home.

In response to the females' song, the males jumped out of the swim pool and raced down the path. Gaining the beach, they dashed across the sand toward the breaking waves, great gouts of black and white crystals shooting into the air from their driving legs. Diving into the waters, they surfaced and whistled to one another. Within moments, the males were spearing fish and gathering crustaceans, which they offered to the females until they were satiated.

The pathway cut and stomachs full, the Swei Swee turned to the protection of their eggs. Young females returned to the cliff top to gather the eggs from the pool. The males began carrying rocks, which had fallen free of the cliffs, and carried them out to the matrons, who stood on a rocky bottom in shallow waters. The matrons directed the positioning of the stones and began cementing them in place.

Alex left the Swei Swee in peace to enjoy their new home. His parting gift to them was an FTL relay station on the cliff top for their Hive Singer, which earned him Mutter's sincere gratitude.

* * *

Three tasks received the majority of Alex's focus, the first traveler's construction, Haraken's military, and the new constitution.

After a typically tough day of negotiations with the Assembly, which had required an enormous amount of control on Alex's part not to strangle Ser Lina Monti, Alex exited the Representatives' habitat. It had been Katie's suggestion to relocate the Assembly Representatives planetside. When Alex had asked Katie why, she had responded, "How would you measure our progress on the constitution, Mr. President?" When Alex admitted it was poor, she had replied, "Perhaps the output of the Assembly would improve if they had a close-up view of their new home." Alex had read between his mother's lines. The Representatives had found their new accommodations quite spartan compared to that of the city-ships. Without the distractions of friends, crowded meal rooms, and entertainment centers, progress on the constitution improved remarkably.

Alex paused to watch an ice asteroid streak overhead, leaving behind a wide trail of super-heated steam. Little Ben had begun delivering ice asteroids to Haraken many days ago, and his efforts had already produced a noticeable change. The hot, dry air had become faintly cooler and had brought the smell of moisture. Clouds had been seen gathering over the mountains, where miniscule amounts of rain were being detected. The SADEs calculated that Little Ben's efforts would allow the planting of trees along the mountainsides and ravines within several years, which would accelerate the oxygen content in the atmosphere. As the nanites sealed Alex's oxygen plugs to his nose, he thought, *I can't wait.*

The SADEs had initiated an emergency over-watch procedure for the Swei Swee as a precaution against Little Ben's activities. Some of the ice asteroids had substantial dust cores. When they struck the ocean, their effects were often felt on distant shores. Upon the detection of rogue waves, Mutter would sing to the Swei Swee to seek shelter.

At one point, Alex had attempted to explain to the First why the walls of the egg dome should be strengthened against the inbound ice asteroids, but he had made no progress. Finally, the leader had beckoned to Alex to follow him, and they had left the cliff top for the beach below. As Alex gained the sands, he had stared at the egg dome. It wasn't the temporary shelter of mottled cliff stone he had seen being built days ago. Blue, green, and cream swirled through walls that glistened as the Swei Swee dwellings did. The matrons had covered the temporary shelter with their permanent crystal building material. Alex had waded out to the dome. Small slots allowed seawater to mix with the inner dome space. He had struck the dome wall with the base of his curled fist. Alex thought he might have been striking a starship bulkhead. That had ended their conversation. As Alex left, he could have sworn the First's warbles hinted at laughter, and his suspicion doubled when Mutter demurred from providing a translation.

* * *

In one of the inexplicable coincidences of life, two separate events would collide, enabling the Haraken's future prosperity.

Early one morning, Mickey had arisen from his cot and hurried to catch a ground transport to a shuttle parked on the runway that had been hastily laid at Espero's future terminal site. The final destination of the shuttle was the *Freedom*, but it made a priority stop at the *Money Maker* for the Chief Engineer.

Mickey made his way to the bridge of the converted freighter and requested some privacy with Mutter. To Captain Menlo, who had lived most of his entire life with an implant, privacy was easily obtained even in a crowd, and he knew Mickey was well-versed in his own implant's applications. But Lazlo also knew Mickey was under a great deal of pressure to deliver Haraken's first traveler, so he was content to order the bridge cleared.

"Mutter," Mickey said when they were alone. "I need your help."

"I suspected dire tidings, Chief Engineer Brandon, when you came to speak to me in person," Mutter replied.

"Please, Mutter, call me 'Mickey.' It will shorten our conversation. I didn't mean to make you anxious. There is no bad news. I've hit a wall, and I need your help."

That the Chief Engineer did not appear harmed in any way from his encounter with the wall was of great relief to Mutter. The SADEs needed Mickey healthy and unharmed to achieve success with the traveler, which probabilities dictated would lead to their personal success. "How may I be of assistance, Mickey?" Mutter asked.

"Once the Swei Swee females create a shell, which the President is pushing us to let them start, we have no means of ingress-egress. It's not like any of us can chew sand, and without an opening, we can't load passengers or freight or even hook up to a station or vessel. We need a standard hatch," Mickey said.

"Have you conducted any experiments that we may not be aware of, Mickey?" Mutter asked.

"We know we can cut a hatch, Mutter. It's slow, but doable. We also know that the moment we cut into the shell, we diminish the resonance continuity, which means the energy collectors won't charge at a sufficient rate. We also know that any attempt to close a cut with nanites fails to restore the continuity."

"We will work to help you resolve the problem, Mickey. Thank you for bringing your problem to us," Mutter replied.

Mickey left soon afterward with Mutter's wish that he avoid walls in the future, unyielding as they were to humans.

* * *

The SADEs' attempts to solve the traveler ingress-egress problem were fraught with failures. It was quite the dilemma for entities who rarely found an impediment they couldn't overcome. Mickey had the matrons build meter-square, flat sheets of shell for the experiments. The engineers applied a wave generator to a plate and attached an acoustic device to measure the square's harmonics and the strength of the signal. First, a plate was cut in half, and following the SADEs directions, the engineers attempted to reconnect them with various methods while still maintaining the sheet's resonance strength. However, the results were abysmal. If the rejoining held, the resonance was diminished, or the method wouldn't rejoin the cut, or the resonance was returned to full strength but the method of rejoining could only be employed once, which would make the technique unusable for a hatch.

After another day of complete test failures and against Mickey's vociferous objections, he and his team readied their first frame, complete with interior instrumentation, charging crystals or collectors, and a drive for transport to the shell construction site. The frame floated on an enormous pair of grav-lifts.

Pools of seawater, specimen tanks, and two mounds of silicate minerals that the matrons had identified as required material stood waiting at the construction site.

Alex, Mickey, and the frame arrived with the dawn. Soon after, the First emerged over the cliff top and scurried to greet Alex. The majority of the females had followed him.

The humans and the First stood aside as the females went to work. Young females took a small sample from one pile while the matrons sampled the second pile. While they masticated, they ambled over to the bow of the frame, where a heavily scarred matron waited. When the females were ready, the elderly matron warbled and another matron took her place at the bow. She was the Swei Swee female whose carapace Terese had repaired. For nearly a decade, she had been relegated to the position of cripple, unable to aid her People. Now she was offered a place of honor. She would begin the first traveler shell for the Star Hunters.

The honoree bobbed her pleasure and turned to the nearest young female. To the humans, it appeared the two females kissed as their mouth parts entangled. The honoree continued to masticate her mouthful of minerals, combining her material with the ingredients of the younger female. When the honoree was ready, she spit her formulation into her true hands and laid it on the crossbar of the bow's frame, shaping and spreading the concoction. Exposed to the air, the material began drying, taking on a lustrous blue sheen shot through with subtle green bands. The matron placed her mouth parts on the small piece of hardened shell and hummed. The harmonics of the shell fragment was picked up by the matrons, who added their voices until all voices were in harmony.

"Black space, Mr. President," Mickey exclaimed. "That old girl just tuned the chorus. That's how they do it."

<Mutter,> Alex sent, <did you capture that sound?>

<Indeed, Mr. President,> Mutter replied.

<SADEs and Mickey,> Alex added. <We will need a library of frame numbers matched to the unique harmonics of the first shell fragment laid on a frame.>

<Done, Mr. President,> Mutter replied. <The fabrication plant will label each frame construction with a resonance-ID. They are fabricating a plate for this frame, and it will be ready later today.>

<Well done, Mutter,> Alex said.

<Mr. President, we need samples,> Julien sent.

<I was afraid you were going to ask that,> Alex replied. <I suppose we need samples from the young females and the matrons before the two materials are combined.>

<Precisely, Mr. President,> Julien replied.

<And do you have any idea how we go about obtaining these samples, Julien?> Alex asked.

<Mickey has a set of empty sanitized containers that were going to be used for salinity tests today. You could employ those. As to how to gain the samples … well … I just asked the most capable human in the vicinity, so I would assume he will invent an appropriate method.>

Alex sent a silhouette of the Sleuth melting into a puddle. Julien just laughed and returned to monitoring the telemetry from his people's implants. With so much at stake, the SADEs were monitoring every conceivable viewpoint.

"Mickey, I need your seawater sampling containers … all you have," Alex requested.

"Mr. President, I can send a tech down to the beach for those collections," Mickey offered.

"They aren't for seawater sampling, Mickey. I need to collect some Swei Swee spit," Alex replied.

There were times such as this when Mickey knew it would not pay to ask questions. So he hurried to fulfill Alex's request.

Once Alex had his set of containers, he approached a young female and sat down in front of her. She immediately lowered herself to the ground without stopping her chewing. Alex opened a container and hawked a loud, noisy spit into it. For a moment, his actions froze the entire cliff top population before work resumed. The eyestalks of Alex's target were fully extended and trained on his container. Alex closed the first container and opened another, offering it out to the female. To her, it was obvious the

Star Hunter First was requesting a tribute, and she hurried forward to comply, spitting her compound into Alex's container, at least most of it. Alex's hand and coat sleeve caught the rest of it.

Alex warbled his approval, and the young female hurried for another mouthful of silicate. He pointed to a second female, whose two closest eyestalks swiveled his way, and he indicated his fresh container. She hurried forward to add her tribute. After that the females began to line up in front of Alex, wishing to add their tribute to the Star Hunter First's collection.

The traveler shell was created mouthful by mouthful, the matrons testing the harmonic of the construction before their portion dried and making any necessary last adjustments. It was incredible to the human observers that the females could unerringly bridge the gaps between the frames as if a laser guided them. It had occurred to Alex that there was substantial value in the males having four eyestalks to watch for hunters in the endless waters, and now it occurred to him the value for the females. With two eyestalks focused in opposite directions, they could align dwelling walls and a shell between frames.

Alex was leaning against the swim pool, and the First, floating inside, clung on the frame next to Alex. All six of their eyeballs were on the females. Alex's head turned at the sound of the First's rush to the far side of the pool. The leader pulled himself half out of the pool, his eyestalks trained on a distant noise. In a rush, he cleared the pool's edge and raced toward the sounds.

Alex cursed. The noise had come from his home site, and belatedly he recalled that construction was to begin today. A committee formed by Harakens had insisted their President have a proper domicile. Alex had foisted them off on Renée, who hadn't enjoyed their well-meaning intentions any more than Alex would have. Swearing at the timing and taking off at run, Alex remembered to plug in his oxygen tube. Over the pounding of his own feet, he heard the slight thumps of Étienne's fleet footsteps keeping pace with him.

Before Alex and Étienne could reach the house site, they heard the shouts of humans mixed with the shrill whistles of the First. *Please not now,*

Alex thought, sending a fervent wish to fortune, hoping not to discover a deadly encounter between humans and Swei Swee. Arriving at the home site, Alex found the First, his claws raised threateningly and snapping rapidly, had backed the crew up against their transport. One of the crew had raised a heavy laser tool in his defense.

"Stand down," Alex yelled as he stepped between the disputing parties.

The First dropped his claws and bobbed urgently in front of Alex. A long song ensued, which Alex's translator only partially managed.

<Mutter,> Alex sent, <did you manage that?>

<Your pardon, Mr. President,> Mutter replied. <While I was able to translate most of the song, he has touched upon a subject not yet encountered. So I must … guess.> In her two hundred years, Mutter hadn't found it necessary to employ the process. It hadn't been necessary. A calculation or measurement was required or it wasn't. After she met Julien and his friend, she had begun employing processes to analyze a question and attempt to surmise the most plausible outcomes. It was new territory that she carefully monitored to ensure it would not jeopardize her responsibilities.

Once Mutter completed her analysis of the leader's song, she sent, <Mr. President, it would appear our First is demanding his people's rights. It is my estimate, my guess, that he is insisting it is the right of the Swei Swee to build your dwelling.> Guessing still disturbed Mutter, yet both Julien and Cordelia relished the process. *The young are creations unto themselves,* Mutter thought.

<Oh, wonderful,> Alex groused. <I have two species fighting to build a home I don't want, at least not now.>

Alex's vision of a timber and stone home, such as his parents had on New Terra, wouldn't be realized on Haraken due to the lack of forests, but he had still harbored thoughts of a traditional stone house.

<Renée,> Alex sent, <we have a problem.>

<As you say, my love, it isn't a problem unless we make it so. What do you need?> she replied.

<I need you to handle the Home Committee. They will be losing their job,> Alex replied.

<Alex, let them do this for us. It's causing no harm.>

Alex sent Renée a short vid of the scene he had encountered at the building site. He heard her intake of breath and a surprised, "Oh, my."

<Apparently the First is claiming Swei Swee rights,> Alex sent, <which Mutter identifies as a demand to build our house.>

<I'll manage the committee. Good fortune with the First, my love. Know that I'll live with you anywhere in any condition,> Renée sent, laughter following her words.

A wonderfully strange woman whom I hope never to lose, Alex thought.

Alex sent the work crew on their way with his apologies. Then he knelt down in a sandy spot and directed the First to his side. Alex spent an hour diagramming his home, careful to match the proportions accurately to his implant's image and relating the drawing to the markers staked out by the committee.

<Julien, I could use your help,> Alex sent.

<Not to worry, Mr. President,> Julien replied. <I've sent a 3-D model to the fabrication facility. They will have it delivered to you in several hours. It should give the First a concept of what you expect.>

Alex and the First went back to observing the building of the shell while Alex waited for the model. Hours later, a transport pulled up and a New Terran tech jumped out with a bundle in his arms and raced toward Alex. He arrived panting, and his eyes started to roll up in his head. Étienne grabbed his arm to steady him, and Alex pulled out his coat's oxygen tube and plugged it into his nostrils.

When the tech's vision cleared and he steadied, Alex admonished, "A few ticks more or less will not matter in what we do, Lamont. At the present time, we have no enemies who threaten us."

"Your pardon, Mr. President. I was told this delivery was critical."

"Understood, Lamont. Oxygen plugs first … hurry later."

After the tech left, Alex walked with the First over to the house site. Alex displayed the model, removing the roof to show the home's interior. Eyestalks compared the model to the outline Alex had made in the sand. His sharp whistle of "Affirmative" pierced the air, and he scurried off to draft his own crew.

"I'm going to space the Home Committee," Alex muttered, taking off after the leader. What he didn't need was to have the Swei Swee females pulled off the shell's construction to build his home. When he caught up with the First, it took another half-hour to get across the idea of traveler first and then his home. Eventually the leader understood, whistling his affirmative, and then leapt into the pool, joining several matrons who were taking a break and wetting their breath-ways.

Mickey, who had been party to the entire episode of the First and the committee, asked, "You sure about this, Mr. President … the Swei Swee building your home, I mean?"

"No, Mickey, I'm not. But if this is what it takes to keep our First happy, it's a small sacrifice," Alex replied. "Besides, Mickey, think of the prestige. Renée and I will be living in possibly the only Swei Swee built home for humans."

"What I'm thinking, Mr. President, is the mood you might be in every morning when you come to work, leaving a home you can't stand the sight of."

* * *

Mickey transported the Swei Swee spit samples back to the fabrication facilities, specifically the transport hatch testing room. The analysis of the saliva compounds gave the SADEs the answer they had sought. There was the briefest moment of celebration between Julien, Cordelia, Z and Mutter before Julien contacted Mickey.

The engineering team felt exhilarated and worked around the chronometer for two days to test the new concept. They combined the Swei Swee process with human tech. Each edge of a cut panel was coated with an application of nanites that had proven to bond with the Swei Swee shell. A second, controllable layer of nanites was laid over the first application. A traveler's controller could signal this second layer of nanites to form or release their bonds.

The concept's true beauty was that the switchable coatings when linked to complete the seal could be tuned to the shell's resonance. Once the process was refined, a final test was performed on a fresh meter-square piece of shell. A square was cut from the middle of the shell, and the fixed nanites were bonded to the cut edges. Then the second nanites coat was applied and the square was replaced in the opening. The opposite edges of the shell were tied into a controller, completing a circuit.

When an engineer activated the controller, sending a signal to the switchable nanites, the square snapped tightly into place. Then Mickey tuned the switchable nanites to match the resonance that had been detected in the shell before the square was cut out. The final step was the application of a wave generator. The engineers and techs held their breath as the strength of the resonance was checked. It worked—the cut-out square stayed locked in place and the resonance level was maintained.

The engineers celebrated, jumping up and down and dancing around. Mickey called for quiet for the final step. The controller sent a release signal to the tunable nanites, and the square dropped out of the shell.

<Mr. President,> Mickey commed, <we've done it. We've created a manner of egress and ingress. We can cut into a Swei Swee shell in any manner we choose.>

<Well done, Mickey. Congratulate your team for me,> Alex sent. Next, he linked to the SADEs. <It appears you four have overcome the first hurdle on your path to independence. You have my sincere congratulations.>

When Alex cut the comm, the SADEs reviewed the next hurdles, as the President had called them, to prioritize their new points of focus. Few Harakens realized the extent to which the SADEs were incrementally managing the efforts of the people to achieve goals that rewarded both humans and SADEs. Actually "few" was a misnomer. Only one human knew the truth, and he was the one requesting the SADEs' help.

-39-

Emotions ran high on the day of the traveler's first test flight, and it wasn't just for a successful flight. Mickey had explained repeatedly that the day's test was only a lift test, but it didn't seem to matter to anyone. Hundreds of people had assembled to witness the historic event, and the entire flotilla was watching.

The traveler floated over its grav-lift cradle in Hellébore's early morning light. Coral light splashed across the translucent shell's blues, greens, and creams. This was no dark traveler, and Alex was infinitely grateful that his people would not be easily reminded of their nemesis.

The engineers had cut a small one-meter-square hatch in the side of the traveler for access by the pilots. Alex had considered requesting volunteers for the test flight until cold, hard logic took over, and he asked Commander Reynard and Lieutenant Ellie Thompson. He had been surprised and pleased that both felt honored to have been considered and readily accepted.

The traveler floated a meter above the cradle, and the hatch was another two and a half meters up the side of the traveler, necessitating a maintenance grav-lift for entry. Alex greeted his two pilots, exchanging polite conversation until Mickey, with the SADEs' approval, signaled all was ready. The pilots turned to board the craft, and Alex followed—only to be halted by the pilots, who had stopped and abruptly turned around. René, Tatia, Tomas, Eric, and the twins took up stances beside the pilots, and Alex's senior officers stood behind them. Alex took a small step back at the faces that challenged him. His anger rose, and he thought to argue, but these were his close friends, and he hadn't the heart to fight them. As quickly as his anger had risen, it subsided. When he felt in control again, he raised his hands out to his sides in surrender, saying, "Safe flight, pilots." In a fluid movement, the pilots saluted and headed for the grav-lift while Alex's people formed beside and behind him again as if nothing had happened.

One senior member who hadn't left Alex's side during the confrontation had been the First, who warbled softly at Alex. The easily translated message said, "Star Hunter First seeks shelter, positive." A sharp claw was held up and Alex rapped it twice with a knuckle.

Renée had resumed her place beside Alex. She felt angry and ashamed at the resistance she had organized, knowing full well what Alex had intended to do. That every participant in her resistance had readily agreed to her request didn't mitigate her feelings. They had denied Alex a once-in-a-lifetime opportunity. He would have been one of the first to ride aboard a Haraken traveler. Renée sincerely hoped her desire to keep Alex safe would not injure their partnership.

* * *

Sheila and Ellie had visited the traveler's fabrication site many times to become familiar with the frame's grav-drive and equipment that had been installed. Mickey had made the decision to create as exact a copy of the dark traveler as he could. Therefore, their Haraken traveler had no human amenities, no shuttle seats, no galley, and no refresher. There were two pilot chairs and a human-built controller to interface with the Nua'll circuitry.

At the test site, the maintenance grav-lift elevated the pilots up to the small hatch, but they were forced to hunch down and crab-walk to reach the interior.

"A little inelegant for such an auspicious occasion is it not, Commander?" Ellie quipped, bent over double and staring at the broad beam of her Commander.

"I don't mind the crawling in, Lieutenant, as long as I will have the opportunity to crawl back out," Sheila replied.

"You have a manner of striking to the truth of a matter, Commander," Ellie said.

Once strapped into their chairs, the pilots reviewed their controller's command-control sequences for the thousandth time. When ready, Sheila signaled the controller to close the hatch, and she was rewarded with a feedback signal of a complete seal. Immediately the controller registered an energy surge on the shell. Per Mickey's instructions, they were to wait until the collectors registered three-quarters full. The grav-drives would require nowhere near that amount of power for the test, but the engineers and SADEs were collecting vast amounts of data at every tick.

For today's test, the pilots would engage the drive, lift the traveler straight up for one hundred meters, hover as they rotated on a horizontal plane for 360 degrees, and then return the vessel to its cradle. There was only one problem—without flight simulation practice or drive power testing, the controller interface couldn't be calibrated. The controller could certainly signal when one hundred meters in altitude was reached, but how much signal was required to drive the traveler to that altitude was unknown.

In addition, Sheila and Ellie flew an empty traveler. There were no hive members and no payload. So when Sheila signaled the controller to direct their flight straight up at 20 percent power, the traveler shot up and out of the atmosphere.

<Commander,> Alex sent, exercising his priority mode, <are you in control of the craft?>

<Affirmative, Mr. President,> Sheila replied, mirth sprinkling her thoughts. <This is incredible, Sir! I want one of these for myself.>

<Commander, please be careful,> Mickey said. <Recall that this craft is a true traveler replica, complete with beam weaponry, and your controller interfaces all systems.

<Understood, Mickey,> Sheila replied soberly. But the look she and Ellie shared was anything but sober. They were two teenage girls who saw the opportunity for mischief. Since they were already in orbit and still accelerating, Sheila chose to stretch the traveler's virtual legs, and the pilots took turns testing the controls while they circled the flotilla's ships.

At one point, Ellie had command control and spotted one of Little Ben's incoming ice asteroids, and she brought the traveler around to keep pace with it. The controller relayed a wealth of energy data it collected from the shell to the pilots' helmets. They were able to monitor the ice and space dust streaking off the asteroid as it neared the planet and Hellébore. Entering Haraken's atmosphere, ice water boiled off the asteroid in great quantities, and the imagery was relayed to the flotilla, courtesy of Julien.

<I believe that concludes today's test, Commander,> Alex sent.

Ellie shared a chastened grin with Sheila and relinquished command control.

<Understood, Mr. President,> Sheila acknowledged. <We're returning to base.>

Once the traveler was resettled in its cradle, the pilots crawled out through the hatch to the cheers and applause of the crowd. As their grav-lift reached the ground, they watched the audience make way for Alex as he marched toward them. Ellie glanced at her Commander and found her wearing the same expression of concern as she did.

Several thoughts raced through Sheila's mind to explain their deviation from orders as her President came face-to-face with her. But instead of the severe reprimand she expected, Alex grabbed her face and planted a full kiss on her mouth.

Alex finished his kiss, but he still held Sheila's face in his hands. He shook it gently side to side, giving her a huge smile and simply said, "Well done, Sheila. You have my deepest thanks."

Much relieved that they were not on the receiving end of the President's wrath, Ellie could not believe she heard herself say, "I was a pilot too, Mr. President."

Alex regarded the slender Haraken with the elfin face and gently cupped her chin to place a chaste kiss on her forehead.

Later, Sheila asked Ellie, "Why the glum face, Lieutenant? We just flew the first alien ship."

Ellie replied, "I was hoping for a kiss like yours, Commander. It appeared … nice."

Sheila smiled, recalling the kiss, and said, "Our President has been practicing, and let's just say he has gotten quite good."

-40-

The success of Haraken's first traveler flight energized Alex's plans. He sat down with his Ambassadors, Tatia, and Julien. The Ambassadors would be his negotiators, Tatia would provide authority and security, and his friend was the only SADE that Alex trusted to manage communications with New Terra and Méridien. By coincidence, the *Rêveur*, with its twin bays, was the only Haraken starship suited for the mission.

The five of them planned out alternatives if the primary gambit failed. New Terra would be visited first, and the Ambassadors would announce the traveler's successful test, inviting President Gonzalez for a viewing to be followed by negotiations. Their next stop would be Méridien.

<I suspect you will not get anywhere with a Council Meeting,> Alex said, <and I doubt you'll get a private audience with Council Leader Mahima Ganesh, but try anyway. We want to appear to follow the rules.>

<As opposed to our last visit, Mr. President?> Tatia asked.

<Yes, well, Admiral, you didn't see me nominate myself as an Ambassador.>

<A good decision on your part, Ser President,> Eric said, completely serious.

Julien refrained from laughing, but only barely.

<You might have an opportunity with targeted invitations to the House Leaders, particularly with Gino Diamanté. There is something about that Leader that is decidedly non-Méridien,> Alex said.

Tomas and Tatia glanced at Eric to check his reaction, but he appeared lost in thought and they were correct.

How many of us were part Méridien and part Independent but allowed only the one face to show in public? Eric was thinking.

After the Ambassadors and Julien were excused, Alex met privately with Tatia. <You are in command, Admiral, and you have mission responsibility. Your priority is the safety of everyone, the ship, and—>

<Your friend,> Tatia finished, sympathetic to Alex's pain. For the first time in nearly two years, Alex would be separated from his friend, whom he had come to depend upon and who had never let him down.

<Yes, safety first, Admiral,> Alex said with emphasis.

<And second, Mr. President?> Tatia inquired.

<These negotiations will be new to our Ambassadors. They will attempt to open doors diplomatically but may encounter opposition. You're there to remind them they mustn't quit.>

The next morning, the crew boarded the *Rêveur*. The liner's original Méridien passengers, except for Renée, insisted on going. Their argument was that it added to the legitimacy of their visit to Méridien, and Alex agreed with their logic. The *Outward Bound* would stay behind, and Tatia kept her Senior Captain, Edouard Manet. The night before, couples had tearfully separated, but in the cool morning air, professional demeanors seemed the order of the day.

Days later, the *Rêveur* neared its FTL exit from the Hellébore system, and Alex sent a signal to Julien.

<Greetings, Mr. President. It's quite late,> Julien replied. It was 4.85 hours on Haraken, and FTL exit was in 0.15 hours. But if Julien could have been certain of anything in his ever-changing world, he was certain he would have received a final comm from his friend. He had counted on it as he had counted on little else in over a century.

<Julien, I want you to do whatever may be necessary to keep you, our people, and that ship safe. I will deal with any consequences, whatever they may be,> Alex sent.

<Mr. President, I calculate that we have a high degree of probability of returning safely. I believe you may have eliminated the only human threat we faced. We should be safe until the Nua'll return or something else crawls out of the deep dark. Besides, Mr. President, I am quite excited to revisit New Terra.>

<Oh, why is that?> Alex asked.

<In my research to locate available node servers for our hidden vid broadcast,> Julien said, <I discovered two repositories of ancient Terra novels. I'm quite eager to acquire them.>

<Be careful, Detective,> Alex said. <I expect to see you return safely.>

<Be careful yourself, Mr. President. I believe you are the one who is less likely to accurately calculate the dangers of your actions.>

Alex laughed. <Oh, I calculate very well, thank you, Julien. I just prefer to ignore the more prudent choices.>

They finished their conversation on an upbeat note, despite their true feelings, but they had wanted that for each other.

There was one final message for Julien which was received mere ticks before the *Rêveur* entered FTL, timing only a SADE could manage. It said simply, "Be safe and return to me."

* * *

Alex headed for a face-to-face meeting with Little Ben. Captain Miko Tanaka landed the *Outward Bound* aboard the *Unsere Menschen,* stationed just sun inward from the system's inner asteroid belt where Ben's operations were focused. When Alex couldn't locate Ben via implant, he requested Z identify his Minister's location.

<Welcome aboard, Ser President,> Z replied, including Alex's companions, Mickey and Étienne. <Minister Diaz is inbound on a shuttle, landing in Bay-8 on Deck-11. Will you require anything else, Ser President.>

<Thank you, Z, that will be all for now.>

<Always my pleasure, Ser President,> Z replied.

"It's hard to believe that's Z, isn't it?" Mickey said.

"Quite the change, isn't it?" Alex replied. "Z is on the road to mobile freedom. He's become a true adopter of the subtleties of SADE-human relationships."

"I'm not following, Sir," Mickey replied.

Alex stopped and regarded Mickey, then launched into an explanation. "You're the Director of a nascent bank with little to show for your title. The first traveler has had a successful test flight, which you hope will lead to business contracts and depositors. The bank will flourish, and you will earn funds for your research and development. Someday the success of Haraken travelers will allow you to walk or fly instead of sit in a prison of metal alloy where you've been for more than a hundred years."

"You know, Mr. President," Mickey replied, running his hand through his short hair, "more and more often, when you talk like that, I'm very happy I'm just an engineer."

"Don't say that, Mickey. I was about ready to appoint you to a ministerial post," Alex said with a straight face.

When Mickey stared at Alex in astonishment and denial, Alex said, "Just joking, Mickey. Come along."

At Bay-8's airlock, Alex found he couldn't signal the corridor-side airlock hatch open. <Z, problem with the airlock hatch?> Alex sent.

Z, who could have wished for Julien's support at this moment, replied, <Your pardon, Ser President, it is a new safety protocol. Minister Diaz's shuttle is in the catch-lock, and the adjoining bay door is open.>

Alex, who thought the safety routine a little overcautious since he only intended to enter the airlock, decided not to voice his opinion and waited patiently for the hatch to release once the bay was secured.

Z was reminded of the human expression "Fortune has smiled on you." There were a good many new safety protocols in place—only, they applied exclusively to Haraken's President.

Inside the bay, Alex waited for the crew to disembark from the shuttle.

<Greetings, Mr. President,> sent Ben.

Alex smiled to himself. Ben had been an abysmal adopter of his implant. Thankfully, Simone, a sublime example of Méridien gene crafting, had taken pity on him one day and helped him. Now Ben had located Alex in his vicinity while he was still inside the shuttle.

<Good day, Ben,> Alex replied.

<One moment, Mr. President. I'm working with Z to correct a g-sling targeting issue.>

Alex almost asked if he could help, but like the new airlock protocol, he decided these things needed to be left in the hands of those who had jurisdiction. Ben was responsible for ore mining and ice water delivery to Haraken's atmosphere, and Ben had delivered far above expectations on the latter task.

Initially Alex had expected Ben to employ the Librans' ore transport craft to ferry ice water asteroids from the belt to Haraken. Instead Ben and Julien had communed over Alex's g-sling program. The program had been transferred to Z, and he and Ben developed a system utilizing the *Unsere Menschen* as a delivery wheel. Mining transports moved small ice water asteroids from the belt to the nearby city-ship, which continually turned on a horizontal axis. The outer doors of six bays, whose locations were distributed equally around the giant city-ship's mid-level, were always open. Beams inside each catch-lock tethered the ice asteroid of a mining shuttle, which had matched the rotation of the city-ship. Once the handoff was complete, Z would measure the mass, set up the trajectory profile in relation to Haraken's position and rotation, and release the asteroid in the g-sling program's cue. Where Alex had expected a delivery rate of ice water on the scale of one asteroid about every twelve to fifteen days, Ben was delivering an asteroid every one to two days.

Ben's huge mass pounded down the shuttle's gangway ramp at a run.

<Like watching a mountain coming at you,> remarked Mickey privately to Alex.

Ben had no sooner come up to Alex than the two of them received a priority message from Z. <Ser President, I require the Rainmaker.>

Alex heard Ben reply, <I'm here, Z.>

<Captain Federico has exceeded limitations again despite my warning,> Z sent.

<Put the Captain and copilot on the comm, Z,> Ben said, turning away from Alex to focus.

Alex sent an image to Mickey and Étienne. "Rainmaker" was stenciled across the back of Ben's environment suit as only the Méridiens could achieve. It was no mere alpha label. The letters glowed delicately in blues and whites with dark blues near the bottoms. A sweep of rain fell from the bottom of the lettering to fade into the black of his suit. It reminded Alex of a summer rain shower.

<Captain Federico, Z has informed you that you are exceeding limitations. That asteroid is too large,> Ben sent.

<Rainmaker, it's just a few kilotons over mass,> the Captain replied.

<Z?> Ben sent.

<Thirteen point eight percent over mass limitation, Rainmaker,> Z replied.

<Captain, you have a choice … drop your load and choose a target that Z approves, or hand over control to your copilot, Ser Valenko. Make your choice,> Ben replied, the authority evident in his thoughts.

The New Terran Captain eyed his attractive ex-Libran copilot, Svetlana Valenko. She returned his stare with one of her own. She was perfectly willing to jump into the Captain's chair, even eager to do so.

<Dropping my load, Rainmaker,> replied the Captain.

<There will be no choice given if there is a next time, Captain. Understood?> Ben asked.

<Understood, Rainmaker,> the Captain replied.

Ben dropped the shuttle pilots off the comm. <Z, my apologies for the Captain disregarding your directive.>

<There's no need to apologize for the recalcitrance of others, Rainmaker. I appreciate your support. Make it rain,> Z replied.

<Make it rain,> Ben echoed, and cut the comm.

When Ben turned back to Alex and company, he found the three men staring at him as if he had grown a second head.

"Correct me if I'm wrong, Rainmaker," Alex said, "but weren't you the reluctant individual who couldn't manage an implant comm to save his life and who near fled at the prospect of ministerial responsibility some eighty days ago?"

"That would have been me, Mr. President," Ben replied with a good-natured grin.

At that moment, implants chimed with notice of midday meal, and the three New Terrans only had thoughts for food. "Shall we join the crew for meal, Rainmaker?" Alex suggested.

"You read my mind, Mr. President," Ben replied.

"Careful, Ben," Mickey said jovially. "He can do just that."

"I had heard that, Mickey. Is that true, Mr. President, what they say, that you can slip past our comm security protocols and read out thoughts?" Ben asked.

"I'm here to discuss reprioritization of your efforts, Minister Diaz," Alex replied formally.

Ben took Alex's answer for an affirmative and was reminded of the rumor—not New Terran, not Méridien, not Haraken.

"I'm at your service, Mr. President," Ben replied carefully.

Conversation was subdued until they made the meal room chosen by Ben, who scanned the room briefly and then led the group toward a corner table near the food dispensers. Since Ben led and blocked the view of much of the room, Alex never saw Simone until a pair of small arms and legs attempted to wrap themselves around Ben's neck and waist. Simone's radiant smile dissolved into a neutral expression when she noticed Alex. As Ben set her down, she tucked herself inside his protective arm and said in quite passable Sol-NAC, "Greetings, Ser President."

"Greetings, Ser Turin," Alex replied. "How fares the Rainmaker's partner?"

The use of Ben's pseudonym brightened Simone's face as she hugged his waist. "He's doing a wonderful job for our planet, is he not, Mr. President?"

"Simone ..." Ben interrupted but stopped when Alex held up his hand.

"He is exceeding my wildest expectations, Ser Turin," Alex said, shifting his gaze from Simone to Ben. "The SADEs project rain will soon be falling over 38 percent of the land, enough to support forest growth before our second year. By then, I will need to appoint a Minister of the Interior who will have the responsibility for water resource management and tree planting in the mountain valleys."

Ben ducked his head, embarrassed by the compliment. Simone hugged him tighter, staring up into her Little Ben's face in adoration.

"Well, shall we eat, Sers?" Alex offered.

"Please sit, Sers," Simone replied, directing the group to a table that was set up primarily for New Terrans. The seats easily accommodated their bulk and were placed farther apart to allow more room at the table for them and their meal. Several attendants hurried to help Simone with trays and drink. When the food was placed before Alex's party, Simone hesitated.

<Please, Ser,> Alex sent privately. <Join us. I'm sure your Ben will tell you everything later anyway.>

Simone acknowledged Alex's courtesy with a nod of her head before she sat in one of the New Terran-formed chairs, almost disappearing beneath the table. She giggled self-consciously before her seat began to elevate and its sides folded inward to meet her slender hips.

"That's new," Mickey said.

"One out of every three meal rooms has been updated with these adaptations to accommodate mixed parties. People love it, but we can't accommodate all the rooms yet—too much drain on our resources," Ben said around the mouthfuls of food he was shoveling. Simone acted as a conveyor belt, swapping out empty serving dishes for fresh ones, supplying more bread, and refilling Ben's cup. No one had ever had the time to create a separate food service system for the New Terrans. They were still eating and drinking out of the frugal, Méridien-designed dishes and cups.

"You just hit on the subject of today's discussion, Minister Diaz," Alex said.

The use of his title caused Ben to pause and set down his utensil. Simone's subtle moue telegraphed her annoyance at anyone interrupting Ben's eating time.

"Are we talking shifting priorities or curtailing processes in favor of others, Mr. President?" Ben asked.

"Shifting priorities," Alex said. "Mickey has met with the other Ministers and Admiral Tachenko on their needs for the next year. With the success of our traveler tests, we need to accelerate ore production."

"To what extent are we curtailing ice asteroid delivery, Mr. President?"

"That's up to you Minister Diaz," Alex replied. "Ore production is the priority. Meet those goals and whatever resources you have remaining you may apply to ice asteroid delivery. Whatever you do, don't start throwing rock asteroids at Haraken."

Simone stared at Alex for the briefest of moments—horrified. When Ben burst out laughing and said, "I'll be careful not to mix them up, Mr. President," she was mollified, saving the exchange later for Ben's interpretation.

"Mickey, you're up," Alex said, and Mickey began walking Ben through the information that he had transferred to Z—ore production totals, refined metals in kilotons, and a delivery timeline, including the final destinations and intended usage details.

While Mickey and Ben talked, Alex connected with Z. <What progress have you made in your mobility planning, Z?>

<Ser President, are you referring to my general theories or my avatar designs?> Z replied.

<Neither, Z. I want to know what you need to enable you to walk around Haraken,> Alex said.

Z halted hundreds of secondary applications. <I do not wish to seem un-SADE-like, Ser President, but do I understand that you are requesting a proposal containing the disciplines, materials, technology, and protocols to enable mobility and maintain SADE viability and security?> Z held his virtual breath. His speech analysis programs reviewed Alex's statement twenty-one times while he waited the ticks until Alex answered.

<Correct, Z,> Alex sent. <You might as well get started, and you may involve the other SADEs as long as the project is not made a priority. Am I understood?>

<Absolutely, Ser President,> Z replied, careful to not begin running programs on the subject while he was still speaking to Alex. One important question did occur to him and he asked, <Is there any specific avatar you require I design, Ser President?>

<For yourself, no, Z,> Alex replied. <But you must ensure the preferred avatar of every SADE is encompassed by your project.>

<I believe if I were to ask Cordelia and Julien, they would request human-appearing avatars, Ser President,> Z ventured.

<And?> Alex asked.

<Understood, Ser President,> Z replied and waited, expecting some qualifying statement on the project.

Alex was silent, but the comm stayed open.

<Ser President, is there anything else you wish to add?> Z asked.

<No, Z, I was just giving you a moment to digest my request,> Alex replied.

Z desperately wished to begin running analysis programs on his research to define the proposal, but the lessons of Cordelia and Julien had risen higher and higher in his program hierarchy. He was reminded of the broader circumstances of Alex's request.

<Ser President, outside of the SADEs and yourself, with whom may this information be shared?> Z asked.

<No one, Z, until I announce the program,> Alex sent.

<Understood, Ser President,> Z replied. He acknowledged the value of his time with Cordelia and Julien and considered the unlikely events that had brought him here. He had been punished for expressing his desire to be mobile and then rescued by a foreign human who was now working to grant him his very wish.

Alex closed the comm, satisfied with the conversation. *Harakens are going to have to be a very flexible people*, Alex thought. Having accepted the Swei Swee, he hoped the Harakens would accept the SADEs walking amongst them.

-41-

Alex assembled an odd assortment of people in a small conference room aboard the *Freedom*. Sitting at the table were Mickey, Lazlo, Alex's father, Duggan, and two other pioneers.

One of the pioneers was Leonard Breslen, a shuttle manufacturer who had uprooted his family from New Terra. He was a close friend of Duggan, whose story of Alex's acquisition of the grav-driven travelers and his intentions to duplicate them gave the struggling company owner the idea to gamble his family's future by immigrating to Haraken. Leo had closely monitored the traveler fabrication processes and the test flights. Then he had approached Duggan, Mickey, and Lazlo to interest them in forming a shuttle manufacturing company.

The third pioneer was the son of a comms manufacturer. The father had built many of New Terra's satellites, but the introduction of the FTL networks was bankrupting the company, and the son decided to venture into unexplored territory as a pioneer.

There was one key individual missing from the meeting … Julien. Several times a day for the first few days after Julien had left, Alex had to halt the start of a comm request to Julien. He badly missed his friend's advice.

Alex's long workdays were stringing together, and it showed in his growing impatience. He sat down heavily in a conference room chair. "Sers, the report from our Ambassadors is that President Gonzalez has accepted our invitation," Alex began. "The *Rêveur* is on its way to Méridien, and we hope to generate some interest there. But I have questions that must be answered before this conference of leaders takes place. What's the price for a traveler … with or without beam weaponry? Do we even allow beam weaponry and to whom? What's the price for a gravity drive? Do we only sell ships or should we also license the technology? Is the price the same for both societies or are they related to an exchange rate of credits? Should we only accept credits or should we barter as well ... trading for things we need? And what do we need?" Alex droned on for several more minutes before he realized he had overwhelmed his audience. "Sorry," he said. He sent them a file with his list of questions and concerns.

"Mr. President," Duggan said gently, recognizing the extent of Alex's exhaustion. "Would you like to hear our suggestions now or should we take some time to organize our responses?"

Looking around the table, Alex realized how quickly he had destroyed the meeting's effectiveness. "Ser Breslen, as the most experienced individual in the shuttle construction business, I would be grateful if you would lead this group. Please manage the responses and contact whomever you need to help you."

Leo Breslen hadn't finished his statement of appreciation before Alex perfunctorily rose up from the table, said "Good night" to everyone, and left the conference room, Étienne right behind him. Alex was intending to return to his quarters planetside to be with Renée, but she met him in the corridor outside the conference room. She linked arms with him, and Etienne melted away for a late-night rendezvous with Ellie Thompson.

Renée led Alex to a vacant cabin two decks up. Once inside, she helped him strip out of his clothes and put him to bed. In moments, Alex was fast asleep. Without Julien, Renée left to appeal to Cordelia. But unlike the previous occasion when Cordelia had refused to violate her protocols to intervene on Alex's behalf, Renée found a willing partner.

<As you have requested, Ser, I've blocked the President's comm reception and rerouted his comm requests to myself and Z,> Cordelia said.

<I had expected your refusal, Cordelia?> Renée replied.

<My apologies, Ser. I was much younger then,> Cordelia replied.

That Cordelia was referring to a decision she had made only a half-year ago made Renée smile. *So many changes so fast*, Renée thought, recognizing she had echoed Eric Stroheim's often-made lament.

* * *

<Mr. President!> Mickey sent excitedly, early the next morning. <Mr. President?> Mickey tried again. <Cordelia, Z, I can't reach the President.>

<Apologies, Chief Engineer Brandon, Ser de Guirnon has requested the President's isolation. Is this an emergency, Chief?> Cordelia replied.

<No, Cordelia, it isn't an emergency,> Mickey replied, <but it is important. Just where is the President?>

Cordelia considered whether to divulge Alex's location since coincidentally Mickey was a mere fifty meters away from the cabin, probably focused on Étienne's implant. The escort had taken up the position in the corridor outside the President's door just a half-hour earlier when Cordelia had informed him the President was stirring. Julien had been her teacher as well as Z's on the intricacy of human interactions. Borrowing from Julien's lessons, she transferred Mickey's comm to Étienne.

<Chief Brandon, how may I help you?> Étienne replied.

<Étienne, I need the President now if he's available,> Mickey said.

<I believe this small cabin's refresher would be quite crowded with two New Terran males and a Méridien female,> Étienne deadpanned.

"Very funny, Étienne," Mickey replied as he rounded the corner a few meters away.

When Alex and Renée emerged from the cabin later, they found Étienne on duty and Mickey sitting on the deck, leaning back against the bulkhead and sound asleep.

"Chief Brandon was very anxious to speak to you earlier, Ser President," Étienne said. "I believe he might still wish a conversation with you."

When Alex shook Mickey's shoulder, the engineer awoke with a start, recognized Alex, and jumped up, grabbing his forearms. "Alex—I mean, Mr. President, I have a great idea. We need to talk now!"

"Join us for morning meal, Mickey," Alex replied. "We can talk over food."

Alex had to calm Mickey several times before they reached a meal room. Alex was in desperate need of a few cups of hot thé in the manner Terese had first prepared it for him, hot and a little sweet. "So tell me about your idea, Mickey," Alex said after his third cup of thé. Both he and Mickey had been making the most of the serving dishes the staff had begun supplying their table.

"Right, Mr. President. We know that we can duplicate a traveler from the crystals up. Good for us! So is there any reason we can't make use of those two frames aboard this city-ship?"

"I don't know, Mickey. Is there any reason we can't make use of those two frames?" Alex returned.

"That's just it, Mr. President. I don't know. From the hardware point of view, I can't think of any reason."

"Are you worried if we employ a dark traveler frame, it will result in some action or comm that you can't control?"

"That's it exactly. We may not know until it's too late," Mickey said, setting his utensil down and wringing his big hands before picking up his cup of thé.

Alex thought through the ramifications of Mickey's concern. On a signal from Renée, the staff retreated so as not to disturb the table. *Where's Julien when you need him?* René thought.

"I don't think we have to worry about it, Mickey," Alex finally said. "The Nua'll wouldn't have enabled the dark travelers to comm outside a system, so hidden comms won't broadcast anywhere that we need to worry about. And as for any hidden actions, that's a negative as well. If the dark travelers could have been directly controlled by the Nua'll, then the Swei Swee couldn't have attacked the Nua'll ringed-ships."

"That was the reason I needed to speak to you, Mr. President. I needed your logic on the question," Mickey said with a satisfied air, sipping on his cup.

"Then what about all those frames on Libre?" Renée asked.

Alex and Mickey turned to stare at Renée. Either of them might have had the same thought later in the day, but that Renée had directed staff traffic, followed their conversation, and leapt ahead of them, had surprised both men. Chuckling, Alex leaned over and kissed Renée on the temple.

"Well, Mickey?" Alex asked.

Mickey sat thinking for a few moments. "I'll need a few things, Mr. President," Mickey replied. "A city-ship, our traveler, some pilots, some engineers, some techs ..." Mickey's voice faded into silence as he switched to comm, involving Cordelia and Z in his planning.

Renée felt Alex's arm drape companionably around her shoulders. She was tempted to climb into his lap. For many days, Alex hadn't been much of a partner in the evening, too tired to do anything but fall into bed.

Alex continued to enjoy his thé while staff began serving dishes again. *Fortune ... we'll have half-a-hundred ready-made frames if this works,* Alex thought.

After breakfast, Alex and Mickey, with Étienne close behind, hurried down to the bay where the two dark travelers sat. As opposed to Alex's last visit, the bay was deserted. All the work stations, equipment, and personnel had transferred planetside as new facilities were completed. The frames stood naked in the center of the bay. Over time, the shells had continued to crumble, and the floor around the grav-lifts had required constant cleaning by the bots.

Very carefully, Alex and Mickey studied the frames for a quarter-hour, climbing over and under equipment, control panels, and drives.

"Mickey, you find anything?" Alex asked.

"Nothing, Mr. President," Mickey responded. "I can't find any corrosion or deterioration. It's like they came out of the fabrication facilities yesterday.

Standing on the decks of their open frames, the two men shared grins of delight. The infamous Nua'll technology, which had destroyed so many worlds, was about to help save one.

* * *

Mickey hurried to design a lift mechanism for their Haraken traveler. Rather than attempting to use tethering beams, which would have required extensive reworking of the vessel, Mickey chose a simpler approach and designed a fixed carrier harness.

The SADEs had calculated their traveler could manage the mass of a Nua'll frame, but Mickey, ever the engineer, wanted a real-life test. Sheila and Ellie piloted the traveler, complete with its new harness, to a position outside the *Freedom* while Mickey and a team of engineers and techs readied a dark traveler frame. EVA crew floated the frame outside the bay and into the harness, locking it in place.

Sheila and Ellie successfully landed the frame at the shell construction site, setting it down on a second grav-lift cradle. Then they made a return trip to the *Freedom* for the second frame.

<We've done it, Mr. President,> Mickey sent. <Both of the dark frames are safely on the ground. We'll begin modifying them with controllers in a few days. After that, it will be the Swei Swee's turn.>

Now that Mickey had done his part, Alex organized another mission to Libre, one in which he wouldn't be taking part. He had Cordelia organize the conference comm and started with Lazlo. <Captain Menlo, turn over command of the *Money Maker* to Lieutenant Durak. You're heading a mission for me.>

<Where are we going, Mr. President?> Lazlo asked.

<You're going to Libre to collect the Nua'll frames that were left on the cliff top. Mickey has a proven retrieval technique, and Commander Reynard and Lieutenant Thompson have practiced it and will be using our traveler as the lift vessel. Mickey will supply you with engineers, techs, and equipment to manage the retrieval of the frames. Captain Cordova will have command of the *Freedom*, but overall mission command belongs to you, Captain Menlo. Any questions?>

<Yes, Mr. President, I have several,> Lazlo stated. <Are any other ships accompanying us?>

<Negative, Captain,> Alex sent.

<Are we taking any fighter escort with us?> Lazlo asked.

<It's your choice, Captain. Talk to Commander Reynard if you feel so inclined, but it's understood that the pilots will be under your control. Anything else, Captain?>

<Last question, Mr. President,> Lazlo replied. <When do we launch this recovery mission?>

<Yesterday, Captain, but I'll settle for the time necessary to transfer personnel to and from the *Freedom.*>

<Mr. President, I am conducting personnel requests as we speak to determine the transfers and timeline,> Cordelia added. <The question is being asked as to the length of the mission.>

<Mickey, Sheila, any ideas?> Alex asked.

<The Lieutenant and I can probably lift and dock seven to eight frames a day,> Sheila replied.

<Cordelia?> Alex asked.

<With flight times and Commander Reynard's estimates, the mission should require thirty-three to thirty-six days, Mr. President. Barring any difficulties, the *Freedom* can be underway in two days.>

<Safe voyage, Captain Lazlo,> Alex said, then left the conference, allowing Lazlo to work through the details with his people.

* * *

The *Freedom* returned from Libre after being gone for thirty-four days. In her hold were forty-nine pristine dark traveler frames. Soon after the *Freedom* achieved orbit, Sheila and Ellie were ready to reverse the procedure and transfer the frames planetside. This time, they had help. Another Haraken traveler was ready, and after some test flights to prove it space-worthy, Ellie took over as pilot of the new traveler, and both she and Sheila picked up new copilots.

-42-

It was another Haraken landmark day. The *Rêveur* exited FTL into the Hellébore system carrying President Maria Gonzalez and three of her Ministers. The Haraken liner was a half-day ahead of the *Il Piacere*, a House Diamanté luxury liner transporting three Méridien House Leaders.

Ticks after exiting FTL, Julien was on the comm to Alex. <I'm home, Mr. President.>

<Julien!> Alex sent. <I'm happy you're back. Communicate to Admiral Tachenko that I need the *Rêveur* stationed near the *Freedom*. Renée and I will be visiting your guests this evening.>

<We look forward to your visit, Mr. President,> Julien replied. He sent a brief comm to Cordelia before he resumed his ship's duties.

* * *

When Julien apprised Maria of Alex's approaching shuttle, she scooped up her Ministers and headed for the *Rêveur*'s bays, meeting Tatia and Edouard on the way. As soon as the bay was pressurized, Maria led the group through the airlock.

The shuttle's gangway ramp had scarcely touched down when Renée came bolting down it, racing across the bay to jump into Maria's arms. Tears threatened to spill from both women's eyes. When Maria saw Alex descending the ramp, she gently released Renée. As Alex's feet hit the bay's deck, Maria extended him an exaggerated curtsy, flourishing her arms broadly and saying, "Your Highness."

"Your Highness, is it?" Alex shot back, his brow furrowing in distaste at the greeting.

"Well, Mr. President, I thought I would take the opportunity to get in some practice. Who knows what your next elevation in status might be?" Maria replied.

"Yes, well, it's just 'President' for now, Madam President, and that's President of a mass of refugees on a nascent world that's not completely terraformed. I think the title translates as 'he whom we blame when things don't work.'"

"As you have taught us, Mr. President, life sometimes brings enormous challenges and the good and brave rise to meet those challenges. Now we're here to help you meet your challenges just as you helped New Terra."

Maria was pleased to see Alex's lopsided grin, and she stepped forward to embrace him.

"Thank you for coming, Maria," Alex whispered.

"I wouldn't have missed it for the universe, Alex," Maria replied. She had hoped this day would come to pass, and now her wish was fulfilled. Maria saw Haraken as a powerful friend and ally, especially with Alex as President. After the flotilla had left New Terra, more than one advisor had counseled her not to count on Alex reinventing the Swei Swee ships, but she, along with Will Drake and Darryl Jaya—her fellow Transfer Team members—would have bet huge credits on Alex and his people finding a way to make the improbable happen.

Alex and Renée greeted their old acquaintances, Ministers Will Drake and Darryl Jaya, and were introduced to Maria's Minister of Finance, Yoshiko Ishikawa.

"And how are you finding your trip so far, Minister Ishikawa?" Renée asked.

"Ser de Guirnon," Yoshiko replied, "I'm experiencing so many firsts, it's making me dizzy … meeting Méridiens, enjoying their food, interstellar travel, and my conversations with Julien."

"Well, I can understand the latter making anyone dizzy," Alex replied drily.

Most of the group was entirely unaware of the image fight that flew between Alex and Julien, except for Renée and Tatia, who picked up on Alex's slight pause. Had anyone been able to observe the onslaught, they might have perceived the host of new images that had been specially created by each individual for just this moment, and the two of them were enjoying themselves immensely.

"I must say, Mr. President," Yoshiko continued, "my family and I enjoyed every moment of the vids sent from Libre. We were especially entranced by Mutter's songs to the Swei Swee. Would there be an opportunity to meet the aliens?"

"Minister Ishikawa," Maria said, "I believe we should take this historical meeting one step at a time, and as it regards the Swei Swee, we shall wait for an invitation."

"Your pardon, Madam President, I was carried away," Yoshiko said.

"Nonsense," Renée told Yoshiko, hooking her arm and leading her toward the airlock. "I have found curiosity has led me to the most intriguing of places."

"Tomorrow," Alex announced to the remaining group, "we will begin formal negotiations, and we will be adding three Méridien House Leaders who will make orbit by early morning. I thought it would be pleasant to have this evening for old friends."

Alex hooked his arm in Maria's and followed Renée, who had Yoshiko's rapt attention.

Maria regarded Alex out of the corner of her eye. That negotiations were to proceed in a communal setting was not what she had expected, and she knew Alex too well to believe it was a mere coincidence created by the timely arrival of the Méridiens.

* * *

Early the next morning, Eric Stroheim joined the three House Leaders aboard the *Il Piacere*.

"Ambassador Stroheim," said Devon O'Shea, the House Leader responsible for planetside, "our SADE reported one of your city-ships is stationed inward of Hellébore's asteroid ring. It was observed slowly spinning. Is it malfunctioning?"

"The *Unsere Menschen* is employed slinging ice asteroids at our planet, Ser. According to the SADEs' estimates, Rainmaker should enable Haraken to achieve a Bellamonde-like atmosphere in another two years."

"Are you not concerned for the safety of your people planetside, Ser?" asked Katarina Pasko, Leader of the House that designed, installed, and monitored Méridien implants. She was especially anxious to meet President Racine, having witnessed his implant powers when he was in the Confederation's Council Chambers.

"As I understand it, Sers, Rainmaker and Z are employing the President's g-sling program. They've already launched hundreds of ice asteroids at Haraken, and each one has struck the oceans as planned. They carefully limit the size and type of the asteroid to ensure the effects of entry and splashdown are minimized. It's quite exciting."

"Pardon, Ser, who is Rainmaker?" Gino Diamanté asked. It was he who had put together this group of Leaders when Council Leader Ganesh refused to meet with Haraken's Ambassadors. However, nothing restricted House Leaders from accepting the invitation, although they were limited in the scope of any business arrangements.

"That would be our Minister of Mining, Ser Benjamin Diaz, Leader Diamanté. He created the concept of hauling the asteroids from the ring, tethering them to the city-ship with the New Terrans' beam technology, and slinging them at the planet."

* * *

Despite the new safety protocols designed to bar the President from entering a bay during a shuttle's arrival, Alex and Maria waited with their contingents inside one of the *Freedom*'s bays for an *Il Piacere* shuttle. Cordelia focused on her sensors, ensuring the outer catch-lock doors were sealed and the space pressurized before the interior door was opened to the bay. When Cordelia had copied the new safety protocols to Julien after his return from his trip, he had laughed, sending, <I have done my best to

restrict our President's predilection for danger for over two years with only minor success. I wish you good fortune in your efforts, Cordelia.>

Accompanied by Eric, the House Leaders descended the shuttle's gangway ramp. Eyeing the beauty of the three visitors, especially that of Katarina Pasko, Maria remarked quietly to Alex, "Does every Méridien look like they stepped out of a holo-vid?"

Alex stared quietly at Maria until she thought she had said something insulting. Then quietly he said to her, "Heart is worth more than beauty any day, and your heart will serve your people well."

Maria glanced at the deck for a moment and then raised her head, holding it up proudly. *A good friend and loyal people*, she thought. *This is a good day.*

The House Leaders and Eric walked through rows of Haraken honor guards, who held no plasma rifles this time. Everyone taking part in the negotiations had been issued the streamlined harnesses to facilitate translations and private conversations between parties. After introductions, Alex explained the day's itinerary, most of which would take place planetside.

"If I may, President Racine," Darryl Jaya asked, "how are the Swei Swee faring after so many generations in captivity?"

"I beg your pardon, Minister Jaya, but of what are you speaking?" Gino Diamanté asked.

"Our government received summary vids of President Racine's entire activities at Arnos. We learned that the Swei Swee had been captured and held by the Nua'll for eight generations."

"Extraordinary!" Gino exclaimed.

"President Racine, did you send these summary vids to Council Leader Ganesh?" Katarina asked.

"No, Leader Pasko," Alex replied, "but then again, I didn't know they were being sent to New Terra, either. Julien was the architect of that operation."

"But … Julien is your SADE, President Racine," Devon O'Shea said. "He must seek your approval … unless … perhaps he has become—"

"Leaders," Eric said, interrupting Devon, "perhaps it is my fault for not preparing you sufficiently for this meeting. This is not the Confederation, and we are not Méridiens or New Terrans here. We are Harakens. Our SADEs are not second-class citizens, tools of Houses and starships. They are equal in status to any Haraken citizen and have free will. One day, they hope to walk among us, and we support that endeavor. Julien is perhaps our preeminent SADE, having supported President Racine in his efforts to save the Confederation from the Nua'll. He deserves your respect for his accomplishments, and you should know that all of Haraken honors each and every SADE as valuable Haraken citizens."

Devon O'Shea glanced at Leader Diamanté. He had been warned to be careful with the Harakens, but the import of that warning did not sink home until now. "My apologies, President Racine," Devon said, delivering a Leader's bow to Alex. "I meant no disrespect."

"And that's the sad part, Leader O'Shea," Alex replied, "that you had not thought your comment disrespectful."

Renée took the opportunity to put the itinerary back on track. "Well, now that our first awkward moment is over," she said, "I believe the unveiling was next on the agenda, was it not, President Racine?"

Renée took Maria's arm and guided her toward a shroud-covered vessel. As Alex and his people followed, Eric ushered the Leaders in the same direction.

<President Racine,> Gino sent in private, <my sincere apologies for Leader O'Shea's comment. Our society's views have been carefully ingrained in us since childhood. It will take time for our people to learn to work together. I hope you will allow us that time. I for one, Mr. President, have no affinity for airlocks that lead nowhere.>

Alex glanced over to Gino Diamanté and grudgingly offered him a nod. Gino's reference to the first discussion Alex had experienced with Eric Stroheim told him his Ambassador had worked hard to prepare the Leaders for their visit. Alex turned to look behind him at Eric and offered him a nod as well.

<Catastrophe number one averted,> Tomas sent privately to Eric. <Well done. It appears our Ambassador duties will keep us quite busy until the Méridiens return home.>

Eric offered his friend a quick smile as he guided the Leaders to the viewing spot. Gone was Eric's impression of Independents as wayward children who required his care, a duty his House had been tasked to perform. His relationships with the Harakens, one and all, were so much deeper than those he'd ever had on his home world. Harakens had become good acquaintances and better friends.

Alex stood in front of the shrouded vessel. "We have discovered some amazing facts about these ships, which we refer to as 'travelers.' The vessel that we will demonstrate today is a hybrid. The entire shuttle, except for the shell, was fabricated on Haraken. The shell has to be tuned, for want of a better word, which only the Swei Swee can do at this time. Three hives of Swei Swee accepted my offer to leave Libre and live on Haraken. In addition to this single shuttle, we have fifty-one frames that had been abandoned on Libre when the Swei Swee were freed. The Nua'll equipment is pristine even after being exposed to salt air for a quarter-year. To date, the Swei Swee females complete a shell about every thirty-two days."

"Could you not co-opt the other hives, as you call them, to expedite your assembly rate, Mr. President?" Katarina asked.

Before Alex could respond—and judging by his body language, it was better he didn't—Gino Diamanté stepped in. "If I may interrupt you, Leader Pasko. Allow me to ask some clarifying questions." Gino turned to Alex, giving him a subtle nod, requesting Alex's patience. "President Racine, what is the status of the Swei Swee in Haraken society?"

"Full citizenship, Ser," Alex replied.

"Do the Swei Swee understand these rights, President Racine?" Gino asked.

"No, they don't, Leader Diamanté. Our language comprehension progresses, but there is little common ground between our cultures to enable us to communicate on these complex subjects," Alex replied. "We have a simple arrangement, one the Swei Swee accept. They are an intelligent species that has been offered sanctuary on our planet, and they have an exclusive enclave on a cliff west of the site of our first city, Espero. While there are three hives, there is but a single leader. The Swei Swee regard their leader as you would your Council Leader, and we treat the First, as he is known, accordingly."

Gino turned to his fellow Leaders and pointedly said, "I believe that clarifies the subject for us."

"Sers," Eric said, addressing the Méridien Leaders, "when a subject confuses you, which may happen frequently during your visit, you might choose to consult privately before speaking. As I have related to you, I myself was in similar circumstances when I first came aboard the *Rêveur*. I was fortunate to have my good friend Ambassador Monti speak for both of us when I might have destroyed negotiations before they had even begun."

"Yes, well ..." Maria said, stepping into the silence that had followed Eric's subtle reprimand. "President Racine, I am anxious to witness what you have fabricated."

Alex acknowledged Maria's request with a slight tilt of his head and signaled to four techs waiting nearby. When they pulled on the dark sheath, it poured off the ultra-smooth shell like water.

Mickey had ordered extra lighting panels installed over the top of the traveler. The blues, greens, and whites of the shell, reminiscent of shallow ocean waters, gleamed in the focused light. The traveler floated on top of its grav-cradle, its graceful shape undisturbed.

Leader Pasko had taken note of Ambassador Stroheim's recommendation about consulting privately before saying something that could come across as untoward. Furthermore, she did not want to earn President Racine's animosity because she was anxious to learn much from him about his implant control. <Leader Diamanté,> Katarina sent, <were they not dark silver before?>

Gino diplomatically rephrased the question to Alex. "Most intriguing colors, President Racine. Quite beautiful. Is there an intrinsic structural reason for the change?"

"Yes, Leader Diamanté," Alex replied. "The original dark travelers were a form of Swei Swee rebellion against the Nua'll."

"Might you share the story with us, President Racine?" Gino asked.

Both Katarina and Devon took note of the deference Leader Diamanté paid President Racine and the ease with which the Haraken responded to his requests.

"The Swei Swee knew that at any moment they might be discarded by their captors," Alex said. "So they built shells with material that would degrade if not maintained. This," Alex said, waving his hand at the new traveler, "is how the Swei Swee build their own dwellings. This shell is extremely durable, and we have had a most challenging time forming hatches."

"Speaking of which, President Racine, I don't see one," said Darryl Jaya, peering at the shell.

On Alex's cue, Sheila, waiting in the pilot seats with Ellie, triggered the hatch. The visitors watched a seam appear in the side of the shell, and then a hatch, pivoting along its bottom edge, levered out and down. Once the hatch descended below the horizontal plane, a set of steps extended from within the frame to reach the deck.

Mickey appeared at the top of the steps. As he began his descent, Alex said, "I would like to present Chief Engineer Michael Brandon, who led the Haraken efforts to build our first traveler."

Mickey received a round of bows and applause from the visitors and his own people.

Next, Alex introduced Sheila and Ellie as the pilots who risked their lives to test the traveler. Both women descended the hatch's steps to stand beside Mickey, and they, too, enjoyed the audience's appreciation. When Sheila scanned the audience, she found Minister Jaya staring at her with a most intent expression.

In a simulcast through his comm and his harness, Alex said, "Next, I would like to present others who share honor with Mickey for our success."

Julien, Cordelia, and Z then spoke to the assembly via Alex's implant and channeled through his belt harness, speaking their names and announcing themselves as Haraken SADEs. The distinction was not lost on the audience, especially the Méridien visitors.

"And lastly, but certainly not least by any means," Alex said, "I would like to introduce to you the entity who did more than any individual to build our relationship with the Swei Swee, saving hundreds, if not thousands, of lives. Her knowledge of music helped decode the Swei Swee language, and on both planets the Swei Swee have adopted her as their Hive Singer, a most prestigious position. Sers, I present Mutter."

"Good morning, Sers," Mutter said. "President Racine flatters me. I have been the SADE aboard my freighter, now known as the *Money Maker*, for more than 231 years. Through the Admiral's efforts, I have been proud to participate in the rescue of both the Libran population and the Swei Swee. Now I find no greater pleasure in my existence than my evening serenades to the Swei Swee. I'm proud to be called 'Hive Singer.'"

The House Leaders could only manage short, stuttered questions via their implants to one another. The world of the Harakens was far stranger than they could have imagined.

As the Minister of Technology, Darryl Jaya was beside himself with curiosity. He whispered into Maria's ear, "I am about to soil my trousers in anticipation, Madam President."

Maria was sympathetic to Darryl's burning curiosity. "We will be allowed to go aboard, will we not, President Racine?"

"Oh, more than that, President Gonzalez," Alex replied. "This is your transport planetside."

On cue, Mickey, Sheila, and Ellie stood aside and gestured to the company to board the traveler. Terese and Pia had the honor of acting as hostesses for the prestigious guests. They stood in the hatch entrance with smiles on their faces.

Throwing aside protocol, Darryl Jaya hurried to the traveler, scampered up the steps, and paused briefly to nod to Terese and Pia before he disappeared inside. Maria and Will shared a laugh over Jaya's uncontrollable curiosity. They quickly followed him, and the Ambassadors directed the Leaders to board.

When everyone was settled in for the flight and the bay had been cleared, Sheila and Ellie guided the vessel out of the bay for the trip planetside. Inside the traveler, the first-time passengers were engrossed in examining the comfortable interior. Méridien-style seating conformed to their individual bodies. From general amenities to interior lighting, the finish cried luxurious styling. There was little that was utilitarian.

"President Racine, do you intend to appoint all the shuttles in this wonderful quality?" Katarina asked, squirming deliciously in her seat.

"Sers, you must keep in mind that this is not a shuttle," Alex replied. "We refer to this vessel as a 'traveler.' It has the capacity to move throughout any system without reaction mass and at a max velocity of 0.91c. You should allow for the comfort of your passengers. However, we will finish the traveler interiors to your specifications, or you may build them out as you please." Alex had noticed Katarina's efforts to catch his attention. It had not escaped his notice that her House was responsible for Méridien implants and probably was the underlying reason for her efforts.

After several more questions for Alex, conversation coalesced among each group of visitors. Their discussions focused on the ramifications to their societies of the Harakens' successful re-creation of a silver ship.

When the New Terrans' conversation dwindled, Darryl Jaya could no longer contain his impatience. "President Racine, when will we depart?"

Alex stood up and turned around to face the seated passengers. "Commander Reynard has informed me that we will be entering the atmosphere soon."

"But the takeoff, the motion, the engines, the acceleration …" Darryl said.

Alex bestowed a huge grin on Darryl. "These travelers are quite remarkable, aren't they, Minister Jaya?"

The visitors urgently whispered or communicated implant to implant. Thoughts of efficient, environmentally neutral, long-range shuttles had intrigued them, but experiencing the absence of the traveler's flight mechanics was proving to be overwhelming. Finally, the passengers felt the disturbance of atmospheric reentry, but it was nothing akin to their experiences in their own shuttles. The traveler's ultra-sleek design and smooth skin slid through the air, and the shell absorbed the friction heat to charge its collectors.

Soon after the ride had become smooth again, the interior lights slowly brightened. "That's the signal that we've landed, Sers," Alex said, accompanying his comment with an apologetic shrug of his shoulders. "There is no other indication of an arrival, not with experienced pilots. Haraken is still a little dry and a little short of oxygen, although we are working on that. Please make your way efficiently on to the transport that's waiting for you."

The visitors stood and headed rearward to where Terese and Pia stood. The hatch seam appeared, bright sunlight streaming through it, and the steps extended from the lowered hatch.

Jaya nodded politely to Maria and extended his hand to allow her to precede him.

"I see, Minister," Maria said. "Now that an inhospitable environment awaits us, you suddenly remember to let your President go first." Maria laughed at Darryl's crestfallen expression and patted him on the shoulder as she passed him by. Will laughed as well and then gently pushed Darryl ahead of him.

As the visitors exited the craft, they looked back at the traveler, which floated on another grav-lift cradle. When they boarded the transport, they sought window seats that faced the ship, staring at its mesmerizing colors as they glowed in Haraken's morning sun. Entranced as they were by the view of the traveler, their attention was snatched away by an ice asteroid shooting overhead, its wide plume of steam streaming behind it.

Maria shook her head in disbelief. Where the Méridiens were content with their technology, entrenched in safety protocols, and New Terrans had yet to become technologically advanced, Harakens surmounted challenges with imaginative innovations. She realized that, given time, the Harakens would change this corner of the galaxy.

* * *

Negotiations lasted nine days. On the subject of monetary exchange, and at Minister Ishikawa's urging, President Gonzalez offered a universal credit, a one-to-one exchange with Haraken credits. Alex recognized a gift when he saw one and accepted it. The House Leaders could offer no such deal. They lacked the authority, but promised to pay for the travelers in Con-Fed credits at par value. Transferring their credits to an exchange run by SADEs seemed imminently sensible to them.

After the question of credits had been settled, negotiations had begun in earnest for the travelers. Alex's team, headed by Leo Breslen, had met with him days earlier. When they had presented the traveler's pricing, with and without finished interiors and with and without beam technology, Alex had been shocked.

"Sers, I have had only one experience with pricing a ship which was my own, the original *Outward Bound.* I find these prices incredible. How did you arrive at these?" Alex had asked.

"Mr. President," Leo Breslen had replied, "we discovered we had no means of establishing a price based on materials and labor. The technology is unique … priceless one might say. So we chose to price our most basic traveler against the real-world costs of Méridien shuttle construction plus the costs of reaction mass and maintenance over the life expectancy of the shuttle, which our SADEs were able to supply."

Alex had expected the Méridien Leaders to balk at the prices. But within moments of conferring, they were all smiles and bargaining for terms and delivery times. Between the three Leaders, they purchased a total of nineteen travelers, agreeing to a 50 percent down payment. Their shuttles would be delivered over a period of two years.

Unfortunately the price of a traveler was a challenge to Maria's government budgets. But Alex had other plans for New Terra. Once he established that Maria was interested in sixteen of the travelers, Alex calculated the total price and offered Maria a deal. Alex's advisory team had identified items that Harakens needed and would be stretched to produce, but that New Terra had in abundance, food stock, raw materials, and manpower.

Alex and Maria sketched out a complex agreement. Haraken would deliver travelers, and New Terra would provide hundreds of kilotons of food stock per Haraken specifications and provide workers and many of the materials to build Haraken's first orbital station. Maria recognized her gift was being returned. New Terra had food production capability to spare and thousands of engineers and techs who would give a digit or two to work on a Méridien-designed orbital station, as well as take part in creating the tens of thousands of items required.

Once negotiations were completed, there was only one item left on the agenda—only, it wasn't on Alex's agenda.

-43-

Maria and Gino had expressed sincere desires to greet the Swei Swee First. However, after Alex had explained the First's greeting ceremony, Gino graciously bowed out. Only Maria had stood her ground, saying she was prepared to consume a fish's flesh for the honor of greeting the First.

Alex, his people, and the visitors took the traveler to the shell construction site, landing it in its cradle. Per Alex's instructions, the group disembarked and remained near the shuttle. He did not want to confuse the First during the introduction.

Two more shells were under construction, the females crawling over the unfinished edges. Leader O'Shea broached the subject that had been on his mind. "Ser de Guirnon," Devon said, "if the Swei Swee are citizens, how do you compensate them?"

"We are still working on that, Ser," Renée responded. "The Swei Swee could request many things for their labors, and they would be granted. Presently, they're focused on returning to a normal life. They fish, build dwellings, and … procreate. The egg domes have tripled since they've arrived. The shells they build are a tribute to the Star Hunter First," Renée added, indicating Alex.

Maria sidled next to Eric. She had found that the Ambassador often offered her valuable and insightful advice, allowing her to glean helpful impressions of first-time contact with Alex and the Harakens.

"Have you greeted the Swei Swee First, Ambassador Stroheim?" Maria asked.

"Fortune forbid, President Gonzalez! Only President Racine has received that … that honor," Eric replied, shuddering at the thought of consuming the ceremonial offering.

"Do you have any suggestions for me, Ser?" Maria asked.

"Ser President, when entering uncharted territory, I advise it is always wise to follow the leader," Eric replied.

Maria's mouth twitched as she controlled her desire to laugh at Eric's reference to the children's game, but a glance at the Ambassador found him staring at Alex. Maria had made preparations for this moment in concert with Julien and hoped Alex would be pleased by her request. Now it struck her how serious the event was for the Swei Swee and the Harakens. The realization wouldn't change her plans, but it changed the emotional overtone.

Alex motioned Maria forward. After crossing half the distance to the travelers under shell construction, Alex's harness cut loose with a loud whistle. A large Swei Swee male burst from the swim tank and raced toward them. Maria's footsteps stuttered to a halt at the furious rush of the alien creature. Vids had not prepared her for reality. She felt Alex's hand firmly grasp hers and was grateful for the contact.

When the claw-snapping First skidded to a halt in front of them, Maria felt too petrified to move. A series of whistles and warbles were exchanged by the creature and Alex, and Maria's harness and ear comm followed their simple greeting. When the Swei Swee's four eyestalks focused on her, she felt lightheaded. She was in the presence of an alien … a true alien. Alex sat cross-legged on the ground. Eric's words returned to her, and she followed Alex's lead. When the First lowered himself to the ground and stopped snapping its claws, it mollified her somewhat and she worked to recall her plan. She watched Alex extend his hands in claw fashion, and the First placed his claws below Alex's in greeting.

The First's eyestalks flicked from the Star Hunter First to the large entity seated next to him. The First hoped he was to greet the Star Hunter First's new mate. His people had been saddened that the leader of the Star Hunter had only the one mate and a puny one at that.

Before Alex could introduce her, Maria triggered her belt harness via her ear comm to issue its initial phrase. "World First greets Star Hunter First," whistled forth, and Maria held out claw-like hands to Alex, who extended his hands to her in greeting. But where Alex sought to touch fingertips to fingertips, Maria lowered her hands below his. From the corner of her eyes, she saw the Swei Swee's eyestalks train on the relative positions of their human claws.

Maria turned to the Swei Swee and triggered her second phrase. Her belt whistled, "World First greets Swei Swee First." Maria waited until the First's claws were fully extended before she reached out and touched fingertips to claw tips—not above and not below. She held her hands still while the First's eyestalks flicked from their touching appendages, then to Alex and back.

The First pulled his claws back. He had identified the entity in front of him as female, and she was not a mate but a leader … a female leader. It seemed confusing, but the female had been brought to him by the Star Hunter First. There was no time to dwell on the oddities … Ceremony was required. He whistled his needs, and a large male shot out of the swim pool and hurried to the feeding tank. With a small fish pinioned in a claw, he scurried to the First, lowering himself to the ground to offer the tribute.

The First accepted the fish, snipping off its head and tail and stripping its skin. In the meantime, the Swei Swee females had stopped work and closed around the leaders to observe the greeting ceremony. The oldest and largest matrons crowded close to Maria, their mouth parts smacking as they tasted the air. Warbles and tweets passed between them. The new leader had been identified as female and presented as an equal to their First, which made this a momentous occasion.

"The females are impressed, Maria," Alex said, his voice soothing her. "It's an important event for them to discover a female leader."

When one of the matrons inadvertently bumped Maria, the eyestalks of the First flicked toward the offender, and his shrill whistle pierced the air. The matrons obediently retreated several meters.

Maria watched the Swei Swee male efficiently strip the fish. He spread his claws to enable him to come close to Alex. Maria could scent the odors of the sea from his body. One fillet of the fish was offered to Alex, who immediately bit into it, chewing noisily. The First whistled softly in response, bobbing up and down. Maria understood the action as excited approval. When the Swei Swee stripped the second fillet, his eyestalks focused closely on the piece of flesh, and he carefully divided it in two. He offered both pieces to her.

"You have presented yourself as equals, Maria," Alex said quietly. "Choose one."

Maria took one of the pieces and held the cool flesh in her hand. While she gathered her courage, the First's eyestalks flicked between her offering, her face, and Alex. She glanced at Alex. In response, he bit a large piece of tissue off his fillet and continued to smack and chew. Maria put the flesh in her mouth, her stomach roiling, but as she bit down a light, sweet flavor covered her tongue. As she chewed, a refreshing flavor filled her mouth. She concentrated on the taste and tried not to think of the creature she was eating. A bit late, she realized her eyes were closed. She opened them to find the Swei Swee First's four eyes staring at her. Maria heard Alex chewing noisily and grunting, so she played "follow the leader" and began smacking her lips and chewing noisily.

The First whistled shrilly, which nearly had Maria bolting back to the shuttle, but she maintained her place. He stuffed his portion of the fillet in his mouth, smacking and chewing on the flesh. The host of Swei Swee burst into a raucous celebration of whistles and snapping claws.

"When is the ceremony concluded, Alex?" Maria asked. She felt she was depending on a younger brother to guide her through treacherous waters.

"When all have finished their share, Maria," Alex replied.

Maria looked at the portion of her share that remained. She glanced to Alex and then to the First. Both were licking their hands, having finished their ceremonial offerings. Maria took a breath and let it out. Then she concentrated on biting, chewing, and swallowing, as if she was in a TSF training regimen. She hadn't made Terran Security Forces General by possessing a mind unable to focus.

When Maria was finished, Alex stood up, but Maria found it difficult to stand. She felt lightheaded again, and her legs were shaky. Alex helped her up, which she greatly appreciated. The Swei Swee extended his dangerously pointed and edged claws to Alex, who formed fists and smacked down on the claws. Then the First extended his claws to Maria, and she tapped them lightly. The claws stayed in place, and the eyestalks swiveled between her and Alex. "Follow the leader," echoed in her mind, and she thumped the colorful blue-green claws with her fists, which felt like striking stone.

The First loosed an earsplitting whistle and the assembly joined in. Maria watched Alex raise his hands over his head, spinning around and snapping his fingers. Maria shrugged her broad shoulders and copied Alex. It had been years since she had danced, although she had loved to as a young girl. The more she spun and snapped, the better she felt. Soon she realized the laughter she heard was coming from her. A great many concerns as President of New Terra fell away as she participated in the ceremony's conclusion. Completing a rotation, she saw that Alex had stopped, and she did the same. Her grin was an echo of the one Alex wore.

Alex was ready to return to the traveler, but as the First backed away, the eldest matrons, those most heavily scarred of shell and claw, came close to Maria. Alex stepped back to clear room for the females since they were intent on Maria. The matrons stopped a half-meter away from her, lifting their claws in the air and bobbing slowly.

"Alex?" Maria asked nervously, her concern returning.

"I believe you have created a new concept for the Swei Swee—a female leader. The matrons wish to share in the moment."

"Do you have a suggestion, Alex?" Maria asked.

"You are the leader of a world, Maria," Alex replied. "Follow your diplomatic instincts."

Maria looked at the heavy, blunt pair of claws directly in front of her. The female's claws and carapace were a torment of scars and scrapes across what probably had been a beautiful shell. Her heart reached out to the female and what she had endured throughout her life, mining for the Nua'll. In her mind, she was a General again, and a trooper who had been injured in the line of duty now stood in front of her, waiting to be decorated. Maria's fists closed tightly and she smacked down on the blunt claws in front of her. The elderly matron warbled softly and briefly lowered herself to the ground before scuttling backward. Another female took her place.

Alex watched female after female stand before the World First, anxious to share in the moment. He would have interrupted, knowing what the constant impact was doing to Maria's hands, but she wore a determined look and was smacking claws with vigor.

<Terese,> Alex sent.

<Standing by with ointment, Mr. President,> Terese returned.

When the last matron received Maria's greeting, Alex guided her back toward the traveler. She was breathing heavily and the edges of her hands bled from the nicks on the females' claws, but she wore the most beatific smile. "I have new friends," Alex heard her say. When they reached the traveler, Terese applied the nanites ointment to Maria's hand.

Tatia stepped up to the two Presidents and handed them small cups. "Perhaps the Presidents would care for a palate cleansing after your ceremony?"

As Tatia filled the two cups with amber liquid, Alex thought to admonish Maria to swallow, not swish and spit while they were within sight of the Swei Swee, but he needn't have bothered. Maria slugged down the ship's brew of cactus alcohol and held her cup out for a refill. It appeared the two ex-TSF officers had shared drinks more than once.

* * *

Back at the Haraken facilities that had been used for negotiations, the House Leaders and Maria approved their agreements as recorded by the SADEs.

Katarina Pasko took the opportunity to ask Alex for a moment or two of his time in private. Alex indicated a small office, and they retired behind a closed door. The Ambassadors regarded each other as did the remaining two Leaders. Renée, however, stared at the closed door.

Once inside the office, Katarina resorted to her implant. <I would appreciate a discussion on the source of the implant power you displayed in the Council Chambers.> She stepped close to Alex, cutting into his personal space, seeking to take advantage of her similar appearance to Ser de Guirnon. The two might have been mistaken for sisters.

Shades of Lina, Alex thought. <It's interesting you should mention this subject, Leader Pasko,> Alex said, holding his ground and putting on what he hoped was a disinterested expression. <I have attempted several times to recreate the experience and have been unsuccessful. I believe it was a one-time event driven by the emotions of the moment.>

<Perhaps, I can help you explore your capabilities,> Katarina sent, stepping so close to Alex that her delicate features filled his vision.

Alex shrugged his broad shoulders in a show of apathy and reverted to voice. "Personally, I have no desire to explore the effect, Leader Pasko. Thank you for your interest and your offer," Alex said politely and then turned and exited the office. With no more business to conduct, Alex led the way out of the facilities to their traveler.

Renée and Terese were focused on the office doorway, intent on gauging Katarina's expression following her conversation with Alex.

<I wonder if Leader Pasko knows how much scowling ruins a beautiful visage?> Terese sent to Renée.

<Yes, it appears our President has been a disappointment to our visitor,> Renée sent back.

As the two women turned toward the exit lock, employed to trap oxygen-rich air inside, their evil grins of satisfaction remained unseen by Katarina Pasko. Renée hurried to catch up with Alex, sliding her hand into the crook of his elbow. His hand covered hers without missing a word in his conversation with the visitors.

* * *

Gino had deliberately sought a seat on the traveler next to President Gonzalez for the trip back to their respective ships. He chatted amiably with her for much of the journey.

"Leader Diamanté," Maria said, in a lull in the conversation, "we will be landing soon. My intuition says you have something to say or ask."

"Your instincts are correct, President Gonzalez," Gino replied. "I've been deciding how to encourage an invitation. In Méridien society, one is required to wait till one is asked."

"Then it's probably good you're not talking to a Méridien, Leader Diamanté," Maria replied.

Gino desperately wished he was communicating via implant. It was easy to understand an individual's true intent when it came from their thoughts. Too much opportunity for change existed when thoughts traveled the pathways from mind to mouth, as evidenced by his observations of children. Then again, the Haraken President was an example of a New Terran who was most direct in his speech, and it was obvious he and President Gonzalez were close compatriots.

"I would like to visit New Terra, President Gonzalez," Gino finally said.

"What would be the purpose of your visit, Leader Diamanté?" Maria asked. "The Confederation has better tech than us, and many of your people believe contact with my people contaminates your society."

"That is all quite true, Ser President," Gino replied. "It would require you and I work that much harder to find common ground for trade, or are you suggesting that two people such as us would fail at the task?"

Maria extended her powerful hand to Gino, saying, "I look forward to your visit, Leader Diamanté."

The traveler landed aboard the *Freedom,* where it had access to a cradle. In the future, the Harakens might develop landing gear, but for now, grav-lift cradles were required at any landing zone.

Maria Gonzalez and her Ministers boarded Captain Lillian Hauser's liner for the return trip home. In fifty-six days, New Terra would receive the *Freedom* and load it with food stocks, building materials, and work force. The latter group would be composed of techs, engineers, and EVA crew who would help the Harakens build their planet's first orbital station. The thought of New Terra's T-Stations operating at full capacity for years to come pleased Maria, but more than that, New Terra would have technological access to the entire gamut of materials created for the Méridien-designed orbital station.

There had been one subject that Maria had not resolved to her satisfaction. Privately she had broached the subject of travelers with beam weaponry for New Terra, but Alex's answer had been conditional. He didn't say no, and he didn't say yes. He stated he needed more time to consider his decision. It was a mature answer for a leader, Maria had thought.

Aboard the *Il Piacere*, the House Leaders and their support staff were an hour ahead of Captain Hauser's liner, bound for Méridien. Gino Diamanté sipped his drink, luxuriating in their mission's success. Every other Méridien House Leader, except for the two in his company, had chosen not to join him for various reasons. Some intensely disliked Alex Racine. Others were incensed at the presence of Independents on Cetus—as they chose to still call the planet. And many other excuses had been offered. However, Gino knew the unstated and fundamental reason they had chosen to stay home—they feared Council Leader Ganesh.

* * *

Word had circulated throughout the flotilla that Alex and his entourage had remained aboard the *Freedom* after the visitors departed, and they were making their way to the central gardens. People began gathering in public places—parks, meal rooms, and any place they could congregate, anticipating the President's announcement. Even the pilots and crew operating in the belt slowed their work to listen.

In the *Freedom*'s central gardens, Alex found a quiet bench for him and Renée. <Cordelia, all Harakens, please,> Alex sent.

<With the greatest of pleasure, Ser President,> Cordelia replied.

<Good evening, Harakens,> Alex began. <We have secured contracts for traveler production for the next two years. By the time they are delivered, Rainmaker should have secured us atmospheric conditions that will allow the planting of our first forests and parks around Espero. At that time, everyone will be able to do without their personal oxygen supply. In addition, we've contracted with New Terra to exchange travelers for food

stocks for the next two years, and materials and labor for the construction of our first orbital station. We have a long path ahead of us, people, but we have our own planet, viable and with wonderful potential, and I know all of you will be working to make a success of our new home. May fortune be with us all.>

Alex's message kicked off celebrations throughout the flotilla and planetside, although only about 9,000 Harakens lived on planet. Accommodations there remained sparse.

Many people tuned their implants to one of the SADE's music channels. Christie and her new friends, Amelia and Eloise, had requested the SADEs set up simulcasts of multiple music channels. It was interesting that none of the SADEs had sought to confirm that the request was authorized. Few young people had more combined clout than the President's sister, the runner organizer, and the great granddaughter of Fiona Haraken.

Around the park, many of the young tuned their implants to the same channel to dance in the syncopated Méridien style. It was interesting to watch young New Terrans imitate the sinuous dance styles of Méridien youth. As the evening wore on, food and drink were dispensed by vendors, and the pioneer restaurateur ventures took the opportunity to introduce their new recipes.

The entourage from the traveler, which had accompanied Alex and Renée, had wandered off, except for Étienne, who stood quietly to the side of their bench, continuing to keep watch. The potential for an incident was near zero, but as the senior people had agreed with the twins, near zero was not zero. Alex was too important to lose. Étienne wasn't alone, though. Ellie Thompson's delicate hand was curled in his.

Couples strolled through the *Freedom*'s grand park, walking hand in hand or arm in arm. It was a pleasurable custom many had adopted from the vids that circulated of their President and his partner. People passed in front of Alex and Renée, but none disturbed the President with comments, vocal or sent. Alex's faraway expression urged them only to nod respectfully, with Renée accepting their honor for both of them.

Alex's thoughts weren't engaged with anyone, not even the SADEs. He was seeing a tug-explorer Captain, sitting alone at his bridge console aboard the *Outward Bound.* It felt like the distant past, but it was only two years ago. Then his thoughts drifted to the here and now. The people under his care were safe, and Haraken had secured a future that heralded growth and prosperity. *I just need this to last,* Alex thought.

* * *

The Swei Swee were gathered on the cliff tops of Libre's Clarion Seas and Haraken's Tranquil Bay, which the people had begun calling "Racine Bay." The hives of both planets assembled every evening, nestling down on grass or soil, walking legs tucked under and eyestalks fully retracted, to hear the serenades of the Hive Singer. The hives of Libre heard Mutter many days later than the Haraken hives, but they were always assembled and waiting every evening for their Hive Singer, who never failed them.

This evening, Mutter was in her glory. She sang a song of celebration for the Harakens—human, SADE, and Swei Swee—and for herself. Her dream, her wish, the first she had held in her long existence, was one step closer to coming true.

One evening, she thought, *I will stand before the hives when I sing.*

— Alex and friends will return in *Hellébore.* —

Glossary

New Terra:

Alex Racine – Admiral of the Libran flotilla, Co-Leader of House Alexander

Amy Mallard – Ulam University professor and Alex Racine's university mentor

Andrea Bonnard – Senior Captain of the Libran flotilla, Captain of the *Rêveur*

Arthur McMorris – ex-President, resided at Prima's Government House

Benjamin Diaz – Pioneer, Minister of Mining, "Rainmaker"

Bobbie Singh – New Terran who saves Amelia on board the *Freedom*

Charlotte Sanderson – Producer at By-Long Media House

Christie Racine – Alex Racine's fourteen-year-old sister

Clayton Downing XIV – ex-Assemblyman, then the new President until voted out

Damon Stearns – TSF Colonel and ex-outpost Commander of Sharius

Darryl Jaya – reinstated Minister of Technology

Delacroix – Pioneer emigrating to Haraken

Duggan Racine – Alex Racine's father

Eli Roth – *Rêveur*'s starboard bay Flight Crew Chief

Eugene Pritchard – Assemblyman

Frasier Brothers – Criminals hired to spirit away Sebastien Velis after the engineer stole the TS-1 database

Fujio – Joaquin Station tech

Gary Giordano – Dagger-9 pilot lost during Libran exodus

Hatsuto Tanaka – Dagger pilot, brother of Miko Tanaka, Sheila Reynard's second

Hezekiah Cohen – Joaquin Station Manager

House Alexander – Méridien House created by Alex and Renée

Jaime – Joaquin Station tech boss

Jason "Jase" Willard – Dagger pilot killed by a silver ship

Jerold Jameson – Naval Base Commander, stationed on Barren Island

Katie Racine – Alex Racine's mother, Haraken Assembly member

Lamont – Haraken tech
Leonard Breslen – Pioneer, shuttle manufacturer
Levinson – New Terran engineer
Lyle Stamford – *Outward Bound* engineering tech
Maria Gonzalez – ex-Terran Security Forces General and new President
Marshall – TSF Colonel and new outpost Commander on Sharius
Michael "Mickey" Brandon – *Rêveur*'s Chief Engineer
Miko Tanaka – Copilot of *Outward Bound*, sister to Hatsuto Tanaka
Nemea Lorne – Senior Assemblywoman
O'bour – New Terran alcohol
Orma – Maria Gonzalez's Chief of Staff
Peters – Terran Security Forces Captain
Prima – New Terra's capital, named after the first colonist baby to survive one year
Randolph Oppenhurst – ex-TSF Captain
Robert Dorian – Dagger pilot who trains the Independent volunteers, Haraken Assembly member
Samuel B. Hunsader – CEO of Purity Ores, a mining company
Sean McCrery – Dagger-10 pilot
Sebastien Velis – TS-1 engineer who stole the Méridien database
Sheila Reynard – Dagger Squadron Leader, promoted to Commander
Stanley Peterson – *Rêveur*'s port bay Flight Crew Chief, Haraken Assembly member
Tatia Tachenko – Commander and XO of the *Rêveur,* ex-Terran Security Forces Major, new Haraken Admiral
Terran Security Forces (TSF) – New Terran system police force
Ulam University – University in Prima named after Captain Ulam
Wayne – student at Ulam University
William Drake – reinstated Minister of Space Exploration
Yoshiko Ishikawa – Finance Minister
Zeke Krausman – *Outward Bound* engineering tech

Confederation:

Ahmed Durak – First Mate of the *Money Maker*

Alain de Long – *Rêveur* security escort for Renée, twin and crèche-mate to Étienne

Albert de Guirnon (gir·nōn) – Leader of House de Guirnon, brother of Renée

Alia – Bergfalk tech treated by Terese

Amelia – Independent teen girl, organizer of the runners

Angelina "Lina" Monti – daughter of the Independent Leader, Tomas Monti; Haraken Assembly member

Asu Azasdau – starship passenger liner Captain and Haraken Assembly member

Bertram Coulter – engineer and Independent on Libre

Bibi Haraken – daughter of Fiona Haraken, Haraken Assembly member

Clarion Seas – ocean waters on Libre

Claude Dupuis (dū·pwē) – *Rêveur* engineering tech

Cordelia – SADE (self-aware digital entity) of the *Freedom*

Dane – starship passenger liner SADE

Darius Gaumata – Libran Dagger pilot trainee, ex-shuttle pilot

Deirdre Canaan – Libran Dagger pilot trainee, ex-shuttle pilot

Delores – Libran tech

Deter Schonberg – Libran philosopher, Haraken Assembly member

Devon O'Shea – House Leader, Planetside Transportation

Diada – Libran tree and Eloise's "perch"

Edouard Manet – *Rêveur* navigation specialist

Elizabeth – starship passenger liner SADE

Ellie Thompson – Libran Dagger pilot trainee, raced atmo-ships

Eloise Haraken – thirteen-year-old great-granddaughter of Fiona Haraken

Eric Stroheim – Director of House Alexander and Haraken Ambassador

Ernst Hummel – Haraken Minister of Energy Production

Étienne de Long (ā·tē·in) – *Rêveur* security escort for Renée, twin and crèche-mate to Alain

Fabrice – Libran implant engineer

Federico – Ore transport Captain

Fiona Haraken – Libran sky-tower building engineer and Elder of Libre's Independents

Gratuito – Libre's only city
Geneviève Laroque (lă·rōk) – *Rêveur* passenger
Gino Diamanté – House Leader, Infrastructure and Environmental Services
Giovanni Tetra – Libre's Elder prior to Fiona Haraken
Gregorio – an elder left on Libre
Guillermo De Laurent – father of young man at Libran town meeting, Haraken Assembly member
Heinrich – young tech aboard the *Unsere Menschen*, who dies fixing jets on the hull
Helena Bartlett – Libran weaver and friend of Cordelia; Haraken Assembly member
House Bergfalk – House responsible for the Independents' colony on Libre
House Brixton – House responsible for the design and creation of SADEs
House Diamanté – House responsible for infrastructure and environmental services
House Ganesh – House responsible for construction of commercial buildings
House de Guirnon – House responsible for building passenger liners
House O'Shea – House responsible for terminals and planetside transport
House Pasko – House responsible for implants
Jason Haraken – grandson of Fiona Haraken
José Cordova – Captain of the *Freedom*
Julien – *Rêveur*'s SADE
Karl Beckert – Station Director on Orbital Station Ein over Libre
Karl Schmidt – starship passenger liner Captain
Katarina Pasko – House Leader of Implants
Lazlo Menlo – new Captain of the *Money Maker* and Haraken Minister of Transportation
Leeson Darden – Captain of the flotilla's second freighter
Leo Tinto – Haraken Minister of Fabrication
Lillian Hauser – starship passenger liner Captain
Lucia Bellardo – Libran ex-Captain, now a shuttle pilot
Mahima Ganesh – Council Leader of Confederation

Marcel Lechaux – Terese's brother and an Independent on Libre
Miriam Dubois – Haraken Minister of City Design and Infrastructure
Mutter – SADE of the *Money Maker* and Hive Singer to the Swei Swee
Patrice – Fiona Haraken's close friend
Pia Sabine (să·bēn) – *Rêveur* passenger, Haraken Assembly member
Rayland – psychopathic SADE left behind on Libre
Renée de Guirnon (gir·nōn) – Co-Leader of House Alexander
Reinhold – Captain of the *Unsere Menschen*
Rosette – starship passenger liner SADE
SADE – Méridien AI (self-aware digital entity)
Sawalie – Elder singer on Libre
Sergio De Laurent – young man at Libran town hall meeting
Simone Turin – Ben Diaz's Méridien partner
Sophie Sabine – Pia's niece and an Independent on Libre
Svetlana Valenko – Copilot of a Haraken harvesting ship
Tomas Monti – Director of House Alexander, Haraken Ambassador
Terese Lechaux – *Rêveur* medical specialist
Willem – starship passenger liner SADE
Z – SADE of the *Unsere Menschen*

Ships and Stations:

Freedom – Libran city-ship headed by Leader Monti
Full Load – Benjamin Diaz's New Terran ice asteroid tug
Il Piacere – House Diamanté premier liner
Money Maker – House Bergfalk freighter converted to Alex's Dagger carrier
Outward Bound – explorer-tug owned by Alex Racine
Rêveur (rē·vœr) – Méridien House de Guirnon passenger liner; Jacques de Guirnon was prior Captain
Unsere Menschen – the *Our People*, a Libran city-ship headed by Leader Stroheim

Planets, Colonies, and Moons:

Bellamonde – sixth and latest Confederation planet to be attacked by the silver ships

Cetus – last Confederation colony established, first colony attacked by the silver ships

Cressida – New Terra's metal-rich moon circling Ganymede

Ganymede – New Terra's sixth planet outward, a gas giant with metal-rich moons

Haraken – New name of Cetus colony in Hellébore system, home of the Harakens

Libre – Independent's colony in Arno system

Méridien – home world of the Confederation in the Oikos system

New Terra – home world of New Terrans, fourth planet outward of Oistos

Niomedes – New Terra's fifth planet outward and site of the habitat experiments

Seda – New Terra's ninth and last planet outward, a gas giant with several moons

Sharius – moon circling Seda and TSF support outpost for explorer-tugs

Stars:

Arno – star of the planet Libre, home of the Independents

Cepheus – original star destination for the *New Terra*

Hellébore – star of the planet Cetus, location of the first Confederation colony attacked by silver ships

Mane – original name of Oikos

Oikos – star of the Méridien home planet, Renée de Guirnon's home world

Oistos – star of the planet New Terra, Alex Racine's home world

My Books

The Silver Ships and *Libre*, the first and second books in this series, are available as an e-book, a softcover version, and an audiobook. Please visit my website, http://scottjucha.com, for publication locations. You may also register at my website to receive email updates on the progress on my upcoming novels.

Alex and friends will return in the upcoming novel, *Hellébore, A Silver Ships Novel.*

The Silver Ships Series

The Silver Ships

Libre

Méridien

Hellébore (forthcoming)

The Author

It's been an eventful journey from Anchorage, Alaska, where I was born over six decades ago, to San Diego, California, where I currently reside with my wife.

Between these two destinations, I've spent years overseas, earned two college degrees, held many jobs, and found a wonderful marriage partner.

My first attempt at a novel was entitled *The Lure*. It was a crime drama centered on the modern-day surfacing of a 110-carat yellow diamond that had been lost during the French Revolution. In 1980, in preparation for the book, I spent two wonderful weeks in Brazil researching the native people, their language, and the religious customs of Candomblé. The day I returned from Rio, I had my first date with my wife-to-be, Peggy Giels.

Over the past thirty-four years, I've outlined dozens of novels, but a busy career limited my efforts to complete any of them. Now the time has come, and I've thoroughly enjoyed planning, researching, and writing each book in this series.

I was a young teenager when I discovered the joy of reading. Today I hope, through my stories, I'm sharing that joy.